About the

Rosie Simpson has a lifelong passion for words and storytelling, writing travel diaries and magazine features as a freelance journalist and teaching English to students of many nationalities. She lives in lovely rural Sussex with her husband, Tim, and dog, Flora. She has a grownup daughter and son, a granddaughter, Josephine, and a grandson, Ivor. This is her first novel.

In memory of my mother, Grace Ashford, who passed on the story-telling gene to me, and for Josephine and Ivor, who I hope have inherited it from me.

Rosie Simpson

IN GREEN PASTURES

AUSTIN MACAULEY PUBLISHERS™

LONDON • CAMBRIDGE • NEW YORK • SHARJAH

A CIP catalogue record for this title is available from the British Library.

ISBN 9781528996426 (Paperback)
ISBN 9781528996433 (Hardback)
ISBN 9781528996440 (ePub e-book)

www.austinmacauley.com

First Published (2020)
Austin Macauley Publishers Ltd
25 Canada Square
Canary Wharf
London
E14 5LQ

Acknowledgements

Heartiest thanks to all at Austin Macauley for having the confidence to take *In Green Pastures* forward to publication and to Matt Shoard and Harriet Main for their perceptive and rigorous editing of my manuscript. I would also like to thank Mike Toynbee and Greg Simpson for their early reading of my first draft, helping me to get a feel for what readers might think about *In Green Pastures*, and to Prof Richard Robinson for alerting me to the condition known then as 'hysterical blindness'. Members of the Halstead and District History Society helped me get the setting right and the National Farmers' Union's *A History of the NFU* put the farming of the time into context. Carol Twinch's book *Women on the Land* furnished me with vital information about the Women's Land Army in World War 1.

I thank my husband for his patient support and valuable observation.

Part One

Chapter 1

In the back kitchen of the East London house, Florence sat with a towel around her neck. Her mother, Marjorie, stood behind her, scissors in hand, trimming her hair.

"With locks like these, Florence," Marjorie said, "you should have all the eligible young men in Stratford at the door."

There she goes again, Florence thought.

The clock ticked on the mantle. Marjorie gathered another lock of hair between her fingers and snipped.

"I like my life just the way it is, Mother."

"There won't be many left to choose from by the time this war's over."

Florence stiffened. How crass. How disrespectful. *Count to ten, Florence. Count to ten.*

"I saw Stan Gifford the other day – he was asking after you," Marjorie said.

"Stan that works at the docks? I remember him from school. What did you tell him about me?"

"Only that you're living in Clerkenwell and working at the bookshop. He seemed very interested."

"Haven't seen him in donkeys' years."

"I know. So I thought I'd invite him round for tea one of these days. It'd be nice to get to know each other again, wouldn't it?"

If her mother hadn't mentioned him, she would never have thought of Stan Gifford ever again. "I'd rather you didn't. Really." She could see her mother's expression in the hand mirror.

"I never had all this trouble with your sister," Marjorie said. "And you're 28. Time's running short."

Dear God ... "I love Nell and George and all their lot," Florence said, "but I wouldn't swap with her if you paid me."

"But why not? Why don't you want a life like hers?"

"Because she's worn out. She walks around with nappy pins in her blouse in a kitchen full of smelly laundry."

"That's how it is with babies."

"I'd go mad." Florence took a deep breath. "Mother, I know what you're *really* worried about. And I promise I won't do anything to make you ashamed of me. There is absolutely nothing risqué about the life I lead. Now. How's the haircut?"

Marjorie took a step back and looked. Florence's hair caught the glow from the range. She smiled at the sight. "It looks fine to me, dear, but you'd better see for yourself."

Florence touched the ends with her fingers and looked at her reflection, turning her head. "That'll do nicely. Thanks, Mother." She shook the towel outside the scullery door and swept up the clippings. They sizzled and flared when she threw them on the fire.

"Have you got time for a cup of tea?"

The mantle clock chimed half past four.

"If it's a quick one – I mustn't be late back – it's Wednesday."

"You and your mandolin. You're like that Don what's-his-name. Giovanni."

"Quixote." She gave her mother a smile. "And that was windmills, not mandolin practice."

The stench from the Yardley soap factory hit the pit of her stomach as she ran for the bus. Still, leaving Stratford's grimy terraces and the Dew Drop Inn on the corner behind her lightened her mood. *A little of Mother and Stratford goes a long way*, she thought.

She turned her key in the front door in Clerkenwell. "Hello Mrs Bartle," Florence called. She could hear the chink of crockery from the kitchen. The landlady was preparing supper. Florence ran upstairs two at a time and unlocked her room. The sight of it greeted her like an old friend. Its still-colourful patchwork counterpane and the brass candlesticks on the chest always cheered her. She breathed in the faint perfume of lavender polish. But there was no time to linger. She looked at her watch, grabbed her mandolin case propped against the bedside cabinet and ran back down the stairs.

"I won't be late for supper, Mrs B," she called.

"Irish stew only gets better with age. Not like me," came the reply from the kitchen. "Have a lovely time."

She always did. Rehearsing with the Holborn Musical Ensemble was the thing she most looked forward to each week. She could hear the tootling sounds of tuning up floating on the evening air as she arrived at St George's church hall.

Alice Johns, forty-ish, birdlike, leaned over her cello, her ringless left hand adjusting the tuning pegs. Her spare shoulders were apparent through her lawn blouse. Florence wondered how so small a woman coped with such a cumbersome instrument. Alice gave her a little smile and a wave as she crossed the hall. "How're you, Florence?"

"On good form thank you, Alice. Can't wait to get going."

"It's lovely to have a mandolinist – such a bright sound."

"I've been practising hard – don't want to let the side down."

She took her mandolin out of its leather case and ran her hand over its sound box. The smoothness pleased her.

"You're better than you think you are." Alice laid a hand on Florence's arm. Florence smiled back.

The swing doors closed noisily behind Bernard Davenport, founder and director of the HME. He swiped a handkerchief across his face and over his bald head, like a giant billiard ball. His cheeks were still shiny with perspiration.

"Good evening, *tout le monde*. Excellent news," he said, pocketing his handkerchief. "The church authorities have agreed we can hold a concert in St George's on a date of our choosing, as long as it doesn't clash with a bring-and-buy sale or sock-knitting session. We must start thinking '*programme*'. No time to lose. So, ladies and gentlemen, to work!"

Chapter 2

The sign above the shop window read 'Messrs Brown and Son Established 1878' in gold script. And inscribed in an arc on the window glass was 'London's Finest Selection of Used And Antiquarian Books. Lending Facilities Also Available'. It was in Charing Cross Road. Florence made her way there on foot six mornings a week to work as an assistant to the Brown father, Mr Arthur, and son, Mr James. Sometimes she walked along Theobalds Road, others Guildford Street, turning left into Southampton Row, depending on her mood. She only took the bus in the foulest weather.

She approached the door with its brass handle and, catching sight of her reflection, straightened the waistband of her skirt. The bell over the door tinkled as she pushed.

The shop was handsome, the bookshelves newly varnished by Florence's brother-in-law, George Ashford. She had recommended him for the job.

"Morning, Mr Arthur."

Brown Senior looked up.

"Good day, Miss Mundy. "We've some new titles in this morning – a bequest. Quite interesting. I'd like you to catalogue them please, and then put them out, if you'd be so good."

"Do you want me to mind the counter, too?"

"If you please. But if it gets busy, just sing out. I'll be in the back office. Mr James will be out all day. He's gone to look at some rather good art books."

Florence was keen to get started. Always something unexpected. Sometimes a rare treat … There were some biographies here: William Wordsworth and Charles Dickens, and a copy of Jane Eyre bound in conker-coloured leather. *Who had owned them. Read them …?* she wondered.

"Excuse me, miss."

She looked up. The man looked tall from where she was kneeling and he was wearing a well-cut jacket. Tweed. Greenish. He looked down at her and touched the wide brim of his hat.

"Oh … Dear – I'm so sorry." Her attention had drifted into Jane Eyre. "I didn't hear you come in. What can I do for you, sir?" She got to her feet.

"It's travel books I'm after. Do you have anything on North America?" His voice was a slow drawl. It reminded her of the flow of the Thames.

"There's a travel section in the lending library. It's through the archway behind you."

"Thank you, miss." He turned towards the library. She noticed he walked with a limp, his left leg stiff at the knee.

Florence went back to sorting the new arrivals. Next on the pile was a selection of sheet music, worn at the corners and faded, but serviceable. She leafed through the booklets, stopping when a title caught her attention. Mandolin concerti. Vivaldi.

"Ooh." She pulled it from the pile.

"Everything alright, Miss Mundy?" Brown Senior called. "Any masterpieces?"

"Not as such, Mr Arthur, though there's a nice leather-bound copy of Jane Eyre in good condition. It'll sell easily, I think. And there's some music here I'm rather interested in. May I look at it during my dinner hour?"

"By all means."

The man with the hat and the limp came back through the archway empty handed. "You don't seem to have what I'm looking for. Besides, I'd prefer to buy than borrow."

"We do have some travel books for sale, but the selection's not exactly comprehensive."

"Hardly surprising in a second-hand shop." He looked vaguely disdainful.

"Foyle's will have a better choice." *Obviously,* she thought.

"Thank you for your help, Miss … Mundy."

He touched his hat brim again and left the shop.

At dinner time, Florence took her sandwich to Victoria Embankment Gardens, pretty with snapdragons. The brightness of the day made her squint after the dim shop interior. She settled down on a bench and when she'd finished eating and tidied away the wrappings, she opened the Vivaldi mandolin pieces and hummed quietly.

"What's that setting your foot tapping?" The voice came from somewhere on her right.

She looked up. The sun was behind him and she could barely make out his features, but she recognised the hat.

"Oh! Was I? I didn't realise …" She cleared her throat as he stood looking at her. "Did you find what you were looking for in Foyles?"

"I had to order it," he said. "It's rather a particular subject – the history of Yosemite National Park."

"Yos … Where? I've never heard of it."

"It's in the United States – California. A wild, mountainous place, so I've read. I'm writing about it, so I'm planning a trip to see it for myself."

"How exciting … I'd love to see the world …" The music book slipped to the ground. She bent to retrieve it. "There must be so much to think about, going so far away to somewhere so … remote. What about the U-boats? The *Lusitania* was dreadful."

"It's a risk … but life has to go on, wouldn't you say?" He smiled down at her, not looking the least bit worried.

She smoothed her skirt and some crumbs spilled onto the ground. Sparrows were onto them in no time.

"You write for a newspaper?"

"Magazines, mostly. I'm freelance. I do travel writing when I can. I'm going for a book about Yosemite."

"A book! How ambitious!" She fiddled with the collar of her blouse.

"And what about you? Are you a musician as well as a bookworm?" He took a step forward and sat down on the arm of the bench.

"I'd really love to be, but whether I'll ever manage to … you need luck as well as talent … and you've got to practise."

"You can make it, I'll bet."

"I don't know about that, but I enjoy my music anyway." She smiled a little nervously and looked at her watch.

"Goodness! Is that really the time? I'll get the sack if I don't get a move on." She stood and gathered up her handbag and the music book, checking the bench to make sure she'd left it tidy, then turned and looked over her shoulder at him.

"Nice talking to you," he said.

After work, Florence climbed the steps to Hungerford Footbridge and watched the river flowing below, barges and lighters ferrying goods upriver from the docks. She breathed in, the atmosphere heavy with the reek of coal smoke, dampness rising from the river. Trains steamed out of Charing Cross Station towards Kent with its hop gardens, oast houses, the sea and Canterbury, the destination of pilgrims … She loved this place. So much life. Commerce. Energy. Noise and vapour filled the air and the bridge shook like an earth tremor beneath her feet. The comings and goings of trains. Brief glimpses of other people's lives.

A cloud of steam, belching from a passing engine engulfed her. The clammy fog filled her mouth and nose and she felt the sharp stab of something in her eye.

"Ow!" Her hand flew to her face.

"Will this help?" A man was leaning on the railing beside her, holding out a handkerchief between two fingers. She reached out to take it from him and dabbed her stinging eye. The material of his green jacket nudged her arm, prickly against her skin. She moved away slightly.

"You again."

He nodded and touched his hat.

"Harry Bartholomew. At your service, Miss Mundy."

"Mr Bartholomew." She acknowledged him with a nod, feeling uneasy but also intrigued about this third encounter. He looked at her and smiled.

"Look, I have to be going, now," she said. "Sorry. Thanks for the hanky."

She handed it back to him, embarrassed that is was now limp and soot-speckled, and ran down the steps, wanting to put some distance between herself and this persistent man.

Chapter 3

Florence got off the bus at Stratford Broadway and made her way via dingy turnings to Gurney Road, where Nell and George Ashford had lived since their marriage. For all its humble setting, number 123 stood neat as a Sunday-best outfit – a testament to Nell's attention to domestic detail and George's decorating skill.

Grace, Florence's niece, nine years old and the middle child of the five Ashford offspring opened the door. "Aunt Flo! Lovely to see you. Mum's in the parlour – she's raring to get going."

"Hello, Gracie, love. Nice to see you, too." She kissed the top of the child's head.

Nell appeared at the parlour door. "Come in, Flo. I've set up the work table in here."

"We're honoured, Nellie. The parlour's normally reserved for high days and holidays." Florence reached out and embraced her sister.

"It's the only room with enough space for the fabric," Nell said. "We're moving the twins into Ellen and Grace's bedroom, you see. It'll be pretty snug in there, so we thought it only right to freshen it up. George has finished the wallpapering and paintwork. It's just the curtains we need. Mother's given me an old pair to remake. Material's quite pretty."

"On top form, Nell. As ever."

"Sorry, Flo. I'm forgetting my manners. How are you?"

Florence opened her mouth to speak, but Nell was unstoppable. "Keen to get this job finished." She turned to her middle daughter still standing in the doorway. "Grace, make sure your father's got a cup of tea – he's in the back kitchen reading the paper. Then it's back to your homework, please."

"Yes, Mum," the child said retreating slowly, "but can't I talk to Aunt Flo for a bit?"

"Maybe later. Your aunt and I have got stacks to do."

In the quiet evening, the two women worked companionably together, the chattering of Nell's hand-sewing machine clacking out a rhythm. Florence sat pinning and hemming as the last rays of the evening sun slanted through the lace curtains at the window.

"Ooh. Better light some lamps in here." Nell stood and reached for the tapers. "How's it going at Brown's, Flo? Still enjoying it?"

"Mmm …" Florence took out the pins she was holding between her lips. "I love working with books – always something new and interesting. Even pieces of music, sometimes," she added, remembering. "A funny thing happened today, though ..."

"Oh? What was that?"

"A chap came into the shop this morning. Wanted a book on some park in America. We didn't have it, so I sent him to Foyle's."

"What's funny about that?"

"Well, nothing, I suppose. But then he came and spoke to me at dinnertime in the Embankment Gardens while I was eating my sandwich. And then he appeared again while I was on Hungerford Bridge after work."

"D'you think he's following you?"

"Well, I'm wondering. It's unsettled me a bit."

"Hardly surprising. What's he like?"

"Didn't really study his looks – I felt rather disconcerted ... He's tall, though, and he's got a limp. Smart jacket. Wears a wide-brimmed hat ... seems rather interesting ... very courteous."

"Well, I doubt you'll take advice from me, Flo, but I'd be very careful if I were you ... D'you think the limp's keeping him out of the war? Surely, he'd be called up if he were able-bodied, now they're conscripting men ..."

Florence caught Nell's uneasy intonation.

"... War's creeping closer and closer into all our lives ... It gives me the jitters."

Chapter 4

A July Sunday just a week after her last visit. The year 1916. Summer sunshine had given way to a chill gloom. As Florence approached her sister's house, she was surprised to see the parlour curtains still closed. It was late morning. *"Hm. That's not like Nell."* She raised the knocker, but the door opened before it struck. Nell stood in the dark hall, her features clouded with worry, her forehead creased in a frown.

"I saw you from the upstairs window, Flo ... I was waiting ... Glad you've come." She bit her bottom lip. "Come in," she said, moving aside. "I've got some news."

Florence stepped over the threshold. "What news, Nellie?" She looked into her sister's face and saw anxiety there.

"George has been called up."

Silence hung on the air for a moment. An image of the daily casualty lists in the papers flashed through Florence's mind ... the deadly reality of war creeping into so many homes.

"Oh Lord."

Nell stooped to pick up a yellow-painted toy duck off the floor and turned it in her shaking hands. "The Somme's still going on – men dying all the time ... They'll send him there, won't they? He's a breadwinner. Father of five ... Why choose him? Oh, God ... How do we face this?" Her voice faltered and she pulled a handkerchief from her sleeve.

"Come here, Nellie," Florence said, embracing her sister.

"We feared his turn would come when conscription came along ... but so soon."

"Where's George now?"

"Gone with Ellen, Alf and Grace over to Wanstead Flats. Iris and Renee are asleep."

"Do the children know yet?"

"No ... Don't know how we'll find the words ..." She gripped the toy. Veins on the back of her hand stood out.

"Let's go through to the back and have a cup of tea and a chat while we've got a few minutes' peace and quiet." Florence's tone was soft. "Look, you sit down, Nellie. I'll do the tea – I know where everything is – and you can tell me all about it. When did you find out?"

Staring at the kitchen range, the glow from the fire reflected on Nell's careworn face. "Got the letter two days ago."

Florence put the kettle on to boil and brought down cups and saucers from the dresser. She found a milk jug with its bead-weighted lace cover on the stone slab in the pantry.

"He'll serve in the Royal Engineers," Nell said. "What good's a grainer and marbler in the Royal Engineers?"

"I don't think things like that count, Nellie. They just want – need – manpower." She was about to say 'cannon fodder', but thought better of it. "He is very practical, though. Maybe that's what they like about him."

"I just don't understand what this blessed war is all about," Nell said. "Surely we're paying too high a price for putting Kaiser Bill in his place. It's mad." Nell's voice wavered. She pulled a clean nappy, stiff from the boil wash, from the clothes horse and folded it.

"It all seems incredible looking back. Mere boys signing up in their thousands at the start." Florence took a mouthful of tea, and set her cup back down in the saucer. "And now ..." She dared not mention the slaughter.

"How much longer ...?" Nell fell silent and folded nappies. She looked up at her sister. "Flo, how am I going to manage on a private soldier's pay?"

"I don't know, Nell ... But you're a coper, you know you are."

"George and I are a team, though. Doing it all on my own ... I just don't know ..."

"Have you been able to put any money aside?"

"Yes. A little, but it won't go far with my five. And believe me, Flo, I'm used to making do, but it's going to be darned hard."

Chapter 5

"Miss Mundy, would you mind retrieving that ornithological reference book – the Audubon we were looking at last week? Mr Jennings has requested it – he's coming in later to purchase it. I put it by for him but it's near the top, I fear. I didn't want anyone making off with it inadvertently. Mr Jennings would be terribly disappointed."

"Not to worry, Mr Arthur, I can reach it." Florence positioned the ladder against the shelves and climbed. With the book in one hand, she came back down and began leafing through the pages.

"The illustrations are sumptuous, are they not?" Brown Senior said.

"Yes," she said. The heavy volume slipped from her grasp and she looked at it splayed face down on the floor.

"Oh!" She gasped and bent to pick it up.

"Miss Mundy, I'm surprised at you. This is not like you at all. I hope you haven't damaged it – it's very valuable, as I'm sure you are aware."

"I'm so sorry, Mr Arthur, I'm not quite myself this morning … I'll pay …"

Brown Senior took the book and checked it over. It appeared unscathed. He looked up at his assistant and noted the worried creases in her brow. "Is something wrong, Miss Mundy?"

Florence drew in a deep breath. "My brother-in-law's been called up. My sister's dreadfully upset."

Brown Senior's expression softened. "Horrible business. And no end in sight."

"How can it have got this bad, when we were so optimistic at the beginning? I wish I understood."

Brown Senior rubbed his chin and looked up at her over his half-glasses. He had a long list of things to do. "Hmm," he said. "The war was brewing for a long time before it finally broke out, I fear."

"People say the Kaiser's got a chip on his shoulder about not having an empire."

"I believe that's true," Brown Senior said. "So he's been looking to expand his sphere of influence. And when he invaded Luxemburg and Belgium, we had to get involved. Too close for comfort … Of course," he went on, "theirs was a standing army – not a crowd of volunteers like ours. And then there's their superior weaponry – machine guns. They've wrought enormous carnage."

"Poor George," said Florence, "and poor Nell, too. It's not going to be at all easy for her."

"I'm sure not," he said, "but we can't let the Germans get the upper hand, can we?"

They both looked up at the sound of the bell above the door.

"Good morning Mr Jennings." Brown Senior stood and shook the man's hand. He dwarfed the customer. But what Jennings lacked in height, he made up for in elegant attire. Starched wing collar, polished brogues. His diamond tiepin sparkled.

"Ah, good day to you, Brown. I see you have the Audubon ready for me. Such a find! Let me look at it."

He examined the covers and flicked through the pages. "Excellent condition! Capital! I regard myself as very fortunate to have tracked it down." He twirled one end of his waxed moustache between his thumb and forefinger.

"I'm delighted to have found it for you, Mr Jennings. Shall I wrap it up?"

"If you would be so kind, Brown, and put it on my account, would you? I'm off to my club where I can really study it. A treat in store."

"Indeed. Good day to you, Mr Jennings."

Florence carried a pile of returned books through to the library. She heard the doorbell again and a muffled exchange between Brown Senior and the incomer. When she'd finished her task, she returned to the shop.

"Miss Mundy. I wonder if you'd mind serving the customer in the map department? He may need help to find what he's looking for."

"Of course, Mr Arthur."

Brown Senior went into the back office. Maps were stacked on a shelf deep in the shop's dim interior. The customer touched his wide-brimmed hat.

"Mr … Bartholomew. What can I do for you?"

"Well, Miss Mundy. Perhaps you can guess what I'm after." He looked at her.

She cleared her throat. "Something to do with your proposed trip to the United States, would it be?

"Right first time. A map – or maps – if you've got them, of the western states. Large scale with plenty of detail. Do you have anything of that sort?"

"I'll have to check the list. It'll just take me a moment, if you'll excuse me."

He turned back to the shelves. Florence ran her forefinger down the catalogue listing.

"Actually, we do have one. It's quite old, but it says here that it's in good condition. It shows California and Nevada. Would you like me to get it down for you?"

"Indeed I would."

She climbed onto the step stool, conscious of his eyes still on her. "Ah. Here it is." She handed him a brown paper envelope. "Perhaps you'd like to look at it over on the table."

She left him to examine the map and returned to the counter. She fanned her face with a magazine until he reappeared.

"I'll take it." He held the map out to her. "It's quite interesting. Topographical. I'll need more, obviously, but this will do to begin with."

"You'll have to look in Stanford's. It's just round the corner in Long Acre. That'll be two-and-six, please."

"Yes, I know Stanford's well," he said, handing her the money, "there's nowhere better for maps."

"So why didn't you go straight there?"

"Can't you guess, Miss Mundy?"

He looked at her and she saw that his eyes were brown. She reddened.

"Excuse me. I must get on." She picked up some books and took them to the far side of the shop.

He followed her and caught her by the elbow. She turned to face him.

"Mr Bartholomew, I must ask you to –"

"What, Miss Mundy? What must you ask me to do?"

"To … stop. Following me. You're making me feel uncomfortable."

"Well if you would stop being so dashed elusive, I wouldn't have to keep following you. I just want to get to know you a little better. What could be wrong with that? Give a fellow a chance, won't you?"

"What makes you think *I* want to get to know *you*, Mr Bartholomew?"

"I don't know that at all. I'm just taking a gamble on it. There's an even chance, isn't there? And it's Harry."

She opened her mouth to speak, but no words came, so she closed it again. He still held her by the elbow and she shrugged herself free.

"I'm sorry," she said, recovering a little, "but I'm really not allowed to conduct my personal life during working hours. Mr Brown pays me to do a job of work and he won't take kindly to your wasting my time, even if you are a paying customer. So I must bid you good day, Mr Bartholomew. And thank you for your custom."

"Au revoir then, Miss Mundy." He touched his hat brim. She watched him as he made lopsidedly for the door.

In the mid-afternoon, Brown Senior left the shop to deliver a 19th century atlas to a customer. Florence was last to leave and locked up, making sure all was secure. Stepping out into Charing Cross Road, she looked about her, more than half expecting to bump into Bartholomew. It had come on to rain, so she put up her umbrella and made her way back to Clerkenwell through streets shiny with rain water, the deepening puddles reflecting back images of passing traffic. Upside-down buses, horses, handcarts, pedestrians.

Tuesday and Wednesday came and went without a sign of him. She wasn't sure whether she felt relieved or offended. But she was intrigued. Wednesday was early closing day.

"You off to Stratford this afternoon, Florence?" Mrs Bartle asked as her lodger came in.

"No … I don't think I'll go today, Mrs B. I've got some mandolin pieces I want to get the hang of. I need to be able at least to have a stab at them before rehearsal this evening."

"Your mum'll miss you."

"She can wait till Sunday. Today mandolin practice takes priority."

In truth Florence didn't think she was up to fending off Marjorie's line of questioning today. And besides, a couple of hours with the new pieces could make all the difference.

Chapter 6

Two days before he was due to join his regiment – everyone referred to it as 'his' regiment, though he felt no ownership in it – George sat outside the back door on a kitchen chair, putting the finishing touches to his kit. He polished the buckles on his uniform belt. Even this inimical task he could not skimp. Skimping was not in his nature.

The view beyond the privy and the back yard consisted mostly of roofs and chimneys. The soap-stink from Yardleys was heavy on the air, but George scarcely noticed it. He looked up from his work, polishing rag in hand. The sun was low in the sky, glinting on the sooty glass of factory windows. Grace, his middle child, came out to join him, carrying a book. She sat down on the step, tucking the folds of her skirt around her.

"Dad, it's going to be really awful without you here to talk to. So I've had an idea." She held up the book. "Grandma Mundy gave it to me. It's a notebook."

"And what're you going to do with it?"

"I'm going to use it as a journal and write about everything that happens while you're not here."

The days running up to their father's departure had been a nightmare for all the Ashford children but especially for Grace, whose bond with him was deep. Coming up with the journal idea had relieved her pain a little.

"Good idea. I'll look forward to reading it when I get back."

"Look." She flicked through the book. "It's got hundreds of pages in it. I can pretend I'm talking to you when I'm writing. I might even draw pictures and stick things in it."

"Dear old Fireworks. What a bright spark you are! Come to your Dad."

George put down the belt and lifted his daughter onto his knee. He drew her close.

"You smell of turps and tobacco, Dad. I love it."

He smiled. She wondered when she would smell it again.

"I'll call my book 'Fireworks' Favourite Fings For Farver. What do you fink?"

In the evening, when the children had gone to bed, George sat with Nell in the quiet of the back kitchen. He told her what Grace had said.

"You know, Nell, these moments with you and the kids, I can hardly bear them."

She put down her mending, laid a hand on his arm and managed to smile.

"Sometimes I think I should draw back so as to protect myself from the heart-ache."

He paused and she took his hand.

"But the memory of these moments is all I can take with me … They'll be all I've got to keep me going."

When the morning of his departure came, George's family found it almost impossible to find the right words to send him on his way.

"Maybe," Grace said to Alf, "all we can do is try to stay cheerful, which won't be easy, and to tell him how much we love him."

On the platform at Stratford Market station, time passed slowly. Nell looked along the platform at other men in uniform, other families embracing, dabbing moist eyes, trying to smile …

The train steamed into the station. George embraced them each in turn. Nell carried his twin baby daughters, one on each arm.

"Take care Nell, my dearest," he said, "and keep safe."

"And you, George, my love. Never forget how much we all love you."

He swung his kitbag over his shoulder and reached out to unlatch the door. He climbed on board the train, slammed the door and released the leather strap that held the window shut. He leaned out. The moment. It was here. *Say something,* Grace thought, *or it'll be too late.*

"I'll write everything down in my journal for you to read when you come home." She struggled to keep the tremor from her voice.

"I'll take care of Mother and help her with the twins," Ellen, the eldest, said.

"I'll do my best to be the man of the house, Dad," Alf added.

The train began to move, slowly at first. He took off his cap and waved it from the window, watching as the sight of them receded. The family stood and waved until the train disappeared from view, leaving only wisps of steam in its wake.

The knot tightened in Nell's chest. "We might as well head for home." She put the twins back in their pram and they made their way back, engulfed in the quiet of their own thoughts. Grace, annoyed with how corny all their parting words now sounded in her head, pushed her fists into the pockets of her cardigan. Ellen linked arms with her mother and Alf lagged behind, kicking stones along the pavement.

Chapter 7

Florence crossed the church hall. Its green and cream painted brickwork was hardly an inspirational backdrop, but two violinists were already tuning up and the clarinettist was practising. "Evening everyone," she said. Bernard was adjusting his music stand. "How far have you got with selecting works for the concert, Bernard?"

"Well, I'm still open to suggestions. I think we'll keep it light, don't you? A couple of gavottes, perhaps a minuet or two. Some jaunty canons and rondos should make for a popular programme. Why, Florence? Do you have something in mind?"

"It's just an idea, and I don't know if I'll be good enough at playing them in time, but I've been working on excerpts from some Vivaldi mandolin concerti. Do you think they're cheerful enough?"

"Indeed. You'll have to play them for us and see what everyone thinks. We want all the members to be happy with the choices, don't we?"

She started, nervously at first and faltered. "Sorry," she said, "I'll start again."

This time, the music's mood and the mandolin's lilt took hold. Her small audience nodded in time and people were smiling.

"Bravo!" Bernard said. "You played that with fluency and expression, Florence. I think we may have a performance here. Do you all agree?"

"Just the ticket!" Alice said. "It'll set the tone for the programme perfectly. We'll enjoy playing along with you, Florence."

The players murmured their agreement and Bernard gave Florence the thumbs-up. She felt light-headed as though she'd drunk something fizzy a bit too quickly.

"It's only an amateur performance in a draughty church, but it's my first chance to play in public," she said to Brown Senior, "and my colleagues in the ensemble really seemed to like it."

"Well done, Miss Mundy. I'm sure you'll be a great success."

At dinner time, she walked to St Martin in the Fields and sat in the quiet of the church. Today the sun streamed in through the arched windows and lit up the interior. She breathed slowly and let her shoulders drop, stilling the giddy feeling inside her. Long moments passed.

"Hello again, Miss Mundy. It's nice to see you again."

She turned to the figure who had sat down on the pew beside her. It took a moment or two for her to recognise who it was. He had taken off the wide-brimmed hat and was rotating it in his hands. A gesture of humility? Reverence? She had not seen him bare-headed before and was struck by the luxuriance of his dark hair. The back of her neck tingled slightly.

"I can see how this tranquil setting is soothing to your soul. Am I right?"

"You are right. I love it in here, especially when I've got things going round in my mind."

"So what is it that's going round in your mind?"

"It's Vivaldi, actually."

He frowned. "Vivaldi?"

"I've been picked to play some of his mandolin music in a concert. I still can't quite believe it."

"Congratulations. Tell me more."

"Do you know Vivaldi's music?"

"I can't say I do …"

"I love it. To me it sounds like sunlight on water. Sparkling. He came from Venice, you know. Vivaldi, I mean."

A smile spread over his face. Florence stopped. Her voice had risen to a pitch unseemly in a church. She raised a hand to her mouth and looked about to see if she had disturbed anyone.

"Well, then. We must celebrate. There's a café across the road. I'd like to treat you to a chocolate éclair … Florence, if I may."

She stood and buttoned her cardigan and wondered how he had discovered her first name. She was about to decline his offer, but instead looked at her watch to see she still had half an hour of her dinner break left. *An éclair. Where's the harm?*

"Oh well. Why not?" She smiled at him.

"Music seems very important to you," Harry said. They sat at a window table as Londoners hurried by.

"Mmm." She nodded and dabbed cream and crumbs of choux pastry from her lips.

"Why the mandolin?"

"Because it sounds so un-English. It takes me away to other places – sunny, beautiful places. In my imagination, at least."

"I enjoy escaping to faraway places, too."

"I'd love to make my living from music, but I've left it a bit late. Besides, I have to earn money to keep body and soul together and performing's a bit of a chancy prospect. My family's not wealthy, you see. They all think I'm dotty … Tilting at windmills, my mother says."

She knew she was going on rather, but it was a novelty to talk about these things – to someone whose expression suggested he was interested.

He sat looking at her with his left elbow on the table, his chin cupped in his hand. "Perhaps this concert could be the start of something big for you."

"It's what I'm hoping."

She took another look at her watch. "I really must be going. Thank you for the éclair … Harry. It was delicious."

"Before you rush off, Florence, I have a question for you. The Romantic Poets – do you like their work?"

She nodded and frowned at the same time. "Yes, I do. But what's that got to do with anything?"

"There's a poetry reading tomorrow evening. The Romantics. Would you like to come? It might be awful, but you never know. It's in a room over a pub in Shaftesbury Avenue. We could walk there when you finish work. What do you say?"

"Um. I'll check my diary." She knew there was nothing in it, but it gave her time. She hid the blank page from his view. Should she trust this man? "Well I … well … Yes. Alright."

The Bloomsbury Tavern was already busy. Its tall, leaded windows let in evening light, illuminating clouds of tobacco smoke rising in misty coils. There were tables in little booths, semi-glazed partitions separating each from the next. *A bit like a confessional*, Florence thought. He drank mild and bitter. She stuck with lemonade.

"Cheers," he said, touching her glass with his.

"Cheers. How's your American research coming on?"

"Pretty fair, I'd say. I've assembled a mass of documents which I've got to get down to reading. I haven't got long – I sail in late August."

"Oh! So soon."

"Why," he said. "Will you miss me?"

"I … hardly know you," Florence said. "How long will you be there?"

"About a year. To see all four seasons."

"Oh …"

"Ladies and gentlemen," came a voice from behind the bar. "Kindly take your seats in the function room. The evening's entertainment will commence in five minutes."

They drained their glasses and made their way across the pub to the stairs. When Florence reached the top, Harry was still only half way up.

"This wretched leg holds me back," he said, "but I'm learning to live with it."

"How did it happen – the leg, I mean?" Florence asked.

"In a climbing accident in the Alps. I fell – slipped on loose stones – scree – on a steep slope – and the leg got caught in a crevice in the rock and it twisted as it broke …"

"Sounds excruciating!"

"It was as well I was roped to another climber, or I'd probably have been killed."

"Good Lord." She gasped.

He sat back, smiling slightly.

"They saved the leg, at least, but it's left me with this infernal limp."

"I suppose it's kept you out of the war. That's one good thing about it, isn't it?"

"Well, no. Not really. I'd have liked to go as a war reporter, but they said I'd be too much of a liability."

"What about Yos … that place in America? How will you manage in such wild country?"

"I'll do a lot on horseback. They ride with long stirrups and nearly straight legs on their saddles, so that will suit me … Shh. It's about to begin."

Dusty curtains drew back to reveal a foursome, each with a buff-coloured folder balanced on one open palm. The applause was polite. The four performers bowed and composed themselves. One, clad in antique attire –breeches, frock coat and cravat, stepped forward. His deep intake of breath swelled his chest visibly.

"She walks in beauty like the night …"

The voice which emerged from this man of modest proportions was not what Florence expected. It was booming, stentorian, the words delivered with an air of studied gravitas. *Too much like a funeral oration,* she thought. And so it went on. The troupe of readers trying so hard. Florence had to stifle a giggle.

"What did you find so funny," Harry said to her when it was all over.

"It's the way the readers took themselves so seriously – trying to sound like Henry Irving."

"But this is the best of English poetry. Don't you think it deserves to be treated seriously?"

"Of course I do. But they made it sound so pompous. I think it should be lilting and rhythmical – like music, almost."

They were sitting in the same booth as before. She'd succumbed to a small sherry this time.

"Their *'Skylark'* had lead boots on. Where was the 'harmonious madness'?" she said.

"But Percy Shelley's asking: 'how is it that we mortals are too burdened with care to express ourselves like the skylark', isn't he?" Harry frowned.

"Perhaps that's the skylark's message: not so much soul-searching."

"You might be right. Maybe the Romantics could have done with some of your down-to-earth common sense."

"Oh, but I love the lyrical words they used – like 'winnowing' and 'murmuring'. They help you see all sorts of lovely scenes in your imagination."

"You know my favourite lines?" Harry asked looking hard at Florence. She shook her head and looped a lock of hair behind her ear.

'And the sunlight clasps the earth,
And moonbeams kiss the sea –
What are all these kissings worth,
If thou kiss not me?'

"Shelley again," he said. *'Love's Philosophy'* Remember it?"

"Um … not very well. I'll … have to look it up. In *Palgrave's Treasury* … I've … got one."

She could not look at him, but he would not take his eyes off her. Her heart was racing. She stood and put the programme from the poetry reading in her bag, fumbling with the clasp.

"I think it's time I was going." Her voice faltered.

He followed her from the pub, but only caught up with her at the bus stop. He slid an arm around her waist and as she spun round, he took her face in his free hand and kissed her lips very gently. The tension left her body and she slipped her arms around his neck.

"There," he said. "That wasn't so bad, was it?"

She shook her head. There were tears in her eyes.

"May I see you again?"

This time she nodded.

Chapter 8

"Right, ladies and gentlemen. I'm happy with the Pachelbel but the Mozart needs some more work, as does the Handel. They're a bit more twiddly, so we'll have another go at them next week. Practise them at home, please. And that goes for you, too, Florence with that Vivaldi of yours, though it's coming along nicely. We're going to give our audience a splendid evening. It's very exciting."

"Heavens, Alice," Florence whispered to her cellist neighbour, "I'm so excited about this concert, I can't tell you."

"There's nothing like a live performance to bring out the best in all of us, I always think. Is anyone you know coming?"

"I don't think my family will show up – my mother's very suspicious of my musicmaking for some reason, and my sister's marooned at home with five children and a husband at the Front. But … I'm hoping … there's a man I've met. He might come, but I haven't asked him yet. How about you?"

"My friend Dorothy will come. She always does. So loyal."

Florence headed for the door. Just two weeks to go. *Tilting at windmills, indeed,* she thought, *I'll show them.*

Harry was waiting for her on the pavement outside. He blew out a stream of cigarette smoke and ground out the stub under his heel. "How did it go?" he asked, taking her free hand and kissing it.

"It was good. Getting better all the time. You will come, Harry, won't you? It's my big moment."

"Just try and stop me, dear girl," he said. "It'll be the highlight of my week. I can't wait. Another week, though, and I'd already be gone. So it will be your parting gift to me … or … part of it, at any rate."

She looked at him, curious. "What else have you got in mind?"

"Ah. Now. That would be telling."

***

For Florence, time seemed to fly. Saturday, 26th August, 1916. A red-letter day for her if ever there was one. She took a last look at herself in the tortoiseshell hand mirror she kept on her washstand and pinched her cheeks.

"You'll do," she said to her reflection. She picked up her mandolin case and left.

As the ensemble took their places, the musicians smiled at one another and crossed their fingers, but each was too engrossed in preparation to exchange many words. They tuned their instruments and set up their music stands, rosined their bows.

Florence glanced up at the empty pews in the nave of the church, thinking how austere, almost threatening they looked. "Do you think anyone will come, Alice?"

"Of course they will. It's still early," Alice said, and patted Florence's hand. "Don't worry."

Gradually, the nave started to fill. There was quiet murmuring. Florence looked up to see if she could recognise faces in the audience. She squinted. Mrs Bartle in her best hat sat with her handbag on her knees near the back of the church. And surely that was Mr Arthur and Mr James making their way towards seats at the front. And then she spotted Harry, carrying a raincoat over his arm and removing his hat as he made his way forward. He caught her eye and blew her a kiss. She looked away hurriedly, adjusting the tuning pegs on her mandolin.

Her stomach felt uncomfortable and she worried that her hand might shake when she played. She closed her eyes and concentrated on breathing ... in ... out ...

"You alright, Florence?" Alice said. "We're all behind you, you know. Just keep looking in Bernard's direction. He's got an excellent knack of quelling performers' collywobbles just by looking at them. If he's smiling, you'll know you're doing well. Good luck, dear."

Florence nodded her thanks. Her biggest worry was that there were several pieces which preceded hers in the programme and she had to keep her nerve through most of the first half of the programme. The Vivaldi was the last item before the interval, after the Hornpipe from Handel's 'Water Music'. How could she stop her hands sweating?

When her moment came, she waited for Bernard's baton to conduct her in. And off she went. Vivaldi's notes spilled from her mandolin like cascading diamonds, sparkling in brilliant light. It was musical cloth of gold, and Florence, elated, knew it was better than ever. She looked up at Bernard and saw he was smiling. And so was she.

The applause went on and on. Harry was on his feet. "Bravo!" he called.

Bernard came to her and presented her to the audience. She stood to take her bow.

At the concert's end, Harry put his arm around her shoulder and escorted her away from St George's. "You were brilliant, Florence, you talented girl." He took her in his arms and kissed her.

"I'm still on my magic carpet, I think. I've no idea how to get off," she said, "Where do you think it'll take me next?"

"Heaven, d'you think?"

She laughed. "I'm not expecting miracles – or my early demise, though I did come close to dying of nerves back there. Perhaps just a little port and lemon to celebrate?"

"I know just the place." Harry took her hand.

"This is cosy." Florence settled down at a corner table in the saloon bar. She propped her mandolin case against the wall, smiling at it and giving it a pat. "Well done," she said under her breath.

Harry returned to the table with glasses in hand. "Don't drink this too quickly," he said, "you'll get tipsy."

She smiled up at him. "Frankly, tonight I couldn't care less. Cheers, Harry." They held hands under the table.

"Do you really think tonight might lead to bigger things?" she said. "I mean, I know it was good, but how good?"

"You might have to think a bit grander than the Holborn Musical Ensemble if you're going to build a decent reputation as a performer."

"Oh, Harry. I can't yet, can I? They're all much better than I am – and they're so nice to play with. It was only my first performance in public, after all, and they gave me the chance."

"You've got to think ambitiously, Florence. Next stop, the Albert Hall."

She gave a little snort of laughter and punched Harry playfully on the arm.

They left the pub and walked slowly on holding hands. The summer evening was fading into darkness, the sky a profound indigo, the last shades of day smudged on the western horizon. The first stars were coming out. Florence hummed her favourite phrases of Vivaldi and swung her mandolin case.

"We can take a short cut down here," Harry said, steering her away from the traffic into a narrow alley.

"Where are we going?" she said. "It's rather dark."

"As I said, it's a short cut. It'll bring us out in Theobald's Road. That's alright, isn't it?"

"Yes, I suppose so, but I'm glad I've got you with me."

They walked on a few yards in silence. Then he stopped and turned towards her. He held her shoulders and pushed her firmly backwards into a doorway. "Just how glad are you, Florence?"

"Hey, not so rough. Harry. Please stop …"

She stumbled as he pushed her until her back was against the grimy door, using all his body weight against her. The mandolin case slipped from her grasp and clattered on the cobbles. She tried to retrieve it, but Harry would not let her. Flakes of old paint from the door lodged in her hair and cobwebs draped themselves over her face. The rusty doorknocker bruised her between her shoulder blades.

"You remember? The parting gift?" He was breathing heavily and his teeth were clenched. "This is it."

"Harry, please don't!"

His strength was crushing the air from her lungs and she could feel him hard, pushing against her belly. It horrified her. Nauseated her. His lips sought her mouth with savage force.

"I told you heaven was next." He breathed heavily and began to gather up the fabric of her skirt. His hand stroked her thigh, making its way towards the top of her stocking. With his other hand, he tugged her blouse until the fabric tore, the buttons scattering on the ground.

She battled to get away from him, but felt feeble under the oppression of his body. His fingers moved relentlessly upward and felt their way into her underwear, his nails gouging her soft flesh.

"*Get off*," she managed to gasp.

The tussle seemed to last for hours and she felt despair overtaking her.

"Come on, Florence. Admit you're enjoying it."

It was then she remembered his weak leg. She managed to hook her foot around it and get him off balance. He staggered momentarily and in that split second, she raised her knee and felt it make contact with his groin. He staggered backwards clutching his crotch and she struggled free.

"How *could* you? I trusted you." Her tears streamed.

"You prissy little bitch. Pretending you're not the *slut* you know you are. You're nothing but a *teaser*. And a *slut*. Do you hear me?"

She grabbed her mandolin, ran up the alleyway and turned into Theobald's Road. *Thank God it* is *Theobald's Road,* she thought. There were people. She clutched her ruined clothing at her neck and ran into the London evening, back to the familiarity of her Clerkenwell lodgings.

Mrs Bartle must have turned in, for the house was in darkness. "Thank God," Florence said again under her breath. Locking the door of her room behind her, she fell on her bed, shaking with anger and shame. Slut. He'd called her a slut.

Chapter 9

"You alright, Florence?" Mrs Bartle tapped on Florence's door. "Only, when you didn't come down for breakfast, I wondered if something was wrong."

"I'm fine, Mrs B. Just a bit slow off the mark this morning." Florence's voice was barely audible from inside the room. "I'll be down in a few minutes."

Mrs Bartle had kept the tea hot and when Florence appeared, she held out a cup to her.

"Wonderful concert last night," the landlady said, "you were so good, Florence. Really professional. And I loved that music you played. Who was it by again?"

"Vivaldi."

"I expect you were celebrating after the performance, weren't you? With that young man of yours?"

"Mmm." Florence felt her throat tightening. "Mrs Bartle, do you mind if I take this back upstairs? I'm feeling a bit fragile."

"Not at all, dear. Can I bring you a slice of toast and marmalade?"

Florence shook her head. "Not really hungry …" She turned and went back up to her room.

The landlady shrugged.

Florence sat down at her dressing table and examined her reflection in the mirror. She ran a hand through her tangled hair. Her eyes were puffy and reddened. *Bereavement must be like this. All the joy suddenly taken away,* she thought. *All ruined.*

But the worst thing was this inescapable feeling. Guilt. He'd called her a slut. Had she brought it on herself? Had she? She didn't feel as though she had led him on. She'd trusted him. What did that say about her judgement? *Tilting at windmills … They were right all along …* and Nell had warned her. One thing she knew for sure, though. She was going to tell no one. Not her sister. Certainly not her mother. No one.

"But," she announced to her reflection, "life has to go on. *I* have to go on. And … he didn't get what he was after." A glimmer of defiance. She poured some water from the ewer into the bowl on her washstand, and splashed it over her face. It was bracing. Then she took her hairbrush and brushed her hair until her scalp felt hot.

Chapter 10

When the Zeppelin night raids on London began, Nell and her children took refuge in the cupboard under the stairs of the house in Gurney Road, Stratford.

"Ellen, you're taking up too much room," said Grace.

"Well, you're hogging the blanket."

Sleep was hard to come by.

"Mum, I can hardly breathe in here," Alf said, "Can't I get out for a breath of fresh air."

"You stay where you are, Alfred Ashford. It's the safest place to be if we're hit," his mother said. "That's what they say, anyway. It's bad enough without Zeppelins dropping bombs on innocent civilians … every day it's closer, this war … we're all in danger, now." Nell shivered.

But one night during a raid, when the streetlights were dimmed, the rattle of gunfire turned to … what was it … voices …? cheering? Making her way along the dark hallway, Nell opened the front door slowly. Gazing up into the night sky, she watched as a great, cigar-shaped mass of flame fell slowly to earth.

"My God. It's like a vision from hell." Her voice wavered. Anxiety flooded in.

All of London saw the Zeppelin fall from the night sky. The three older Ashford children emerged from the cramped cupboard, woken by the jubilant sounds coming in from the street. They made their way to the front door and peered out.

"What's going on, Mum?" Ellen asked, rubbing her eyes.

"Just look," was all Nell could say. The spectre of war, random death. Nearer, ever nearer.

Alf was gaping in amazement. "Oh! Good shot!"

Grace watched the flaming airship fall. "Those poor men … I can't bear it!" Tears filled her eyes.

Nell put an arm round her. "Shush," she said, "That's one less to drop its bombs on us."

"But the men inside will burn to death."

In the morning, Grace picked up the 'Fireworks' journal and wrote to her father: *Everyone cheered last night when the airship came down. There were even bagpipes playing. But all I could think about were the men dying in that terrible fire. They might have been dads with sons and daughters like Alf and me. Those poor children.*

In the next day's newspaper, Nell read the full story of the night's action. Lieutenant William Leefe Robinson, Royal Flying Corps pilot of 39th Home

Defence Squadron had pursued the airship in his BE2c open cockpit biplane, flying at 11,000 feet. His top speed, the article said, was 70 miles an hour. Robinson had fired two drums of incendiary ammunition at the airship to no avail. At the third attempt, the ship ignited and crashed with the loss of all 15 crew members who either burned in the inferno or jumped to their death.

A few days later, Robinson was awarded the Victoria Cross for his feat of airmanship that night. The press was full of reports.

"Golly. A VC already. That was quick," Nell said.

"Mmm," said Florence.

"You alright, Flo?"

"Sorry, what did you say?"

She sat stirring her tea in her sister's back kitchen. It was Wednesday afternoon.

"I asked if you're feeling alright. Not off-colour, are you? Only we haven't seen you for a couple of weeks. It's not about that bloke with the limp, is it?"

"No!" Florence said a little too quickly. There was a steely edge to her voice. "That … didn't come to anything …" She took a sip of her tea and the drew breath. "I'm fine. I just … haven't been sleeping too well, that's all. And I've been quite busy. At work." She summoned a smile. "How's George?"

Nell sighed. "He's alright, I think, but his letters tell me precious little … I feel so … disconnected …"

She sat with the two babies, one on each knee. "Flo, d'you think you could hold on to one of these for me? Then I can top up the tea."

She handed Iris, with the blue eyes and blonde curls across to Florence. The baby beamed toothlessly, a stream of dribble escaping from her mouth.

"Oh, here," Nell said, holding out a muslin cloth, "she's teething. She'll slobber all over you."

Nell put Renee down on a mat in front of the range and retreated to the scullery. Florence sat Iris on her arm.

"Hello, little one. How are you?" Iris reached out, took hold of her aunt's nose and chuckled.

"Oi, let go of me, you little monkey," Florence said, releasing her nose from Iris' grasp. She found she was smiling at the baby.

Nell returned and put the pot back under the cosy. "And since George left, it seems to me the war's come knocking on our door. The Zeppelins … they put the fear of God into me, I don't mind telling you. My nerves're on edge all the time these days. At least the children are a comfort. Ellen's an enormous help when she's not at school, and Alf does his best. And Grace … well, she's Grace. No trouble, but something of a dreamer – a bit like you, really."

Florence let it pass.

"But I worry about them, too. And money's tight, of course. Sometimes I wonder about taking in a lodger. I could make room with George away."

In a moment of quiet, Nell picked Renee up and sat down. Florence ran her fingers through Iris' curls.

"Why don't I move in with you all, Nellie? Be your lodger?" It was like a moment of brightness on a dull day.

"You? Why would you want to do a thing like that?"

"I've … well, I've been thinking of leaving Brown and Son for a while … business has been a bit iffy there recently. It's the war, I think … As I said, I'm not sleeping too well … Feeling … unsettled."

"Would you feel any better here? With babies waking in the night and Alf running through the house like a herd of elephants?" Nell's face was a picture of amazement.

Florence shifted Iris onto her shoulder. The baby burped. Florence smiled again.

"Excuse me!" she said to the child, and then "Do you know, I think I would, Nellie."

"And what if we fall out? We're very different, you and I."

"Yes, I know. But I'd be another grown-up to talk to. And much better than a stranger, surely."

"You'll have to get a new job. Near here. In Stratford."

"There's no shortage of work – I'll find something."

"But in Stratford. You couldn't wait to escape Stratford."

Florence shrugged and smiled. "Oh, well," was all she said.

Renee began to whine. Nell picked her up.

"Here," she said. "You have this one and I'll take over that one. You'll have to learn how to stop them grizzling if you're going to live here."

**

"I'm so sorry, Mr Arthur. I hate to let you down, but my sister needs my support, so I'm moving back to Stratford. I must hand in my notice."

"I can't say I'm not disappointed, Miss Mundy. You've been an exemplary member of staff. We shall miss you at Brown and Son."

At dinner time on her last day, Florence took herself on a little odyssey to visit all the places that had meant so much to her in her time at the bookshop. Looking along the Thames from Hungerford Bridge, she hoped desperately that one day the memory of Harry Bartholomew would disappear into thin air like the steam from the locomotives. *Not yet … But maybe one day.*

Brown Senior shook her hand. "You can rely on a good reference from Brown and Son, Miss Mundy. And I'd like you to have this as a token of our esteem. And if you ever want to come back, there'll be a place for you here."

He handed her a handsomely bound first edition of *Far From The Madding Crowd*. It smelt richly of leather.

"Oh Hardy. How lovely. Thank you."

She ran her hand over the cover and opened the book at random and began to read: *"'Oh!' she cried out in affright, pressing her hand to her side. "Have you run me through – no, you have not! Whatever have you done!"*

"I have not touched you," said Troy, quietly. "It was mere sleight of hand. The sword passed behind you. Now you are not afraid, are you?"'

Hm. Troy, Florence thought. *A bad lot.* She closed the book. "I can't wait to read it all, Mr Arthur. It'll be a treat."

***

"I'll have to ask you to pay till the end of next week, I'm afraid," Mrs Bartle said. "It'll take me a few days to relet the room."

"You've been the best landlady anyone could wish for, Mrs B. Thank you for taking care of me."

She took a last look round her little room. It had been a haven. A refuge.

"And you've been the nicest lodger. I only hope I can find another half as good."

She smiled at Florence and put an arm around her shoulder. "Good luck, dear. You deserve it."

***

And so Florence moved back. The Yardley reek. The Dew Drop Inn. An ache of defeat and humiliation in her soul like a dead weight.

"What about a job?" Nell asked her. "Why don't you go into a munitions factory? They say the money's really good."

Florence shivered and hunched her shoulders. "Not for me, Nellie. I couldn't be part of making those weapons. They're killing young men wholesale."

"German young men, though."

"Still men. Flesh and blood. Fathers, sons, brothers, husbands … Not for me."

"You sound like Grace."

"Good for her if she feels that way."

"Surely there are plenty of civilian jobs around if you don't fancy war work," Nell said. "What about the buses? I read an advertisement at the bus stop on the Broadway the other day. Haven't you seen it?"

"What are they advertising for?"

"Bus conductresses. With London General. It says you have to be at least five-foot-tall and aged between 21 and 35. How tall are you, Flo?"

"Five foot seven … I quite like that idea."

"I think you'd make a really good bus conductress, Aunt Flo," Alf said.

"And the uniform's very smart," Ellen added.

"Terrific idea," said Grace. "Standing room only! No standing on the top deck!"

"Well, with you lot ganging up on me, I can hardly say no, can I?"

***

"They couldn't have been keener," she told the family. "I've got to have a medical and then there's two weeks' training. It's in Chelsea – I can get there by bus."

Then she got her navy-blue uniform.

"The skirt's rather short," Nell said.

"It has to be ten inches above the ankle so you don't trip going upstairs."

"The hat's a bit funny," Grace said, "why's it got that chinstrap?"

"So it doesn't blow off on the top deck, of course. I'll have to go up on top in all weathers."

"What route will you be on?" Nell asked.

"Route 10. Elephant and Castle to Wanstead. I can pick it up at the end of the road to get to and from the bus garage. I couldn't wish for better."

Better? Well of course she could wish for better. Better was life before Harry Bartholomew. Life with a job she enjoyed, where she was valued. Life with joy and music in it. Now life was the ache of shame, guilt. There. All the time. No matter how she tried to pretend otherwise.

Part Two

Chapter 11

It was approaching mid-summer, 1917. On a June afternoon, Nell was pegging out washing. The quiet of the day was interrupted by a deep droning. She looked up to see what was causing the sound. Low on the horizon, heading towards the city, she could make out what looked like a swarm of immense insects.

"My God! Bombers. In broad daylight."

Soon, away to the south of where she stood in her Stratford back yard, she heard the booms of exploding bombs and watched as plumes of smoke rose skywards, like some infernal funeral pyre. She was shaking. "No!" She shook her head and hot tears started. "No. No. No!"

"Have you read the news?" Florence asked when she got home at the end of her shift. "Those planes dropped bombs on a school in Poplar today. Dozens of children were killed. Here, it's all in the evening paper." She held out The Evening News to her sister.

"Children?" Nell sat down.

Fourteen Gotha aircraft had raided London, the report said. More than a hundred and fifty people died, including the Poplar schoolchildren. Unprepared, hundreds more Londoners were injured, many by falling anti-aircraft shrapnel. People had crowded into the street to watch.

"This is the last straw, Flo. Too close for comfort. Much too close. I can't carry on like this. It'll do me in, I swear." Nell bit her lip. "It could be us next ... it's just not safe here anymore."

Florence sighed as she reached for Nell's hand. "Steady, Nellie. Our boys will get the measure of the Germans ... the RFC'll see 'em off, just like they've done with the Zeppelins. You'll see."

"No. I can't just sit here and hope. I've got to do ... Something. Get out of here. I mean it, Flo. The East End, the docks. It's just too dangerous."

Nell's face was pale, her skin papery. She swayed and gripped the back of the chair for support.

"Sit down, Nellie. Can I get you a nip of brandy?"

Nell nodded weakly. "It's in the top cupboard in the scullery ... out of reach ... you'll need a stool ..."

Florence went out to the back, her mind on its own train of thought ... *Getting away from here – from London – would be good ... Bartholomew will be back soon ... I'm a sitting duck on the buses ...* Guilt and self-disgust still plagued her like evil characters in a puppet show, and the sight of a man in a wide-brimmed hat made her blood run cold. She rummaged among the dusters and metal polish, found the miniature of brandy and went back to her sister.

"Here. I'll pour you some."

Nell pulled a face as she sipped the fiery liquid, but it warmed her and she felt steadier.

"Tell you what, Nellie. Let's do some dripping toast for the children's tea. I'll cut the bread and you can toast it."

"Alright, Flo."

"Have the twins eaten?"

"Mmm. I scrambled an egg for them … they're in bed now."

Florence kept the mood of busyness and inconsequential chatter going.

"Someone got on the bus today with a double bass, of all things. Took up a whole seat. Had to charge him …"

She spread the toast slices with the meaty dripping and set the plate on the range to keep warm. All the while she searched her brain for a way forward. And then an idea struck her.

"Nellie! I've had a thought. Right out of the blue. It's a bit of a wild card, but you know what they say – 'Nothing ventured' …"

"What is it, Flo? What have you got in mind?" Nell sniffed and wiped her nose on the tea towel in her hands. She looked up at her sister. "The way I feel right now, I'm game for anything."

"Who do we know who's moved to the country?"

"Don't play games with me Flo. I'm not in the mood."

"Cousin Ivy? Moved to somewhere in Essex? When she married Sidney Rayner?"

"Oh, yes! What's the name of the town where they live?"

"Halstead. North Essex. Miles away from here. A different life."

"But we're hardly close to Ivy and Sidney."

"Blood's thicker than water, Nellie. And I'll come with you. I've got nothing to keep me here. I'm not wedded to London General."

Nell frowned, pondering Florence's idea. "But what about Mother and Dad? Should they come too?"

"They'd never leave – Stratford runs in their veins. Besides, Dad *is* wedded to Tate and Lyle's. He'll leave that company feet first. No. It's you, me and the children."

"Maybe you're right, Flo … Oh, let's do it."

"That's my girl, Nellie! I'll write to Ivy. If she can come up with some ideas, we might be able to make a run for it."

"And I'll speak to the landlord about shutting this house up." Nell was smiling now.

"Let's call the children in for their tea, shall we?"

Halstead. A bolt hole.

Chapter 12

"Dear Florence and Nell," Florence read, *"I'm sure I can help you find somewhere to stay here in Halstead. With so many menfolk away at the war, lots of people are finding it difficult to make ends meet. And with the extra space, taking in lodgers is quite popular. I must admit, though, that finding room for seven of you might prove a bit of a problem, but I'm sure we can find something suitable. Besides, Iris and Renee don't take up much room, do they?"*

"All their clobber does, though," Nell said.

"I know you'll love it up here as much as I do." Florence continued reading. *"I wouldn't come back to London if you paid me. By the way, I've heard people say that the name 'Halstead' comes from old English meaning 'place of refuge'. That's just right for you, isn't it?*
I'll keep in touch.

With love from your cousin,
Ivy Rayner.

"'Place of refuge', eh?" Florence said. "Just what we need."
"And the landlord says we can pay him a retainer and take a year's leave of absence from Gurney Road. So I've signed up to that."
"We're as good as on our way!"
In the ensuing days, Ivy forwarded a list of possible lodgings for Florence and the Ashfords. Florence and Nell scrutinised the inventory of possible billets, weighing up the relative merits of each. In the event, it came down to a trade-off between space and rent. At length they settled on Mr and Mrs Everitt at number 25, Stanley Road, Halstead – the accommodation was hardly spacious, but it was cheap. Florence felt empowered for the first time in months. Nell wiped tears away with the back of her hand. These were tears of determination.
"Stanley Road, Halstead. Here we come," Nell said.

***

The remainder of the summer of 1917 passed in a fever of preparation. Nell sorted the family's belongings into piles of things to take, things to ask her mother to store and things for the rag and bone man. Florence planned the journey.

47

Grace's 10th birthday in August was barely acknowledged in the flurry of activity. Then, one morning, the postman knocked at the Gurney Road house with an envelope for Grace. "It's come all the way from France. Must be something extra-special," he said.

Grace grabbed the envelope, thanked the postman and ran with it clutched to her chest till she reached the outside privy. *No one's going to barge their way in here*, she thought, bolting the door. She ran her thumb along the top of the envelope, scared she might damage whatever was inside if she ripped it open in too much haste.

She caught her breath as she withdrew the contents. It was the most beautiful thing she had ever seen – a card with a gauze panel, embroidered in silk: purple, yellow, pink and green, with pansies and cherry blossom and the words 'HAPPY BIRTHDAY' in silver thread. "Dad." She turned it over in her hands.

'On Active Service Somewhere in France', George had written. 'To My Dear Daughter Grace, To Wish you many Happy Returns of the Day, August 7th, 1917. From Your Loving Dad. Grace could not stop the tears as she read and reread the words – stilted, but written by her darling father. She ran her fingers over the card.

"I wonder where he was when he wrote this." And then: "This card's going with me to Halstead. In fact, I'm going to treasure it for the rest of my life."

Grace held the card and thought about the family's impending move. Stratford was all she and her siblings knew. Her whole life had been played out against the backdrop of Grandma Ashford's, Grandma Mundy's and 123 Gurney Road. Part of her was curious to see how other people lived and what 'the country' was like. She thought she might like it, that it might appeal to her love of beautiful things. Seeing things in nature that she'd only seen in pictures was exciting. On the other hand, there seemed to be something … what was it? … disloyal about leaving London. She looked to her Aunt Florence for reassurance. They were sitting together at the parlour piano, picking out familiar tunes.

"Aunt Flo," she began, "I wish I could see into the future."

"How so, Gracie?"

"Well, it sort of feels as though we're just running away – not just from the air raids, but from everything we know."

"In a way I suppose we are. But sometimes it's the sensible thing to do. And your mum's at her wits' end."

"Maybe it's silly," the child went on, "but I think I'll feel further away from Dad if we leave his home. There'll be fewer things to remind me of him. I don't want to forget him …"

"Carry on."

"If it's nice in Halstead, I'll feel guilty about enjoying life while Dad's hating what he's got to do in the war. D'you think Dad minds us leaving home like this?"

"Gracie, my love," Florence said. "Of course not. Just think of all the stories you'll have to tell him when he gets back. It's an adventure. Who knows what this year will bring for all of us?"

Chapter 13

They set out for their new life on an early September morning. Spiders' webs outside the bedroom windows spilled droplets of dew and sparkled in early sunshine. Halstead, straddling the meandering River Colne and surrounded by the soft north Essex countryside, was a formidable train journey from Stratford.

"Now then, you children." Nell spoke to her elder offspring like a commanding officer addressing troops. "It's a long walk to the station, and you can't dawdle or we'll miss the train. And you've got to do your share of carrying things."

"And at Marks Tey," Florence continued, "not only have we to change trains, but also platforms. It won't be easy."

Nell had crammed the twins' pram with as much luggage as she could and still leave room for the babies without risking them falling out. There were bags and parcels hanging from the pram handles. Ellen carried a bulging haversack stuffed full of winter coats, as well as a holdall of her own clothes. Alf and Grace were loaded down with packages almost as big as themselves, while the two women tackled heavy items of hardware and utensils.

They felt like a troupe of travelling tinkers. Progress along Stratford streets was slow. Ellen was stoical and tight-lipped. Grace and Alf exchanged glances. Each of them had insisted on adding their most cherished possessions to their burdens. Grace held her diary and her Dad's precious birthday card close to her chest. Alf clutched the pad of drawing paper he'd bought with the sixpence Grandma Ashford had given him for boot-cleaning services.

Stratford Market Station came into view.

"Phew, Nellie!" Florence said. "I'm done in already."

"Me too." Nell fixed her hatpin more securely. "What a slog! And we've only done Round One."

Florence looked at her watch. "We've got a few minutes to sit and recover. Thank heavens."

"So tiring with all this lot to carry," Nell said.

Florence put her baggage down and shook her hands to restore the circulation. Nell dabbed at her cheeks and forehead with a handkerchief.

"I don't know why you've brought that old mandolin, Flo – you haven't played it for months."

"I know … but … I might feel like taking it up again in Halstead …"

They waited for the arrival of the 9.27 from Liverpool Street with quiet anticipation. Renee and Iris were snoozing peacefully amid the baggage heaped on their pram.

"Listen," Florence said, cupping an ear, "you can hear the whispering in the rails."

Several moments later, the engine puffed into view. As it slowed in a cloud of smoke and steam, Grace felt dwarfed by the immensity of the thing and reached for Florence's hand. Oiled and polished piston rods drove back and forth, propelling the wheels whose diameter was at least twice her height. It let off steam in a deafening rush. The shock was tremendous. Grace clapped her hands over her ears and pulled a screwed-up face. The twins woke up and bawled.

"All aboard!" called the guard, flag in hand. "Now then," he said, addressing the Ashfords and Florence. "You'll have to travel with me in the guard's van with all that clobber. Come along, now. I'll help you up with it all. You'd better hang on to them little 'uns," he added. "We don't want no one fallin' down the gap, now, do we?"

After handing everything and everyone up into the guard's van Florence and Nell brushed smuts off their high-necked blouses and smoothed their skirts. Nell licked a corner of her hankie and dragged it over her children's faces. They grimaced in turn.

"Get off me, Mother," said Alf.

"I'm not having my children turning up looking like street urchins."

The train steamed out of the station, conveying the family into the unknown. At Marks Tey, they had all of nine minutes to haul the household entourage over a footbridge to the platform for the 11.21 Colne Valley Railway service to Halstead. Nell carried Renee and Iris, while everyone else dealt with the pram and its contents.

It took just half an hour to cover the last leg of the journey, but it was like travelling into a new world where greenness prevailed and placid animals roamed the gentle landscape.

They got out at Halstead Station and the train steamed on its way. Florence watched as the red tail lights receded to their vanishing point up the line. The steam cleared and the quiet seemed almost unnatural after the clatter and hiss of the train had died away. Taking a few moments to get her bearings, she shouldered her baggage.

"Right!" she said. "Let's get ourselves to Stanley Road. I could murder a cup of tea. Follow me!"

"Hello." The voice came from the doorway of the ladies' waiting room a little way up the platform.

Florence looked up at the figure emerging from it. "Ivy!"

"I thought I'd come and meet you. Here. Let me help you with those heavy bags. Welcome to Halstead. I hope you'll be very happy here. Come on, I'll show you to Stanley Road.

"What are they like, the Everitts?"

"Honest, straight talking, I'd say," Ivy said. "She can be a bit sharp, but he's a sweet old codger."

The little procession turned left into a neat street of red brick cottages, grouped in terraces of four, each bearing a small stone plaque with a name carved into it. Number 25 was part of Prospect Cottages, 1905. Built on two floors, it presented its front door and just one downstairs window and one upstairs towards the road, a classic 'two-up-two-down'.

"I'll be on me way now," Ivy said. "Let you get settled in. Come and have tea with Sidney and me soon." She turned and left them at the gate, waving as she withdrew.

The tiled path was swept. Florence lifted the knocker and set her face into a smile. There was a rustling from within and then the rattle of a lifting latch. Mrs Everitt was a plump red-cheeked woman, but there was no warmth in her piercing eyes. She greeted Nell and Florence a little stiffly, and showed the family into the living kitchen. There was a kettle heating on the range.

Looking round the room, Florence was struck by the lack of comfort. *Spartan*, she thought. Wooden floor with just a rag rug in front of the stove, a hard chair with no cushion and a table that was hardly big enough for them all to sit round at once. But the china was not chipped, and the tea revived the travellers.

"Now," said Mrs Everitt. "These are the rules of the house ..." Her accent was broad. Country. Nell and Florence smiled and nodded, while Alf and Grace nudged each other. Ellen took it all on board. A chapter of Mrs Everitt's prohibitions related to the young and were listed under the rubrics of 'not makin' no noise', 'not trampin' mud into the house' and 'not disturbin' Swank at mealtimes'.

'Swank', it turned out, was Mr Everitt. Florence wondered what it was short for.

"And you needn't expect me to do no cookin' for you," Mrs Everitt said. "You can have the run of the kitchen while I'm at work, so you can look after yourselves. It's lights out at 9.30 of an evenin'. Swank's got to get a good night's kip afore he starts work at 6. I'll show you the sleepin' quarters."

There were just two bedrooms at 25 Stanley Road; Nell, Ellen, Grace and the twins were to sleep in the larger one, while Florence and Alf had to share the smaller. Mrs Everitt and Swank had arranged to sleep on the settee and a canvas camp bed in the parlour.

Florence and Nell thanked Mrs Everitt, but wondered how they could accommodate the contents of the pram as well as all their clothes in the confines of the tiny bedrooms. The pram itself was destined for the Everitt's minute shed, where the hens would more than likely roost in it.

"Come on," said Ellen, "there's lots to do. We can shift the beds around and store the things we don't need every day underneath them."

They hauled their bags up the narrow staircase, bumping on every tread. Alf remembered his drawing pencils and, carefully withdrawing them from his sock, placed them under his pillow. Florence dandled Renee and Iris on both knees while Nell and Ellen began unpacking the bags and finding places to stow their belongings. Alf and Grace passed the contents of the pram up the stairs from one to the other. When that was done, they felt a little superfluous.

"Look," said Nell, cramming the twins' cardigans into a chest drawer. "You two," indicating her son and second daughter. "Why don't you make yourselves scarce? There isn't enough room for all of us in here. You might as well go and have a look round. Make sure you're back before dark."

Grace and Alf couldn't escape quickly enough. They raced to the end of Stanley Road, which lay on the edge of the town. Beyond it were fields as far as they could see. Green meadows running down to the river. The trees in woods and spinneys were just beginning to turn russet. The Colne Valley basked in the glow of afternoon sunshine, the sky a deep ultramarine, rosebay willow herb spikes still a ravishing pink. Grace caught her breath. It was love at first sight.

"Oh, Alf! How lovely it all is! Quick. Let's get down to the river. There's a bridge over there. We can look for fish!"

"Yeah!" Alf waved his fist. "I bet I get there first!"

"Oh, no you won't!" Grace was already running. The soft air ruffled their hair as they tore across the meadow and they were gasping by the time they reached the wooden bridge spanning the Colne winding its way towards Halstead.

"Just look," said Alf. "Fish! When you said we could look for them, I never thought we'd actually see any."

There in the lazy flow of the river, camouflaged against the stony bottom, but still visible, trout swam along the shallows. Neither of the children had seen live fish before, save for the goldfish in glass bowls given away as prizes on the hoopla stall at the fair on Wanstead Flats. But that was in another world.

The two children leaned over the rail watching the water flow quietly under the bridge, small rafts of reed coursing along between the river banks.

"Funny thing," said Grace, "The sky's jolly blue, but the water looks even bluer. How do you think it does that, when the water's only reflecting the sky?"

"No idea," said Alf after a pause for reflection. "But you're right, Gracie. Further down it looks like a silver ribbon … I like it here by the river, I think I'm going to learn to fish, if I can find anyone with a rod who'll teach me."

They took their time to wander back to their lodgings. This freedom. So exciting. So novel. Looking out across the meadow, Grace spotted some pale discs nestling in the grass. She pointed them out to Alf.

"What do you think they are?"

"Hmm, they look like toadstools or something."

Grace ran across to take a closer look. "They're *mushrooms*! And they're like *saucers*, Alf. Come on! Help me pick some!"

"How d'you know they aren't toadstools?" Alf asked. "They could be poisonous. You could die if you eat them."

"They're mushrooms, I tell you. Look at the underneath side. I think they're called gills. And if they're pinky brown like these, they're definitely mushrooms – I read it in a nature book. Just look at the size of them!"

Grace scooped up the hem of her skirt to make a sort of pouch and began gently to ease the white mushrooms from the ground. Soon, she and Alfred had filled the skirt-pouch. With care, they carried the precious harvest back to the house.

"Yes, young lady," said Mrs Everitt. "Them's mushrooms alright. Tell you what," she suggested, turning to Nell, "You can have an egg or two from me hens, fresh today, and I can let you have some of Bill Broyd's good bacon to go with 'em. It'll make a nice supper, will that."

Nell thanked Mrs Everitt and offered to cook some for her and Swank.

"That's right good of you," the landlady replied. Perhaps her initial bark was worse than her bite.

' ... and we picked tons of wild mushrooms', Grace wrote in her diary, 'I've never eaten anything so delicious in my life. It was a banquet.'

Later, she lay in her bit of the shared bed. I wonder what Dad's had for his supper tonight, she thought.

Chapter 14

"Look Gracie." Florence pointed a finger at Halstead on a local map. "X marks the spot."

The roads linking the Essex towns of Braintree and Colchester with Sudbury and Haverhill in Suffolk intersect there in the Colne Valley. The town was neither handsome, nor pretty, though it harboured charming corners. It was more what Florence called workmanlike: purposeful, and with an air of self-confidence. Its main street, broad, like many English market towns, rose quite steeply from the river crossing at the Town Bridge to the Jubilee Fountain, Halstead's tribute to Queen Victoria's Golden Jubilee.

There at the top of the town, the flint solidity of St Andrew's Church with its square tower dominated the townscape, its chiming clock marking out the rhythm of Halstead life. Halstead people had worshipped on that site since Saxon times. Beyond the Town Bridge at the bottom of the hill, a little road, The Causeway, turned away from the main highway through the town to run alongside the Colne for a couple of hundred yards to Townsford Mill, standing astride the river. Once a flour mill, it later became a silk weaving factory of the Courtauld company, which flourished in Halstead, providing much local employment in the heart of the town.

Waking on her first morning in Halstead, Grace rubbed her eyes. Remembering where she was, she leapt out of bed and, drawing back the curtain, saw that it was another bright day.

"Right," she said, "I'm going to explore this town today. Who wants to come with me?" She caught her mother's expression, one of slight disapproval.

"Sorry, Mum," she added quietly, "I should have asked you first. Do you need me to help you today?"

Nell smiled slightly as she changed Iris's nappy. She hadn't the heart to squash Grace's excitement. "No, dear," she said. "You can go. Perhaps Alf and Aunt Flo would like to go too. It'd do Flo good to get out and have a look round. Ellen and I can manage here."

They breakfasted on porridge which had steamed itself to a delicious gloopiness on the range overnight. It tasted divine with milk and honey from local hives.

"You must go by the Public Gardens," Mrs Everitt said. "What we call 'The Rec'."

"What's it like?" Grace asked. "Are there any swings?"

"No, but it's got right nice gardens and a little bandstand. In the summer months they hold dances there. On the dancing green."

"Let's go there first," Grace said.

The Public Gardens were less than five minutes' walk from Stanley Road. By now, the floral displays were past their best, but still pretty. Narrow footpaths, punctuated with park benches, circumscribed a central mown green, and wended their way between flower beds. At one end of the grassy sward stood a bandstand, painted green and with a weather vane on top.

"This must be where they hold the dances in the summer," Florence said. Grace held out her skirt and did a pirouette on the grass. Her aunt smiled.

"Lots of things to look forward to."

They did a tour of The Rec and, emerging onto the main street, stopped on the Town Bridge to watch the waters of the River Colne as they streamed through the town. The High Street was quiet and virtually bereft of traffic save for the odd delivery bicycle or horse-drawn cart. Alf was smitten by the drawing possibilities in every courtyard and under every archway. He disappeared down alleyways and cart tracks to see what might be hidden out of sight of the main street. Florence and Grace looked in shop windows – Broyd's the butchers, whose bacon they had already enjoyed, a greengrocer under the name of Cooper, Pountney's ironmongery and hardware stores. Hardly glamorous.

"D'you think you'll like living here, Aunt Flo?" Grace asked. "What will you do to fill your time?"

"Well, Gracie, it's too early to say just yet. But I'll make the best of it whatever. And you never know what's round the corner, do you?"

Uncanny, that child. It was as if Grace had tapped straight into her thoughts. For though Florence felt safe in Halstead, the same demons still stalked her. How was she to reinvent herself here? Apart from those who were too old, too frail or needed for the domestic war effort, most of the men had been packed off to fight. The community was lopsided. Women were running family shops and businesses, and most of Courtauld's workers were women. There had to be opportunities.

Florence and Grace meandered on, arm in arm. Alf reappeared after one of his solo forays. "D'you know, there's an old workhouse round the corner. 'Cept it hasn't got paupers in it any more, it's full of soldiers. All getting ready to go off and fight, I expect."

"Oh, really?" said Florence. "Did you meet any?"

Chapter 15

"You've got to go to school," Nell said to Ellen, Alf and Grace. "Education's too important to ignore."

Nell made an appointment for the children to meet the head of Halstead Council School, Mr Morton Mathews. On an afternoon when the school day was coming to an end, she accompanied all three, scrubbed clean and dressed in their best, to the school tucked away among the complex of weaving factories clustered together in the shadow of Townsford Mill.

Mathews' task of managing 340 pupils with a teaching staff of just six women teachers was often challenging. A slight, bespectacled man in his late middle years with a luxuriant moustache, Morton Mathews ran his school with quiet dignity. He greeted the three Ashford youngsters.

"One must never lose sight of the need to respect both staff and pupils in this job," he said, "but you have to be tough as well, or control goes out of the window. I can be hard on miscreants."

Alf looked apprehensively at Mathews. The Head caught sight of the boy's face and a smile spread across his features.

"Don't worry too much, Alfred, I'm not a complete ogre. Life would be dull without laughter, wouldn't you say?"

"Yes, Mr Mathews."

Alf was excited to learn that Morton Mathews was an artist of talent and not a little fame. His lithographic prints regularly featured in exhibitions at the Royal Academy. And many portrayed local buildings.

"And what are your favourite subjects?" he asked, appraising the three youngsters.

"Drawing! I love drawing buildings – just like you … Sir," he added, aware of his mother's stern glare.

"Oh," replied Mr Mathews. "I look forward to having a look at your efforts. But I would urge you, young man, not to neglect the principal aspects of your education – and I mean by that the Three 'Rs'. You may find you need them in later life."

"Yes, Sir," said Alf, chastened.

"And what about you two girls? What is it that enthuses you?"

"I love words, Sir," Grace said. "English and composition and spelling. Sometimes I write poems. And music and nature are the things I like most."

"Very good," said Morton Mathews. "I'm sure you'll enjoy your school life here. And you, young lady," he asked, turning his bespectacled gaze on Ellen. "What can we do for you?"

"I can do arithmetic," said Ellen. "That's what I'm best at, Sir," said Ellen, respectfully, but without enthusiasm.

"Excellent! I see no sense in delay. You'll need a week or so to get yourselves kitted out, so I'd like to see you here on the Monday two weeks before the half-term break. That way you'll have a little while to get used to how we do things here, get to know your teachers and classmates, and be ready to *get down to business* after the break. How does that suit you?"

"Very well. And thank you for your time, Mr Mathews," Nell said, nodding and rising from her chair. "I'll see that the children fulfil your confidence in them."

***

"I really want to make the most of these lovely autumn days before we have to start going to school," Grace said at breakfast time next morning. "There's so much to discover and it's so pretty here."

"You ought to take yourselves over to the Brawkes," said Swank Everitt as the lodgers sat around the kitchen table. "It's nice there, and you can gather nuts an' blackberries by the pailful."

"Ooh! I'd like to go there," said Grace. "Can you tell us how to find it?"

She really had no idea what 'it' was. The word 'Brawkes' meant nothing to her. But Swank explained the route, pointing it out on Florence's map. She discovered it was in fact Broak's Wood which lay to the north west of the town, accessed by a series of footpaths over open farmland.

"Can we go tomorrow, if the weather's still nice, Aunt Flo?" Grace asked. "We could take a picnic and spend all day there, if you have the time."

"Well, young Gracie, we could make ourselves useful and bring back some blackberries for tea, couldn't we? If that's alright with your mum." She glanced in Nell's direction.

Florence and Grace set out looking like explorers equipped with stout shoes and waterproofs in case the weather turned nasty. They took an assortment of cans and jars, tied with string handles for foraging, and a hearty picnic. The world was theirs. And Broak's Wood fulfilled its promise for Grace that day.

"I can't believe the colour of the leaves on those trees. It's as though they're on fire."

Hazelnuts abounded, and the two of them crammed them into their containers. Blackberries, likewise, were so prolific they felt intoxicated by the plenty. Nature's riches poured out on them. They followed all the little tracks they could find, russet fallen leaves crackling under their feet. Grace scooped them up between her two hands and tossed them into the air to watch them gently tumble back to earth. Florence took care of the fruit and nut harvest and stood watching her niece.

"This place is revealing a new you!" She smiled at the child's exhilaration.

"I know, Aunt Flo. I can't believe how lovely it is."

They sat by a little pool to eat their picnic of hard-boiled eggs, ham sandwiches and apples, washed down with ginger beer, Aunt Flo's special treat. The water in the pool was muddy, opaque. Grace trailed her fingers in it.

"It's the colour of a soldier's uniform." She stared into its rippling surface and saw, floating there, indistinct, her father's face, his army cap tipped back on his head, his mild, brown eyes looking back at her. She smiled at the reflection, wondering how his day was going.

"A penny for them," said Florence.

"Oh." Grace sighed, her eyes glistening. "I feel so guilty enjoying myself while Dad's over there with all that barbed wire and guns. Supposing he … Supposing I never see him again?"

"Come and sit by me," said Florence. She put her arm round Grace's shoulders. "You know, your Dad wouldn't want you to sit around moping. Just think of how much you'll have to tell him when he comes home. And you must believe he will come home."

Grace realised her aunt was right. So she recorded it all in her diary. The glorious autumn colours, the harvest of blackberries and nuts – 'all free!' she wrote – the apparition in the quiet pool water, the comforting conversation with Aunt Florence.

Chapter 16

Another afternoon, Florence, Nell and all five children walked to a fruit farm to buy windfall apples. The day was still, the sky cloudless and bees buzzed among the ivy. The air was full of the scent of the orchard. There were plenty of windfalls to be had, but the trees were also laden with fruit – *crimson and gold globes, tempting and luscious*, as Grace wrote later – that remained unpicked. Florence and Nell could not resist the temptation to stow some of the perfect fruits under the twins' pram cover.

"Who's going to miss them?" said Nell.

"But why haven't they been harvested?" Florence frowned. "The wasps'll get them if they're not picked soon."

Florence asked the same question over Nell's baked apples that evening.

"Not enough labour to do it," said Swank Everitt, who worked as an agricultural carter, hauling fodder, crops and milk churns for local farms. "Farmin's the same everywhere. No blokes to do the work."

"That's terrible," said Florence. "Almost a crime in wartime."

"Government's never had any time for farmin'," Swank went on. "It's not even a reserved occupation."

"So where does all our food come from?" Grace asked.

"The empire and America," Mrs Everitt said, "Always been cheaper than 'ere. But now them German U-boats're blowin' up our shippin'. Blockadin' ports, too."

"So even though it looks so plentiful around here, it's all an illusion," Florence said.

"Yup. This year's harvest's nothin' short of a disaster. People'll be starvin' afore long. And what's this useless government's answer? Get women workin' on the land. I ask you."

"Isn't that a good idea?" Florence said. "In London thousands of women are doing men's jobs. Why not farming?"

"Not tough enough," Swank said. "And it'll mean wages'll fall."

The Ministry of Food, which had only come into being the previous year, was exhorting women to take to the land. 'God Speed The Plough' read one recruiting poster, 'And The Woman Who Drives It' against a picture showing a besmocked and gaitered female driving a team of heavy horses turning a straight furrow into a radiant sunset.

"I've seen the posters," Florence said to Nell. "They've set me thinking. The Women's Land Army – why not? I've nothing else to do, and this is important work."

"Are you quite sure?"

"My mind's made up."

"But farming's gruelling work. You're not used to it."

"I'm still young, I'm healthy and I could be a farm worker."

"But the winter's coming. You'll have to turn out in all weathers …"

"I know all that. But how can I sit around here buffing my finger nails while the likes of George are risking everything in France, fighting for a country that's facing starvation? There are already a quarter of a million women out there who've signed up, apparently. Why not me?"

**

On the appointed Monday morning, Nell accompanied Ellen, Alfred and Grace for their first day at Halstead Council School. Ellen, now 12, was escorted to the classroom of Miss Hobbs, while Alf and Grace found themselves classmates in Miss Moore's class of some 60 children aged 10 and 11.

"I'm very pleased to meet you, Alfred and Grace," said Miss Moore, though her pursed smile told a different story. Two more pupils in her already overcrowded class was something she could do without. "I'm sure you'll fit in here."

"Good morning, Miss Moore," said Alf and Grace together, their gaze ranging over the sea of faces seated two-by-two at desks arranged in rows across the classroom.

"I've arranged for two children from the class to look after you and help you settle in," said Miss Moore. Looking towards the ranks of children, she said: "Doris and Donald, would you come to the front, please?"

Donald, his hair untidy, his tie askew, offered his hand to Alf. "How do," he said as Alfred returned the gesture. Donald's grip was firm.

Doris raised her brown eyes to meet Grace's blue-grey gaze. She smiled. "Come along, Grace, you can 'ave the desk by me," she said to the new girl in her country accent. Grace followed her back to her place.

Ellen, too, palled up with tall Madge Dixie who played the piano in morning assembly. Ellen took Madge back to Stanley Road for tea. The twins called her Mash. Alf, Grace and Ellen settled in quickly. Their classmates were fascinated by the way they spoke; the other pupils were all local children and had rarely heard London intonations.

Doris, Grace soon discovered, was the daughter of Mr and Mrs Cooper, whose greengrocery shop she and Florence had seen in Halstead High Street. Doris' dad, like Grace's, was away at the Front in France.

"It's awful, ain't it, Grace. Don't you miss 'im?"

"Yes, but I keep a diary that's meant just for him. And I can pretend I'm talking to him."

Grace recorded the importance of meeting Doris in her diary: *'I've never had a really close friend before. I'm having such nice times with Doris, and we like doing the same things. I believe she likes me, too.'*

"Are you any good at singing, Gracie?" Doris asked as they walked home from school.

"I absolutely love it."

"Well, you can join the choir at St Andrew's. I sing there every week."

"I'd like that."

"Right. Then you must ask your mum if you can come to practices on Thursdays at 6 o'clock with Mr Davage, he's the choirmaster.

***

Florence set about applying to join the Women's Land Army. The application form listed the terms and conditions for signing on. There were three sections of the WLA: agriculture, timber cutting and forage, and a choice of six months or a full year to sign up to. Florence pondered her options, and decided to join for six months.

"If I really like it and want to carry on, I'm sure I'll be able to renew the agreement," she said to Nell, as they read through the documentation. "And if I can't stand it or we go back to London, I won't be committed."

She decided to opt for agriculture, seduced as she had been by the image of the Land Girl driving the plough in the poster.

"It's not going to be apple picking in the autumn sunshine, you know," warned Nell. "All it mentions here are cereal and spuds – and mangolds for animal fodder. It'll be all about digging and hoeing and humping heavy loads, won't it?"

"Yes. It'll be hard work. I'll be wet through, I'll be muddy, but I'm damn well going to do it." Indeed, the self-flagellation aspects of what lay in store for her held a certain appeal. Atonement. A good way to expunge guilt. Rebuild self-respect. And she rather fancied the boots and breeches.

The application form set out a reciprocal bargain: applicants were required to sign up for six months, to attend a selection board and medical examination, to take up work when required and – this section was printed out in block capitals

– TO BE WILLING TO GO TO ANY PART OF THE COUNTRY YOU ARE SENT.

In return, the government promised an initial wage of 20 shillings per week, a free uniform, two weeks' free maintenance and free rail travel.

'No training will be given, therefore the initial wage is only 20 shillings,' explained a note at the foot of the page. 'Should the worker be able to pass an efficiency test, it will be raised to 22 shillings.'

"Fair enough," Florence said to herself. She was concerned about the requirement to go where she was sent. But, she reasoned, there was plenty of farming around Halstead, "And if I work from home, I'll cost the government less." *They'll be reasonable,* she thought, *why wouldn't they be?*

She applied straight away. The older Ashford children now at school and Nell with her life revolving around the twins' needs, Florence couldn't wait to roll up her sleeves, literally, and taste the life of a farm worker. She took the opportunity of chatting to Swank Everitt, when she got the chance. He got to see the life of local farms at close quarters.

"It'll be comin' on for winter when you join up. Not much field work, but there'll be plenty to do wi' animals, specially if it's a cold 'un. It ain't easy, though, Miss Mundy, hauling great loads of hay out to the sheep."

Florence was not expecting the bureaucratic wheels of the Board of Agriculture to turn with any sense of urgency in spite of the circumstances. She had read excerpts from a speech by the Board's President, exhorting women to sign up for the WLA, but warning them: "This is no occasion for lilac sun bonnets ... " Florence, who'd never worn a sun bonnet in her life, thought: *patronising so-and-so* and hoped that he was not typical of the WLA hierarchy.

In a bid to do something useful during the dog-days of waiting for a response to her application, Florence went to the apple orchard she'd visited with the family and offered her services to harvest as many of the ripe fruits as she could. To begin with, she took them home to Stanley Road, where Nell got involved in cooking tarts, crumbles, cobblers and apple dumplings – as much as rationing would allow. Before long, the two women were able to supply small batches of home-baked apple desserts to the baker in the High Street.

"I bet Doris' mum would love some apples to sell," said Grace. And she was right. Molly Cooper was pleased to stock this local produce and she put other local greengrocers in touch with Florence.

"We've got a thriving little business in the making here," Nell said, smiling.

Ellen, Alf and Grace helped with the apple picking after school and during weekends. Swank Everitt tucked into mouth-watering 'afters' each evening. Nell's cooking talents were a revelation in the Everitt household. Mrs E, whose job cleaning at the 'big house' left her exhausted, had no energy left for cooking at the end of a working day. Nell Ashford's arrival was changing Swank's life. He'd never been fed this well before.

Chapter 17

"Florence Mundy." The receptionist beckoned her forward. She smoothed her coat, straightened her fairisle beret and stepped out over the oak floor.

There were three members of the Women's Land Army recruitment panel, all women, each sensibly dressed in felt hats and tweed suits. *County set*, Florence thought, presenting them with a frank, open look. *They're not pulling social rank on me.*

She found, gratifyingly, and somewhat surprisingly, that her look was returned in kind. They had class superiority written all over them, these women. The pearls, the twinsets, the careful makeup. Yet the eyes looking back at her were not supercilious – she'd seen that regard many times before. These eyes were candid, yes, but she didn't mind that. There was something else. What was it? Not begging, surely not. Entreaty. That was it. These women really wanted – needed – her to be a good candidate. It was a look that boosted Florence's confidence.

"Do sit down, Miss Mundy." The chairwoman indicated a straight-backed chair facing the panel. "My name is Matilda Fairfax, and these are my colleagues, Mrs Beryl Jupp and Miss Laetitia Allen-Jones."

"How do you do?" Florence said with a slight nod.

"Now, I don't imagine I need to stress how badly Britain needs the help of women like you at this critical time. Agriculture is in a parlous state with so many men away, and we can no longer rely on imports with our shipping a prey to enemy submarines," Matilda Fairfax said.

"Yes," Florence said. "So I've read. It's why I'm here."

The panel of ladies asked Florence about her background and work experience, her health and her expectations of the Women's Land Army.

"There'll be no shortage of physical effort required of you, Miss Mundy," Beryl Jupp said, her tone almost pleading with Florence not to decline the modest terms on offer.

"Now you've heard what the WLA expects, are you still interested in taking on this challenge?" asked Matilda Fairfax, pen in hand.

"Yes, I am, very definitely. But I have one request to put to you …"

Florence stressed her preference for working within reach of Halstead. The ladies whispered among themselves for a few moments, before turning back to Florence.

"I think we can agree to your request – we really can't afford to lose promising candidates."

Florence emerged from the interview with a printed requisition for an official medical examination. The local doctor's surgery in Halstead was authorised to carry them out. She could fix it up in the next couple of days.

***

At Stanley Road a bombshell was about to drop. Mrs Everitt chose her moment with care.

Nell sat at the table peeling onions. Bill Broyd the butcher in the High Street, who had sympathy for the young Londoner with her growing family and absent husband, had let her have a bagful of marrow bones, which now stood simmering on the stove. Nell was in the process of producing some hearty soup. Served with satisfying suet dumplings, it was a meal which rendered its partakers replete and mellow. Renee and Iris were engaged in preparing a tea party for their shared toy dog on the rug in front of the range.

Nell had got into the habit of making enough quantity to offer the Everitts a portion each. It was a way of repaying them for sharing their tiny home. She knew how much Swank appreciated her cooking, and she was happy to do it.

"I've got to 'ave a word, Missus Ashford," said Mrs Everitt. Nell looked up from her task, mopping her eyes, moist from the onions.

"Of course, Mrs E. Is there anything wrong?" Nell had not succeeded in striking up the kind of warm relationship she'd have liked to have with her landlady, but she believed they had a good enough modus vivendi.

"Well." Mrs Everitt cleared her throat. "I got to ask you all to leave," she said, her hands clasped in front of her pinafore.

"What?" Nell looked up, shocked. "But why? I thought we'd settled in so well!"

"What with this house bein' so small, I feel we're all too crowded in." She looked awkward. "And then there's all this feedin' Swank his dinner." A pause interposed while Mrs Everitt arranged her features into her most serious expression. "Are you tryin' to lure him away?" She took a step back, placing her fists on her hips.

Nell looked at her open-mouthed, hardly believing what she was hearing. Swank was old enough to be Nell's father. She felt the urge to giggle rising in her chest, but she knew it would be a mistake to laugh out loud.

"Of course not!" Nell shook her head. She raised the handkerchief once again to her eyes, but now it wasn't the onions causing them to water. "Mrs E! How could you think such a thing?"

"Well," said the landlady again. "There it is. I've made me mind up. You got to go. I'll give you time to find somethin' else, but I want you gone afore Christmas."

Mrs Everitt turned and left the room.

"Very well," said Nell to the woman's retreating figure. "We know when we're not wanted."

Nell quite literally didn't know whether to laugh or cry. *What a preposterous situation*, she thought. Her shoulders shook with silent laughter. But where were they to go?

When Florence arrived home with the daily apple quota, Nell broke the news. "What?" said Florence. "You and … *Swank*? God, give me strength!" The two sisters fell into each other's arms, helpless with laughter. "We'll have to get Ivy on to it again."

"Well, I dunno," Ivy said. "Most could take two at a pinch – but seven!"

"Not likely," said one potential landlord after another.

It was the vicar, Rev Curling, who suggested the Mizens in Factory Terrace. Of their four children, only one, Elsie, remained at home.

Factory Terrace was a row of brick cottages built by the Courtauld family to house workers at the neighbouring weaving factory. Arranged in two blocks, each house had pretty latticed windows and three floors, enabling residents to provide lodgings for silk weavers living too far distant to travel to and from work each day. Between the two blocks stood a massive brick chimney, conveying waste vapours away from the factory's power house.

Jane Mizen worked day shifts at the Courtauld's factory overlooked by Factory Terrace, where they wove synthetic silk fabric pioneered by the company. She was a big-boned, grey-haired woman with a pleasant manner and the tolerant demeanour begotten of raising four children. Mr Mizen – Monty – a burly man, was an engine driver for the London North Eastern Railway, a job which kept him from home for many hours at a time, returning dog-tired at all sorts of hours in serious need of his sleep. Monty's face seemed to Grace to be always smeared with oil and coal dust, his finger nails deeply encrusted with black grime. Monty's bath times in the galvanised tub before the kitchen fire were hallowed. Number one house rule was not to disturb Monty's bath. Rule number two was never to waken him from his much needed sleep. But Monty was a cheerful man, and chuckled a lot, his laughter filling the house.

For the Ashfords and Florence, life in Factory Terrace was a distinct improvement on Stanley Road. With two spacious bedrooms and a sitting room at their disposal, they were far less cramped.

'*The chimney scares me*', Grace confided in her diary. '*When I look up at it, the whole thing seems to sway and fall towards me. I know it's just because the clouds are moving that makes it seem that way, but I don't think I'll ever get used to it*'. She was drawn by the constant hum and rattle emanating from the factory and would peer in through the ventilation gratings on a scene of intense activity where women in caps and overalls tended the great looms, the shuttles flying back and forth.

Elsie, the Mizen's 12-year-old daughter was in Ellen's class at school. Nell began to invite Elsie to join the Ashford children at breakfast time for a helping of porridge. Elsie's loose-lipped mouth seemed to slide about when she spoke. Eating porridge, she struggled to control each mouthful. Grace would stare, transfixed. '*It's rude, I know,*' she wrote, '*but I can't help it. All that slurping – I just want to giggle all the time!*'

Chapter 18

Swank Everitt hadn't been wrong about the approach of winter when Florence received her orders to present herself for duty with the Women's Land Army. She was assigned to Valley Farm, a three-mile bicycle ride from Halstead by metalled road and then unmade lane. Tenanted by Frank Davis and his wife Annie, Valley Farm kept Shorthorn cattle for dairy produce, sheep for meat and wool, chickens and ducks for eggs and for the table, and grew a small acreage of cereal, grass for hay, mangolds for fodder and potatoes and vegetables for market.

Florence bought a used bicycle from Clarke's Second Hand shop in the High Street and spent some time oiling the chain and checking the brakes and tyres for roadworthiness. She was required to be at Valley Farm by 6am sharp. It was barely light as she mounted the bicycle, but all the Ashfords apart from the twins had roused themselves to see her off. Nell had made drop scones, which Florence had savoured with bramble jelly.

She rode away from Factory Terrace with a sense of excitement, though her new WLA uniform felt stiff and unyielding, the heavy-duty twill breeches restricting her freedom of movement as she pedalled. Instead of gaiters, she'd been issued with puttees, just as soldiers wore. It had taken her a while to learn how to wind them and tie the fastening tapes. Her storm-proof hat had a deep brim to keep the rain off her face and neck, but she could turn it up at the back when it wasn't raining. She felt quite proud of the armband, bearing the red and green emblem of the Women's Land Army, which she wore on her left sleeve. It gave her a sense of purpose, a visible indication that she was contributing to the war effort. She liked that.

The buildings at Valley Farm were arranged around a cobbled quadrangle. The cow byre and milking parlour ranged along one long side. At the far end stood the stabling and beside the stables was the muck heap, neatly stacked and steaming gently, where the daily barrow loads of soiled animal bedding were deposited, for later use to enrich the soil. Opposite the stables a low building housed the dairy where milk was separated, butter churned and cheese produced. A flock of chickens and a few ducks scratched about in the yard, foraging for seed and spilt horse fodder. On the far side of the yard stood the farmhouse with its oak door at the top of a short flight of stone steps.

Florence leaned her bicycle against the cow byre wall. There was no one around to greet her. Slowly she circled the yard, noting its tidiness. The dairy had been left in apple pie order, all the vessels scrubbed and stowed neatly and surfaces spotless.

Two draught horses were tied up in the stalls and Florence went into the stable building to acquaint herself with them. Clover and Campion – each horse had his name inscribed on a wooden panel screwed to the lintel above their stalls – lowered their muzzles into her hand in search of titbits. Florence had none, but she rubbed their warm noses with the palm of her hand, and they whinnied. They were not as she imagined working horses on a farm to be – Clover and Campion were smaller, short in the leg, and lacked the long-haired coats and feathery feet of the Shire horses she was familiar with. And they were chestnut in colour. A grey pony, Cherry, according to his nameplate, occupied the neighbouring stall, nuzzled Florence's elbow, intent on his share of the attention.

The sound of cattle lowing engaged Florence's attention. Looking towards the yard gate, she saw a tallish, well-built man, clad in tan overalls and a cloth cap, herding a dozen or so cows up the field. A black and white border collie ran around behind them, making sure none was left behind. Unlatching the gate, she stood aside as the herd made its way to the byre, the cows letting themselves in via some slip rails which lay on the ground.

"Go on, then," said the man. "Close them rails."

Florence figured out as she picked up each rail that it had to slot into brackets screwed to posts either side of the gap where the cows had gone into the byre.

"Not bad." The man scratched his head under his cap. "Frank Davis," he said, holding out his hand. The dog ran up to her, its tail wagging. "That'll do, Jack."

"Florence Mundy," said Florence, returning the farmer's firm handshake. "The Women's Land Army sent me here."

"Yeah, I know. 'Ave you done farm work afore? Or are you one o' these prissy townies what's never set foot in a field?"

Florence bristled slightly. "I am a Londoner, it's true, but I don't doubt I can do farm work. I've passed the interview and the medical examination. I'm in good shape, and I want to do this. I just need your guidance and I know I can help you with running your farm, Mr Davis." She bent and fondled the dog's ears. "Good boy, Jack," she said. He sat and looked up at her.

"Well," said Frank Davis, "we'll see about that, but I 'ope so. This war's made a mess of farmin'."

"So I've been told," Florence said.

"I had me own boy and another lad workin' with me afore. The pair of 'em's in the army now. Soon as 'e turned eighteen, Wilf was off."

"Lots of young men were very keen, weren't they?"

"Yeah, too keen. I didn't want him to go – we need him here, his Ma and me. But he feared the white feather – thought folk'd think him a coward – and he wouldn't listen."

Florence nodded.

"We're hard put, me and Annie, to keep things goin'. Some things just don't get done. Who was it said an army marches on its stomach?"

"I think it was Napoleon."

"Yeah, well ours won't for much longer unless the government changes the rules."

"I was thinking how shipshape the yard looks. The dairy, too. They're a credit to you and your wife," said Florence.

"Thank you. We're doin' our best, but some things 'ave gone by the board. Hedges are sprawlin' all over the shop for want of a good cut. Ditches, too're full o' muck and weeds. Plus we got fields lyin' fallow."

"But why, when we need the grain harvest?"

"It's 'cos we can't get 'em ploughed and sown. And they won't pay enough to break even on the arable … And you're right. The country's well nigh on starvin'. About time we got some help."

"Well, I'm here now."

"Anyway, er … what's your name again?"

"Florence Mundy."

"Is that miss or missus?"

"Please, just call me Florence."

"Fair do's," said farmer Davis, rubbing his chin. "Anyway, like I was sayin', we better get started. Them cows won't milk theirselves."

He strode off across the yard and picked up pails and milking stools stowed in a shelter at the end of the milking parlour.

"This time of year it's all about lookin' after the beasts. Cows can't go out in the bad weather, and if there's snow we have to take hay out to the sheep. It's hard work. It's cold work and it's long hours. I 'ope you know that."

"Yes, Mr Davis. Everyone from my sister to the WLA panel has been warning me. But I'm prepared for it … I was admiring your horses. They're unusual. Not like the draught horses I've seen before."

"That's because they're Suffolks. Some call 'em Suffolk Punches. They're the local breed. Tough as old boots, they are. Can haul a plough all day and still pull a cart in the evenin'. Nothin' like 'em for stamina."

The back door of the farmhouse opened and a solid woman, her sandy hair secured in a bun at the nape of her neck, stepped out into the yard. She wiped her hands on her apron, and came across the quadrangle.

"Mornin'!" she said. "Miss Mundy, ain't it? It's good you're here. I'm Annie Davis. The dairy and the fowl and the veg are my department. I can put you straight on all you need to know about the cheese and butter makin'," Annie said, giving Florence the benefit of her candid gaze.

That look again, thought Florence, smiling back at Annie. There would be no messing with these people. They were a team, a working partnership who'd run this farm through good times and bad. But the war was delivering up, unbidden, the toughest times yet.

"First off, you can help get them cows into the parlour, and I'll tell you how we do the milkin'. Afore long, you'll be doin' it yourself, so make sure you pay heed to what me and Annie says," Frank said. "Next, I'll hand you over to Annie, along wi' the cream, and she'll show you how we go about churnin' the butter."

Florence couldn't remember when time had gone by so rapidly. Her head was reeling with all she'd taken in during the few brief morning hours. After milking, she had helped Frank turn the cows back out into the pasture. She could not believe how much mess they'd made in the byre and the parlour in the short time they were in there.

There wasn't a lot to learn about mucking out cows, except that it had to be done scrupulously. Twice her full barrow slid off the ramp as she pushed it to the top of the muck heap, depositing its contents onto the cobbles. She'd had to reload it and sweep up the mess. The stables, too, had to be cleaned out while the horses grazed in the paddock. She had to pile the clean straw up at the back of the stalls with a pitchfork and sweep the exposed floor, allowing it to dry off before relaying fresh straw beds. Everything else had to be barrowed to the muck heap.

Annie Davis invited Florence to a brief lunch of soup and a doorstep wedge of home-made bread in the farm kitchen. The beam above the inglenook gleamed with horse brasses and the high-backed oak settle stood at right angles to the fireplace. Patchwork cushions piled on a rocking chair suggested creature comforts were not forgotten.

Annie talked Florence through the essentials of butter- and cheese-making. Florence did her best to concentrate. It would take a few practice runs before she got the processes firmly lodged in her brain.

Before she knew it, afternoon milking time had come round again, and the whole performance she'd watched early that morning had to be repeated. This time Frank gave her an enamel pail and milking stool, and showed her how to gently squeeze the cow's teat to release a jet of milk.

"You have to get up real close to 'er flank and feel 'er heat on your face," said Frank. Florence did, and she found the warmth of the placid creature moved her. As she relaxed into the task, so did the cow and the milk flowed.

It was fully dark by the time she wheeled her bicycle into the front garden at Factory Terrace. Nell thrust a mug of tea into her hand as she stumbled through the kitchen door.

"Sit down and get those boots off," she said. "I'll heat some water and pour you a bath. You look all in!"

"I am. But it was terrific! You know what, Nellie? I can milk a cow!" Florence realised with a start of surprise that the state of her self-esteem had not entered her mind all day. *Oh!* she said to herself with a small smile of satisfaction.

Grace expected a full account of 'absolutely everything' Florence's day had yielded. "Have the cows all got names?" she asked, as Florence pulled on her most comfortable cardigan. "How many eggs do the chickens lay every day? What colour are the horses? When can I come and visit the farm?"

"All in good time, Gracie," said Florence. "I'm a bit worn out right now ..."

Later, Florence sat with her niece in the warmth of the kitchen range. "D'you know, Gracie, if you put your face against the cow when you're milking her, she gives up her milk more freely. It feels nice, too. Lovely, in fact."

"Gosh," Grace said, "it sounds almost too good to be true!"

"I know," said Florence, "I can hardly believe it myself."

Chapter 19

"What are we going to do for Christmas this year?" Ellen asked.

Nell sighed. "I don't know, Ellen. But it certainly won't be like Stratford Christmases – all the family round the parlour piano."

Nell didn't think there was a chance that George might get leave. His letters had become bleak and brief … the chill of the absence of her shared life with George had stolen into her soul. She yearned for the togetherness she and George had shared.

"We'll do our best to make it special with what we have … but we'll all miss your Dad …"

"I try not to think of Dad not coming back," said Ellen.

"So do I." Nell sighed. Coping alone. Fatherless children. *Dear God! Spare us*, she prayed.

Grace and Doris were attending several practices a week at St Andrew's to satisfy Mr Davage's expectations in the run up to the Christmas schedule of carol services and concerts.

The Ashfords had never been a churchgoing family in Stratford, so the glowing interior of St Andrew's, with its vaulted ceiling, stained glass windows, murals of apostolic life, gilded fretwork and candlelight inspired Grace with a sense of reverence. And she loved being part of the beautiful sound of voices raised in harmony and soaring within the ancient stonework. She committed to all the dates Mr Davage had announced, including a special concert for the soldiers billeted in the old workhouse.

Back at Doris' house, Molly Cooper allowed the two girls to practise their parts using the harmonium in the living room at the back of the shop.

"Doris, d'you think Ollie Davage'd let us do a duet for the first verse of 'Once In Royal David's City' at the soldiers' concert?" Grace asked.

"I don't know. No reason why we can't ask. 'He ain't asked no one else yet."

Mr Davage thought about it. "Why not?" he said, "If you work hard on it." The girls smiled with satisfaction and thanked the choirmaster.

In contrast to her mother, Grace was looking forward to Christmas, in spite of her father's absence. She and Doris had embarked on a project to make everyone something Christmassy from the pine cones, tree bark and evergreen fronds they'd foraged in Broak's Wood, and were spending hours gluing them together and decorating them with red and green enamel paint Monty Mizen had given them. Alf was making cards with his own drawings of Halstead's landmarks on the front. Ellen was knitting mittens, socks and little vests for the twins from unravelled woollen garments. Nell was touched by her children's industry and set about putting aside provisions to make a plum pudding and mincemeat. At least there'd be something seasonal on the table.

"Mum, Mum!" Grace burst in through the back door, her face glowing from running in the chill air. A grin lit up her features. "Mrs Cooper said would we like to have Christmas dinner at their house with her and Doris. Can we? Oh, please say we can!"

Nell's expression brightened. What she'd seen of Doris' mother, she liked. And they were women in a similar predicament.

"Well ..." Nell said, mulling over all the implications, "doesn't Mrs Cooper mind that there are seven of us including Aunt Flo? Is she sure she can cope with us all?"

"Yes, yes, she says it's all fine. She and Doris will be lonely on their own. She wants us there *because* there are so many of us. It'll brighten up their day as well as ours."

"I think you're right, Grace. And I can help with food and cooking. It'll be a joint effort. We'll have to see what Ellen and Alf think about it, and if they agree, we'll accept their kind offer."

"Better than staying here with Elsie," said Alf.

"It's good to have something to look forward to," Ellen said.

***

"Will you come to the soldiers' Christmas concert, Mum?" Grace said. "Mr Davage says you can, and Doris and I are doing a duet. You've got to come and hear us."

"As long as Mrs Mizen can babysit Renee and Iris, it would be lovely. Can Aunt Florence come too?"

"Of course she can."

Nell felt almost carefree, walking to the top of the High Street, past the Jubilee Fountain, in the company of her two eldest children. Grace was already rehearsing with the choir. St Andrew's clock struck seven as they turned left into Hedingham Road.

The hall at the old workhouse, arranged with a small platform for the singers and a podium for Mr Davage at one end, was a sea of khaki. Nell caught her breath. To one side near the front a block of chairs had been reserved for the public and supporters of choir members. A tall, pleasant-looking man in officer's uniform greeted them with a bow and a welcoming smile.

"Captain Forbes – Andrew Forbes – at your service, madam," he said. "May I show you to your seats?"

"Please do, Mister ... um ... Captain Forbes." Nell reddened. "My daughter's a member of Mr Davage's choir ... My sister's arriving directly. She's in the Land Army. She's coming straight from the farm."

"Very well," said Captain Forbes with a nod. "I'll be sure to save the seat next to you for her."

"Look, Mum. Over there. It's Doris' mum," said Alf.

"So it is," said Nell, catching Molly Cooper's eye as she looked in her direction. "I can talk to her about Christmas later."

The choir had already filed onto the platform by the time Florence, breathless, tiptoed into the hall. Nell waved her gloved hand, not too ostentatiously, she hoped, and beckoned her sister towards the spare seat.

Florence slumped onto the wooden chair, still wearing breeches and greatcoat. She dragged her hat from her head and ran her fingers through her hair, attempting to arrange it into some sort of order.

"Phew! Sorry, Nellie. We were late back from the blacksmith. Couldn't get away any sooner. Where's Gracie? Oh, look! She's up there out the front with Doris. Heavens! It's her big moment – and I almost missed it!"

"Sshh, Aunt Flo," Ellen said in a whisper. "Everyone's looking at us. And it's about to start!"

Florence settled herself, and a moment of silence followed. Mr Davage raised his baton and, on his signal, Grace and Doris began. The clarity of their voices captivated the soldiers. As their final note died away, the two girls nudged each other and beamed at their appreciative audience.

"Makes you think of home, don't it?" said one private soldier to his neighbour. The other man nodded and blew his nose.

Returning to their seats at the end of the carol, Mr Davage gave them the 'thumbs up'.

"Can I get you a glass of punch, Mrs Ashford? And what about your sister," Captain Forbes asked at the interval. He turned to Florence, "May I bring you a glass, too?" Florence inclined her head and smiled back at him.

"And you two youngsters. Would you like some lemonade?"

"Yes, please!" Alf and Ellen said in enthusiastic unison. "Thank you very much."

He returned with a full tray and handed glasses round to the family party.

"I hope you're enjoying the concert," the captain said. "Which choir member is your daughter, Mrs Ashford?"

"She's one of the two soloists in the first carol. The fair one."

"My goodness," he said, "she has a lovely voice – they both have – and such confidence! I'm a bit of a singer myself – I love it. But I doubt I'd have pulled off such an assured performance at their age."

"What kind of music do you like, Captain Forbes?" asked Florence.

"Well, I've quite a broad taste, if I'm honest. I like almost everything from opera to music hall, not that I'm very proficient – especially at the former. I know quite a lot of Gilbert and Sullivan, but I think my favourite songs are Neapolitan ballads. You know – 'O Sole Mio' and numbers like that."

"Really? I can play that on the mandolin …" *Can I still …?*

The Drill Sergeant's piercing voice penetrated the hum of conversation.

"Ladies and gentlemen. The second half of the concert is about to begin. Will you all kindly return to your seats?"

The concert concluded with the audience joining in a rendition of 'O Come All Ye Faithful'. The deep strains of the soldiers' voices dominated the melody, but the choir's soprano section sang a descant in the 'Sing, choirs of angels' verse, bringing the carol to a spirited climax.

"What did you think, Aunt Flo?" Grace asked as they all walked back to Factory Terrace, their breath making clouds of steam in the frosty air. "The audience did give us a good clap, didn't they? Do you think they liked it?"

"I thought you and Doris were nothing short of splendid. The whole concert went beautifully. There are lots of good voices in the choir, and Mr Davage has rehearsed you all so well. Those soldiers have got to go back to the Front soon. Your lovely concert has given them a chance to forget that, just for a little while."

Grace considered what her aunt had said and drifted into her own thoughts. She wished she could sing for her own dad and take his mind off the war. And why couldn't he be home on leave for Christmas? She tucked her gloved right hand under Doris' left elbow and they fell into step together.

Chapter 20

"You'll find Clover's the 'orse that knows the ropes – he's a bit older'n the other one."

Frank began teaching Florence how to harness and hitch up Clover and Campion. It was strenuous work, throwing the leatherwork over the horses' backs, but they knew the routine and would lower their big heads, allowing Florence to put the heavy collars on them. Once she'd worked out which strap fastened to which buckle, it all became easier. And before long, she'd grasped the technique of backing the two great beasts between the shafts of the farm waggon.

"We 'ad another 'orse, same age as Clover, but the army come and requisitioned him," Frank said. "Cowslip, his name was. Good lad, 'e was. I often wonder where 'e is now, poor beast. They wanted to take the pair of 'em. But I said we couldn't do without no 'orse at all. How'd we run a farm with no 'orse? I ask you! So in the end they let us keep Clover, thank God. And we got Campion as a young 'un. He's doin' alright. Quick learner. Keen to please."

He scratched Campion's ear. The horse inclined his head, leaning into the farmer's hand.

"We got to start takin' fodder out to the sheep, now they've finished all the grass. I'll teach you how to drive the waggon. The 'orses know what to do. You'll pick it up in no time."

"You'd better stay over these short nights, Florence," Annie said. "I can fix up the attic room where the labourin' lad used to kip down. What d'you think? You can eat with Frank and me – no trouble."

Cold weather and short hours of daylight were making Florence's days increasingly challenging.

"Annie, that's so kind of you. To tell the truth, I'm a bit torn. You see, I love it at Factory Terrace with Nell and the children, but the cycling's not much fun in the dark and cold."

She took a moment or two to ponder Annie's offer. "If it's alright with you and Frank, I'd like to stay over some nights, but maybe go back home on others when Frank doesn't need me to work too late in the evening."

Annie looked at Frank, who nodded. "Thing is," he said, pointing the stem of his pipe to emphasise his point, "we're still a body short, an' no mention of anybody else comin'. So winter ain't goin' to be easy. We'll need all the hours you can do."

"So, what you suggest'll be fine," said Annie, wiping her floury hands on her apron. "Come on, I'll show you the room."

Annie and Florence climbed the attic stairs. They had to duck under the lintel of the door at the top. Annie had brought a candle which she used to light the bedside oil lamp. The room did not have much furniture, but was cosy for all that, the sloping roof beams adding to its snug feeling. The bed was covered by a patchwork counterpane. The lamp, on its tatting mat, stood on an elm pot cupboard beside the bed and, against the far wall was a marble-topped washstand, its bowl and ewer decorated with a floral motif and gilded edge. A pine chest with a mirror and a slightly battered ladderback armchair were the only other pieces of furniture. A rag rug lay alongside the bed, and a print of Holman Hunt's 'Light of the World' in a mahogany frame hung on the wall over the washstand. A tiny wood-burning stove, its flue running obliquely along one wall towards its outlet in the roof would warm the room nicely, Florence thought. She liked it at once. It smelled of polish and linen.

"It's not much," said Annie, "and it gets cold up 'ere, but you can fire up that stove and it'll warm the room a treat."

"Just what I was thinking," Florence said.

"We got plenty of wood you can use."

A brief flashback to her Clerkenwell digs came into her mind. A haven.

"Do you mind if I bring my mandolin? I'd like to play it in the evenings, if it won't disturb you." The conversation with the captain at the soldiers' concert had made her realise ... *It's time* ...

"Good Lord, no! You can play for us of an evenin'. We'd enjoy that."

Chapter 21

Jane Mizen tapped on the Ashford's sitting room door. "There's someone 'ere to see you," she said. "A young gent in uniform. Says his name's Forbes – I think that's what 'e said."

Nell was sitting on the floor, the hobbing foot between her splayed legs, her skirt bunched up above her knees. Hammer in hand, she was repairing the children's worn shoes.

"Oh, my good lord!" she said. "I'm in no fit state to see anyone – just look at me!"

"Now then, no need to panic," said Jane Mizen. "I'll keep him talkin' a few minutes while you get yourself organised, then tap on the door when you're ready for him to come in."

"Alright. I'll just be a moment or two. Thanks for the breathing space."

Nell tugged at her skirt and smoothed it with the palms of her hands. Hastily, she gathered up all the shoes and tools and shoved them behind an armchair. She tidied her hair with her fingertips. Why would *he* be paying her a call?

"I'm ready now." Her knuckles tapped on the door.

Jane Mizen led Andrew Forbes up to the Ashfords' landing and Nell ushered him in.

"Hello again, Captain Forbes." she extended her hand to the soldier. "How nice to see you."

"Please forgive this unorthodox intrusion, Mrs Ashford," the Captain smiled and took her hand.

She showed him to a chair by the fire. "Can I get you a cup of tea?"

"Yes. Thank you." Andrew Forbes took off his cap and turned it round in his hands. Nell filled the kettle and set it on the hob.

"I hope you don't mind my coming. The choir master gave me your address. I shouldn't have asked, I know, but I didn't know how else to contact you."

Nell fiddled with the cups and saucers, then sat down opposite him, setting the tea tray on the low table beside the chair. She noticed perspiration on his brow. He took out a handkerchief and mopped it.

"The thing is, we're having a Christmas tea party for some of the men's families on Sunday afternoon and I was wondering if you'd all like to join us."

"Do you mean me to bring all my children as well? I've twins of twenty months, too, you know."

"Yes, of course. And – please – will you ask your sister to come and bring her mandolin? If you agree to come, that is. You see, we'd like to have some songs and …" he shrugged slightly, "people doing turns …"

"Turns?"

"Music. Skits … Some light entertainment … Does that mean you'll come?"

"Well … Yes, I suppose so, though I can't speak for my sister. She's working flat out at the farm, and hardly comes back into Halstead these days. But of course I'll ask her."

"You won't forget to mention the mandolin, will you?" Forbes asked.

When she saw him out, she turned to look at her reflection in the hall mirror. Still pretty.

Two days later Nell sent Alf round to Hedingham Road to let Captain Forbes know they would all be there, Florence included, on Sunday at three. She wrapped up a jar of her bramble jelly in a scrap of red cellophane she'd been saving to take as a 'thank you' present.

Florence, rusty after the long layoff, used the evenings at Valley Farm to practise her mandolin playing. Echoes of her old life were inescapable. The demons played havoc with her resolve, but she persevered. She had a performance to prepare for.

***

Florence put down her broom and stowed the wheelbarrow. The horses and cows were turned out, the yard swept clean. She had grown to enjoy her Sunday morning chores. Frank and Annie were regulars at St Andrew's and left for Matins after morning milking, leaving her to carry on alone. She savoured the tranquillity. But this morning the peace was shattered when Alf and Grace appeared on borrowed bicycles.

"We thought we could help you collect the eggs and get ready to feed the sheep," Alf said unwinding his scarf.

"That way you'll have time to get ready for the party," said Grace. "Can I help separate the cream?"

"Well, alright." Florence placed her hands on the children's shoulders. Their faces were turned up towards her. The frisson of annoyance at their interruption ebbed away.

"Alf," she said, offering him the egg-collecting basket, "be careful the girls don't peck you – and I don't want any smashed eggs, alright? Mrs Davis has said I can take a dozen to the party as a present this afternoon, so be careful!"

"Yes, Aunt Flo. You can trust me."

"Gracie, you come with me and we'll sort out the cream for the dairy. After that, we've got to load the waggon with hay and hitch up Clover and Campion so Mr Davis can take the fodder out to the sheep."

"Can't you drive the waggon, Aunt Flo?"

"Not yet, and certainly not without Mr Davis here. I'm still a rookie."

"Golly, this is hard work," said Alf, forking up forage onto the waggon, "it's much more strenuous than I thought."

"Phew!" Grace said as she tossed her final forkful onto the waggonload. "D'you have to do this every day, Aunt Flo?"

"Every single one. You can't leave animals to starve in winter weather, you know! It gets easier as you get used to it, though. There's a knack to it. And being taller helps."

"Can we help harness the horses now?" Alf asked.

"Yes. But just make sure they don't tread on your toes. You'll know all about it if they do."

***

"The men have done their level best to make this drab old billet look festive." Andrew Forbes met them in the entrance hall, festooned now in coloured paper streamers. "Welcome. Do come through and help yourselves to some tea," he said.

They made their way to the back room where teas was being served. The hall was crowded with soldiers and their families, the babble of conversation rising to a pitch.

"They feeding you well, son?" a young private's mother was saying.

"Did those socks your aunt knitted for you arrive?"

"Your sister sends her love."

"How long till you go off?" a father asked.

"They haven't told us yet," his son said.

"We've brought you something to say thank you," said Nell, raising her voice to make herself heard. She handed the jar of bramble jelly to the captain.

"How kind!"

"And I thought you might enjoy these," Florence added, handing him a box, lined with straw, in which nestled a dozen eggs from Valley Farm.

"Ah," Forbes said. "I can't thank you enough."

Forbes held Florence's gaze until she lowered her eyes. His eyes were hazel, she noticed. He cleared his throat. "Come on, children. We've got Father Christmas here. He's got something in his sack for each of you … Carry on, Corporal," he called over his shoulder.

A figure clad in a padded red suit and army boots, his dark moustache visible beneath a white cotton wool beard, came into the room.

"Ho, ho, ho!" He shook his shoulders in mock mirth. "I've got presents for you – as long as you've been good children." The twins eyed him with suspicion.

Delving into the hessian bag, they each pulled out a package wrapped in brown paper, with their name written in neat copperplate on a luggage label.

Ellen's was a pin cushion on a red ribbon she could wear on her wrist. Alf had a cardboard cut-out of Westminster Abbey he could slot together to make a 3-D model, and Grace's was a book of poems.

"Thank you," they said in turn.

For the twins, someone had whittled two little wooden birds, a thrush and a robin, from wood.

"How did you know what we'd like?" asked Ellen.

"Ah," said Captain Forbes, tapping the side of his nose with an index finger. "Call it intuition. Now!" He clapped his hands together. "It's time for the fun to begin!"

Since Nell's acceptance of the invitation, they'd each been practising a 'turn', just as they had done most Sunday evenings back at Gurney Road – singing round the piano, recitations, comedy.

In among the soldiers' and their guests' juggling, ventriloquism, tap dancing and jokes, they each performed. Even Nell, leaving Renee and Iris with Florence, sat at the piano and sang a duet with Ellen – 'The Temple Bells', one of the Four Indian Love Lyrics by Amy Woodforde-Findon.

Alf carried off a passable impression of Charlie Chaplin in an over-sized bowler hat and a walking stick both borrowed from Monty Mizen. A small square of brown blanket stuck on with flour and water paste passed for a moustache. Florence accompanied him in the manner of a pianist in a film theatre. The audience loved it and cheered him loudly.

Grace had settled on reciting 'The Rose', a poem of her own she was rather proud of, inspired by the show of blooms which had graced the garden at Factory Terrace until the frosts had brought their riotous season to an end. She'd already committed it to her diary, written out in her best handwriting, knowing how much her father would love it when he came to read it. "With soft, blushing petals of a beautiful hue ..." she began. The soldiers listened, and cheered her at the end.

Florence felt good to be playing before an audience again, in spite of the legacy of That night. Farm work had taken its toll of her fingers, and she'd had to practise hard to restore their dexterity. She had tried to think of something to play that would take these soldiers' imaginations as far away from the war and the Front as possible. But still she could not face Vivaldi. "I'm going to play a minuet by an 18th-century composer called Boccherini," she said. "I want you all to close your eyes and imagine yourselves in the Italian city of Lucca, where he came from." She played with a lilt that transported her listeners clean away from wintry Essex and they cheered as she drew the performance to a close. "Not very Christmassy," she observed with a grin, "but never mind!"

Andrew Forbes walked onto the small stage. "Thank you so much, Miss Mundy. That was like a magic carpet ride." He was still applauding.

"Oh!" Florence said, "That's just what I think."

"Now, I wonder if I might ask you to help me out." He turned towards her. "You see, I have a song I'd like to sing which I believe you know, and I'm hoping you wouldn't mind accompanying me."

"Well ... no, Captain. I'll give it a try, if I can. But what's the song?"

He broke into a brief extract from 'O Sole Mio' in a clear tenor voice.

"Oh! Yes." Florence recalled their earlier conversation and smiled, looking down and blushing slightly. "Fancy you remembering!" She steadied her hands and began the well-known air, so beautifully suited to her instrument.

They left the stage together, their audience stamping and whistling their approval.

"Thank you for making that possible, Miss Mundy." She laid her mandolin carefully on a chair. "It gave me the chance to share a moment of common humanity with my men. In the normal course of soldiering I don't often get the opportunity. It meant more to me than you know." His right hand clasped hers in a firm handshake and then he laid his left hand over hers. Something in his gaze made her look away. She withdrew her hand gently.

Nell appeared in the doorway, an impatient look on her face. "Oh," she said, "I didn't mean to interrupt, but … the twins are about at the end of their tether, and the others have got school tomorrow. We must get going. Florence, are you coming now?"

Florence looked at her watch. "Heavens. I've only just seen the time. Nell's right – it's getting late and I've got my usual early start …"

Forbes cut her short. "It's fine, Miss Mundy. I'll see you back to the farm, it's the least I can do. And I'll ask Sergeant Crawford to help your sister back to their lodgings." He turned to Nell and the children. "You've all made this a splendid prelude to Christmas for my men, and I thank you most sincerely. Please, enjoy your Christmas, won't you?"

"Er, yes. Thank you, Captain." Nell turned to Florence. "Is this alright with you, Flo?"

"I suppose so …" How else was she to get back out to Valley Farm this late? "It's … fine, Nellie. I'll speak to you soon."

Nell turned and left the room.

Andrew Forbes turned to face Florence. "I'll take you back to the farm, Florence – May I call you Florence? I can use a motor from here. It's not a problem."

"Alright …" She felt uneasy … *Slut* … That word swilled in her brain. Could lightning strike twice?

The vehicle was a small truck with a cramped cab. She sat staring fixedly out of the windscreen, her mandolin case across her knees.

"How long have you been playing the mandolin, Florence?"

"A few years … on and off."

"You play well."

"Thank you, Captain."

"It's Andrew. Please call me Andrew."

At Valley Farm, a lamp was still burning in the Davis' parlour.

"I must go in – Annie and Frank must be waiting up for me." Florence reached for the door handle.

"No. Please stay, Florence. I'd like to talk to you. I know nothing about you, and in a very short time I'll be gone."

"Why me?" She said simply, frowning at him.

"I hardly know. But the moment I saw you at the concert, I sensed something different about you. Something sensitive. Generous."

He turned off the ignition and dowsed the lights. It was suddenly impenetrably dark. Black, velvety dark … *Slut* … *That's what he means, isn't it?*

"So, who are you, Florence Mundy? I really want to know."

"I don't think … I should be doing this …" she began. *Slut … Why should I trust this man?*

"Please …" he said.

She could not justify to herself what drove her on … But she began to tell him about her Stratford background, Brown and Son, even the Holborn Musical Ensemble, and how it was she'd become a Land Girl in north Essex … *This is dangerous ground … and yet …* "Until the last few weeks, I wasn't sure I knew who I was. I think I'd been chasing rainbows and burying my head in the sand about where my life might lead … " She broke off. *Am I really any surer now? Slut …!* "Sorry about the bad metaphors …" She cleared her throat to give herself a breathing space. *Shut up, shut up Florence,* she said to herself. *You barely know this man. Why trust him?* "… But now I feel I'm where I should be. The Land Army life – the animals, the hard, physical work, the new skills, the independence – it's good for me." *That is true.* She took a deep breath. *But enough is enough.* She shifted the focus. "What about you, Captain Forbes … Andrew? What makes you tick?" *Do I care …? Do I?*

He sighed. "If we're talking bad metaphors, I'm the proverbial square peg in a round hole. I hate the army. And I hate this war. Don't get me wrong – I love my men, and I've seen heroism of the kind I'd never have thought possible. But I've also seen lives wiped out before my eyes. Young men crippled and maimed. By other young men – just like us. We have no animosity towards each other as individuals – we could be friends. But we blow each other to kingdom come. The whole thing's completely insane. And I have to pretend I believe in it all. I ask you. What a farce! It's me giving out the orders – and most of those boys'd do anything for me – we have a good relationship. Yet I've already sent many to their deaths." He paused. "You seem so independent, Florence. You've gone your own way. But I merely toed the line in my family. My father was a career soldier, decorated in the Boer War, mentioned in dispatches, and all that. Expected it of me. He's not a man to be gainsaid and I lacked the courage to rebel … And now, here I am, dreading going back. It's harder the second time; I know what's out there, now, and frankly I'm scared."

His voice faltered, and he reached out to her. She found herself holding him close and felt his shoulders heaving. "Meeting you has changed everything." His face was buried in her hair, his voice muffled.

What? she thought. *So soon?* She felt wrong-footed, out of her depth as she rocked him gently in her arms. He sobbed against her. "Come on now." She struggled to find words. "I understand your fears. God knows! I'd loathe it in your position. But … Andrew … you can't – you just can't – let despair swamp you. You've got to summon up the nerve to face it."

"You're right, of course. I have no option."

"Maybe the tide'll soon be turning in the war. You never know, the Yanks might start to make a difference before long."

He raised his flushed face and wiped away the evidence of his unseemly tears. He blew his nose, shook his shoulders and cleared his throat.

"I'm so sorry. I don't often lose control. It's just that I've been keeping all my feelings to myself. There's been no one else I could share them with. Until you." He touched her hair. "Thank you. And please forgive me."

"There's nothing to forgive," she said. "But look, I've really got to go now, or I'll never be ready for the morning … I'm touched by all you've shared with me … Andrew." Picking up her mandolin case, she fumbled again with the door handle.

"It's a bit awkward," Andrew said, reaching across her to release the latch. "Please. May I kiss you goodnight?" His mouth was on hers before she had time to consent. He was tender. His kiss was warm. Different. But was it really? How could she know?

"I must go," she said and climbed out of the cab. "Goodnight." Slamming the door behind her, she looked back only briefly to see his face, shadowy and indistinct, his eyes fixed on her.

"What *am* I getting myself into?" *Slut … Slut … Slut.* Her footfalls on the stairs accused her.

Chapter 22

"Well done, all of you," said Nell to Ellen, Alf and Grace. Their school reports reflected a good term's work.

In the week before Christmas, envelopes arrived from France for all of them. Grace retreated to her bedroom with hers. She could feel the firm edge of a card and she withdrew it gently. It was gorgeous, like the one she was already treasuring. This time, the silk embroidery on a gauze panel depicted a Union Flag tied with red, white and blue ribbon to sprigs of green holly with scarlet berries. A bell, worked in the stripes of the French Tricouleur was also tied to the ribbon. 'XMAS GREETINGS' was stitched in gold thread and an embossed frieze of four-leaved clover and horseshoes framed the embroidered panel. Good luck motifs. Grace crossed her fingers.

She ran her finger along the row of 'X's her father had drawn along the bottom of the card. 'Somewhere in France'. *I wonder where*, she thought, *and what was it like where he'd sat and written the card*. She tried to picture him, sitting maybe in a trench, thinking of her. She wished he could say more. "Keep safe and come home soon," she said, pressing the card close to her heart.

Nell, too, sighed as she read George's words. *Still alive, thank heaven ... But ... these brief messages ... so aloof ... perfunctory, almost*, she thought. "Oh, George, my dear, I do so miss you," she said aloud. "The sharing, the caring, the confidences. I miss it all." She felt safe here in Halstead, and God knows, she was grateful for that. But she found it hard to feel festive. Would he ever get leave?

Grace poked her nose out from beneath the bedcovers on Christmas morning. She could feel the nip of frost in the air. The inside of the bedroom window was a tracery of frosty fern shapes, which looked pretty, but presaged just how arctic it was going to feel when she emerged into the chill of the room. She jumped up and down on the spot to keep warm.

"Brr! Come on, Ellen, wakey-wakey, it's Christmas Day. We're going to Doris' soon. I can't wait! Oh! Merry Christmas, by the way."

"Keep your hair on," Ellen said. "There's lots to do before we're ready to go round there."

"Well, I've got to sing in church first. I can't be late for that – Mr Davage'd never forgive me." Grace was off like a small tornado, dragging clothes out of the drawer, washing her face and hands with water from the bedroom ewer, then pulling on her stockings.

Nell was already getting breakfast ready in the kitchen. Grace burst in, still thrusting an arm into her pullover.

"Good morning, Mum. Happy Christmas!"

"Same to you, dear," her mother answered with a little smile. "Would you like an egg for breakfast? They're from Aunt Florence's farm."

"Ooh yes! Rather! Can I have it boiled with toast soldiers, please? I need to be quick so I can meet Doris outside her house. We've got to sing this morning – it's important 'cos it's Christmas Day."

"Well, I know all that, Gracie. You've told me umpteen times."

"Can you come to church?"

"I don't think so." Nell tidied Grace's hair, still tangled from sleep. "I'd like to, but Mr and Mrs Davis have given us a lovely chicken for Christmas dinner. I've got to stuff it and take it round to Mrs Cooper's. Then there are the giblets to cook up for the gravy. I've really got my work cut out. You go on, and sing well. Say a prayer for your Dad."

"Yes, I will. And for Doris' Dad, too." She sliced into the top of her egg with a spoon. "I'll go straight back with Doris and see you there, shall I?"

Soon she was gone, skipping up the High Street, her breath billowing in steamy clouds in the morning air. Doris was waiting for her, carol book in hand outside the family shop.

"Happy Christmas!" They hugged each other briefly and ran off up the hill towards St Andrew's. The bells were ringing to welcome Christmas morning.

Shafts of sunlight flooded into the church, picking up the intense colours of the stained glass windows. Halstead residents filled the church, each with his or her own priorities of praise or supplication. Or grief. But all to reflect on the birth of a baby in Palestine over 1900 years ago and to pray for an end to Europe's bloodshed. The carols were familiar and sung with energy, voices resounding.

Grace spotted her Aunt Florence in the congregation. She was sitting next to Mr Davis, the farmer, and his wife. Grace was surprised – Aunt Flo was not a regular at St Andrew's, and yet there she was. Her expression was one of … well, it looked like prayerfulness. Or deep thought. Maybe both.

Florence came out of St Andrew's with Frank and Annie.

"Aunt Flo!" called Grace, emerging from the church porch. "I didn't know you'd be here. Are you coming back to Doris's with us? Happy Christmas – and to you, Mr and Mrs Davis!"

"Yes, Gracie. I'll walk back with you and Doris. The Davises gave me a lift into Halstead and asked if I'd like to come to church, so here I am."

She took her leave of Frank and Annie, patted Cherry, standing between the shafts of the little dog-cart, and, joining hands with Grace and Doris, the three set off towards the Coopers'. The savour of roasting chicken hit them as they burst into the kitchen behind the greengrocery shop.

"Gosh!" said Doris, "that does smell so good! I'm starvin'!"

"Well," Molly said, "you'll have to be patient. We're not quite ready yet. You can go and set the table – and mind you use the good linen and the best china."

Alf was already in the dining room, working out how to pull out the extra leaf on the dining table and trying to find enough chairs for everyone.

"It looks fit for a king," said Grace, setting a candle in the centre of the table. "I think we're all ready now." She put everyone's presents beside each place setting.

Molly said grace, giving thanks for their good fortune in sharing such a feast, and remembering absent loved ones: "We pray it won't be long afore they're back in our midst, with peace prevailin'. Amen."

The children fell upon their meal as though they hadn't eaten for days and they each opened their gifts with murmurs of appreciation.

"Thank you," said Doris to Alf, pleased with his drawing of St. Andrew's. "You got a fine talent there."

The children cleared the table, scraping the scraps into a bin destined for Bill Broyd's pigs, a small recompense for the butcher's donation of the sausage meat Nell had used to stuff the chicken.

"That was amazing, Mrs Cooper," said Alf, "and so was Mum's pud. Thanks. I'm really full."

"Now, you lot." Nell raised her voice to make herself heard. "Why don't you take yourselves into the parlour and play charades till we're done out here. The fire's lit. Molly, go and put your feet up for a few minutes. You've worked so hard – you must be all in."

Molly opened her mouth to protest, but Nell hushed her and insisted.

"You and I can clear the dishes in no time, Flo," she said, handing her sister a tea towel.

The two women were silent for a while, each in her own thoughts. It was Nell who spoke first: "How is it out at the farm? I haven't seen you since the party at the old workhouse."

"Oh, you know, jolly hard work. But I'm coping, and the Davises are grateful for every little thing I do. And they're so generous, what with all the eggs and the chicken for Christmas dinner and everything ... wasn't it delicious ...?" She trailed off, a little wistfully, Nell thought.

"Have you seen anything more of Captain Forbes since that night?"

Florence tried to get her thoughts about Andrew Forbes into some sort of order.

"No," she replied at length, returning clean cutlery to the dresser drawer, "I haven't. And I don't know if I should. Oh, Nellie, I just don't know what I should do. I'm getting into a real state about it."

"But why, Flo? He's not married, is he?"

Florence put the tea towel down on the table.

"No. It's nothing like that." She sighed " ... He told me everything about how wretched he feels about the war; how he hates being a soldier – you'd never have guessed at the party, would you? So good with his men! And then he kissed me. Told me I'd changed his life – can you believe it? The thing is, I like him. Yes, I do. He seems warm and honest, and the music was such fun. But I got the distinct impression he was really reaching out to me for some sort of deep commitment. And I don't think I want that – not now ... and not with him." She sat down on a kitchen chair and looked up at her sister. "And he's got to go back to France. I can't just ignore what happened. Leave him dangling – it's too cruel. But I don't want to raise false hopes. Make promises I can't keep and, in all honesty, don't think I want to enter into."

Nell wiped her hands on her apron. "You know, it's a funny thing. When he came round to Factory Terrace that day, I wondered if he was after *me*. I was flattered, I can tell you – handsome chap like that … But when I saw him with you at the party, I pretty soon realised how wrong I was … And heck. Married with five children. Who was I kidding? Besides … George …" She grinned and Florence saw in that instant that loneliness was imprinting itself on Nell's features. "If he's fallen for you – and it looks as though he has – you have to respond to him. Do you think he's right for you? Isn't he rather out of your league?"

Florence frowned. "Meaning what?"

The noise coming from the parlour had been rising for some time to a level that Nell felt she must address. At that moment, the kitchen door was flung open and Ellen came in, her arms folded across her chest.

"I can't play with that lot anymore! They're just being stupid!"

Nell and Florence went to investigate. The cushions from Molly's chairs and settee were piled up on the floor with Alf, Grace and Doris rolling around in fits of laughter. The twins, sitting on little chairs, bashed each other with soft toys, laughing too.

"We're being mountaineers," said Grace, wiping tears from her face with the back of her hand. "And this," she pointed to the mound of cushions, "is Mount Everest. We're trying to climb it, but we keep falling off."

Florence had to turn away to stifle a giggle, but Nell was white-knuckled.

"Get up this minute! And put those cushions back before you reduce them to rags! You should be ashamed of yourselves!"

Molly came into the room, carrying a tray of tea things. She felt revived, and grateful for the short rest. "Oh, come on now. No harm done. And it is Christmas. Don't come down too hard on 'em, Nell. They're still kids. You got to expect some high spirits now and then. Let's have a nice cuppa. The young 'uns can have some lemonade." She set the loaded tray down carefully on a table beside an armchair. "Y'know, I ain't had as good a time as this since my Fred went off to war. You lot've made our day, ain't they, Doris? And I tell you somethin' else – the sound of kiddies laughin' beats the silence of an empty house, and that's a fact. Let 'em enjoy themselves!" She patted Nell on the shoulder.

The children, chastened by Nell's outburst, put the furniture to rights.

"Let's play 'Consequences'," Doris said. "We can go in the other room when we've finished our lemonade."

Molly continued in a soft voice, "I know how it is for you, with all your lot and the older 'uns gettin' bigger and more boisterous. You worry they'll run amok."

"Yes, Molly, I really do." Nell breathed a small sigh. "I've always had George to back me up where discipline's concerned. But it's so much harder now, on my own – like everything else. You must feel it, too."

"Yes, that's true, but I've only got the one, and Doris is a good girl and helps a lot. I was worryin' she weren't gettin' enough fun out of life. But now she's made a friend of your Grace, she's happy as a lark. They're a grand bunch, your lot."

"Molly's right," said Florence. "It does you good to see children having fun, hear them laughing. And heaven knows what life's got in store for them."

"Here. Sit and drink your tea. And stop worrying!" Molly said.

The children ran back in, giggling.

"Listen to this consequence!" Alf said: "Elsie Mizen met Mr Mathews at the Rec. She said to him: "Can I have a penn'orth of dolly mixtures?" He said to her: "I don't like liver and bacon!" And the consequence was: they sailed away to Darkest Africa!"

The women smiled.

"Very amusing, Alfred," said his mother and, turning to Molly and Florence, "You're right, of course. I just worry too much."

Chapter 23

"Hah," Florence said at breakfast on Boxing Day. "A day off! it's good to have a lie in for once. I've almost forgotten what it's like to stay in bed till the sun's up."

She took Renee and Iris out in the makeshift twin pushchair Nell had acquired now they were toddling. Alf and Grace went with her, and they headed for the Public Gardens. Then they stopped on the bridge and watched the ducks. It was cold, and everyone was grateful for the mittens Ellen had given them for Christmas.

Later, Florence and Grace settled down together by the range.

"Aunt Flo," said Grace after a few moments, "is everything alright with you?"

"Why do you ask?"

"Well, I saw your face in church on Christmas morning. I've never seen you looking like that before – kind of distant and thoughtful. Were you saying your prayers?"

"In a way I was." Florence took a deep breath. "Do you say your prayers, Gracie?"

"Yes I do – every night! I pray Dad will come home safely, and I pray that this awful war will stop."

"Do you think your prayers are answered?"

"Um, yes … and no. You see," Grace frowned, putting her thoughts in order. "I believe God has given us this beautiful world, which I love. But I don't understand how all the fighting and cruelty fits in with His plan for us. But if you don't say your prayers, you'll never know whether they get answered or not, will you?"

"You're right there, Miss Philosopher."

As the light of day faded, Florence left Factory Terrace to get back to Valley Farm. She'd hitched a ride with Swank Everitt who had a load of cattle feed to deliver to the Davises. Swank and his cart had become quite a boon to Florence as a means of transport these short days. Valley Farm was one of Swank's regular ports of call, and he was always happy to give her a lift if she needed one. She repaid him with portions of whatever Nell had been baking. Today, she'd brought him a helping of cold Christmas pudding.

"Thank you, Miss," he said with a flash of irregular teeth and a chesty gurgle. "Much obliged." This was the high spot of Swank's week and a well-kept secret from Mrs E.

Letting herself quietly into the farmhouse, Florence found Annie, crocheting in hand, and Frank, reading in front of the inglenook fire.

"Weather's set to turn colder still," Frank said. "Threat of snow, dammit. We'll have to shift the sheep in case we can't get hay out to the field where they are now. We better get goin' early in the mornin'."

"Alright, Frank. I'll be up and about in good time. Goodnight."

She was getting ready to turn in when there was a tap at the door. Annie was standing on the little landing at the top of the attic stairs. She had two steaming cups in her hand.

"Come in, Annie. What is it?"

"I've brought you some hot milk with honey and a drop o' whisky in it," she said. "Thought you might like a nightcap."

"That's kind of you."

The room was glacial, so Florence built a fire in the little stove. It ignited quickly and took the chill off the air before long. Annie sat down on the bed and gestured to Florence to sit down beside her. She handed her a cup and Florence took a sip.

"What is it, Annie? I haven't done something wrong, have I?"

Annie cleared her throat. "No, no. It ain't that, silly girl. It's that young serviceman what brought you home afore Christmas. He's been out here twice today. Desperate to see you, he is. I know it ain't none of my business, but I think he's keen as mustard. I was just wonderin' if you're tryin' to avoid him."

Florence looked deep into her cup … *slut* … "Well, yes – I mean no! I'm not trying to steer clear of him. I know what you say is true, and I simply don't know what to say to him."

"Aren't you keen, then?"

"I just don't know. But I don't think so. Or not in that way, anyway. And I don't want to say anything I might regret." Florence got up and poked the fire. "I've been agonising about it all over Christmas and I still don't know what to say to him."

"P'raps you don't need my advice, but for what it's worth, my feelin' is you got to be honest. It wouldn't be right to go givin' no false impressions, no matter what's in store for the young man."

"He's going back to war and probably wants some answers … but the ones I feel I can give him aren't the ones he wants to hear …"

"I don't say it'll be easy sayin' things he won't like afore he has to go off to fight, but life's not about takin' the easy way out, and if your heart ain't in it, you've got to tell him. Findin' the way to do it is another matter."

Florence took a sip of the toddy. Annie put an arm round her. "I'm gettin' on now and I've seen a few ups and downs in people's lives. I can understand how it is for young 'uns like you. These times is about as bad as bad can be, but we've still got each other to help us through. You've been the answer to a prayer for Frank and me, m'dear, as good as any daughter, and we'll do all we can for you."

Honesty. Telling the truth. Florence knew it was the way forward. But how to frame the right words? And that word … *Slut* … still stalked her.

"He'll be back again tomorrow, you can be sure of that." Annie gathered up the empty cups. "Maybe as you sleep on it, the right words'll come to you. Goodnight, Florence."

"Annie."

"Yes dear."

"D'you think I can trust him?"

Annie stood by the door looking hard at Florence. "I think so, dear. He strikes me as an honest man."

Florence listened to Annie's receding footsteps on the uncarpeted stair. Harry Bartholomew's presence stalked the room. Sleep eluded her.

Chapter 24

Florence was already in the yard, sweeping and tidying as Frank and Jack approached. Daybreak was little more than a faint smudge on the eastern horizon. It would be a good hour before it was daylight.

"We got to get the sheep back near the farm if the weather's takin' a turn for the worse," Frank said. "It's a fair old way, so we'd best get goin'." Jack trotted in circles around Frank's feet, dying to get going.

"Ready when you are, Frank."

"Here. Take this. It'll 'elp you stay upright and you can use it to keep the ewes in order, too." 'This' was a sturdy stick with a knobbly handle.

Travelling on foot by the feeble light of a couple of lanterns, the trio set off from Valley Farm. Out there on the hilly pasture, the sheep could be anywhere within a wide radius. *We've got to get this done before milking*, Florence was thinking, *but it could take hours*. Tramping over tussocky terrain in the half light, she was glad of the stick that gave her the sure-footedness she needed as they moved on as swiftly as they could.

"How're we going to track them all down, Frank?"

"You wait till you see Jack goin' into action. He's a four-footed miracle when it comes to roundin' up sheep. Got a sixth sense – can find 'em anywhere. He'll have them ship-shape and Bristol fashion in next to no time."

Once the ewes came into view, Frank issued a series of commands and whistles to Jack. They were unintelligible to Florence, but the dog circled and parried, rounding up the sheep into a neat flock.

"Now." Frank handed Florence a stout stick. "You go over on the left flank of the flock. Keep up with 'em and waggle that stick if any of 'em drifts off. If you lose any, give a shout an' I'll send Jack over yon to get 'em back. You'll have to keep movin' sharpish, mind. They may be only sheep, but they can get a shift on."

Florence nodded, shouldered her stick and strode off to the far side of the flock. Jack was still running back and forth keeping the animals together. On Frank's signal, they set off back towards the farm. Jack worked like a demon. It seemed he knew what the sheep would do before they did it and so pre-empted any groups of ewes from breaking away. Florence didn't take her eyes or her mind off the sheep for a single moment and did her job just as Frank had asked. The roofs of Valley Farm came into view, and Frank called a halt.

"We got to go left of Valley. And it's narrower, so the sheep don't have so many places to run, but they'll make a longer line, so we won't be able to see the ones at the front. Just keep drivin' 'em forward and the front runners'll have to keep goin'. Anyways, Jack'll make darn sure they do. At the end of the track, the land gets wider again, so things may go haywire. Just keep your eyes peeled for stragglers and Jack an' me'll do the rest. You know the fold we're makin' for and the gate's open."

As the flock emerged into the open field, for a few moments it seemed to Florence as though everything had gone wrong. A cacophony of bleating deafened her as the sheep ran about everywhere. She ran, waving her stick at escaping sheep and cursing them for their unruliness. But Jack, the consummate master of this business, steered the beasts towards the open gate. As the last ewe crossed into the fold, Frank latched the gate and sighed with relief.

"That's a job well done!" He took off his cap to wipe his perspiring brow on his sleeve. "Copybook, that. You done a grand job there, Florence. It's not often it goes like clockwork. Full marks!"

"Thanks, Frank."

He clapped her on the back with his gloved hand and she nearly lost her balance. "Now all we got to do is get as much fodder out to 'em now, afore the snow starts, 'cos once there's deep snow on the ground, there ain't no way we can get the horses an' waggon out here. So we got to prepare now."

Frank saw the look of anguish on Florence's face. "But not afore we've had a warmin' in the kitchen and a bite of breakfast to revive us."

She smiled a weary smile back at Frank.

Annie had laid on a feast of a breakfast – eggs, bacon, black pudding, fried bread, bubble and squeak. The aroma was so mouth-watering, Florence had to stop herself picking up a rasher of bacon and munching it on the spot.

"I'll go and wash my hands," she said.

Gallons of tea quenched their thirst.

"It's a good job I got a big teapot." Annie was touched by the way Florence tucked in and turned away to hide her amusement.

"Nothin' like a hearty breakfast to set you up for the rest of the day." She cleared away the empty plates.

Frank's next task for Florence was to drive laden waggonloads of hay out to the sheepfold and stack it neatly so it could be covered with a canvas tarpaulin to keep the weather off it. Florence was glad to have the chance of driving Clover and Campion on her own and she felt pleased that Frank trusted her with the responsibility. *Mind*, she thought, *he and Annie have got the milking to do, so there's no choice but to let me do this by myself.* She harnessed the horses up and backed them between the shafts, feeling deft and capable. Frank helped her pile a towering load of hay on board the waggon before she moved off, reins in both hands and clicking the team into action.

Frank had chosen this sheepfold partly because it was close to the farm, and also because it had a free-flowing brook running through it, keeping the ewes supplied with fresh water. This was a potential emergency and he was not a man to let nature catch him out. "You can't run a farm just crossin' your fingers and hopin'," he was fond of saying. "You got to ACT!"

The light was fading as Florence drove the waggon back into the yard for the last time that day. Frank had come with her to secure the haystack and tie down its canvas sheet.

"Phew. I've lost count of the loads we've ferried out to the fold, Frank. Now I've got to do the right thing by the horses." She rubbed them down with handfuls of straw to dry off their sweat-streaked flanks before the frost set in. Frank had said: "A horse wet with sweat can take a chill if it gets cold." She mixed them each a warm bran mash and tossed extra straw and big piles of hay into their stalls before 'putting them to bed'.

"'Night, boys." She patted their strong shoulders and scratched them behind the ears. They whinnied softly as she made her way back to the farmhouse.

A galvanised tub was set before the fire, half full of steaming water. Annie held out a bath towel to Florence. "I think you've earned this. I've sent Frank off to stack the butter pats in the dairy with strict instructions not to come back till I say he can. You have a good soak my dear. You've worked like a Trojan today, and now we're ready to face whatever Mother Nature chucks at us. There's a plate of stew and dumplin's waiting for you, and I've stoked up the stove in your room so it's nice and cosy when you're ready to go up."

"Annie, you're an angel." Florence peeled off clothes damp with sweat. She didn't know when she'd felt so tired. Or exhilarated. She stepped into the steaming tub, luxuriating in the warmth that eased her fatigue. She hummed absently as she soaked and looked down at her slim body in the water, a body she'd never given to any man. Since Bartholomew had tried to take it by force, she'd recoiled from the very idea … But what about Andrew? She shivered slightly and soaped the loofah energetically. Well, she was going to say 'no' to him, wasn't she?

Later, she, Annie and Frank ate in comparative silence, too weary for conversation, registering their satisfaction with the savour of Annie's supper with nods, grunts and smiles. Florence, now dressed in her twill nightdress and a dressing gown, the tassled girdle knotted at her waist, stood beside Annie at the sink, drying the plates as Annie passed them to her. In the contented quiet of the room, only the crackle of logs burning in the grate and the clock ticking on the mantelpiece broke the silence. The knock at the door shattered the quiet like a gunshot.

"I bet I know who that is," Frank rose to his feet.

"I'm so sorry to disturb you this late."

The voice from outside in the yard was by now familiar to Florence. She looked down at her unseemly outfit and ran her fingers through her still damp hair, hanging loose about her shoulders.

"We've been expectin' you," Frank said. "I'll have to ask Florence if she's ready to talk to you. She's had one heck of a day!"

"Help!" Florence mouthed rather than said. Annie placed a hand on her forearm. The older woman looked Florence in the eye and nodded. "Don't put it off no longer," she said quietly to Florence. "Ask the young man in, Frank."

Andrew Forbes stepped over the threshold, muffled up against the frosty night. Florence turned to face him.

"Hello again, Andrew."

A silence interposed. Annie broke it with comfortable words. "Come and sit youself down by the fire." She gestured towards Frank's fireside chair. "Keep the fire well tended so it stays in till mornin', and brew yourselves a warm drink if you like. Frank and me are makin' tracks for bed now, so we'll bid you both a good night. Sing out if you need anythin', Florence."

Andrew was removing his boots on the mat inside the door.

"Andrew. Take off your scarf and greatcoat. You'll fry in here. I'll make us a toddy." She busied herself with the kettle and Frank's whisky bottle. "It's getting jolly chilly outside ..."

"Florence. You look so beautiful. I can't get you out of my head ... or my heart. I've come here to tell you I love you, and to ask you to wait for me till I come back."

Dear God, Florence thought. "Andrew," she began, "I ..."

"Wait! Please wait." He held up a hand to silence her. "I want to tell you what I have to say before you go any further."

She handed him a steaming cup and sat down. "Alright. Go on."

"Ever since our last meeting, I've been cursing myself for a fool. You must think me a coward, a weakling for breaking down like that."

Florence shook her head.

"Well, I need you to know I'm nothing of the sort. And the last thing I want is for you to pity me because you think I've reached my breaking point. I haven't, and I'm fully resolved to go back to the Front and lead my men with the determination they deserve from their CO. You said I must find the courage, and I'm doing just that." His resolute expression struck her as she watched him. "But after the war ... After the war, I have other plans, and I've been hoping you'll want to be part of them." He took a deep breath. "I've seen more pain and suffering than any human being ought to. And I'm realist enough to know that it's not finished yet. But when it's all over, I'm done with the army. I'm going to train as a doctor. I want to relieve pain, not inflict it—enhance life, not annihilate it. And I can't tell you how much I want you to be part of it."

"Andrew, I..."

"No, Florence, I haven't finished. This war's a war of old men, like my father. It's all about power and control, not people's wellbeing or a better world – or anything honourable and civilised. Our generation, Florence, yours and mine, has got to do a better job of creating a world where peace and justice can flourish. This is my dream, and I pray it could be yours too." He took both her hands in his, his eyes bright. "Florence, I felt drawn to you from the moment we met. And everything I've learned about you since convinces me that I'm right. We could be such a good team, you and I. If it weren't for the war, we could take our time, get to know each other bit by bit, but ... it's not like that for us. We don't have that luxury."

She struggled with the tightness in her chest. She'd expected a declaration of love, but not one of such intense commitment to values that she admired – a better, more civilised world.

"Andrew … I thought I'd know what I would say to you when this moment arrived. I'd made up my mind to say 'no' to you. Because … I hardly know you. And because I don't think I'm ready to commit. To anyone. But what you've just told me has set the cat among the pigeons."

He smiled at her and took her hand.

"Please. Let me have my say now." She sat a while, trying to get her thoughts straight. "Since coming here, I've started to glimpse a life that suits me. Today's been the toughest, physically speaking, that I've ever had to face. But I can't describe the exhilaration I felt when Frank congratulated me on a job well done. I think I've arrived somewhere I want to be. And now I find that place is where you are, wanting to do things that matter to people. It's changed the whole picture, and now I'm all at sixes and sevens."

"I'm listening to you, Florence … Do you have an answer for me?"

"I … I'm going to ask you if we can meet up again after I've had time to reflect on what you've said to me tonight. Please, Andrew. Believe me, I'm no flibbertigibbet. I'll neither leave you in the lurch, nor give you an answer now I'll want to take back later. But after the day I've had, and as tired as I am, I don't think I can make a decision right now that'll affect the rest of my life – our lives. At least." a grin lit up her face. "I'm not sending you away with a flea in your ear."

"My dearest girl. You must take the time you need. I'll be waiting for you. Can I hold you now?"

Their kiss, their embrace lasted long minutes. At last, Andrew held her at arm's length his eyes never leaving her face.

"I'm going now. I'll be in touch to let you know when I've got some time to meet again. And thank you – so much – for giving me hope." He kissed the top of her head. "You're even lovelier than I dared believe."

Chapter 25

"Oh, goodness! Just look at that! Alf! Alf!" Grace screwed up her eyes against the brightness. She pulled on some socks and ran over the bare floorboards to her brother's room. "You've got to come and have a look at this!"

The snow had started in the night. It was a good foot deep on the roof of the weaving factory across the road, and along the railings, little puffy balls of the stuff were perched in delicate balance on each finial. Every branch and twig was weighed down with it. Barely a footprint had sullied it.

Alf stumbled back, being careful not to disturb Ellen, still sleeping in the bed Grace had just vacated. He rubbed his eyes. "This'd better be good, Gracie, I was in the middle of a really nice dream, then. I'd just caught this huge pike ..."

"Never mind fishing – just come here!" Grace pointed to the white world outside the window. "Isn't that something? We've got to get out there and build a snowman. He'll be the biggest in Halstead. We'll get Doris to help – she'll be able to bring a carrot for his nose. And we'll need a hat and a scarf and coal for buttons –"

"Whoa, whoa! It looks like fun, I'm not saying it doesn't, but I'm going to have my breakfast before anything else. So you'll just have to keep your hair on till I'm ready."

"Oh, Alf. You drive me mad sometimes. Get a move on, can't you?"

But Alf was a good sport, so she contented herself with dressing in the warmest clothes she could find before going downstairs. In the living kitchen, warm with the heat from the range, Grace had to take off several of the layers she'd just put on.

"Have you seen the snow outside, Mum?" Her grin would not have disgraced the Cheshire Cat.

"Good morning, dear. Of course I have. My eyesight's as good as yours, you know. Aunt Flo's going to have her work cut out at the farm while this lot's on the ground."

"But isn't it beautiful?" Grace said. "Snow's never as white and lovely as this in London. It goes slushy and sooty in no time."

"Yes, you're right, Grace, it is prettier here."

"Alf and I are going to get Doris and build the best snowman ever!"

"But first you're going to eat some breakfast." Nell was firm. "There's some toast and dripping keeping warm on the range. You need to eat well to keep out the cold. And before you set off having fun, I've promised Mrs Mizen that you and Alf will help Elsie clear the snow from the front path."

"That's alright," Grace said, taking a great bite of the dripping toast, "we can use the snow we shovel off the path for the snowman! Perfect!" She finished her mouthful. "Mum, can we have some lumps of coal for the snowman's buttons?"

"Grace, you know the price of coal. We can't afford to waste even a few pieces on a snowman. You and Alf can pick some clinker out of the ash pan under the range and use that. It'll look just as good."

Alf wandered in and, following the savoury scent of the dripping, made straight for the plate of toast.

"Honestly! Where are my children's manners? Have you forgotten how to greet your mother in the morning, Alfred?"

"Sorry, Mum. How are you today?" He produced the bowler hat Monty had lent him for his Chaplin skit. "What do you reckon, Grace? I don't think Mr Mizen'll mind if we use this for the snowman, d'you?"

When they'd eaten as much toast as they could manage, Grace handed Alf the coal shovel from beside the range. "Take this," she said, "and hold it steady while I fish out some decent sized lumps from the ashes with the tongs. They're going to be Mr Snowy's buttons – and his eyes."

"Grace!" She turned towards her brother just as he let fly a snowball that hit her square in the chest.

"Now you've asked for it, Alf Ashford." She ran towards him and shoved a fistful of snow down his neck."

"We'll never get this path cleared at this rate," Elsie said. "Can't you two be sensible for a minute?"

When they'd finished, the path was easily passable by the grownups, they thought, and they'd stacked up enough snow to make a sizeable mound for the snowman's body. Grace set off for Doris' house and soon the two returned with a crooked carrot to make a hooked nose. The children rolled an increasingly large ball of snow along Factory Terrace and felt they'd made Mr Snowy's head big enough. It took all their effort to lift it and lodge it in place on top of the snow 'body'.

"Goodo!" Doris hopped with delight. "Now for all the bits and pieces!" She picked up a twig. "This'll make a good arm and hand, don't you think?"

"We just need a scarf," said Grace, eyeing up the striped muffler looped round Elsie's neck. "Elsieee …" She tweaked the end of the scarf.

"No!" said Elsie. "My mum'll kill me."

"Oh, go on. It's only for a little while, and I'll explain to your mum. It's just right – and he's got to have a scarf. Your dad's hat looks terrific!"

Elsie unwound the scarf reluctantly and placed it round the snowman's neck. The children stood back to admire their handiwork. Nell came to the door, holding a twin's hand in each of hers, the toddlers muffled up to their ears.

"Very impressive as snowmen go – he's about the best I've seen. And now you've finished him, you can play with your little sisters. They'll like the snow, too."

"I know!" said Alf. "If we can borrow a couple of tin trays, we can give them rides up and down the road. Can we, Mum?"

"Good idea, Alf. Can we, Mum?" Grace said.

"Oh, alright. But you must be very careful and not let them fall off." Nell went into the house and came back with the trays. "Grace," she called as Alf sat the twins down on the trays, "I thought this would do for the snowman." Opening her hand, she held out a pipe. "It's one of your Dad's favourites ... I brought it in case he gets leave."

"Oh, thanks, Mum!" Grace slid the pipe into the corner of the snowman's clinker grin. "Perfect."

Renee and Iris giggled with excitement as the older children sent them slithering along the snow-covered cobbles.

'I don't think I've ever, ever had as much fun in a single day,' Grace wrote in her diary. She did not neglect to mention the pipe.

***

Out at Valley Farm, it was a different story. Snow clearing was a serious issue in the farmyard just to enable barrow-pushing. Once she and Frank had cleared enough space, Florence led the horses out to the paddock. Their hooves repeatedly balled up with hard-packed snow, so they slipped and slid on the icy ground. She used her hoof pick to clear out the accumulations, only for the build-up to refill their hoof cavities within a few paces. There was no way the team could work in conditions like these. It was all down to human effort.

"Now I understand your sense of urgency, Frank. Once the snow's on the ground, it's too late."

"Exactly, missy."

She set off for the sheepfold, pitchfork in hand, to replenish the hay racks and make sure the water was still flowing. With the cows in the byre, the need for fresh straw to top up their litter seemed never-ending. And all their forage had to be fed to them by hand. Her body ached by the time Annie called her into the farm kitchen for a reviving cup of tea.

"Here," she said. Florence eased herself into a chair with a groan. "A cuppa'll do you good. An' I've made some drop scones – they're good with honey."

"You do look after me, Annie." Florence loosened her boot laces.

"A note came for you when you was out with the ewes. A young soldier brought it – not *your* young soldier, but one of his men, I think. Here it is."

Annie handed her a brown envelope with 'Miss Florence Mundy, c/o Davis, Valley Farm' written on it in a sloping hand. Florence opened it with difficulty, her fingers feeling clumsy. Inside, a note was written on a single sheet of lined paper, torn from a memo pad:

'*Dearest Girl,*' it began in the same handwriting, '*We have our embarkation orders – we leave on 2nd January by train from the station here in Halstead. There's so much to do to prepare for departure, I have so very little time to see you But I must see you, my darling.*

'What with all this snow, it's so much harder getting around, but I'm hoping – you don't know how hard I'm hoping – that you could meet me tomorrow night. Is there any way you could get back into Halstead and meet at about seven? I was thinking by the bandstand in the Public Gardens.

'I know you won't be able to get a message back to me, but I'll be there, and I'll wait as long as it takes. I can hardly wait to see you and to hear what you have to say, my dearest love.

Andrew'

"Oh, Annie, I can't possibly do what he's asking! How on earth can I get back to town with the snow as bad as it is? I can't ride my bicycle – even Swank Everitt can't get his waggon out here till the road's clearer. And just look at me! I'm a complete wreck! I only have my WLA kit here at the farm."

"Let's talk to Frank about it when he comes in for his tea. You got to see that young fellow afore he goes, there's no doubtin' that." Annie had noticed Florence's bright mood since Andrew Forbes' visit, but she had not confided any change of heart, and Annie hadn't asked. *She'll tell me when she's good and ready,* Annie thought.

Frank lifted the latch and let himself into the kitchen on a gust of icy air. He stamped the snow from his boots and took them off on the mat. "Still bloomin' chilly. But I think we're winnin'. We got things under control, as long as it don't get no worse."

"Frank, we've got to help Florence get into Halstead tomorrow. The army's movin' out in a couple of days, along with her young officer. He can't get out here, and he needs to see her."

"But Frank," Florence began, "you've got enough on your mind without worrying on my account ..."

"No, no, Florence. You're one of us and it's down to us to give you a hand. It'll mean walkin', mind, but if it don't snow any more, there'll be plenty of footprints that've flattened the snow out – people have had to get to town for all sorts. As a matter of fact, I've got to go myself to get to the bank and to the feed merchant's. If we get ourselves well fettled for the mornin' chores, and get a shift on first thing, we could set out after a bite at dinnertime. I expect you'll be able to stay over with your sister, and we'll worry about gettin' you back out here when the time comes."

Frank helped himself to a drop scone and spread honey on it. Annie handed him a mug of tea. He took a great swig of tea, then bit into the scone. "That's better. Good pancakes, Annie, girl!"

"But Frank –" Florence began again.

Frank raised a hand. "No 'buts', missy. It's best foot forward now and in the mornin', though. Somehow, we've got to squeeze a quart into a pint pot!"

***

A light sprinkling of new snow was falling as Frank and Florence set out from Valley Farm. The road into Halstead, quiet at the best of times, was deserted.

"Take this," Frank said. "If you lose your footin' and take a tumble, you could find yourself with a twisted ankle, or worse." He handed her the stick she'd used when they moved the sheep. She was glad of it. Something to rely on. They exchanged few words. Her gaze strayed out across the snowy terrain, indistinct with the gentle, still-falling snow.

"Don't you feel small in this vast white landscape, Frank? I do."

"Yeah. Like ants, ain't we?" They plodded on, lapsing back into their own thoughts.

So much human history's been about war. Just like now, she thought. *Greed, vanity, hatred and jealousy. Little room for love and justice.* Love and justice … Her thoughts came back to Andrew and his vision. *It's right and good. We can make it work …*

"Frank," she asked, "did you ever have any doubts about marrying Annie?"

"Nah!" He guffawed into the crisp air. "We knew it was right from the moment we clapped eyes on each other."

"You're quite different, though, you and she. Didn't you worry it might not work out?"

"She's a good woman, my Annie." He turned to look at her and she could see he really meant it. "We kind of *complement* each other … like bubble and squeak, if you like."

Florence laughed.

The tower of St Andrew's church came into view through the veil of snowy spindrift.

"I'll leave you here, if that's alright," Frank said as they reached the junction with the High Street.

"Thanks for the company, Frank. You'd better get your business done quick – the light's not going to last long."

"Don't you worry about me, Florence, I'll be fine. And with luck, I'll see you tomorrow back at Valley." He cleared his throat and offered her his right hand. She took it, and he covered it with his left one. "Annie and me, we hope it goes well for you tonight."

"Thanks, Frank." She looked at him and smiled.

She turned her back and headed towards Factory Terrace. The children's snowman fixed her with his unblinking stare as she approached the front door. She found it surprisingly unnerving. She let herself in and called out for her sister.

"Nellie! It's me!"

Nell appeared from the back kitchen, where she was ironing the children's school clothes for the new term.

"Flo! How the devil …?"

"I walked in with Frank. Have you got any tea on the go? I'm gasping!"

"Yes, of course. But what's brought you back from the farm? I didn't expect to see you till the snow cleared."

"Andrew's asked me to meet him tonight. At the Rec. They're leaving for France in a couple of days … The kids've been enjoying the snow, haven't they?"

Nell sensed a tactical change of subject. "Yes, they have. But why the meeting? Is it still on with him? I thought –"

"Well, we've got some things to sort out before he leaves, and tonight's our only opportunity. I don't want to talk about it with anyone else till we've had a chance to discuss it together. It wouldn't be right. So, if you don't mind, Nellie, I'm going to keep it under my hat till I've seen him. Right now, I've got to freshen up and try to make myself look reasonably presentable. Is there any chance of a bath?"

"Oh, alright." Nell shifted the wooden clothes horse standing in front of the range. She wasn't keen on having her routine disrupted. "But you'd better be quick before the children want their tea."

They lugged the zinc tub in from the scullery and filled it with jugfuls of hot water from the range. Florence bathed swiftly.

Her next concern was drying her long hair. Many times since she'd taken up farming, she'd been tempted to cut it short into a fashionable bob that would dry quickly and be much less trouble. Florence was not vain about her looks, but she was proud of her hair. She brushed it in front of the range, glossy in the fire's glow.

Grace came in with a book under her arm. "Hello, Aunt Flo. You look nice."

"Thank you, Gracie. Would you help me decide what to wear tonight? I'm going to be outside in the snow, but I want to feel happy about how I look." They rummaged through Florence's meagre wardrobe and settled on the same skirt and coat she'd worn for her WLA interview. There were few alternatives.

"You can cheer it up with that little hat of mum's with the feather and the veil," Grace said. "It would really suit you. I'll ask her if it's alright for you to borrow it." And she was off, calling her mother from the stairs. She came back in, clutching the hat. It was hardly proof against the weather, but it was pretty. Shaped rather like a Robin Hood cap with a turned-up brim and a point in the front, it was fashioned from brown velvet and had a pheasant's feather sweeping backwards and a spotted veil that came just to Florence's chin. She pinned it on, a little on the slant, with the point just above her left eyebrow, and pulled the veil down.

"I like that," Grace said.

"Yes. So do I. Now. I've got some nice leather gloves somewhere." She looked down at her hands, no longer smooth as they'd been in her London days. "Oh well," she said. "Honest toil."

In all other respects, the work at Valley Farm had been good for her. She felt strong and fit, trim and supple and her complexion glowed. She was not displeased with her reflection in the bedroom mirror.

"Well, I'd best be off." She'd already heard the church clock chime a quarter to seven. "Wish me luck, Gracie!"

"What for? Where are you going?"

"I'll tell you in the morning!" Florence said over her shoulder, making for the front door.

Chapter 26

New Year's Eve, but the town was quiet. Parlour windows were lit, but there was no sense of celebration to greet the arrival of 1918, just people gathering quietly, hoping, some praying, for a better 1918. For an end to the war. For the return of loved ones and a return to normality. Some mourning soldiers who would never return. Others learning to live with maimed bodies, ravaged identities. Florence passed no one as she walked the snowy pavements towards the Rec.

The lamp standards cast golden light over the gardens. The incessant light snowfall had obliterated every footprint on the dancing green spread before her as she approached the bandstand. A figure sat on a park bench in a halo of lamplight. She saw the fleeting red glow of a lighted cigarette and a small cloud of exhaled smoke. And she could just make out the silhouette of a military cap, the light picking up the polished brass of its regimental badge. He turned and stood as he sensed her approach. Then she too was bathed in the lamp's soft glow as the snowflakes fell.

"Florence!" His dark eyes took in every detail of her. "I ... I worried you wouldn't make it in all this snow. I can't believe you're here. How did you get back from the farm?"

"I walked. With Frank. There was no other way. Hello, Andrew."

He took her hand and drew her towards him and kissed her fingertips. "Hello, you wonderful girl!" He smiled at her. "Let's sit down here." He gestured towards the bench. He'd already cleared away the snow.

They sat close, their shoulders touching. She could feel the warmth of him and did not shrink from it. He took out his cigarettes and offered her one. She reckoned this occasion called for a smoke and she took one from the packet. He flicked his lighter and she drew the smoke in. There was something reassuring about the tobacco's fragrant tang. But she didn't smoke often and the first inhalation made her feel light-headed.

"How've you been?" He put an arm round her shoulder.

"Fine. It's darned hard work, but we're coping ... You?"

"Flat out. No one's had the chance to think about what the future holds – too much to do. Probably just as well. The longer this farce goes on, the more like 'The Grand Old Duke of York' it seems. We're all either up, down or half-way up. Us, the Germans – everyone. Going nowhere. If it wasn't so tragic it'd be comical. But – I don't know ..." he broke off and sighed. "I can't believe it can go on much longer. We're fighting ourselves and each other to a standstill. Surely someone will stop it before we completely wipe each other out."

"Dear God, Andrew. I hope so."

"Still. We're not here to talk about the blasted war. I just can't wait till it's all over and we can get on with living. I've been thinking about medical school and the challenges of study and learning something totally new. It's a far cry from Staff College, but I reckon I can do it – I'm good at science."

"And you'll be doing what you want to do. What you believe in."

"Mmm. Of course, we'd be pretty hard up until I'm qualified, but then we could settle wherever you want to – town or country, the choice is yours. I know I'll be happy anywhere as long as I'm with you –"

"Andrew." Florence rested her hand on his arm. "I haven't answered your question yet. In fact, you haven't made your intentions very clear at all. But you're making some fairly sweeping assumptions." She smiled and tipped her head to one side.

"Of course! How could I be such an unromantic fool?" Taking her hands in his, he knelt before her in the snow. "Florence Mundy, my dearest, my darling girl. Will you wait for me? And when peace comes, will you be my wife?" He looked at her, unblinking.

She took a deep breath. "Yes, Captain Andrew Forbes, I will. I … think … we'll be good together." *Well, I've said it … In at the deep end,* she thought.

He stood and took her in his arms. "Well." He grinned at her. "If you're going to be the future Mrs Forbes, I'd better find out if you can dance!"

He led her out onto the dancing green, the snow soaking the hem of her skirt. He held her right hand and slipped his right arm round her waist. Taking a breath, he began humming 'On The Beautiful Blue Danube'. He swept her off round the snow covered green, and before long, he was singing at the top of his voice. Florence found herself singing along with him as he swung her round the green step for step.

"So that's alright, then." They fell back onto the park bench, out of breath and laughing. "Now." He was suddenly quiet. "I have something I want you to have." He felt in the breast pocket of his uniform jacket and pulled out a flat tin.

"The men call this my 'Snout Tin'," he said. "'Snouts' are what they call cigarettes. It used to have cigarettes in it."

"I do know what a snout is – I come from Stratford, remember? – I bet I know more slang than you do!"

"One day we'll put it to the test, but right now, I want to show you what's in the Snout Tin." He opened it. Inside, set on a little piece of red velvet was a gold ring. "It was my grandmother's," Andrew said. "I've been carrying it around with me as a good luck charm, but now I want you to have it while I'm away. It probably doesn't fit you, but you could always wear it round your neck on a chain. And when I get back, I'll buy you the loveliest ring I can afford."

He took the ring from the tin and laid it on his open palm. Florence ran her finger round it, but then closed Andrew's hand over it.

"No. I can't take it now, when you're going back there. It's your talisman. You should keep it with you!"

"You surely don't believe all that superstitious poppycock, do you? You're my good luck charm now. What do I want with meaningless symbols?"

She shook her head and covered her face with her hands. "I don't know what to think. But if it's kept you safe till now …"

"If it's with you, I shall feel far safer than keeping it with me in some stinking trench. Please, Florence, my love. Please take it."

She opened his fingers and took the ring. It was tiny and bore traces of the engraved design which had once decorated it. Andrew fitted it onto the little finger of Florence's left hand.

"There. Grandmother was quite a character. She would have approved of you."

"Thank you. I shall treasure it. But you must take something of mine to keep in the tin." She tried to think of what she had with her that she could give him. Reaching up, she disentangled a tortoiseshell comb, inlaid with mother-of-pearl, from her hair.

"Here. It's all I've got, but please take it with you." She kissed it and gave it to him. It was a perfect fit for the Snout Tin. Andrew closed it and put it back in his tunic pocket.

"It's a funny thing," he said, "here we are, pledging our lives to each other, in an Essex country town that's alien to both of us. Is it coincidence or kismet do you think?"

"Who knows? You're here because it's where the army sent you. I'm here because I decided to help my sister get out of Stratford. And now look at me – callouses on my hands, shovelling farmyard manure all day … It only goes to show, you never can tell what's round the corner."

"You're so right. I imagined myself ending up with the insipid daughter of one of my parents' friends by default. How glad I am I've found you!" He described to her his comfortable home in Dorchester, of cricket and tennis and garden parties.

"Casterbridge! Hardy country," Florence said. "They gave me 'Far From the Madding Crowd' when I left Brown and Son. A first edition. It's just about my favourite novel."

"Are you anything like Bathsheba Everdene, do you think?"

"Gosh, I hope not. She did some rash things." She bit her lip and frowned.

"Broke some hearts, too …"

"But I love Hardy's sense of Wessex country, don't you? He takes you right there when you read his books. It's one of the reasons I knew I'd like it here."

They talked of places they knew, books and music they loved, people they admired and didn't admire and didn't feel the cold.

"I've got to go now," he said at length. "So much still to do … My darling Florence, I shall keep the memory of this magical evening in my heart while I'm gone. I shall think of you all the time and imagine your beautiful hair every time I take the comb out … 1918 is about to dawn. Hope and pray with all your heart and soul that we shall emerge into a peaceful world before this year ends. And don't let any Sergeant Troys turn your head while I'm gone!"

She gripped his arm and shook her head, smiling. They walked along the snowy streets back to Factory Terrace. The embrace that followed brought them both to the verge of tears, but neither wanted to part on a melancholy note. He smiled as he held her at arm's length.

"That snowman's giving us his blessing," Andrew said as they acknowledged Mr Snowy's clinker smile.

Florence tugged at his tunic collar. "Look after yourself, Andrew. And come back soon."

"Just as soon as ever I can!" He smiled and turned on his heel.

She watched him walk away. He tipped his cap back and stopped to light a cigarette under a street lamp. He turned and waved, and was gone.

She let herself into the house as quietly as she could and took off her boots in the passageway. She tiptoed into the bedroom, trying not to disturb Alf's sleeping form on the divan. She heard a quiet tapping at the bedroom door, and Grace appeared. She rubbed her eyes and yawned.

"You alright, Aunt Flo? Had a good time?"

"Yes, I did. Thank you, Gracie. We danced on the green. My skirt got all wet!"

"But there wasn't any music."

"We sang. Now. You must get back to bed before we wake the whole household. Happy New Year, Gracie."

"Same to you, Aunt Flo."

Chapter 27

"You said *yes?*" Nell said. The sisters sat together at the kitchen table next morning.

"I did."

"But only last week you didn't think you would. You made it quite clear you didn't love him. What's changed?"

"Lots of things. And I had plenty of time last week to reflect." Florence stared into her steaming tea and watched the bubbles on the surface slowly revolving. "I liked Andrew from the outset. You know I did." She raised her head and looked at Nell. "We've got a lot in common – music, for a start. We even like the same books, I've discovered. And when he told me about his plans to become a doctor after the war and start doing some good in the world, I knew I could go along with that. We'll make a good team, he and I. We'll be helpmates … And I haven't lied to him. I haven't once said I love him, but I mean to go through with the promises I've made him." There was a pause. "Besides, I do love him in a way. I admire him and care about him. He's a good man … I believe I can trust him."

"But still a man. He'll expect his conjugal rights. They all do. Are you ready for that? With someone you love like a brother?"

Harry Bartholomew's violation began to crowd her thoughts. Again. She shivered.

"I'm not completely naïve, Nellie. Believe me, I've gone all over this time and again in my mind this past week. I believe I want to be with him and that we can be happy together. Lots of people marry without feeling the kind of physical passions you're talking about. It can still work."

"You still a virgin, Florence? I bet you are. You haven't got a clue. And there'll be kids. You never wanted any … Still, a doctor's wife. At least you won't have to worry about where the next meal's coming from, hm? You sure you're not getting ideas above your station? Did you tell him about being a bus conductress? I bet you didn't."

"Nell! That's not worthy of you! All that class nonsense means nothing to me – you know that. Besides, we'll be pretty hard up while he's training. I'll do whatever I have to. Children will have to wait anyway."

An uneasy silence ensued. It was time to leave. "Look, Nellie, have a heart. How could I have sent him back to the Front without a hope? I simply couldn't do that."

"Well, when you're the leading light in the local Gilbert and Sullivan Society and have your work cut out running charity whist drives, as well as raising a tribe of kids, I hope you won't regret the deception – and opportunism!"

Florence pushed her chair back noisily. *How dare she?* "I'll be off, then." Her voice trembled. "Give my love to the children. I'll see you when I see you. The hat's on my bed." She hurried from the room, put on her overcoat and boots by the front door and walked away into the cold morning, slamming the door behind her.

The air sparkled, the sky was cobalt. The sub-zero night chill had rendered the snow layer crusty underfoot. Florence, though, was oblivious to the beauty and clarity of the day. As the snow crunched beneath her boots, guilt and self-doubt were there in her conscience. Again. *Damn you, Bartholomew ... And damn you, Nell.* Opportunism? Deception? Social climbing? No such scurrilous motives had entered her head. So Nell's words rankled ... But she hadn't mentioned working on the buses to Andrew. Why hadn't she?

Her thoughts meandered back over her life since arriving in Halstead. Less than four months ... Valley Farm, the Davises – *how good it's all been. Given me a sense of purpose ... If it weren't for Nell's fears, I might still be in London.* Working on the buses. Fearing the reappearance of Bartholomew ... *I'm in a much better place ...* And now Andrew. *Admirable. Yes. Handsome and humorous. Yes, yes. But ... but ...* She hadn't looked for love, romance, physical contact – any of it – since Harry ... She'd escaped him with her virginity intact – just. But she *had* felt physical desire for Harry before the assault ... *Slut ... Surely it'll be different with Andrew, won't it?*

The shoulder of her greatcoat caught against an overhanging tree branch heavy with snow. The branch snapped back, setting off a shower of snow, tumbling through the air. She watched it drift to earth and brushed it from her sleeve. No point in hypothesising further. *I am where I am.*

She set off again, a new determination in her step, one hand in a coat pocket, the other planting the stick Frank had given her in the snow. She couldn't wait to get back to Valley Farm. To work. She heard the sharp, piercing whistle of a train in the station. One such train would be taking Andrew and his men off to war tomorrow...

"Mornin'! It's good to have you back, m'dear. Happy New Year. Let's hope, anyways." Frank was in the lane with Jack. The dog's tail thrashed and he ran to greet her.

"Yes, indeed." She stooped to fondle Jack's ears. "How's it going, Frank? You and Annie been managing? I see the lane's a lot clearer than yesterday."

"Not bad. Swank's been out, helpin' us shovel it away so as he can get his cart up here. If we crack on this afternoon, we'll be able to get the horses back to work. Roll your sleeves up, missy!"

Chapter 28

Two days later, it was back to school for the children of Halstead. The boys had been dying to gain access to the playground so they could construct ice runways in the still-unblemished snow. 'Windy' Clark and his best pal, Lennie Plumb were quick off the mark.

"Come on, Lennie – there's the best bit. Let's bag it quick." They buffed and burnished the snow layer with the soles of their boots, packing it into a slick of blackened ice that they could launch themselves along, cheeks glowing in the keen slipstream. Grace and Doris looked on, impressed.

"It's not a bad slide," Doris said. "You any good at slidin', Gracie?"

"Not bad …" She stood watching. "D'you think Windy and Lennie'd let us have a go?"

"Dunno. Let's try 'em." In the art of guile, she could show Grace a thing or two. "Good slide, boys. Can we have a go?" She eyed Lennie.

"It's not for girls," Lennie said. "Girls can't do slidin'."

"Bet we can."

"Look, Doris. Alf's on a slide with Donald over there," Grace said. "Why don't we just go and ask them? Alf'll let us have a go – he's my brother."

"I'm not givin' up here." Doris had a determined look on her face. "This 'un's a much better slide. I'll get Lennie to say yes – you wait and see, Gracie." Doris turned towards the boys. "Now, Lennie Plumb, you've got to let us *prove* we can slide as good as you!" Lennie and Windy discussed the matter for a moment. "Come on. Your lives'll be hell if it gets out you've backed out on a challenge with *girls!*"

The boys knew she was right. There was nothing else for it. "Alright, then," Lennie said. "But don't blame us if you fall over and skin your knees!"

Doris took a deep breath before her run-up and launched herself like a skater, spreading her arms as if about to take flight. She sailed along the ice slide, smiling, and elegantly disengaged herself at the far end.

"Fair do's," Windy said. "One down, one to go. Come on, Grace, let's see what you can do."

Grace felt nervous. Almost all the children in the playground were now watching Windy and Lennie's slide and the normal hubbub had diminished to a murmur.

"Go on, Gracie," whispered Doris.

She stepped forward and attacked the slide, concentrating … It couldn't have gone better. She skipped off the end, smiling. Doris was already heading towards the boys. "Are we on for another turn, then?" she asked them.

Miss Moore placed a hand on Alf's shoulder and pulled him from the line. The boy wondered what he'd done wrong.

"No need to panic," said Miss Moore. Her benevolent look told Alf he wasn't in trouble. "Mr Mathews wants to see you at play time. So when the bell goes, run along to his office, please."

"Yes, miss." He spent the next hour and a half in a complete daze. The spelling and history lessons were just a blur.

When the play time bell rang, he straightened his tie and went off to Mr Mathews' office. Grace watched him go, but was not able to say anything encouraging to him. He knocked on the office door and stood back till he heard Mr Mathews issue the invitation to enter.

"Hello, Alfred. Happy New Year to you. Did you and your family have an enjoyable Christmas?"

"Yes, Mr Mathews, thank you. Happy New Year to you, too."

"I've called you in today to congratulate you on your superb Christmas card." Alf had almost forgotten.

"Your drawing skills are really very good indeed." Mathews produced Alf's card, a pencil sketch of Townsford Mill. "Your perspective is good, the proportions are accurate and your pencil work is first rate. I'd say you have a very promising future if you stick with it." He broke off and, resting both his elbows on the desk, leaned towards Alfred, addressing him with a directness which slightly intimidated the boy. "I believe you have an exceptional talent – one which could help you earn your living in time to come. I'd like to help you develop it, if you'd agree to some extra lessons with me."

"Oh, yes please, Mr Mathews! There's nothing I'd like more," Alf said, amazed. "But I'll have to ask my mother …" He trailed off, aware that Nell was less than enthusiastic about his obsession with drawing. In Nell's book, drawing was just a pastime, not the route to a career. Besides, where was the money to pay for Mr Mathews' lessons to come from?

"Why don't you ask her to come in and see me?" said Morton Mathews. "That way I can reassure her about the value of such tuition, and explain to her what I've got in mind. Perhaps early next week? Shall we say Tuesday at noon? And I'd like you to be there to have your say, too. What do you think?"

Predictably enough by Alf's reckoning, Nell objected, and was on the verge of dismissing the proposal as a silly idea. But the look on her son's face made her think again.

"Well …" She took some moments to reflect. Ellen had had piano lessons back in Stratford when money was not so tight and Grace was getting excellent singing tuition thanks to Oliver Davage at the church. Alf was receiving no such benefits.

"I suppose it wouldn't hurt to go and listen to what Mr Mathews has got to say, but I'm making no promises, mind."

Nell lifted the latch on the school gate and made her way between the ice runs. She reached the door, where the ash pan cinders from the boiler had been strewn since the start of term.

"Do come in and have a seat, Mrs Ashford," said the Headmaster, "I've sent for Alfred – I'm sure his teacher will send him along presently." He indicated a straight-backed chair with a gesture of his hand. "But before he arrives, I'd value a moment just to put you in the picture, so to speak, about Alfred's drawing skills."

Nell cleared her throat. "Before you begin." Her tone was matter-of-fact. "I'm keen for my children to make the most of their intelligence, and hope that their educational success will take them far. I also want them to take pleasure in their artistic gifts, but must tell you that I do not possess the resources to indulge them ..."

A firm knock came at the door.

"Come in, Alfred!"

The boy pushed open the door and entered, his socks pulled up and school tie straightened. Nell turned to watch her son as he came into the Head's study. She was pleased he'd bothered to smarten himself up. *So like his father,* she thought.

"Please sit down, Alfred. I was on the point of explaining to your mother how I think developing your drawing skills could help you towards a successful future. On reflection, it makes sense for you to hear my views as well." Mathews put his elbows on the desk and intertwined his fingers. "It's important to realise that drawing skills are not simply of recreational value. A gift of the sort that you possess, Alfred, could lead you into engineering. Or architecture. Has anything of that sort occurred to you?"

Alfred shook his head. "N-no, Mr Mathews. But I –"

Without waiting for the boy to finish, Mathews continued. "There's a good living to be had as a draughtsman in many technical industries, and further qualifications could take you a long way."

"I really like the idea of being an architect," said Alf, "but apart from being able to draw buildings, what else would I have to do?"

"Mr Mathews." Nell interrupted, an anxious note in her voice. "I feel I must stop you there before Alfred gets carried away." She stopped and rearranged her position on the hard chair. "I have to be honest with you. Frankly, our family circumstances are insufficient to support any of my children through a prolonged period of study ... they'll have to work for their living as soon as they leave school. I'm sorry ..."

Morton Mathews put his elbows on the desk and clasped his hands together. "Mrs Ashford. Far be it from me to pry or to suggest any course of action which might embarrass you. I am merely keen to convey my opinion that taking Alfred's drawing abilities seriously may not be mere frivolity. For the present, I am prepared to give him the benefit of extra tuition at no cost to you. I spend many hours in my studio, and I would relish the prospect of nurturing Alfred's talents while I'm getting on with my own work. Demonstrating new techniques to him and correcting errors will not interfere with my projects, and helping him develop would be payment in itself, so I beg you, please do not reject the idea on financial grounds." He turned to Alf. "As for you, young man, if I am to expend extra time and effort on you, I shall expect you to keep your end of the bargain."

"What *is* my end of the bargain, please sir?"

"If your buildings are not going to fall down or have the wrong proportions, you will need to work hard on your mathematics so that you can understand structures. If you want to be able to explain your plans grammatically and fluently, you must not neglect your English. In short, if I am to help you, I want to see you helping yourself by doing your best in all your lessons. What do you say?"

Morton Mathews waited for Alf's reply.

"Yes sir. I'll try my best."

"Can't say fairer than that, my boy. Now. Mrs Ashford." Mathews turned to Nell. "What do you think now you've heard what I have in mind?"

Nell sat, her gloved hands folded in her lap. Alf noted that she was beginning to smile.

"Well ... what can I say? Your suggestion is most generous, Mr Mathews. And if you're really sure that Alfred won't get under your feet in the studio, I'm happy to accept your kind offer. Rest assured, I shall do all I can to make sure Alfred fulfils his obligations. And thank you. Very much. This means a great deal to me – and, of course, to Alfred."

"I won't let you down, sir." Alf said.

"Good." Mathews took the boy's hand. "Shall we say Saturday morning at 10, then? I'll ask my wife to bake some of her rather good gingerbread."

Chapter 29

"Hey, look at Mr Snowy! Dad's pipe's fallen out of his mouth!" Grace ran to pick it up.

"So it has." Alf said. "And one of his arms has dropped off! Oh dear." He assessed the snowman's dishevelled appearance. "I think the snow's starting to melt."

"Well, it had to sooner or later," said Ellen. "It's two weeks since you built him. Winter won't last forever."

There was no doubt. Mr Snowy was past his best. The battered bowler hat had fallen over one clinker eye, giving him a drunken look, and his carrot nose was drooping. The snowman became a sad sight in Factory Terrace, until his remains were the only signs left of the snow. The playground slides melted away.

Nell resumed her daily round, taking the twins out in the makeshift push chair, passing the time of day with Molly Cooper as she went about her shopping, dropping in on cousin Ivy for a chat and catching up with the life of the town.

"It's good to see you, Nell." Molly dumped a couple of pounds of potatoes from the brass scoop of her scales into Nell's shopping bag, her finger tips showing red and raw from the ends of her fingerless gloves. "It's been that cold, I've had trouble gettin' the veg in from my smallholders. Life must be tough for them. How's your sister doin'? It can't be easy on the farms."

"No, indeed." Nell fumbled with the clasp on her purse. "I expect it's hard going … but I haven't seen her since New Year's Day. The children've enjoyed the snow, though, haven't they?" she said, changing the subject. She looked at Doris' mother with a smile. "Mine have had a whale of a time – I think Doris has too, from everything Grace has said."

"Yeah, they have! Them playground slides've been a lot of fun … I've had no news from France this past week or two, have you?"

"No," replied Nell, "I expect it's because of the weather."

"I'm sure you're right, Nell. But it's funny they can get the soldiers away from here, but they can't get the mail back! I miss the letters, even if they are a bit curt. I bet you do, too."

"Yes …" Nell sighed. "Any news is better than no news. Well … almost any news. I feel so … Disconnected, don't you?"

"I do indeed. How much longer can this lot go on? We've just had our fourth Christmas at war. And business is a far cry from 'usual', ain't it?"

"We can only hope and keep on writing. We've got to keep our letters going – they're a lifeline to the boys at the Front. I just hope they're getting through.

Anyway, Molly. Better get on – got to go and see what Bill Broyd's got in his window today. What do I owe you?"

"Eightpence ha'penny, please, Nell."

She counted the coins into Molly's hand and turned the pushchair towards the shop door. The twins waved to Molly, their hands warm in the woollen mittens Ellen had made.

"You always get more than you bargain for with Mr Broyd," Nell said over her shoulder. And she blushed slightly. "I don't object to the extra offcuts and such, in fact I'm very grateful for them. But I don't know what to say when he starts dishing out the compliments … I'm never sure whether he's serious or not … and whether he's … you know … a bit too familiar … Does he expect, well, how can I put it? Payment in kind, so to speak, for his little extras?"

"Oh, don't you worry on that score, Nell. That rascal Bill's been like that as long as I've known him, cheeky so-and-so! He just does it to brighten up his day – and your day, too. There ain't no malice in him. And he knows where to draw the line."

Nell set off along the High Street. The twins' breath made misty clouds and their cheeks glowed rosy like ripe apples as Nell's boot heels clacked on the pavement. Outside Broyd's shop window, Nell tried to assess its display without the butcher noticing her. Bill raised his own pigs in a little yard with a sty behind the shop. The meat was always tender. Home-cured ham hocks were good and economical. But if there was a small hand-and-spring of pork in the window, she could be tempted. It would feed the family for several days.

Broyd came out from behind his counter and stood in the shop doorway. His shadow fell on Nell and the twins' pushchair. Nell looked up at the butcher, tall and hefty, a smile on his jovial face. Bill's mutton-chop whiskers were greying now, but his thick hair was still dark. He wore a straw boater, as befits a traditional butcher, its hatband black since the loss of his nephew on the first day of the Somme Offensive. He lodged his fists on his hips, his forearms like hams.

"Well, good day to you, young Mrs Ashford. May I say how charming you look today. And how are them twins? Bonny little lasses!" His tone was avuncular, as always, and disarming. Nell blushed as she looked away.

"I'm well, thank you, Mr Broyd. And very glad to see the back of the snow. Perhaps life can get back to normal now – whatever normal is, these days."

Nell wheeled the pushchair into the shop, fragrant with the smell of sawdust on the floor. She chose a breast of mutton, which looked good and meaty, which she could stuff with breadcrumbs and herbs. She counted money into the butcher's hand and smiled as Broyd slipped a small package of giblets into Nell's bag with a wink. She thanked him again, and was on the point of leaving, when Broyd called her back.

"Mrs Ashford, I've a proposition to put to you."

Nell looked aghast.

"Don't you panic," he said, chuckling, "this is a business proposition. I'd like to know if you could see your way to makin' brawn for me to sell in my shop. Only my last lady had to stop on account of her husband's come back from the war in a bad way and she can't spare the time no more. You've gained quite a reputation in Halstead for the good food from your kitchen. And at the moment, most of my pigs' heads're goin' to waste. It's a cryin' shame. I'd pay you, of course … Have you ever made brawn, Mrs A?"

"Well, I have once or twice, Mr Broyd, when I had my own kitchen in Stratford. But I'd have to ask Mrs Mizen if she'd mind – and I'd have to pay her something for using her range. And there'll be the cost of the fuel. Brawn takes a lot of cooking, as I'm sure you know. Leave it with me, and I'll see what I can do. I'd like to help if I can, and the extra money would be welcome. Thank you for thinking of me."

She set off back to Factory Terrace. She felt gratified. It would be good to have something useful – and lucrative – to do. She hoped Jane Mizen would not dismiss the idea.

"That's fine with me, so long as you pay your way," Jane said, "I can't afford to be out of pocket."

"I'll make sure you're not. But I'm really keen to do this. It's perfect! If it weren't for the twins, I could do a little part time job while the others are at school. But Iris and Renee tie me to the house, and there's just not enough to keep me occupied."

"Monty and me, we like a tasty bit of brawn. Elsie's partial, too. Perhaps you can pay us in kind, like, some of the time?" The landlady grinned and hunched her shoulders. "By the way, there's a letter from France for you. I expect you'll want to read it quick. I'll fetch it up for you."

Chapter 30

Leave! Nell could barely believe what she was reading.

"Oh Jane! My husband's got leave. He's coming home!"

"My dear! That is good news. I'm so pleased for you."

"And so soon! I can hardly believe it!" Nell felt giddy and reached for the newel post. "At least with Florence at the farm we'll be able to fit him in ... It is alright if he stays here, isn't it?"

"Of course, dear. Where else is he going to kip down if not with his family? We can shift the furniture round to make enough room."

Nell smiled gratefully at her landlady. She tried to see George in her mind's eye but the image was elusive, indistinct. Her failure shocked her. It had been so long, and his letters told her so little.

"I'm so worried about what the war may have done to George. He's a peaceful, kind man ... Shell shock might ... Well, it might have turned his mind. You hear such stories ..." She frowned and bit her lip.

"Don't meet trouble half-way. He's more'n likely survived better than what you think. Let's hope so, anyways." Jane laid a hand gently on Nell's arm. "Now then, let's get this place ship-shape for a soldier's return, shall we?"

After school Nell broke the news.

"Dad? Here? When? How long for?" Grace danced about the kitchen.

"Any day now. So, you three." Nell sat the older children down in a line. "Listen to me, please. I know you're all excited, but you've got to remember where your Dad's been all this time. He'll be tired and weary and he'll need rest. You mustn't pester him. Take it gently. Give him a chance to settle in."

In his letter, George had asked the family not to meet him at the station. He preferred to take in the unfamiliar townscape without the distraction of his wife and children fussing and asking him questions. He'd need a little space. And he'd need a pint.

***

At No.5 Factory Terrace, the excitement was palpable. Alf was the first to spot his father rounding the end of the road by the silk factory.

"There he is!"

At a time when servicemen in uniform were a common sight, Alf would know his father's silhouette anywhere. George was a lightly built man who walked with one shoulder a little higher than the other, owing to years of carrying ladders, so he leaned ever so slightly to the left.

116

"He's here!" Alf said in a stage whisper, though he didn't really know why he was whispering.

When the knock came at the door, the whole Ashford family crowded into the hallway.

"Let Mum get to the front," said Ellen. "She should be first to greet Dad."

The others knew she was right and retreated, shuffling, up the passage. Nell opened the door. George, she saw, had lost weight. His neck emerging from the khaki collar of his uniform jacket looked almost scrawny and his cheeks were hollow.

"Oh, George!" She looked into his eyes and saw sadness in them. She clasped his upper arms, still gazing at his face. "We've all been longing for this moment."

He stepped into the house and noticed how his family had all grown.

Alf offered his father his right hand. "Hello, Dad." His voice wavered. "It's wonderful to have you home."

George took Alf's hand in both of his and shook it. "Alfred. It's good to know you've been the man of the family while I've been … gone. Well done, lad. And you, Miss Ministering Angel," he said to Ellen, who blushed and kissed his whiskery cheek. "Your mum says she doesn't know how she'd cope without you. And just look at these little twins! Not babies anymore!"

"Say hello to your Daddy, little 'uns," Nell said. Iris and Renee looked at George shyly from beneath their blonde mops and withdrew to their mother's skirts. "They'll have to get to know you, George."

Grace had stood back, her heart bursting. Now she flung her arms round her father's neck.

"Hey! Fireworks! Steady on, eh?" George regained his balance with the aid of the banister rail.

"Oh Dad! I've missed you so much!" she said against his chest.

"And me you. All of you!"

"Dad looks all in," Alf said. "We've got to take it slowly, like Mum told us."

"But we've got to make this time really special, too," said Grace.

Later, when George had removed his boots and military kit and Ellen had brought tea with bread and bramble jelly, the children sat at his feet. Alf had brought his drawing book, whose pages showed the good work he had done in his weekly sessions with Morton Mathews.

"This is good, Alf." The boy's natural gift for drawing and his eye for line and form were talents he'd inherited from his father, and George was gratified to see how his son's skills were coming on.

"Mr Mathews says if I keep working hard at my school subjects too, I could be good enough to become an architect."

"Did he really?" George ruffled the boy's hair. "And how would you like that?"

"Capital." Alf nodded. "I think it would be capital!"

"Well, keep up the good work then."

Next it was Grace's turn. She handed him the diary she'd been keeping with all her observations and private thoughts. She'd not shown it to anyone.

"This is for you, Dad. I've written down everything important since you went away. It's got all about how lovely it is here and what we've been doing. Singing with Doris and exploring. You must come to visit The Brawks and the Rec …"

"Whoa there, Fireworks. All in good time. And you can be my personal guide. But give us a bit of a breather first, then I'll be right as rain."

He began leafing through his daughter's diary, and she watched him in silence, noticing how his hand shook.

Over the next few days, George kept falling asleep in the chair by the range. Yet at night his sleep was erratic and he whimpered often. Nell woke him gently. "George, my love … you're safe now." Cradled in his wife's arms, his demons would gradually subside and his breathing return to normal.

He revealed nothing of what had befallen him in France during those early nights back in a comfortable bed with his wife beside him. Most evenings he withdrew to The Bull down by the Town Bridge, coming back much later with drink on his breath. He smoked incessantly, taking the tobacco smoke deep into his lungs and letting it out in a long sigh.

Nell felt helpless. Before the rift, she'd had Florence to talk to. Now she confided in Jane Mizen. "I can't reach him." She bit her lip. "I think he's too far gone down a dark road where I can't follow."

"You've got to keep strong and give him time. It's you and your kids that'll get him through it, you mark my words. Stick with it and with luck you'll get him back. Perhaps not like before, but maybe you'll have to settle for good enough. He loves them kids. They'll pull him round, I shouldn't wonder."

Come the weekend, Grace decided she must do something. "Dad. It's time for me to show you all the beautiful places I've discovered here. I've planned it all with my friend Doris and two boys called Windy and Lennie. Windy knows so much about the country – he'll make it really interesting for you. And I want to prove there are still wonderful things in the world." George opened his mouth to speak, but Grace cut him short. "I won't take no for an answer. You're going to love it."

George relented and smiled at Grace. He wasn't proud of his behaviour. He just couldn't help it. But he'd read Grace's diary and was moved by it – there was poetry in it, little sketches and notes about things she'd found out. It was charming, and in spite of himself, he found he was looking forward to her day out.

Nell prepared a picnic for them, with brawn sandwiches, hard-boiled eggs and some little pork pies like the ones she'd started to make for the butcher. Alf tagged along and the three Ashfords met the other children at the end of The Causeway. They set off across the fields towards Broaks Wood, the air bright, though it was cold with a bitter edge to the wind. George was still wearing his army uniform. He preferred it that way. In mufti, people might think him a shirker.

Doris pointed out snowdrops in the banks and golden celandine in wooded niches.

"It's a miracle how the flowers start to bloom so soon after the snow goes." said Grace. "Snowdrops and crocuses – they're so brave! It's still jolly cold!"

As they walked across the meadows lying fallow for want of manpower to cultivate them, George picked up the exquisite song of a bird he could not even see. Its trills and cadences cascaded down the still air in a torrent of bright sound. He looked up and searched the heavens in an attempt to identify its source, but could not.

"What … what *is* that … that beautiful sound?"

"It's a skylark, Mr Ashford," Windy said. "Ain't it a treat? Them birds make their nests on the ground, and that one's tellin' the skylark world that he's just found a good place. He's way up there, just a tiny speck up above, and yet you can hear him clear as a bell, can't you?"

George swallowed the lump that had just caught in his throat. In his mind he could see a different picture. Stumps of trees full of machine gun bullet holes. Barbed wire in hideous coils stretching across the ruined earth. Shell holes filled with water and mud as far as the eye could see. Yet that sound. That music. He'd heard it there, too.

"He don't look like much, the skylark," Windy said, "but he makes up for that with his singin'."

"You're right there, lad. It's like a message of hope," George said to the boy.

In Broaks Wood, the beech trees were yet to emerge into leaf. Their russet remains from last year still lay deep on the earth. Grace noticed emerald shoots like small spears pushing up among the leaf litter.

"What are those, Windy?" She cleared a space round a little clump with her fingers.

"Them'll be bluebells come late April and early May. You'll have to come up here then, Gracie, it's really nice."

In a clearing they found enough rocks and tree branches for everyone to sit on for their picnic and they fell silent, save for grunts of satisfaction, while they tucked in. George thought he'd never tasted anything so good. He reached out for Grace's hand and squeezed it. She turned to face him, her cheeks stuffed with a mouthful of brawn and crusty bread, and tried to smile.

"I wanna say a big thank you to you and your pals for this expedition of yours, my old Fireworks, it's just what the doctor ordered."

"S'alright, Dad," Grace managed to splutter as a piece of sandwich went down the wrong way. Her eyes watered and she struggled for breath. Doris clapped her on the back and dislodged the fragment. "Choke up, chicken!"

Grace wiped her eyes on a corner of the napkin Nell had packed in the picnic bag.

"Alright now, Gracie?" Grace nodded.

After lunch, the children climbed trees. Doris and Grace, were keen not to be outdone by the boys, so they tucked their skirts into the legs of their drawers to make climbing easier.

In a moment of quiet as the children lay breathless on the leaf litter, a rattling sound echoed through the woodland.

"Hell!" said George, his face turning white, his eyes darting from left to right in search of the source of the sudden interruption. "What's that?" He thought: *machine-gun fire – No! No! Not here. For God's sake.* He started to shake and his hands were sweating. Tears coursed down his face.

"Easy does it, Dad," Alf placed a hand on his father's shoulder.

"It was that noise …" George tailed off. He dabbed his cheeks with his napkin.

"It's alright, Mr Ashford," said Lennie. "Nothin' to worry about. Just an old woodpecker a-drillin' into a tree. It's what they do come early spring. Great spotted. Noisy beggars."

The spell was broken, a signal to pack up and make their way back to Halstead.

"We can't round off the day without taking you to the Rec, Dad," Grace said.

"The flowerbeds are lovely at the moment," Doris said. "Full of Lenten roses."

George bent to examine the down-turned flower heads, some creamy, some plum-coloured.

"And over there's the dancing green and the bandstand. They have music and dancing there in the summer. Aunt Flo came here to meet her soldier friend on New Year's Eve. They danced in the snow and Aunt Flo got her skirt all wet," said Grace.

Chapter 31

"Why haven't we seen Florence?" George asked.

"Busy at the farm," Nell said.

He felt there was more to it than that. There was an evasiveness in Nell's manner when he mentioned Florence's name. He'd heard nothing about a soldier in her life.

"Tell me about this soldier and your Aunt Flo, Fireworks."

So Grace told him what she knew. " ... and then Aunt Flo disappeared on New Year's Day, slammed the front door, and we haven't seen her since." She frowned. "I think they had a row about a hat. It's probably all my fault."

"A hat?" said George. "Is that all?"

Grace told her father how she had found the hat Florence had borrowed thrown on the bed just as Florence left the house.

"Look, Fireworks," he said, his hand on Grace's shoulder, "I'd like to see your Aunt Flo. After all, if it weren't for her, you and your Mum and your brother and sisters wouldn't be in Halstead. We owe her a lot, and she must be missing all of you. D'you think we could walk out to the farm tomorrow? If your mum says it's alright?"

"I'd love that, Dad, I miss Aunt Florence a lot – we're really good friends. And if she's fallen out with mum because of something I did, I'd feel awful."

On the following day, after Grace had sung in St Andrew's choir at Parish communion, father and daughter set out to Valley Farm. When they arrived, there was no one around, though the yard looked as ship-shape as ever. Clover and Campion's stable doors were open, but there was no sign of the big horses out in the paddock. Grace noticed that the muck heap, stacked beside the stable block and steaming aromatically had diminished in size. A broad scar along its length showed where forkfuls of the winter's spent bedding had been pulled out.

"Maybe they're muck-spreading. I think they do that this time of year before they sow the seed."

"Can I help you?" Annie emerged from the dairy and was wiping her hands on some muslin.

"It's me, Mrs Davis. Grace. And this is my Dad. We've come out to see Aunt Florence, if she's around. My Dad's home on leave."

"Hello, my dear. And welcome, Mr Ashford. I think Florence'll be back with the waggon and the horses directly. Why don't you come inside and have a cup of tea while we wait for them? I made scones this mornin'. You'd be welcome to one." She led them into the farm kitchen and set the kettle to boil.

"How is Aunt Flo? We haven't seen her since the new year."

"She's workin' all the hours God sends," Annie said. "And now we've got the go-ahead from the government to plant more arable, we're goin' to be busier than you could possibly imagine. There'll be no let up for months, what with plantin' and lambin' and the potatoes and mangolds … I just don't know how we're goin to fit it all in. If it weren't for Florence, I reckon we'd go under."

There were noises outside. The two Suffolks pulling the waggon were returning to the yard. Sitting in the driving seat, reins in hand, was Florence, driving the team through the gate, turning them in the confined space and bringing them to a halt by the muck heap, ready to reload.

George watched it all from the kitchen window. Annie went to the door and called Florence over. She jumped down from the waggon and made much of the horses. "There's good boys." She patted their steaming necks.

"Your brother-in-law's here!" Annie called.

Florence ran across the yard, taking off her rough leather gauntlets. "Oh George!" Florence beamed. "It's so good to see you! And Gracie! Thank you so much for bringing your Dad out here to see me!"

"Come on inside and have some tea with your family."

"I'm so pleased to have the chance to see you while you're home!" Florence was breathless and glowing. She hugged George. "Have you got long?"

"Not very, worse luck, though this one's making sure I'm using every minute to the full." He nudged Grace and she grinned back at him. "This new life's suiting you, Florence. I can see it is."

"I'll say. I've taken to it like a duck to water."

Annie poured the tea and set scones, butter and jam out on a tray. Then she slipped away, back to the dairy. Grace followed, eager to help.

Florence chattered on about the farm and everything she'd learned since the day she arrived. George sat listening until she caught sight of his expression and slowed to a halt.

"Sorry, George. I'm blathering on. It's probably a bit boring to you …"

"Nah!" His laugh was wheezy. "It's smashing what you're doing, Flo."

"How's it been going for you, George?" She barely knew how to frame the question, but she couldn't not ask it. Her voice was gentle. George looked down, studying his own boots. Florence could see the tension in his jaw.

"It's about as horrific as you could possibly imagine, Flo … Don't ask me to describe it. Any of it, for Gawd's sake." He turned away, battling to retain his self-control. Florence laid a hand on his trembling arm. He looked out over the farmland for several long moments and drew a deep breath.

"Anyway. Fireworks has told me all about your Captain What's-his-name."

"Forbes. Andrew Forbes … Back in France now … He agrees with you about the war, George."

"Funny thing, Flo. Nell hasn't said anything about him to me. Not one word."

"Nell doesn't approve, I'm afraid." Florence shrugged. "She thinks I'm fortune-hunting and taking advantage. It's because Andrew's an officer and plans to take up medicine after the war … not my station in life."

"So you and Nell have had words – and not about a hat."

"A hat?" Florence said, puzzled. "What hat?"

"Fireworks knew there was something amiss between you and Nell – she thought it was about the hat you borrowed."

"Sweet child," said Florence, "she wouldn't understand."

"Well, neither do I, for that matter. I can't see the problem if you care for one another."

"Ah. That's another thing. Nell doesn't think I do care ... But look! I've got to get back to work before those poor horses catch a chill, and Frank gives me my marching orders ... Oh, heck! Poor choice of words, George. Sorry."

"Yeah, well, not to worry. It's been really good to see you."

They went back outside and crossed the yard to the dairy. Annie was skimming cream and she'd put Grace to work on the butter churn.

"Good little worker, your niece, Florence. She can come out here whenever she's got time. Like I said, we can do with as much help as we can get. There's always somethin' to do."

"Come on, Fireworks, we gotta be gettin' back."

Florence hugged him. "God's speed, George."

Chapter 32

I have to stay cheerful for him, Nell told herself. *He's got to face going back there ...*

That fact was not lost on George, either, but he resolved not to waste a moment of this precious time with his wife and family.

"Look, kids," he said to the children, "I'd love to take your Mum out to The Bull so we can have a little drink together. D'you think you could take care of the twins for an hour or two if we went this evening?"

"Of course we can, Dad," Ellen said. "And if they give us any trouble, we can always knock for Mrs Mizen to help us sort them out."

"Good! I'll go and tell Mum to put on her best bib and tucker."

Nell had given them all their tea, washed the twins and got them ready for bed before giving her own appearance a thought.

"What are you going to wear?" Grace asked.

"Heavens, it's been so long since I got dressed up," Nell said, "I've forgotten what I've got to get dressed up in." She rummaged through the bedroom cupboard and unearthed a suit of bottle green velvet with little covered buttons down the front and on the cuffs.

"That'll look lovely, Mum."

"Thank you, Gracie."

Nell and George opened the door to leave.

"Just you be careful, you lot!" Nell called out over her shoulder, "I don't want anyone hurt or anything broken, thank you very much! And don't let those little ones get too close to the range."

George took her arm as they set off along Factory Terrace.

"You're doing a marvellous job with the family, Nellie. They're a real credit to you. I know it can't have been easy all this time. And I take my hat off to you for this cooking work you're doing for the butcher. Ruddy brilliant! I hope he's paying you properly."

"Bill Broyd's not a mean man – he pays me well, and I'm grateful for the extra income, I can tell you."

They pushed open the saloon bar door, and the beery smell of the pub greeted them. George steered his wife towards a small table near the fireplace whose coals were glowing in the grate. She sat down and took off her gloves. George went to the bar and returned to the table with a pint in one hand and a port and lemonade in the other. He sat beside her and they clinked glasses.

"Here's to an end to this war. Soon." George raised his pint.

"You've said so little about the war, George. Your letters have been so … Sketchy. I've been at a loss to know how you've been in the midst of it all. And since you've been back, you've been so jumpy and at times …" she searched her mind for the right word "… morose. I can't help worrying. And it makes me feel so … alone. I suppose the censor doesn't let you say much …"

"That's true." George took a deep breath and looked at Nell, his brown eyes moist and bright in the firelight. He filled his pipe and lit it from a match.

"It's not the easiest thing to talk about, y'know Nellie. Soon as you start, all the memories replay in your brain and drive you nearly hysterical. Easier just to hold your peace. Try to keep it out of your mind, so it doesn't haunt you. Except it still does." He drew on his pipe and puffed out blue-grey smoke. "But I tell you, those kids have done so much to help me believe there are still some good things worth surviving for. And you have, too, Nellie." He paused. "I believe I could tell you a bit about it, now – if you want me to, that is. It doesn't make very cheerful listening, mind."

"Go on, George." Nell's voice was low. "I really think I want to know. And perhaps it'll be better for you if you tell me."

"Well. I don't know how to begin … I haven't actually had to go over the top. Turns out, because I'm good at fixing things, they put me in a maintenance trench behind the Front Line. I thought what a lucky blighter I was – and it's true, it's safer back there. But the noise and the mud's just as bad – and there's still the risk of a shell falling on us in that trench …" he paused and Nell could see him shudder. "And the worst thing's been the stretcher bearers having to come right past us on their way to the dressing station … It's awful, Nell. All those poor lads with limbs blown away, faces shot off, insides all hanging out … all the moaning and crying out for their mothers … sorry … I can't go on any more …" He was quiet for a moment and drank from his pint. Nell dabbed at her silent tears. "They're only boys," George continued, "just a handful of years older than Alf, many of them. The hardest thing to bear is the guilt … while those lads were out there in that hellfire, I've been safe by comparison."

He brought a handkerchief out from his pocket and wiped his face. His hands were shaking again. Nell stroked his shoulder.

"Don't say any more if you don't want to, George, dear. I see now why you couldn't write all this in your letters. Impossible." Their eyes met, and they felt for each other's hand and hung on tightly.

"Come on, let's be gettin' back." George rose to his feet and Nell followed, still holding George's hand.

The house was quiet as they prepared for bed.

"Nell." He felt warm beside her.

"Yes, George."

"I'm sorry – so sorry – I haven't made love to you since I've been back … I just haven't … been able to. Because of … Well. What I've told you about."

"I understand, George … But I need to know. Do you still think I'm pretty? Find me … attractive?"

"Nell. Sweetheart. Of course I do."

"There isn't anyone else, is there? In France?"

"No, Nellie. No, there isn't. In fact, tonight, my dearest, tonight I want to show you how much I do still love you. I want the warmth and smell and softness of you. If you'll have me."

After, they lay in each other's arms.

"I love this feeling of closeness, George. I've missed it so much."

"Nellie," George said in the quiet of nighttime, "I've never been with any of those French women, y'know. Honest. It must've been on your mind. Lots of the blokes do, and I can see why – especially with the young 'uns, so homesick for their loved ones. Scared and angry. It's a way of forgetting about it all, just for a while." He turned towards her. "But not for me. For one thing, you and the kiddies are on my mind most of the time. Besides, I get to thinking this war's all about ordinary people's lives being trampled on. And it seems to me that going with those tarts – friendly, they are, even motherly – is just another kind of taking advantage. Using another person for selfish reasons. I know it's freely offered, and that the boys pay what's asked, but I don't see it that way."

"Thank you for your honesty, George. You're good and loyal. And I love you still. So much."

***

There was just one weekend left before George's return to the war.

"Nell," George said. "I want to take something to remind me of you and the children back with me. Do you think we could get some photos done?"

"Well, there is a chap in Halstead who takes pictures at weddings and things. But we'll have to get our skates on – we haven't got much time left."

"I want you all looking your best for these photos. They're for your father, so it's very important," Nell told her children.

Ellen and Grace had slept with their long hair wound up in strips of rag and wore the resulting ringlets falling loose about their shoulders and with satin bows on top of their heads. They and their sisters wore their best dresses, the twins' little robes trimmed with broderie anglaise. Alf, his hair brushed and his Eton collar chafing, wore his tweed suit, steamed and brushed so it looked like new. The minute Alf had returned from his drawing lesson and Nell had run a critical eye over his appearance, they set off for the photographer's studio at the top end of the High Street.

Mr Jenkins the photographer was far from speedy.

"How long's this going to take?" whispered Alf. "This collar's killing me."

"Shut up, Alf. Remember this is for Dad," Ellen said.

"I'll have to send the pictures on to you." Nell sighed. "I didn't think he'd be able to get them done in time. We'll just have to hope they catch up with you wherever you are. And I'm so glad I shall have a snap of you, George, so I won't lose the memory of how you look as I did before you came back."

"This leave's been a real tonic," George told his family. "You'll all come and see me off at the station, won't you?" The children nodded. "'Course, Dad," Alf said.

When the time came, they were uncharacteristically quiet. Grace bit her lip and gave him a poem she'd written about a bird with 'wings like shovels'. Windy had told her it was a lapwing. "To help you remember," she said.

Ellen had knitted him a muffler and wrapped it in some tissue paper. "It'll still be cold there," she said.

Alf had drawn the bandstand at the Rec. "Here you are, Dad," he said.

He hugged them one by one, Iris and Renee no longer shy. Then he put his arms round Nell and clung to her. "Look after yourself, dear girl. And all of this lot."

"I will ... and come back to us in one piece." She couldn't help thinking of what he'd said about shells ...

"I'll do my best. And Nellie, I've got one little thing to ask you before I go. Make it up with Flo, eh? Life's too short and too precious to waste it on daft feuding."

Nell opened her mouth to speak, but George's train puffed to a halt. She managed a small nod. He shouldered his kitbag, picked up the bag of food Nell had prepared for him for the journey and opened the carriage door, with a last, longing look at his family, he smiled and waved.

"Don't forget to send them snaps." The train pulled away from the platform.

Chapter 33

"Now then," said Frank, shielding his eyes as he looked out over his fields, "if we're goin' to get the sowin' done afore the lambin' starts, we got one heck of a lot to get through."

Florence was standing beside him, thick gloves on her hands. The cool weather, borne on a stiff north-easterly, was delaying the start of the growing season and the landscape lay, a washed-out palette of ochre, brown and lifeless shades of green beneath a sky which was no colour at all.

"It might still look like winter, but soon as the wind changes, everythin's goin' to kick off like nobody's business. And the lambs won't wait, anyhow." Frank took a pull on his pipe, the wind carrying the smoke away on a feisty gust.

"But what with the Prime Minister's support for a ploughin' policy and a guaranteed price for wheat, we can go on and plant up some of that land what's been out of cultivation for years." He pointed out the terrain in question with the stem of his pipe. "It's just about gone back to scrub, some of it, so it'll be a tough job gettin' it back in shape. But at least we know if we do, we ain't goin' to lose money this time. Wrong time of year for ploughin' up. Should've been done last back end, like the rest of the arable, so we got a lot of catchin' up to do ... Ploughin's hard work for the team on the heavy ground we got here. Can't do more than an acre a day, and that's pushin' it. You can't overwork your horses."

It was as though Frank was thinking aloud, but Florence was listening. "Will you let me help with the ploughing, Frank?"

Frank turned to Florence as if registering her presence. "Sorry, my dear, I was off on my own train of thought ... What did you say?"

"I asked if you'd allow me to do some ploughing. Or should I carry on with routine farm chores?"

"Both, I shouldn't wonder," Frank said, his pipe gripped between his teeth. "We won't get it all done without turnin' all our hands to the plough, so to speak. You've got enough mileage under your belt with the 'orses now – you'll soon get the hang of ploughin'. Besides, they know what they're at, specially the older 'un. You know how to talk to them right already, and they know your voice. Your job's keepin' the furrow straight and even. And I'll show you how to do that."

The following morning, as soon as it was light, Florence harnessed Clover and Campion while Frank saw to all the other livestock needs.

"Plough's already in the field," Frank said. "I got Swank to take it down the other day when he was passin'."

They walked the horses down the track and turned into the fallow meadow as Frank indicated. He showed Florence how the plough attached to the harness and walked the team forward along the field headland until they were halfway across.

"This plough'll only turn soil to the right, so you can only plough clockwise," he said. "I'm goin' to turn the first couple of furrows to show you how it works. We're goin' to start in the middle of the field, then you add your furrows each side of what's already been ploughed, always turnin' right when you get to the headland, see?"

"Mmm." Florence nodded.

"Next thing you got to learn is how to adjust these two wheels, because they're what'll keep you on the straight and narrow, like."

There were two metal-rimmed wheels, one larger than the other, either side of the central shaft supporting the ploughshare. Florence could see their position could be adjusted up or down by releasing the nut on a bolt which held each wheel fast to the vertical column. She watched as Frank loosened each one in turn and reset them in such a way that the plough stood level on the ground.

"Now. If you take a look, you'll see the plough's got two blades. A curved one what turns the soil over and a straight one what cuts down into the ground in a straight line. If you've got your furrow wheel set right, that's your bigger 'un, it'll follow the line of your last furrow, and you'll hardly have to steer. Your little wheel's got to roll along on top of the unploughed ground. Ruddy child's play, ain't it?" He grinned at Florence. "First furrow's always the hardest because you've got nothin' to go on. Once I've ploughed a couple, you'll have the grooves to work into. It's easy with these boys – they know more about ploughin' than you'll ever learn!"

Frank jammed his cap down on his head and, gripping the two handles of the plough, he whistled up the team and they took steady paces forward. The ploughshare gouged the surface of the ground, exposing the umber soil, the curved blade turning it over to one side. The pungent smell of earth wafted up. "The secret's in keepin' the angle right and the pressure even," he said. "That's what them little wheels do for you."

Florence strode out alongside Frank as Clover and Campion threw their weight into the work. At intervals, Frank halted the team with a 'whoa!', took out his spanner and readjusted the two wheels, the smaller running along the uncultivated ground, the larger in the furrow's groove.

"You'll have to do this quite a bit on this rough old ground," he said, "or the plough'll go lopsided."

Reaching the field's far headland, he slowed the team. The horses turned their ears back towards Frank, waiting for his spoken command. "Away, boys!" he called, lifting the ploughshare blade from the soil. The horses turned to their right, crossing their forelegs and half-pirouetting in little more than their own length. Frank sidestepped with the plough until horses, plough and farmer were facing back along the field, with their newly ploughed furrow, a clean cleft, on their right. "Walk on," Frank called to the horses, flapping the guide ropes he held in each hand, along with the handles of the plough. They set off, once again engaging the ploughshare blade in the ground. Campion on the right walked in the trough of the first furrow while Clover walked on the unturned ground. "Away, boys!" Frank called out again at the far end, and the two horses again turned a half-circle to the right and stood ready to start on the next furrow.

"Right-o!" Frank beckoned Florence to come forward and take up the plough handles. "Now it's your turn!"

Florence, adrenalin coursing, took hold of the wooden hand-grips, worn shiny by years of use, in her gloved hands. She looked to Frank for reassurance and prepared to move forward.

"Whoa!" he said, addressing Florence as well as the horses "You've got to set them wheels so the plough's level first. Once you get that sorted out, then you can set off, and the blades'll take themselves through the ground. He gave her a nod and handed her the spanner. She adjusted the wheels. She was sure she'd got it right.

"Walk on!" The horses moved forward at a marching pace, and before she had time to move, the plough was out of her hands. "Oh, my good lord!" She gasped with surprise. Frank was doubled up with laughter.

"Whoa, boys!" he managed to splutter through his mirth. "Nice try!" He clapped an arm round Florence's shoulders. "Don't you worry – it gets lots of folks like that first time. When the horses get a shift on, you got to be careful not to trip up. Specially when the mud's sticky, like it is now!"

She rechecked the level, and when she was happy, they set off again. This time the ploughshare bit into the soil and Florence's first furrow began to take shape. She gripped the handles as the team walked up the field, but found they took very little guiding, so long as the plough remained level and the furrow wheel hugged the wall of the previous furrow. Treading in the heavy soil in the wake of horses and plough, the earth clung to Florence's boots, making them heavy. It was difficult to put one foot before the other. She trudged on up the field, determined to keep the thing under control. Frank paced the distance beside her, calling out encouragement as they moved forward. Florence brought the team to a halt before the turn, red faced and breathing hard.

"Phew! It's quite tiring!"

He offered her an open bottle of Annie's lemonade and she took a long swig. She looked back along the furrow to assess her work. The cleft in the ground was a bit wavy. "Ah. It's not as good as yours, is it?"

"That's because you didn't set them wheels often enough. Your furrow wheel was too high some of the time, so it didn't hug the other furrow tight enough. You got to be ready to keep resettin' the levels on this bumpy ground."

The more Florence did, the better she became. When they stopped for a break, she looked back at what she had done and was pleased. She thought back to the WLA poster which had first inspired her. *Not bad,* she thought.

"Now then," Frank said. "I think you're ready to carry on by yourself, if you feel you can."

Florence nodded. "I don't see why not."

"Normally, I'd give a novice a bit more tuition, like. But we ain't got the time. It don't have to be perfect, just serviceable's good enough. I'll make sure Annie gets some vittels out to you come dinner time, and you can carry on like you've been doin'. Don't forget to give the horses a drink every now and then. And keep adjustin' your levels!"

"Of course, Frank. Off you go. I'll be fine."

"That's marvellous," Frank bashed the soil off his cap on his trouser leg. "I've got a ton of things to work on. It'll give me the chance to take the shears to that untidy hedge along the next field. So I'll leave you to it."

Florence stroked the horses' warm noses. "You're the bosses here, boys. Thank God you know what you're doing!"

Chapter 34

Florence sat by the window of her attic room, watching the westering sun bathe the North Essex landscape in a golden glow before slipping below the horizon. If she stood on tiptoe and craned her neck, she could just glimpse, beyond the lane, a corner of the field she'd ploughed. The turned soil looked rich and moist. Maybe not the ruler-straight-and-level furrows Frank could turn, but her first. And therefore something special.

In the still-leafless ash tree that stood below the window, a bird sang a scherzo of intricate notes. She sat listening for many minutes. She picked up her mandolin and tried to mimic the bird's exquisite song on it.

"Florence!" Annie's voice drifted up the narrow staircase. "Supper's ready down here!"

Florence put the mandolin aside, the spell broken.

"Coming, Annie." She made for the door in her stockinged feet.

Frank was knocking out his pipe on the hearth while Annie stirred a steaming stew pot on the range.

"There's a letter for you up there on the mantle beside the clock," she said, pointing with a wooden spoon. "Another one from Captain Forbes, I shouldn't wonder."

Though in fact she was in no doubt. Letters from Andrew were arriving almost daily since his departure, first from Aldershot, where troops were mustering, and more recently from France. They were full of his optimistic vision of a future made new. It would have Florence in it – a point he made time and again. She was his rose-coloured spectacles. She knew it, and while it amused her, she felt uneasy that the post war world might not measure up to his expectations … Her fingers played with his antique ring which she was wearing on a chain around her neck. Annie watched her.

"'He alright, then?"

"Ye-es." She folded the flimsy paper and slipped it into her breeches pocket. "He's living in the sunlit future."

Andrew seemed to be spending nearly all his free time writing to her. For her part, she wrote him brief notes, mostly about events on the farm. These, after all, were what her life consisted of these days. *I must tell him about the bird in the ash tree*, she thought.

"There was a bird in the tree outside just now. I couldn't see it from my window, but it's got a heck of a lovely song! What could it be? A nightingale?"

Frank chuckled. "Not yet. They haven't arrived. You have to wait till middle of April for your nightingales. We're still in Feb'ry, just. It'll have to be a resident – probably a common or garden robin. They can sing real well, robins. And they're one of the few what sings all the year round. Seein' off the competition, he'll be."

"Oh. You live and learn." *Still a townie*, she thought.

Florence did little more than eat, sleep and prepare the new fields for sowing in the next couple of weeks, dashing off quick notes to Andrew when she could. Annie hoped her strength would hold out.

"Here," Annie held in her hand a jar which had once contained mint humbugs. "I've made some bath salts from soda crystals and lemon verbena. I thought you might like them for your bath. Nice and relaxin' they are. Help relieve them tired muscles."

"You are kind, Annie. Thank you." Florence took hold of the jar.

"You alright these days, Florence? I must say you seem chipper enough in spite of the work."

"It's because of the work. It's doing me no end of good. This life's a real treat for me."

"What about, you know, I mean ... Personally? I don't want to pry, but ..."

Florence knew what Annie was getting at – Andrew away, no word from Nell ... "Annie, I'm fine. And keeping busy's the best antidote to becoming wrapped up in myself. Funny thing, though, the one I do miss is young Gracie!"

Come Saturday morning, Frank hitched up Cherry to the dog cart and set out for Halstead. He had a list of errands which he was consulting in the doorway of Pountney's the ironmongers on the corner of High Street and Factory Terrace. He needed to stock up on a whole range of supplies: paraffin and creosote, wire nails and sandpaper. The interior of Pountney's shop was stacked floor to ceiling with so much merchandise, it was a wonder that bearded Pountney could find anything in the murky depths of his premises.

Frank folded his list and slipped it into the inside pocket of his jacket. Looking up, he spotted a small figure making its sluggish way with along Factory Terrace towards him. He stopped. The figure looked familiar. "Hello there, young Grace," He raised his cap. "It is Grace, ain't it?" The child looked up at Frank, an anxious look on her face. "You look as though you've lost a quid and found sixpence! What's the matter?"

"Oh! Mr Davis. Hello. I'm doing some shopping for my Mum. She needs washing soap and some brads for shoe repairs, you see, so I've got to get them at Mr Pountney's." Frank looked down at her as she examined her feet.

"You don't want to go in there by yourself, do you?"

"It's so ... dark, and Mr Pountney ... he's so thin ... and his eyes frighten me."

"Old Pountney's a funny cove, but he's alright. I know he's an odd lookin' bloke, but he won't hurt you. But look, why don't you come in with me?"

"Thank you. I'd like that."

They went into Pountney's shop, their boots making a hollow sound on the bare boards. A single oil lamp cast illumination too meagre to penetrate the

133

farthest corners and the air was thick with the smell of Pountney's wares. Grace put her hand over her nose. Pountney grunted as he rummaged among his stock for the items Frank and Grace had requested, his spare frame bent almost double. Then he disappeared into the back yard to fill Frank's paraffin cans. Not a single pleasantry passed his lips.

Emerging back into the daylight, Grace held on to the brown paper bag containing her purchases and Frank lugged his tin cans now full and heavy. "Thank you, Mr Davis. You've been very kind!" She turned to walk back along Factory Terrace.

"Wait a mo," Frank called after her, "I've got an idea. If you're not too busy doin' things for your Mum, I could take you out to the farm to pay your aunt a visit. I happen to know she'd quite like to see you."

"Oh, please!" Grace said with a little skip, "but I've got to take this back to Mum first. And I'll have to ask her if it's alright."

"Of course you have. Why don't you hop in the cart so Cherry and me can take you, and we'll wait outside while you ask her."

Grace ran up the front path, calling out for her mother as she went. Nell met her on the doorstep and acknowledged the farmer with a wave.

"It's all very well," Nell said, "but how are you going to get back? I don't want you walking all that way by yourself."

"Oh. I hadn't thought of that."

"Well." Nell sensed her daughter's disappointment. "Let's ask Mr Davis what he thinks. I've no objection in principle, as long as you've done all your school work for Monday."

Frank took off his cap and scratched his head. "Hm. How about if Grace brings a nightdress and somethin' to wear tomorrow? Then she can stay over and Annie and me can bring her back into Halstead for church in the mornin'. How's that?"

"Oh! Yes! Please say yes, Mum!" The girl hopped from foot to foot.

Nell drew breath. She hated being beholden to anyone.

"Don't you worry." Frank guessed her misgivings. "Annie and me, we'll put her to work while her aunt's busy. There's always a pile of things needs doin' on a farm. She'll earn her keep."

"In that case I can hardly object, can I? You're most kind, Mr Davis, and I hope your wife won't mind."

"She'll be as pleased as punch! An' it's Frank to you!"

Grace was already upstairs, stuffing her things into a canvas holdall.

"Mind you take something respectable to wear to church," her mother called up to her, "and don't bundle it all up like rags – I don't spend hours ironing for the good of my health!"

Grace was back in the hall, her bag packed, in less time than it took Frank to turn the pony and cart round in the road outside.

Nell came out of the pantry with a jar of pickles. "Give this to Mrs Davis and be sure to thank her for having you."

Grace grabbed the jar and ran out of the front door. "See you tomorrow, Mum," she said over her shoulder.

"And tie up your bootlaces before you break your neck!" Nell called after her.

Chapter 35

"Windy, d'you think your sister might lend me her bike so I can ride it out to see my Aunt Flo at the farm?" Grace's tone was wheedling, but Windy smiled.

"'Spect so," he said, "she never rides the thing."

So Saturday visits to Valley Farm became a feature of Grace's week. Often Doris came with her if Molly was able to spare her daughter from the shop.

Those weekly visits gave Grace a baseline to watch the spring emerging. First the osiers along the river banks flushing the palest green imaginable, then the hawthorn hedges gradually coming into leaf. After the snowdrops, the primroses and violets. The girls did anything Annie Davis asked them to do from collecting the eggs, warm from the chicken coop, and feeding the fowl to scrubbing feed buckets and mangers. Sometimes they went in the cart with Florence to check on the ewes. Others, they helped Annie in the kitchen garden where her spring planting was getting under way. Florence showed them how to pick out the horses' feet and soap the harness. And there were always dairy chores to do.

It was a couple of weeks before Easter which fell at the end of March. Grace and Doris were having a yard-sweeping race, seeing who could push the stiff brooms across the farmyard the quickest. There were penalties if bits of hay and straw were left lying.

Two men, unknown to either girl, pushed open the gate and came into the yard. One, mousy-haired under his cap, wore the familiar khaki of the British army, the other was tall. He wore what looked like a uniform, but not one they recognised. He was bare-headed and his hair was fair. The men stood, looking around, not speaking to one another. Grace and Doris called a truce and stopped their sweeping. Neither of the Davises appeared, so Doris approached the men.

"Can we help you?"

"Ah!" The British soldier looked down at her. "I'm looking for Farmer Davis. Could you tell me where I might find him, young lady?"

Doris looked at Grace. Grace shrugged. "Out on the farm somewhere. Is he expecting you?"

"Well, not at this precise moment, but he knew we'd be here sometime today."

The blond man was looking about the yard. He said nothing.

"I think it's best you have a word with Missus Davis. She's in the house." Doris gestured towards the farmhouse back door.

"I can go and get her, if you like," said Grace.

"Thank you." The soldier gave a nod.

Grace ran across the yard and up the steps to the door. She knocked gently and went into the kitchen. Annie, seeing the young men's arrival, had just tidied her hair and was taking off her apron. "I'm just comin'," she said, "I know who they are."

"Good afternoon." She nodded in the soldier's direction. "I'm Annie Davis. My husband'll be back any minute. He's not gone far – he's expectin' you."

Annie nodded towards the house. "Off you go, you two. There's bread and jam in the kitchen. Make yourselves at home."

In the kitchen Grace and Doris cut hunks of bread and toasted them on a long-handled fork before the fire. They applied butter and jam and took up positions by the window. It was frustrating not to be able to hear what was being said, but they found they could infer quite a lot from people's movements.

Frank had returned and was shaking hands with the soldier, who spoke at some length and gestured towards the tall fair man. Frank looked at him and talked to him briefly. The young man brought his heels together and inclined his upper body forward in a stiff bow. Frank and Annie turned their backs on the strangers for a moment or two and exchanged quiet words. Then they nodded to one another and seemed to be smiling. Turning back to the men, Frank nodded again and held out his right hand to the soldier who shook it.

Grace and Doris crept to the door and opened it a crack, just in time to hear Frank speak to the light-haired man in clear tones.

"We need your help here and we'll treat you fairly, you can be sure of that."

The man looked blankly at Frank, but accepted his hand, bowing once more.

The eavesdroppers looked at each other and frowned. The soldier and the other man turned to leave the yard. Annie and Frank, his arm round her shoulders, were already making their way towards the house.

"Quick!" said Grace.

When the Davises re-entered the house, the girls were sitting by the fire trying to look innocent. They knew they mustn't ask. If their mothers knew they'd been listening in to Frank and Annie's private conversations, they'd be banned for good from coming to Valley Farm. Yet they could not keep the look of curiosity from their faces.

Frank filled his pipe from the tobacco pouch on the mantle. Turning, he caught sight of the girls' expression and let out a guffaw. "No prizes for guessin' what you two want to know. Shall we tell 'em, Annie?"

"Hmm. No harm in it, I expect. They'll know all about it soon enough anyway."

Frank sat on the arm of the settle. "Well. The tall man you saw outside, he's a German." He put his hands on his knees and, hunching his shoulders, he peered at Grace and Doris. "What do you think of that, then?" He put his pipe in his mouth and took a puff.

Their eyes grew big. "No, really?" said Grace.

"Did you think they've all got horns and a tail?" Frank asked. "That's just what some people'd have you believe. But y'know." He sounded serious now. "Most of them're just like us. They got families and folk what love them, same as us. An' the war's just as horrible for them as it is for our boys. This lad you just seen, he's a prisoner of war an' it don't make any sense at all for the likes of him to sit around all day doin' nothin'. We need labour on our farms to feed everyone. These blokes'll work hard. It's better than bein' in the war, wouldn't you say?"

Grace and Doris nodded in unison, lost for words for once.

"Now then," Frank said. "Do you want to know anythin' about him?"

"Why is he in Halstead?" Grace asked, a resentful note in her voice. It felt to her like a violation. Germans were putting her father's life at risk every day. And Halstead – *her* Halstead – was heaven on earth. They had no place here.

"There's a load of 'em arrived in the old workhouse – where the soldiers were before. It's a good sign! If we're takin' prisoners, it means we might be gainin' the upper hand. We got to hope that's true. And meantime, let's put 'em to work for us."

Grace supposed he was right.

"What's his name?" Doris asked.

"He's called 'Olger."

"Olga?" Doris exploded into laughter. "That's a woman's name, ain't it? From Russia, or somewhere? Is he actually a lady dressed up?" She dissolved and Grace giggled too, in spite of herself.

"It's H-Holg-ER," Frank's shoulders were shaking. "It's got a 'H-aitch' on the front and an 'ERRR' on the back. H-Holg-E-R-R. It's a German man's name. But I grant you, it is a bit of a daft *one*. I think we'll call him Fritzy instead. What do you think?"

The girls nodded. "That's better," Doris said.

The door opened and Florence came in and stood on the doormat. "Can someone give me a hand with the horses, please? They need a rub down and a bran mash before we turn them out for the night."

Grace leapt to her feet. "I'll help you, Aunt Flo."

Florence and her niece worked away, wiping the sweat from the horses' flanks. Grace was not tall enough to reach their withers. She worked in silence, preoccupied, Florence thought. "You and Doris had a good afternoon, Gracie? What've you been up to?"

"Umm … We were sweeping up the yard. It was good fun – we made a game out of it. And then …"

"And then what?"

"These two men came in. One of them's a *German*. And Mr Davis says he's going to come and work here, on the farm, with you. Aunt Flo, I'm worried. He's *German*."

Florence stopped what she was doing and took hold of her niece's hands. "I know, Gracie. Mr Davis has told me all about it, and I've agreed to it. The fact is, there's simply too much for us to do by ourselves. And making sure we have as good a grain harvest as we can, not to mention the other crops and raising animals is all so important."

"But doesn't he – the German, I mean – think of us as the enemy? His country and ours are fighting each other. Mr and Mrs Davis' own son is out there in the war. How can they …?"

"We don't know what he thinks of the war. He hardly speaks any English, so he can't tell us much about anything. But one thing we do know, his job in the army was to look after horses – not fire machine guns or shells at our soldiers. He can't be all bad."

"I suppose not. But I'm still not sure."

"It's his experience with animals that's good for this farm. Mr Davis was lucky to get him – he'll be really useful with lambing just about to start. And don't worry, little love. I'm touched that you're concerned about me, but I'll be alright."

She wiped the horses' damp ears with a cloth. "Have you forgotten already what you said about the Zeppelin crew? How you felt such sadness for the death of those men? Someone's fathers and sons and brothers? That's still true, no matter what you hear people say." Florence paused. "Come on, let's get these hard working boys fed, eh?"

"Have you met him, Aunt Flo?"

"Not yet, but I soon will. He's going to start on Monday. He'll go back to the old workhouse every night – he's under curfew. The camp commander'll keep tabs on him. Honestly, Gracie, I don't think he'll step out of line. He knows what will happen to him if he does. And if he tried to escape he wouldn't get far. Besides, don't you think he might prefer it here to being at the Front?"

"I suppose so, Aunt Flo, but you must promise to be careful. What does 'under curfew' mean?"

Chapter 36

Nell was pleased with the photographs of the family, proud of their appearance. She packaged up the pictures for George and posted them. There was a picture of George himself in uniform, boots and puttees, his gentle eyes and kind face looking out from the snapshot. She kept that one for herself and the children to keep him in their memory. Jane Mizen found a dusty frame which Nell cleaned up, buffing the glass so the photo's clarity was not dulled. Now it stood on the dressing chest in the bedroom.

"You're lookin' more cheerful these days," Jane said, handing Nell another letter from France. Nell opened it with a vegetable knife.

"Yes, I really am, Jane. George's leave's done me so much good. And him, too, judging by his letters and the cards he's sending the children."

"There. What did I tell you. Nothing like the closeness of your loved ones to put you right."

"Jane, I've been meaning to ask you."

"Yes dear. What is it?"

"Bill Broyd wants me to do more baking for him. The brawn and pork pies are selling so well, he's asked me to start making scotch eggs and pasties in time for Easter. I'd love to take on the extra work, but would you mind?"

"It's fine by me as long as you keep up with the payment in kind, like you've been doin'. It really helps with the housekeepin', as well as tastin' so good. But how will you be able to fit it all in?"

"Ellen loves helping. And she breaks up from school soon, so she'll have more time. And the others will be there for the twins. I should be alright for time."

"You copin' with wicked old Bill's cheeky tongue?" Jane asked her.

"Yes – I've got him well trained. And I just laugh it off. If I took him up on one of his propositions, he'd probably run a mile!" Both women laughed. "One thing is bothering me, though," Nell said. "It's my sister. I still haven't made it up with her. And I promised George I would."

"Ask her down for tea. The tea table's a suitable forum for buryin' the hatchet. Nice atmosphere round a teapot."

"Hmm. I think I will. It's the twins' birthday on April 8th – she could come then, and it wouldn't seem so ... obvious. And I could ask cousin Ivy ... haven't seen her in ages. The 8th is a Monday, but we could do it on the Sunday afternoon. What do you think?"

"Ideal." Jane nodded.

"What've you got there, Gracie?"

Grace had held the envelope tight in her hand as she pedalled out from Halstead.

"Sorry, Aunt Flo, it's got a bit crumpled. It's an invitation. It's the twins' birthday soon. Mum wants you to come to their tea party." Grace held it out to her.

"Well. Let's have a look." Florence opened the envelope with a hoofpick.

Her sister's neat cursive script requested the pleasure of her company on the afternoon of Sunday, 7th April.

"You will come, Aunt Flo, won't you?"

Chapter 37

"Oh God. It's happenin' again." Frank put down his knife and fork and turned the page of the newspaper to read the full report.

"What is?" Annie asked.

"It's all kicked off again on the Somme. The Boche've got troops to spare, now the Russians are out of it. They're headin' for Paris. Makin' a run for it before the Yanks join in, I s'pose. Says here they're makin' rapid progress."

"Lord, Frank. And there'll be more killin', more maimin'. We all thought Passchendaele was the last straw. How can it just go on and on? We got to pray for Wilf – an' all those poor men out there."

In every home, anxious families drew together once more and hoped their husbands, sons, brothers and lovers might be spared. For those who had lost loved ones, the grieving was never ending.

Florence, despite her agnosticism, prayed for Andrew. It seemed as though that was all she could do. *Just like 'The Grand Old Duke of York'*, he'd said about the war. And she could see now exactly what he meant. Backwards and forwards over the same ground.

The day before Good Friday. Annie was thinking about roasting a shoulder of lamb for Easter Sunday dinner and inviting Holger. A knock at the farmhouse door interrupted her train of thought. Frowning she made for the door. A slight youth, little more than a boy, stood at the top of the steps, an envelope in his gloved hand.

"Telegram for you," he said without a smile, holding the envelope out to her. She felt her knees weaken and she reached for the door jamb to steady herself. The boy turned and descended the steps, got on his bicycle and was gone.

A telegram. She sank onto the settle, barely able to breathe. From France. She sat unable to make herself unstick the envelope. Missing presumed dead ... Died of wounds ... She forced herself to look at the scrap of paper in her hand. It came, it said, from a field hospital outside Amiens. She inserted her shaking thumb under the flap and prised open the envelope. Unfolding its contents, she tried to focus on the printed strip gummed to the flimsy paper. 'Lance Corporal Wilfred Davis 5th Army seriously injured' it read. 'Immediate repatriation Moorfields Hospital, London EC1'.

Not dead! Was all she could think. She let out a wail of relief. But seriously injured. How? How seriously? Maimed? Disfigured? Her lovely boy. Impaired. In pain. She read the telegram once more. "Moorfields," she said out loud. "That's the eye hospital ... Not blind! Please, God. Not blind!" Wilf's eyes, always alive, had brightened her life since his boyhood. Again she moaned, covering her face with her hands. He'd grown strapping, muscular, but in Annie's heart Wilf was still her little boy. The life she'd borne into this world. As a baby he had crawled across this very floor and buried his fingers in the softness of the dog's ears. She recalled him fetching in the eggs as a toddler, and later helping his dad, or playing football with the other lads. She'd been so proud of him when he left in his khaki with a salute and a "Don't worry, Ma, I can take care of myself."

It must be like this for all mothers of war casualties. But knowing that didn't help. She wasn't sure why, but she heaved herself to her feet and made for the yard. She stood and breathed in the familiar scents of the farm. "Wilf, my darlin' boy, my pride and joy," she said through her tears. "Dear Lord!" She raised her fists to heaven. "Give us strength. Give us hope. And send healin' to this world that mankind's broke to pieces!"

She stood for many minutes before beginning to think more clearly, her courage renewed.

"Must carry on," she said quietly to herself, wiping away her tears with the handkerchief she kept in her apron pocket. "Can't give in. He'll need us. And we'll have to help him get through this. Fowl need feedin' … No earthly use in makin' them suffer." She brought scraps from the kitchen and scooped a measure of grain from the bin in the barn. The hens and ducks came scuttling, clucking and quacking at the prospect of rations.

She took herself to the kitchen garden and, selecting a hoe from the tools in the shed, started dislodging seedling weeds from between her young broad bean plants. "How dare you?" She was addressing the weeds.

"What the devil's got into you? You're goin' at that hoein' like a thing possessed!" Frank was standing, enjoying the spectacle of his wife giving her garden work the hammer-and-tongs treatment.

"What's that you say?" Annie kept on hoeing. "And what's so funny?"

Frank was standing with the young German beside him. Clearly amused by the picture before his eyes, Holger was concealing a smile behind a hand.

"There you are, Fritzy. That's what I call hard work."

Jack sat at the men's feet, his tongue lolling. They had been checking the ewes. They were a couple of weeks at most from the start of lambing, and they'd spent time preparing the fold which Frank had picked out for the arrival of the new lambs.

While she'd been working, thoughts of Wilf's injuries had slipped from her mind. But on seeing Frank and, more particularly, the German, who still wore his army uniform jacket to work on the farm, it came back to her. The sorrow, the anxiety. She reached into her apron pocket for the telegram. "Frank." She held out the rumpled envelope to her husband, "Oh! Frank! It's our boy. It's Wilf …"

"Not … dead, is he?"

"No. Thank the Lord. But seriously injured, it says. They're sendin' him home – well, to London. Moorfields Hospital. Frank, it's his eyes. Got to be.

P'raps he's been blinded." Frank came over to her and rocked her in his arms. Jack crouched, his ears flattened.

The smile had left the German's lips. He had not understood much of what had passed between the Davises, but he got the gist well enough, and withdrew to retrieve his bicycle, and to give the farmer and his wife some moments alone. It was almost two weeks since he'd come to Valley Farm, and he felt he was settling in well. But now this. Their son injured. By one of his countrymen. Did they blame him? For being German? He wouldn't be surprised if they did. He wheeled his bicycle over to where the Davises were now standing talking about their boy.

" … and how can we think about goin' up to London with all that's goin' on here in the next few weeks?" Frank was saying, shaking his head. Annie shook hers, too.

"Excuse me," the German said. "I help." He pointed to his own chest. "I do more here." He nodded.

Frank put a hand on Holger's shoulder. "Thanks. Annie and me, we appreciate it."

The Easter Sunday dinner never happened.

Chapter 38

"Oh Annie. No. Not Wilf. I am so sorry." Florence said. "You and Frank feel like family to me – I almost feel as though I know him. And I know how proud you are of him."

"I've always done me best to make this farm as good as it can be so Wilf would have something to come into. But if he can't see …"

"You don't know that's the case. You've got to find out."

"We've got to go and see him," said Annie.

"But how can we with lambin' in the offin' and so much hangin' on the grain harvest?"

Florence laid a hand on Frank's arm. "When the time comes for you to go to see Wilf in London, Fritzy and I will be able to hold the fort for – what? Thirty-six hours? Neither you nor Annie can do this on your own – you've got to go together to see your son."

"But –"

"No buts, Frank. I know it's lambing time, and I've never birthed an animal in my life. But Fritzy has and he's already let you know he wants to help. And Jack knows his job around the sheep inside out and backwards. He'll keep us in line."

"We don't even know if Wilf's arrived at Moorfields yet," said Annie.

"So we've got a few days at the very least till we do know. We've got to use that time to get ourselves organised." Florence's tone was firm

"But," Frank said again, "Fritzy doesn't even speak English."

"Neither do the ewes." She shrugged and smiled.

Chapter 39

"Annie, how can I go when you need me here?" Florence had mixed feelings about Iris and Renee's birthday tea. She genuinely wanted to heal the rift between Nell and herself. It had been three months, now. And she knew it would please Grace, who was caught in the middle of this argument for reasons which she could not understand.

"You got to go, Florence. You owe it to George for one thing. You know how he felt about you and Nell fallin' out. And to young Grace."

"We're in good enough shape here," said Frank. "Most important thing is the plantin's done. You and Fritzy'll only have the lambin' to think about. Apart from the other animals, of course, but we fit them in all the time anyhow."

Florence knew he was right.

On Sunday 7th April, Florence wheeled her bi...cycle, which had been in the hay barn for weeks, unused, out into the yard. She had to take a brush to it to remove wisps of hay and a layer of dust.

She hoisted her mandolin on her shoulder and cycled off to Factory Terrace. *You never know*, she thought, *the children might enjoy a bit of a sing-song*.

Grace met her aunt on the doorstep with a huge hug. "Factory Terrace hasn't been the same without you in it, Aunt Flo. Come in!"

She led the way through to the back kitchen. Iris and Renee sat in their highchairs, their pretty frocks and cardigans protected from food spillages by linen tea towels tied round their necks. Alf was practising his 'magic' trick of making marbles seemingly disappear and reappear in his mouth. The twins loved it.

"Stop that, Alfred," Nell said, "you'll give them ideas, and then they'll be putting all manner of things in their mouths, too. And I don't mean food!"

Alf scratched his head thinking what else he could do to entertain his little sisters. He did love it when they laughed at him. He put the tea cosy on his head and pulled a face.

"Off!" said Nell. "The tea'll be stone cold!"

Florence stood in the doorway. "You have to keep on top of them all the time, don't you? Hello, Nellie."

"It's only because he's stupid," said Ellen, approaching the table with another plate of scones.

Nell stood and the sisters embraced. "It's been too long, Flo."

"You look well, Nellie. Halstead life must be suiting you."

"Yes, it is, apart from having to keep this lot in line."

146

"I've brought these for the birthday girls." She gave them each a small parcel, wrapped in white tissue. They ripped off the paper to reveal wooden egg cups, each with their name on.

"Swank made them," she said.

"Thanks, Flo. That was thoughtful."

Ellen poured Florence a cup of tea, and plumped up the cushion on the chair by the range. Grace showed her the birthday cards she'd made for each of the twins. "Iris's one's got an iris on it and Renee's has a lily. I wish Mum and Dad had called her 'Lily' – it's much prettier than Renee."

"They're lovely, Gracie. And is Alf keeping up his drawing lessons?"

"Don't ask, Aunt Flo!" Ellen said. "If he does much more drawing, we'll all have to move out – there won't be enough room in here for us."

Alf left the room and returned with a sheaf of paper under his arm. "I've got one or two I'm quite proud of. This is my favourite." He held out a sheet. It was a sketch of the font in St Andrew's church. The symmetry, the three-dimensional perspective, the highlights on the wooden lid, the look of solidity of the iron ring on the top, Alf had captured it all. "It's 15th century, you know. Mr Mathews got the vicar's permission for me to draw it."

"It's remarkable, Alf." Florence was genuinely impressed.

She had forgotten how enjoyable it was spending time with Nell's children. The little twins had grown and were starting to talk. By the end of the afternoon, they were calling her 'Aunt Fo'. She was glad she'd come.

"Aren't you going to play your mandolin for us?" Grace asked. "You've brought it all this way."

"Yes, of course. What would you like to hear? Or shall we sing a song?"

They wanted something the twins would like, so they all joined in with 'Little Jack Horner', 'Mary, Mary Quite Contrary' and 'Jack and Jill', while the little girls clapped. When Alf mimed Jack falling down and breaking his crown, they laughed. 'Old Macdonald Had a Farm' ended in a riot of noisy animal impressions.

Cousin Ivy dropped in, bringing some little peg dolls she'd made for Iris and Renee.

"When's the baby due, Ivy?" Florence asked.

"End of June," Ivy said. "Stan and me, we're that excited. Stan's workin' overtime, tryin' to get a bit extra together to cover the added expense … I'll have to give up work when the baby comes. Things'll be tight … Wonderful sausage rolls, Nell. I don't know when I tasted pastry that light."

Jane and Elsie Mizen joined them for a short while. Elsie slurped her tea and bits of sponge cake kept escaping from the side of her mouth. Grace winced.

"I ought to be on my way, too," Florence said, "I want to get back before it's completely dark. Here," she said to Nell, holding out a ten-shilling note. "This is for the twins. Put it towards some new shoes, or something. "Here, you lot," she called to the older three, and she pressed a florin into each of their hands."

"Wow! Thanks, Aunt Flo, that's jolly generous."

"Well, I don't have much to spend money on. But you make sure you behave yourselves, alright?"

Nell stepped in. "Now that you've cleared the table, you kids, you can go and do the washing up in the scullery. Off you go!"

"I … I was wondering if you'd heard from Captain Forbes recently, Flo," she asked once Ellen, Alf and Grace were out of earshot.

"Yes, of course. He writes regularly."

"Is he … alright?"

"As alright as anyone could be over there."

"Flo. I know I was a bit hard on you –"

"A *bit* hard! I'll say!"

"Well, George made me realise how unkind I'd been. And I see now what I said was … not … fair." She took a breath. "And I'm sorry, Flo, and I've missed you. Please say you forgive me."

A brief silence followed. Florence stood and offered Nell her hand. "Well said, Nellie. Let's put it behind us." The sisters embraced, more warmly this time.

"Lord, Nellie. I should have said earlier. The Davis' boy, Wilf. He's been injured. They say it's his eyes – they're sending him back to hospital in London."

"Oh, poor them. I must send them a note. Can you wait a minute while I write it? Then you could take it back with you."

"Of course." Florence waited in the hall.

Nell reappeared with an envelope in her hand.

"Here," she said, handing it to Florence. "Do tell them how sorry we are. But … Flo, I'm so glad you came. And thanks for the presents. Stay in touch, and mind how you go on that old boneshaker of a bicycle."

They waved her on her way until she disappeared from sight at the end of Factory Terrace.

She loved the clarity of early evening light above all others. But columns of dark cloud were massing, the westering sun throwing the clouds into sharp contrast.

She was glad she'd patched things up with Nell. *Life* is *too short for bitterness and recrimination,* she thought. George was right. Pulling into the farmyard, Annie came running from the house.

"D'you think you can ride that contraption down to the lambin' fold? The first ewe's givin' birth – you might like to go and see what it's all about."

Chapter 40

Florence pedalled hard, avoiding as best she could tussocks and ruts in the track leading down to the fold. *Birthing. New life ... motherhood ... the next generation.* She jumped off the bicycle and ran across to where Frank and Holger were kneeling, concentrating on the pregnant ewe. Jack lay with his head on his paws, still and watchful. The ewe was standing, her back end facing the two men. She pawed the ground and pulled a strange face, her top lip curled back, head in the air.

"She's doin' alright," Frank said. "And everything looks fine. I want you to come and watch this."

Florence squatted down next to the two men and waited. The ewe bleated and then something appeared at the opening of her birth canal.

"See those?" Frank pointed an index finger. "Them's the lamb's front feet. Her lamb's the right way round. That's just as it should be. Next contraction, we'll see its nose."

Again, the ewe bleated and something small and pink appeared.

"Good! Once its head's out, it's all over bar the shoutin'. It'll slither out like a fish on a slab!"

Within a minute or two, the lamb's whole head was born. The ewe pushed and bleated again, and the shoulders appeared. Then the rest of it flopped out onto the grassy pen, and the ewe began to nuzzle it and lick the fluid from the lamb's body. "Good," said Frank again. "Actually it's a ewe lamb, so we'd better call it 'she'. Now. This bit's important, so you'd better watch carefully. You got to clear her nostrils, so's she can breathe, smack some iodine on her navel, and make sure she gets up and starts sucklin' pretty quick. You can see this ewe's acceptin' her little 'un, because she's alickin' her and encouragin' her to get up." Soon, the lamb was on her feet, the birth fluid drying on her woolly skin. And she began searching for the ewe's teats. Finding one, she thrust her muzzle against her mother and began to suckle.

Florence could think of nothing else she'd ever seen to match this. She looked at Frank and shook her head. "Wonderful," she said.

"Don't go all dewy eyed, Florence, this is serious work, and there's more you got to know about."

Holger watched. Now he looked up and smiled. "Is good," he said. "Nice lamb." He pronounced it 'lemb'.

Just as those clouds had foreshadowed, rain set in, making the lambing process uncomfortable for humans and sheep alike. Frank, though was not unhappy, as it meant there was plenty of moisture to help his cereal seedlings grow on.

"The cycle of life doesn't wait for fine weather, does it?" Florence was glad of her WLA hat to keep the rain from going down her neck. The lambs started to arrive one after another.

"Right." Frank stirred his tea. "I've drawn up a rota. Florence – now you're alright with routine lambin', you can do early mornin's and evenin's. That way you can do the milking and chores in the stables and milking parlour during the day. Fritzy, you'll have to do daytimes because o' your curfew, so I'll take care of things through the night."

They sat in the shepherd's hut by the lambing fold. "This little Tortoise stove's worth its weight in gold," he said. "And if this weather keeps up, you'll feel you'd sell your soul for it. It'll dry your waterproofs and your socks and it'll boil up the teakettle in a brace of shakes. And while it's quiet out in the fold, you can warm your feet in here. There's a stack of wood round the back under a tarpaulin. You'll have to check that nothin' out of the ordinary's kickin' off, but Jack's marvellous at spottin' when you need to step in. I love lambin'. You were right to be amazed by it, Florence. Circle of new life. It's the real rewardin' part of farmin'."

***

"I don't know whether to be relieved or apprehensive or both." Annie said when they learned of Wilf's admission to Moorfields. She wanted to drop everything and go, but Frank was more circumspect. "Now then. Let's not jump the gun." Annie winced at the word 'gun', but let it pass without comment.

"Trains'll be hopeless over the weekend, and we've got to fix up how we're goin' to get to the station. We'll have to hitch a ride with Swank when he comes for the mornin' milk churn – and get him to bring us back, too … Besides, our boy's goin' to need time to get his bearings …"

"You're right, Frank, but we got to know how it is with him so we can begin to work on where we go from here. And God knows, I want to see my Wilf! I can't bear the waitin' no longer. And the letter didn't say we got to hold off."

Wednesday would be the day.

"I wrote to my mother," said Florence, "she's more than happy to put you up overnight. You can't do it there and back in a single day. The last thing you want is to feel rushed when you're with Wilf."

"So," Annie said. "Let's catch the mornin' train into London, as early as Swank can make it, go straight to Moorfields … And after, we can go back to Stratford for the night. We'll be back here around dinnertime Thursday."

"Good. I'll let Mother know. But you've got to promise me one thing." Florence fixed Frank and Annie with a steady look. "Don't believe anything she tells you about me!"

Chapter 41

Annie and Frank felt dwarfed, insignificant in this big city. "How can folk live here?" Annie said. "It's like they're just tiny specks of dust."

The entrance doors of the Moorfields stood before them. They pushed them open and made for the reception desk where a young woman greeted them.

"What name?" she asked.

"Davis."

"Patient's first names?"

"Wilfred Francis. Lance Corporal." Annie splayed her hands on the desk top.

"Very good. Please wait a moment."

The receptionist searched in a card index box, her fingers toing and froing. Annie and Frank felt uncomfortable, impatient.

"Ah! Here we are. I'm sorry to have kept you waiting. You'll find Lance Corporal Davis on the second floor. Ward 9B. But I have a note here to say his doctor would like to see you before you visit your son. He'll meet you on the second-floor landing, if you'd like to go up and wait there." She gestured towards the stairs.

There were some straight-backed chairs grouped round a low table with a collection of old eye medicine periodicals. Annie straightened them. They sat down. "I don't want to read about what can go wrong with people's eyes," Frank said, "I wish I had a newspaper."

"Mm," was all Annie said. The atmosphere was suffocating. "I'm goin' to find the ladies' room. Wash my hands." She was gone a while, and Frank sat fiddling with his hat and thinking about how badly he could do with a pipeful of tobacco. Annie returned, and the waiting continued.

"Where on earth can he be?" Annie began to sound desperate.

"He's a busy man ..." Frank said.

It was almost an hour before a short man in a pin-striped suit and a diamond tie pin appeared through some swing doors. He hurried across to them, running a hand through his thinning blond hair. He extended his hand to Frank and Annie.

"How do you do, Mr and Mrs Davis? I'm Doctor Hoad and I've been treating your son. I'm most awfully sorry to have kept you waiting so long. My ward rounds took longer than I anticipated."

Annie and Frank stood and had time only to mumble 'good afternoon' and nod as Dr Hoad continued. "Do sit down, won't you? Now. To put you in the picture about your son's injuries and not to put too fine a point on it, he's been the victim of a shrapnel injury which, I'm sorry to say has destroyed his sight."

"Oh Frank, Frank!" Annie pulled a handkerchief from her bag and dabbed her nose. Frank slumped in his chair and shook his head.

"But all is not gloom and doom," continued Dr Hoad. "We're seeing so many injuries like this as a consequence of the war. And what we're discovering is that in some – not all – but some cases, there has been partial improvement. Some of our patients have had some sight restored."

"And you think our Wilf might be one of them patients?"

"It's very difficult to say at the present moment, Mrs Davis. It's very early days – and there's a great deal we don't yet understand about what's going on. We're learning all the time from these cases, and there have been some very encouraging results. However, I don't want to boost your hopes unduly. Lance Corporal Davis has sustained a severe injury, and at this stage, we don't know what sort of recovery is possible." Dr Hoad put his elbows on his knees, clasped his hands together and looked at Annie and Frank. "One eye, his right, is quite clearly damaged beyond repair. His facial flesh wounds should heal reasonably well, but there's nothing we can do for the eye. His left one, on the other hand, although he can see nothing at present, appears undamaged. It may be the shock of the wounding and his present mental state which has caused the sight loss. It's what we call 'hysterical blindness' and may well be reversible if that's what it is. Or there could be internal damage to the eyeball itself which we are unable to identify in which case the blindness will be permanent. It's a very tricky business, I'm afraid."

"Hysterical blindness. Well I'm blowed." Frank shook his head. "I've never heard of such a thing."

"So what happens next?" Annie asked. "How long till we know, Doctor?"

"It's likely to be a slow process. If there is internal damage to the eye mechanism, it will not mend. We must be patient. And hope. However, the best opportunity we can give him is to keep him very still and quiet. We've put him on a slight sedative to help him stay calm … He has been a little … agitated since he was admitted. It's not unusual. Lots of casualties come in here like that. They've had a tough time."

Frank took hold of Annie's hand. "One more thing, Doctor," Frank asked, "How long's he goin' to have to be in here? Only bein' farmers, it ain't easy to get away to visit."

"I do see, and I sympathise. But I would advise against moving him for the present for the reasons I've explained to you. We'll keep him here for a while yet and see how he responds. Then we can consider transferring him to your local hospital. I think you have quite a good one in Halstead, haven't you?" Dr Hoad did not wait for a reply. "Now, I expect you'd like to see him." He broke off and rose to his feet. Frank and Annie stood. Annie rearranged her hat. "Don't expect too much too soon," Dr Hoad said placing a hand on Frank's shoulder. "It's early days, as I said." He shook hands with them again. "I'll make sure you're kept informed." He turned to go. "Now, if you'll excuse me, I'll send Sister to show you to the ward." He nodded and was gone.

"Thank you, Doctor," Annie said to his retreating figure.

A nurse, impeccably uniformed, approached them. "Mr and Mrs Davis? Follow me, please."

They walked the length of the ward, between rows of iron beds occupied by men, mostly young men, with either one or both eyes bandaged. Some appeared to be sleeping.

Wilf lay in the last bed on the left. The Sister beckoned to a nurse to bring another chair to his bedside. Annie looked at her damaged son. Both his eyes were bandaged, but his nose, mouth, chin, jaw looked just the same as ever. Even the lobes of his ears, visible below the white dressing, were achingly familiar to her. "Wilf, my boy, it's us. It's your Ma and Pa."

Silence. There was no smile on his lips at the sound of her voice, as once there would have been.

"You awake, lad?" Frank said.

Silence.

Annie took his hand as it lay on the hospital counterpane. Wilf withdrew it. Firmly. "Oh, Wilf, Wilf!" But she was determined not to let her voice betray her distress. She cleared her throat. "The farm's doin' really well now the Women's Land Army's sent us Florence. She's a godsend."

"The spring sowing's lookin' good," said Frank, "and lambin's started. I remember how you used to love lambin'." He drew the line at mentioning the German. *All in good time*, he thought.

Silence.

Annie looked at Frank, distraught.

"Son," said Frank, "we're lookin' forward to havin' you home, but it won't be just yet awhile. Dr Hoad says you've got to keep real quiet and maybe you'll be able to see again ..."

Wilf's expression did not register a response to his father's words.

" ... When he says the time's right, we'll get you back to the hospital in Halstead, so we can see you more often."

The beleaguered parents sat mute, as though shipwrecked on a foreign shore where they did not know the language. "We'll just stay a while," Annie managed in a whisper, "and if you want to say anythin', you just go right ahead. We'll be listenin'." They sat hand in hand gazing at their stricken son, while the bustle of the ward went on around them. They were unaware of the passage of time until the same nurse approached the bedside on quiet feet.

"Mr and Mrs Davis. I'm sorry, but visiting time's coming to an end, now. I'll have to ask you to leave, I'm afraid." There was a note of sympathy in her voice. Annie and Frank got stiffly to their feet.

"Well, bye for now, son," Frank said, "we'll come again when we can."

"We love you, Wilf, my darlin'," said Annie as the Sister began to usher them away.

"Pa." Wilf's voice was unemotional. Flat.

"Yes, Wilf. I'm listenin'."

"There's no point. In carryin' on."

"Wilf. Son. Don't say that!" was all Frank could think of to say.

Chapter 42

Half way through the Davis's absence. *So far*, Florence thought, *so good*. She'd moved herself into the shepherd's hut for the duration, returning to the farmhouse only for necessities and a bite to eat. She'd even managed to get some shuteye between lamb deliveries, and she planned a couple of hours off-duty after milking, while Fritzy was at the fold with the ewes.

It was 5.30 on Thursday morning. There were six new born lambs suckling on their dams since Frank and Annie left. Florence felt proud that she and Fritzy had seen these new lives into the world. Something about lambing brought a lump to her throat. She was wide awake now, and poked her nose outside. The air smelt of moist earth, tangy and perfumed with the scents of the country spring.

Jack and she took a turn round the fold, Florence making a mental note of which ewes looked as though they might be on the verge of dropping their lambs. The dog had spent the night in the open, on the lookout for foxes, ready to see off any bold enough to come close. There was just one ewe that Florence thought was nearing her time. She could see it turning circles, pawing the ground and pulling that odd expression.

She returned to the hut, Jack trotting at her heels, and set the kettle to boil on the Tortoise stove. Soon it was steaming. Florence warmed the teapot, spooned tea into it and left it to brew under a woollen cosy. She retrieved a jug of milk from a wooden foxproof box under the hut, and poured herself a cup of tea. There was, she thought, nothing quite like a freshly brewed cup first thing. *A miracle of the highest order.*

She took her mandolin and sat on the steps of the hut as the sun came up, bold and golden, flooding the fold in morning light. She strummed the instrument, and began to put together some chord sequences which she felt suggested this idyllic setting. Jack came and rested his head on her knee. She offered him half a biscuit. He gobbled it. She was half way through her second cup of tea, when Jack took himself off to take a look at the ewes. He trotted to the far end of the fold and stood with his ears cocked. He woofed and trotted back to Florence. He barked again, more purposefully this time, his forefeet left the ground with each bark. "What is it, boy? Is she ready?" She stroked his ears. Jack shook her hand off and began to dance in circles. Florence knew better than to ignore him. She put down her cup on the steps, picked up the iodine, some clean towels and the tube she used for sucking mucous from the new lambs' nostrils and followed the collie towards the fold.

The ewe she had identified as near her time was down on the ground, panting and bleating. There was no sign yet of the lamb. Florence went through her usual

154

preliminary routine, thinking the lamb's forefeet would emerge any minute. The ewe strained again but still the lamb did not appear.

This isn't right, Florence thought. She inserted her hand into the ewe's birth canal and groped for the lamb's little hooves and the shape of its forelimbs, but could not locate them. The ewe's body tensed as she contracted once more, but, it seemed, she was unable to push the lamb towards taking its first breath.

Now what do I do? This lamb needs help if it's going to get itself born. But she didn't know how to do it. She withdrew her hand and tried palpating the ewe's belly with pushing movements towards the animal's rear end. Nothing happened. "Dear God," Florence said out loud. She felt inside the ewe again and found the lamb's nose, but it seemed as though its legs were folded backwards, making it impossible for the ewe to push. She tried to get a hold on the legs and bring them forward, but the ewe let out a painful bleat, and Florence feared she might tear its birth canal if she continued. The thought of a haemorrhaging ewe filled her with terror.

For want of knowing what else she could do, she continued to massage the ewe's flank as best she could. The ewe was clearly tiring, her head lying listlessly on the ground. "Keep going, girl," Florence whispered to the ewe. "You and I, we mustn't give up. We've just got to keep trying."

Florence was concentrating so hard that she didn't notice Jack jump to his feet and career back to the shepherd's hut. A figure on a bicycle had just arrived and Jack approached him flat out, once again dancing in circles and barking.

"Jeck. What is it?"

Jack led the way back to where Florence knelt over the ewe. Holger followed and vaulted the fold's perimeter hurdle without breaking his stride. He knelt down beside Florence and nudged her, politely but firmly, to one side. He got to work, palpating the ewe and making rotating movements with his hand inside her. The only words he uttered were unintelligible to Florence. She wondered how long they'd got before the lamb simply suffocated in the act of being born. She offered up a silent prayer. Holger let out a straining sound from deep in his throat. Then a long sigh.

When Florence looked again at the ewe, the sight of the lamb's small nose brought her to the verge of tears. Then its head appeared. "Is it alright?" she whispered.

"A moment." Holger eased the lamb into the world. It looked limp and lifeless and Florence could see it wasn't breathing. Holger picked up the frail lamb by its back legs and swung it from side to side.

"Fritzy! For God's sake!" Florence tried to stop him. "What do you think you're doing?"

"Wait. Please." The German set the lamb down next to its mother, who pushed at it with her nose. The lamb twitched and lifted its head and let out a small sneeze. The ewe nudged it again. Little by little, it struggled to its feet and took its first faltering steps. It shook its woolly head and sneezed again, then sought the ewe's udder, head-butting her to stimulate the let-down of her milk.

"It starts lemb to breathe. Is old ... thing," Holger told her, not knowing the right word, "I learn it in my home."

Florence was so relieved to see the lamb revived, she barely heard what he was saying, but she had the grace to thank him. "Fritzy, you're a hero!" Taking his hand, she gripped it and slapped his shoulder.

"Aach!" But he too was smiling.

Chapter 43

They sat together in the third-class carriage and left the smoke of the city behind them.

"What if he never gets any sight back?" said Annie.

"Well," Frank cleared his throat. "At least that's one thing where there is a glimmer of light, even if it is a small one. I'm just as concerned about what he said right when we left. Sounds like he wants to give up. That ain't no good to man nor beast – he's got to want to try!"

They travelled on without speaking.

Frank had been brooding on fears of his own since the arrival of the telegram. "Annie, have you given a thought to the tenancy?"

She turned to face him. "No, Frank, I haven't. What about the tenancy?"

"If – and let's remember, it's still an 'if' – if Wilf don't recover enough to take on Valley Farm, and when I'm past bein' able to carry on farmin', plain fact is, we'll lose it."

"What d'you mean, Frank. Lose the farm?"

"That's exactly what I mean. If the farm don't make money, how're we goin' to pay the landlord? He's not a charity! It's the main reason I've been so particular in my farmin' – so we got somethin' *viable* to hand on to Wilf … In time, you and me, we could move to a little tied cottage to see out our days near the place we've devoted our lives to …" He took out a linen handkerchief to wipe his nose. "I hadn't said nothin' to you because of the worry …"

"You're not thinkin' of packin' it in yet, are you? We've got best part of another decade in us."

"I know, but we've got to think ahead."

"Now, Frank." Annie laid a cotton-gloved hand on his. "We got to face this together. You can't be bottlin' up worries like that and leavin' me out in the cold. We're a partnership, you and me. When all's said and done, we got each other, and that's a source of strength. We'll have to face it when and if the time comes. Together. With the good Lord's help."

Frank raised the gloved hand to his lips and kissed it. "Annie, my old girl, I don't deserve you."

"Course you do, you old softie, we deserve each other."

They sat in silence again. England's landscape, green with spring grass, flashed past the carriage window.

"You know, I can hardly believe I left our farm in the hands of a townie with a few months' experience and a foreigner that we know nothin' about. I'd never have done it except in these dire circumstances … If it weren't for Jack, I don't think I'd have dared. I wonder what we'll find when we get back?"

***

"All quiet at your place when I collected the milk churn yesterday and again this mornin'. Didn't see no one," Swank Everitt told Frank as he and Annie climbed aboard his waggon at Halstead station.

"I guess that's good news, Swank. Hope so, anyways."

Frank was twitchy all the way back to the farm. He cracked his finger joints, putting Annie's teeth on edge, but she said nothing. It was mid-afternoon when the familiar gateway of their home came into view. Florence and Holger had spruced up the farmyard in preparation for their return. Now they and Jack stood waiting for them in the sunshine.

"How's it been?" They were barely within earshot.

"It was nerve-wracking!" Florence said. But she was smiling.

Chapter 44

"You two fancy a picnic on the Brawkes on Saturday?" Lennie asked. "Bluebells'll be out now. You remember, Gracie, we talked about it when your Dad was home. It's a right nice time to go. What d'you think?"

"I think I'd like that very much. How about you, Doris?"

Doris nodded. "So long as my mum'll be alright without me. I'll have to check."

They agreed to meet outside Cooper's greengrocery shop at 10.30.

"Lovely mornin' for it," Lennie said. "Anybody got any ginger beer?"

"No," said Doris, "but I've got lemonade –"

A shrill squeal filled the air.

"What the devil –?" Windy said. They all turned in the direction of the noise to see a pig, running out from the narrow alleyway beside Bill Broyd's butcher's shop.

They all knew Broyd had a slaughterhouse behind his shop. This pig looked like the next candidate for the chop.

"He's havin' none of it, is he?" Doris began to giggle.

The pig ran up the High Street, squealing. The butcher appeared at the mouth of the alleyway, a knife in his hand. "Stupid beast!" He ran after the pig, but was no match for it. Nervous shoppers ran for shelter shrieking with alarm.

"I don't know who's makin' more noise," Windy said. "The pig or those women."

The saddleback's route led it towards the group of children outside Mrs Cooper's shop.

"Quick!" said Windy. "Link arms! He can't see much with them floppy ears – we can trap him." They formed a human barrier. The pig ran into them and stopped. "Stand your ground. Now! Come round to the left so we've got him cornered. Then we can get him through the shop doorway!" The human chain did not disintegrate and the pig quietened. The children closed on it, easing it into Mrs Cooper's doorway. "Now." Windy said. "Shut the door, then we've got 'im!"

Grace got hold of the shop door with her free hand and gave it a shove. It slammed shut.

"What d'you think you're doin', lettin' that clumsy creature loose in my shop?" Molly Cooper was less than happy. "It'll ruin all my stock!"

The still-intact human chain moved the pig across the shop towards the counter.

"Mind out, Mrs Cooper," Windy said. "We're goin' to trap him behind your counter. We can keep him out of trouble there till Mr Broyd comes to get him."

Bill Broyd appeared with a length of rope. He tapped on the glass pane. "Can I come in, now?" Broyd said, "Have you got him pinned down?"

The butcher approached the pig, attached the rope, nooselike, around its neck and hauled on it making sure it would hold. Then he stepped astride the animal to anchor it between his legs.

"Don't let go of him now you've got him, Bill," said Molly Cooper. "I'll have to charge you for any damage he does in here."

Broyd drove the pig out into the High Street. He could feel Halstead's eyes on him. How long would he be the laughing stock of the town?

***

When Grace sat down to write her diary that evening, she hardly knew where to begin. *'The colour and scent of the bluebell carpet and the delicacy of the nodding flowers was so wonderful'* she wrote. But thoughts of the pig's escape and recapture kept bubbling into her mind. *'You won't believe this, Dad. It was absolutely hilarious ...'*

Chapter 45

"Look at all that boisterous young life. It's good to see." Frank smiled as the lambs gambolled on the spring grass.

"Isn't it?" Florence said. "You know, Frank, I'd rather be back in the lambing pen than bent double banking up potatoes."

"Got to be done, though, missy. It's the next thing on the list. Swings and roundabouts. That's farmin' for you. You and Fritzy can work together on it for the next few days. You aright with that?"

"Ye-es ... Come on Fritzy, let's get started."

"Oh! My aching back!" Florence straightened up and stretched. She took off her coat and ran the back of her hand across her brow, looping a strand of hair behind her ear.

A bird call echoed through the warm air. Even Florence recognised it.

"A cuckoo!"

"Ein kuckuk!" Florence and Holger said together and laughed briefly at the coincidence.

"I'm usually wrong," Florence said, looking away from the German and picking up her hoe.

"Nein – no. Is good."

She began hoeing again. The cuckoo kept up its simple call which carried across the fields. Holger was trying to say something to her. "Is ... music ..."

"What is, Fritzy?"

"Handel. Die Kuckuk ... und Die ..."

"Nightingale. You mean 'The Cuckoo And The Nightingale', I think. Do you know it?"

"Ja." He smiled. "You know?"

"I do! It's lovely." She hummed a little of the melody.

"I play," he said.

"Oh ... " she said. "Can you?"

***

Next morning, Florence was forking new straw into the cow byre when she heard the clack of the gate latch. Holger was late. It was unlike him. He came stumbling in, pushing his bicycle. She put down her pitchfork and approached him, breaking into a run. His face was stained with blood, his fair hair matted with it.

"Whatever's happened?" She took his arm and sat him down on the clean straw. She took a close look at the wound and lifted his hair to see the extent of it. He winced.

"Sorry, I didn't mean to hurt you, Fritzy, but we need to clean this out and dress it properly. How did you do this?"

"Ein … stone." He gestured with his hand that it had hit him on his right temple. "Ich … I … fall down." He indicated that the bicycle had gone over and he'd hit the ground. As he moved his arm, Florence noticed a crumpled piece of paper in his hand.

"What have you got there?"

He opened his hand and she took the torn paper and smoothed it out. 'BOCHE BASTARD' was written on it in untidy capitals.

"Damn!" Folding the paper, she put it in her breeches pocket and reapplied her attention to Holger's injuries. "Look, Fritzy, you stay there for a minute. I'm going to get some iodine and witch hazel and a bandage. I'll just be a moment or two. Just stay put." She spread her hands to indicate he wasn't to move.

Returning with a basin of warm water and some laundered muslin, she set about cleaning him up. "Gosh, it's bled a lot, and it's really jagged." The bloodstained muslin strips turned the water red as Florence bathed the wound. The iodine brought tears to Holger's eyes. His hands made fists.

"I know it stings, but it will help the healing." She folded a wad of the muslin and placed it over the wound. Then she bound it in place around his head. "You'll be alright but you'll have to take it quietly. I'll ask Annie if you can rest up in the kitchen. Here." She offered her arm for him to lean on.

Annie was just finishing off in the dairy and came out as Florence and Holger made their way past the window. "What's happened here?"

"Someone's thrown a stone at him and knocked him off his bicycle. I think he should rest up for a while – he's a bit groggy. Is it alright if he sits in the kitchen for a bit, Annie?"

"For sure. Make him a cup of tea, Florence. Hot and sweet. And tell him to put his feet up on the settle. I'll be in in a while. He can have some soup with us for his dinner, if he feels like it."

"Thanks, Annie." Florence installed Holger by the inglenook and made him some tea.

"Must get back to work." She smiled as she made for the door, "I'll see you at dinner time."

"Florence."

She turned towards him. "Yes, Fritzy."

"Danke."

She held his gaze for a moment. "Think nothing of it."

Annie was at the door, just as Florence was leaving, wanting to know more about the incident, so Florence stayed a while longer.

"Take off that bloodstained shirt, Fritzy. I'll get you one of Frank's." Annie mimed the shirt removal.

Florence helped the German out of the soiled shirt while Annie went to search for an old one of Frank's. Holger folded his arms across his chest, and, slightly embarrassed, turned his back. Florence noticed the freckles across his shoulders.

"So how did it happen?" Annie asked.

Florence told her what she knew and showed her the scrap of paper.

"I think that's nothin' short of disgustin'." She shook out the twill shirt that had lain folded in Frank's tallboy. "War's not his fault – he didn't ask to be in it and he seems a gentle soul. He's just another victim, like all the young men what's suffered. And besides, look what he's doin' for us here. Frank'll give 'em what for if he finds out who done it."

Florence felt inclined to do the same.

Chapter 46

Bill Broyd went to great lengths to rebuild bridges with his Halstead customers following the slaughterhouse breakout. He called on the mothers of each of the captors of the escaped pig and presented them with a cut of pork as a token of his thanks. As it turned out, every Halstead household, or so it seemed, was eager to buy a piece of 'that old pig what got out of Broyd's slaughter 'ouse'. Bill wondered whether orchestrating regular 'escapes' might be good for trade, but decided that it probably wasn't worth the risk.

"I'd probably be breakin' the rationin' rules if I kept lettin' me pigs out," he said to Nell.

"Well, if it means we get a piece of pork like this every time, you won't find me complaining."

She took her sharpened knife to the beautiful piece of rolled loin and carved off a thick slice and gave it to Jane Mizen.

"Thank you for your generosity!" Jane said. "There's goin' to be some lovely cracklin' on that. Nothin' my Monty likes better!"

"There's much more here than we can get through. It seems only right to share it." Nell cut another slice from the pork and then called to her older children. "I want one of you to run this round to cousin Ivy's. And when you've done that, you can ride out to Valley Farm and ask your Aunt Florence if she can join us for dinner on Sunday."

"I'll go," said Grace. She had not been to the farm since before the lambing. "I've got lots to tell Aunt Flo."

Florence was still hard at work in the potato field as Grace pedalled by the field gate. Holger was hoeing, too, his wound still bandaged.

"Grace!" called Florence from across the potato planting.

Grace dismounted at the sound of her aunt's voice and leaned her bicycle against the hedge. "Hello, Aunt Flo, I've come with an invitation from mum."

"Oh good! Well, it's about time we stopped for a bite of dinner, so come and join us."

Grace looked shyly at Holger, his head still bandaged. "What's happened to him?"

"Oh, he fell off his bicycle," Florence said by way of a half-truth. "Not very dignified ...

Fritzy, this is Grace, my niece. She was here the day you came to the farm for the first time." Florence put her hands on Grace's shoulders. Holger bowed.

"Hello," Grace said, holding out her skirt in both hands and bending her knees in a small curtsey.

Florence stifled a grin. "Have you ever met anyone from another country before, Gracie?"

"No, Aunt Flo, I don't think I ever have."

"Well, now's a good time to get the hang of it. They don't bite – well, not all of them, anyway. And I don't think Fritzy does." Grace smiled at the German and he smiled back.

They sat together on a woollen rug and unwrapped the sandwiches Annie had packed up for them. Cold mutton and tomato chutney.

"We've got this huge piece of pork to roast," Grace began, "Mr Broyd gave it to us for catching his runaway pig …" Grace's account left nothing out. "… And that's why mum would like you to come to lunch on Sunday. To help us eat it."

"Gosh! What a story. I'd love to come. Now. Will you help us with these wretched spuds, or are you going to leave it all to us?"

"Well … I'd really like to see the lambs."

"Oh, come on then."

***

"That was out of this world, Nellie." Florence leaned back in her chair and stretched. "*Delicious* pork."

The children had cleared away and Ellen was supervising the washing up in the back kitchen. Grace had just brought the two women a cup of tea.

"It was really good to see Grace at the farm again. So much seems to have happened since she and Doris were last out there."

"True," Nell replied, "including the arrival of that German …"

"Holger, you mean. Or Fritzy, as we call him."

"Is he … alright? Only I've been a bit worried about letting the girls come to the farm with him around …"

"How do you mean 'alright'? Does he have two heads? No. Does he wear jackboots and a pointed tin helmet? No. He seems a perfectly nice sort of bloke, as far as one can tell with an English vocabulary of about a dozen words. One thing I can say in his favour, though. He's terrific on the farm. I'd have really messed up lambing without him."

"But you read such awful stories in the papers."

"Holger's not some caricature of the evil Hun, you know – in fact he's been the victim of some rather ugly behaviour just the other day on his way to the farm." She searched in her bag for the scruffy piece of paper. She smoothed it out and handed it to her sister. "One of our loyal compatriots lobbed this at him, tied round half a house brick – or so it looks from the gash on his head. I don't know about you, but I'm not very proud of someone doing that in my name."

Nell was indeed shocked by the message. "Hm. I wouldn't have expected something like this in Halstead – in London, maybe. But you can see why he should attract such … well … hatred, I suppose. He represents our enemies."

165

"Oh, come on, Nell. Would you feel the same if George were a prisoner of war in Germany? Would it be alright if upright German citizens threw stones and abuse at him?"

"Well, of course not. But *they're* the aggressors …"

"No buts! It's just plain wrong! Unjust and uncivilised! Even Frank and Annie were outraged and they've got cause enough to hate the Germans!" Florence fiddled with the ring hanging on a fine chain around her neck. Reconciliation, she reminded herself. "Oh, come on, Nellie, let's not fall out again. Life's too short. Remember?"

"No, you're right."

"That roast was utterly delicious. Thank you for inviting me. And don't worry. I'll make sure that Grace comes to no harm when she comes to Valley Farm. Please say she can still come."

Chapter 47

Dear Mr and Mrs Davis,

I am writing to bring you up to date with Lance Corporal Wilfred Davis' condition following several weeks of recuperative care at Moorfields Hospital.

As I explained when we met, there remains a chance that the sight in his left eye may be restored, at least partially, maybe more. It has been our intention to stabilise his condition and promote the healing he needs if there is to be any improvement. This is the course of treatment which we have pursued and we are satisfied that his ocular function has not deteriorated. Indeed, we believe that it is no longer as fragile as when he was admitted to our care. However, I regret to say that there has, to date, been no discernible restoration of his sight.

We are satisfied that we at Moorfields have done all we can and we feel it would be in Lance Corporal Davis' best interests if he were transferred to your local hospital where he will be able to continue the restorative therapy, which offers him the best possibility of some recovery of his sight. Of course, you will be able to visit him regularly there, which may prove valuable in the rehabilitation of his temperament following his experiences in the war.

I would urge you not to give up hope with respect to Lance Corporal Davis's prospects for improvement. You will, however, need to be patient.

I can arrange for the patient's transfer to Halstead Hospital, organise transport and liaise with the hospital staff regarding his admission. You will hear directly from the almoner when the plans are in place.

I wish you and Lance Corporal Davis all the very best of luck for the future.

Yours very sincerely,
Justin M. Hoad.

Annie refolded the letter. "Thank the Lord he's comin' home. All this waitin's driven me nearly mad."

"I know, old girl. You haven't been yourself at all."

"I'm sorry, Frank. I just couldn't help it … But now what? We've just got to wait to find out about his sight. But I'm just as worried about his spirits. Kind words and hugs aren't goin' to be enough to bring him back to us, but that – and prayin' – is all I know how to do."

"Well, we'll have to do our best. And hope. Not much, I know, but it's all I can suggest at the moment."

Frank drove the dog cart towards the town with Annie sitting beside him. He urged Cherry forward. Fizzy clouds of cow parsley lined the verges of the lane and elderflower blossom the size of saucers whizzed past them at eye level.

Halstead Hospital in Hedingham Road looked westward over meadows towards the River Colne. Patients recovering from all manner of illnesses sat out in wicker chairs on the hospital's terrace reading, snoozing, taking in the good air.

Wilf had known that view all his life. The irony of now being a patient here without being able to see it in all its pastoral beauty was not lost on him. He sat aloof from the other patients, a cup of tea turning cold on the table beside his chair. His left eye was no longer bandaged, and lacerations visible around the white dressing covering the right one had partially healed to purplish scars.

A nurse showed the Davises out to where Wilf sat.

"Hello Wilf," Frank said and patted his son's shoulder. Wilf shrugged slightly.

"Pa," Wilf said, by way of salutation, "Ma with you?"

"I'm here, Wilf. How are you?"

Wilf shrugged again but said nothing.

"It's good you're here now," said Frank.

"Have you got everything you need?" Annie asked him. "I've brought you some of your own pyjamas ... and some shortbread – your favourite."

"Ta. I don't need nothin'."

Frank cleared his throat. "Crops're comin' on a treat, and this year's lambs're a perky little lot."

"We'll have peas and broad beans soon ..." Annie began, but the vacant look on Wilf's face told her he was not listening. It wrenched her heart to see him like this, so like her dear Wilf of old and yet so altered. His skin had not lost the bloom of youth, despite his injuries, and his left eye was still as dark and beautiful as before. Yet he stared unseeingly from it.

"Well, me and your Pa'll be able to see you regular now you're here ..." Stating the obvious, she knew, but still ... "Takes no time at all in the cart."

"Don't trouble yourselves. I don't want no company."

"But chattin' with some of the other patients'd help pass the time." said Annie.

"Ma! I don't want it. Any of it! Got that?"

Annie and Frank got to their feet, not knowing how to take their leave of Wilf.

"Well ... we'll be off, then, son," Frank said.

"God bless." Annie kissed her fingers and touched them against Wilf's forehead. He flinched slightly.

"Ma, Pa," was all he said.

***

"We just don't know how to get through to him." Frank and Florence were putting the cows out after milking. "He's so bitter. It's like he blames everyone – even me and his mother. Yet all we want to do is make him know we love him and we'll take good care of him no matter what."

"But that's just it, Frank. He's a man now. He doesn't want to be looked after. He wants a life – an active life – of his own, like you've had. But that's been taken away from him. No wonder he's angry! So would you be in his position."

Frank leaned on his stick.

"But you and Annie mustn't give up. You've got to be strong for Wilf and somehow not let all his anger get you down. Your love's the best thing you can give him at the moment. It's probably all you can give him."

"That's just what Annie says. She plans to carry on with the visits and parcels of food and clean pyjamas and just take the cruel words and the silences and try to let them wash over her like water off a duck's back. But I just don't know if I'll be any good at that ..."

The cows were back in the field now. He latched the gate and leant against it. "And there's another thing on my mind." He took his pipe from his pocket and lit up. "We're just tenants here, as you probably know. I've always thought Wilf'd take over when I'm past it. Not for a few years yet, but still. Wilf loved workin' with me on this farm afore he went off to the war. It's in his blood, like. But if he can't see, how's he goin' to carry on here after me? We'll lose this place, Valley Farm, that's been our home for so many years. And where'll we go? I don't mind tellin' you it scares the livin' daylights out of me." He exhaled a stream of smoke.

"Oh, Frank. That's an unthinkable prospect." Florence thought for a moment. "It's not much, but it's all I can do to help. The six months I signed up to with the WLA expires at the end of May. This month. I want to sign up for another six – that's if you'll have me, of course. It's not much, but at least it'll give you a bit of a breathing space. And who knows what might happen in that time? Wilf might get his sight back ... the war might even come to an end."

"Yeah, you're right, Florence. It might never happen. But as for keepin' you on, we'd like it if you did. In fact you leavin' would put the cat among the pigeons good and proper."

Florence sat by her attic window as the sun was going down. She had 'Far From The Madding Crowd' open on her lap. She could not get enough of the way Hardy evoked his Wessex landscape. *Even Hardy would struggle to do justice to this sunset,* she thought. *Nowhere else I'd rather be ...*

Chapter 48

"Ow! Mum! Help me – I'm in agony!" Alf, came through the front door at the end of his school day.

"Alf! What's the matter?" Nell ran to the top of the stairs to see her son doubled up in pain, his hands clutching his abdomen. "You were fine when you went to school this morning, weren't you?"

"It started at dinnertime with bellyache. Now it's moved downwards. I can't stand up – it hurts too much."

Nell came down quickly and put her arm round Alf for support.

"I think I'm going to be sick." The boy groaned.

"Quick, then. Let's get you back outside." She opened the door and steered Alf into the front garden, where he vomited.

"Ugh!" he wiped his mouth and nose with his handkerchief. He tried again to straighten up, but the pain in his gut got the better of him and he stooped forward once more. "Ugh!"

Nell looked at his face. It was pallid, greyish. His skin felt clammy under her hand. "No better?"

Alf shook his head.

"I'll get you a drink of water to take the taste away. But first, we'd better get you to bed with a hot water bottle and see if that does the trick. Come on, Alf. Upstairs.

The hot water bottle did nothing to relieve the pain. Alf lay writhing, his bed sheets damp. Nell bathed his sweating forehead with a moist cloth.

Jane Mizen put her head round the door of the Ashfords' quarters. "Can I help with anythin'?"

Nell emerged from Alf's bedroom, a towel in her hand. "Oh, Jane, I'm so sorry about the mess in the garden. I'll clear it up as soon as I can …"

"Don't worry about that, my dear. Better outside than inside. But I knew somethin' was up soon as I saw it."

"It's Alf. He's got this terrible pain, and it's not getting any better even though he's been sick – in fact he seems to be getting worse."

"He must have a fever, being so sweaty. I think he needs to see the doctor. Can you send your girls?"

Nell called to Ellen and Grace, who were preparing tea for the twins.

"I'll go," said Grace, already making her way to the door. She ran all the way to the doctor's house and found Dr Gibbons clearing up at the end of his afternoon surgery. She arrived hot and out of breath, and knocked at the door of his consulting room. "Dr Gibbons, can you come? It's my brother. He's been sick and he's in awful pain."

Gibbons listened to her and turned to pick up his bag. He pulled the door closed behind him.

"What do you think it is, Doctor?"

"I really can't say till I've examined him," he said, but he stepped up the pace as they headed back to Factory Terrace.

He took the stairs two at a time, following Grace's directions to Alf's room. Nell was still mopping Alf's sweating body. She had opened the window a crack in an attempt to get some fresh air into the room, but did not want to put him in a draught. Dr Gibbons shouldered his way in. He palpated Alf's abdomen and took his temperature. The boy groaned again and drew his knees up.

"He's got a high temperature. I think he's suffering from appendicitis. I'm not going to prod and poke around too much now – he's in enough discomfort as it is. But we must get him to the hospital as soon as we can. They can make him much more comfortable there, and prepare him for surgery first thing tomorrow morning. Do you have access to any transport, Mrs Ashford?"

She shook her head. "No."

"Don't worry, I'll get my car. It'll only take a few minutes to get this young man up to Hedingham Road. Why don't you pack him a bag while I'm gone? I won't be long."

"Thank you, Doctor." Nell looked down at Alf. "I can't imagine how we'd manage to get him all the way to the hospital under our own steam."

Alf was virtually a dead weight in her arms as she helped him down the stairs. Grace followed with a holdall she'd packed for him. In the car the boy shivered and retched. Nell thought he might vomit again, but there was nothing, apparently, left in his stomach to bring up. The car sped up the High Street, lurching as it rounded the left hand corner at the Victoria Memorial. The doctor drew the car to a halt in front of the hospital's main doors. He ran inside in search of a nurse and a trolley, returning swiftly with both. He lifted Alf out of the car and laid him carefully on the trolley. The boy lay on his side with his knees drawn up. He looked awful and Nell stroked his hair. She looked anxious as the nurse began to wheel the trolley away.

"Try not to worry, Mrs Ashford," Dr Gibbons said. "The night staff can make him comfortable. If you leave his bag, I'll see that the nurse takes it to him."

"Is it safe to leave the operation till tomorrow, Doctor?"

"I know what you're thinking, Mrs Ashford. What if the appendix bursts before the morning? Of course, there's always a risk, but in my judgement it will be better to operate in the morning, when he'll be better prepared and I'll have more nursing support. Please try not to worry about the operation too much. We're quite used to doing appendectomies these days. Medical science doesn't stand still, you know."

"When … will I be able to see him?"

"I think the best thing is for me run you home now, and I'll let you know how it goes tomorrow. It's probably best to leave visiting till the day after – he'll be pretty groggy for a good while when he comes round."

"Yes," Nell said. "Yes. Thank you, doctor."

She barely slept that night, the 'what-ifs' playing and replaying in her mind.

Chapter 49

" ... and the doctor drove him in his car straight to the hospital for an operation on his appendix because it was infected. All full up with poison, it was, and Alf had terrible stomach ache – it made him sick and everything. And Dr Gibbons said if it had burst, he might have died!" Grace told Florence the whole story.

"He even had an anaes ... you know, they put him to sleep so he couldn't feel the pain."

"What a dreadful worry for you all. How's your mum been coping?"

"She was really worried and couldn't wait to see Alf after the operation, but the doctor wouldn't let her come till the day after because of the effects of the anaesth ... What *is* that word? I just can't remember it."

"It's 'anaesthetic', Gracie. How's Alf now?"

"Well, he's alright, but it still hurts a lot if he moves too much, and he's got to stay in hospital for ages while he heals up. Miss Moore says he's got to do school work while he's in there so that he doesn't fall behind." She sighed. "I expect I'll have to take it in to him, and probably help him with things we've learned in class. I can't help thinking he's going to get very fed up in there with all those old people."

"Not all the patients are that old – Mr and Mrs Davis' son's in there, and he's only twenty."

"Oh! That's good. They can cheer each other up."

"Well, maybe ..."

They talked as they pulled weeds from the kitchen garden. "Blessed weeds're growing like billy-o, what with this sunshine after rain," Florence said.

"Look – you can see there are peas growing in those pods, and tiny marrows." Grace examined the young growth.

"The marrows'll be huge in a week's time."

Annie came out of the dairy, a pat of butter in her hand. "That's lookin' a real treat. Best kitchen garden I've had in an age. Mind you, I haven't had the help these last few years, so the veg has had to look after itself, pretty much. Slugs have had a field day! This year, there'll be beans, cabbages, beets, carrots – all sorts – to spare. I'll be able to sell some to your friend's mother at the greengrocer's, I shouldn't wonder. Come on inside! I've got some scones to take down to the hospital, but I can spare a couple for you hard workers."

"My brother's in the hospital with your son, Mrs Davis. He's had acute appendicitis and he's even got stitches."

"Is that a fact? I hope he's feelin' better afore long. How long's he in there for, d'you think?"

"Oh, weeks, I think. What about Wilf?"

"They haven't said. Depends how he is. But I'd like to get him home soon as possible. He's got too much time to brood in there … Still, perhaps he'll start to enjoy your brother's company."

"I expect he will – Alf can be very funny."

"Gracie," Florence said, "there's a bucket of scraps for the hens by the door. Why don't you take them outside and scatter them in the run?" Grace grinned and ran outside.

"Annie." Florence buttered her scone. "Frank's told me about the threat to your future here if Wilf can't see. I know there's nothing I can do to help matters but if you ever feel like talking about it, I'm here, and glad to listen."

"That's good of you … I'm of a mind to face it like everythin' else we've had to tackle in life – do what seems right, work hard and put our trust in the good Lord. Ain't no use in meetin' trouble half way – it might never happen. And even if it do, sittin' around wringin' our hands won't help one bit."

"Good philosophy."

"It's the only one I've got. And, you know, you're one of our heaven sent blessin's, and if I'm honest, so's young Fritzy. He could've been a complete waste of time – or worse. Anyways, I'm grateful for your offer of a listenin' ear, Florence, dear. Frank and me we're a good team, but we don't always see things in the same light. Men, they've got a different way of lookin' at life."

Later when chores were done, Florence, Grace and Annie got into the dogcart with Grace's borrowed bicycle in the back. Cherry was not to be chivvied with all that weight on board, but the afternoon was pleasant as they made their unhurried way back to Halstead.

"I ought to be thinkin' of makin' some elderflower cordial while the flowers are at their best. Shame to let 'em go to waste." Annie carried a waxed paper bag containing the scones for the hospital inmates to share. "D'you think your brother would like one, Grace."

"I don't know if he'll be better enough yet. Oh! By the way, Aunt Flo, I almost forgot to tell you. I think I know who threw that brick at Fritzy – Mum told us what *really* happened to him. There's a boy in Ellen's class at school – Joe's his name. Joe Wilkes. He's been bragging about how his older brother, Billy – he's about 16 … well, he said he'd 'scored a bull's eye with a Hun'."

"Oh really, Gracie? Go on."

"I didn't understand what he meant at first, so I listened in to what he was saying. He was telling all his friends how his brother'd knocked a German off his bicycle. Cocky, he was, like it was something to be really proud of. All Joe's friends thought it was really funny and kept on laughing, but not everyone agreed. Doris and I, and Ellen and Madge – and some other people – said it was wrong and they should be ashamed of themselves, but Joe's lot were just rude to us, and wouldn't listen."

"Has anyone taken this Billy to task for what he did, Gracie?"

"Not that I know of. I think he got away without being seen, so there's no one can swear it was him … I don't really like Joe. He swaggers and bullies the younger children, so Doris and I steer clear of him and his lot. Some people in my class say that Billy's just the same."

"I know that family," Annie said. "Doesn't surprise me a bit. They're a bad lot by all accounts."

"What happened to Fritzy's left a really bad taste in my mouth. I wish there was something we could do to get back at them for Fritzy's sake." Florence bit her lip.

Chapter 50

"Can I draw you?" Alf asked each of the nurses.

"As long as you don't expect me to sit still," one said.

"Hey, that's really good, Alf. Can you do me now?" said another.

Alf Ashford was feeling better. Now that he was strong enough, on mild afternoons he pushed the tea trolley out to the terrace, passing the time of day with other patients. Those who felt well enough enjoyed his corny jokes. His attempts at engaging Wilf Davis in conversation did not, however, succeed. And so he gave Wilf a wide berth.

Lance Corporal Wilfred Francis Davis still couldn't see the point. All these people keeping him going. His mother bringing in little treats – scones, for God's sake. His father going on about the farm ... They didn't have a clue.

Nurses, with more work to do than seemed fair, bathing him, doing hospital corners on his sheets, trying to jolly him along. As if that were possible. It was all over for Wilfred Francis Davis. At 20. *For king and country? My arse*, he thought. *Why couldn't that friggin' shrapnel have done the job properly?* He sobbed and shook. And in the small hours nightmares dragged him back to sweaty consciousness with a reprise of the din of battle. The screams, the moaning ... was it in his head or was he crying out? He couldn't make it out ... until gentle hands smoothed his brow, quiet words calmed him in the dark.

I'd do away with myself right now for two pins. But how to? Where did they keep the drugs? Breaking into whatever secure room harboured them would be impossible anyway. How could he rig up a noose from his sheets? Smash a teacup and slash his wrists? They'd be onto him. They'd resuscitate him. Hunger strike? They'd force feed him, wouldn't they? A prisoner of war with a lifetime's sentence. He couldn't see the point. He couldn't see anything. At 20.

His mother said she wanted to get him back home to Valley Farm. Valley Farm, where he'd spent the best times of his life. Where he'd hoped for a future doing the things he loved. Taking over the reins from his father, doing as good a job – maybe even better. That was so obviously not going to happen for this son of the Colne Valley. Thanks to king and country.

Now there was a woman doing the work he used to do. And a German, for God's sake. What kind of mockery was that? Left on the scrap heap of life in the wake of a female and a Hun. His impotence, his humiliation was complete. Bring down the curtain.

Chapter 51

"*Please* come with us, Aunt Flo," said Grace. "Our mums won't let us go by ourselves, and we *do* want to see what goes on!"

As the late spring evenings lengthened, the Rec came alive every Saturday evening with music and dancing. Local bands came to play in the bandstand, drawing in the townspeople to stroll around the gardens, relax on the park benches under the gas lamps or dance on the mown oval of the dancing green.

The Rec. What memories! Florence could see Andrew even now, turning up his collar in the lamplight. The way they'd danced in the snow. The promise she'd made. *Andrew*, she thought. *Almost half of 1918's passed since that night, the last time I saw him ...*

"Well, I could do with a change of scene, I suppose," she said, "and it'd be nice to hear some music for once, other than my own mandolin. If it's alright with your mothers, I'll come into Halstead and change into something a bit tidier than boots and breeches. Then we can wander along together and see what all the fuss is about."

The Rec was already lively by the time Florence and the two girls arrived.

"Ah! It looks so pretty with the lights and the flowers," said Grace. "No wonder everyone comes here! It must take their minds off the war, don't you think, Aunt Flo?"

"Yes, Gracie. At least for a while."

"Let's take a turn round the gardens, and go and listen to the band," Doris said.

"Alright. You coming too, Aunt Flo?"

The atmosphere was almost merry. The sounds of conversation, laughter and a Viennese waltz drifted across the Rec. People were dancing to the rhythm.

Away from the music, at the far edge of the gardens, a group of boys and youths sat lounging on a bench. Their cigarette smoke cast a cloud in the lamplight. Their laughter sounded raucous.

"Look, Gracie! Over there! It's them Wilkes boys and their pals. Typical! Noisy lot – showin' off as usual! All they do is swagger. Let's steer clear, eh?"

Grace had never seen the older Wilkes boy before, but she recognised Joe, sitting with his arms folded across his chest, a cigarette hanging from his lips. She nodded. "I don't want to get mixed up with them." She turned to her aunt and pointed surreptitiously. "Aunt Flo, those are the boys I told you about – the ones who we think attacked Fritzy. Over there."

"Is that them?" Florence felt a rush of indignation. "They don't look a very savoury lot, do they? Come on, I don't want you two getting mixed up with them. Let's go round to the bandstand. They're playing a polka."

The dancers were responding to the lively tune.

"Hello, Gracie, how're you, then?" It was Windy, standing grinning with Lennie beside him. Doris turned, too, and smiled back at the two boys.

"Oh! Windy! I didn't know you'd be here. Do you and Lennie like to dance?"

"No fear," Lennie said, "you won't catch us at that caper! We just came down to have a look. Evenin', Miss Mundy."

"*Please,* Windy – just one little dance," said Grace.

"We'll do your arithmetic homework for you," Doris said.

"'Fraid not." Windy said, "There's some things blokes like us just can't do. And dancin' with girls is one of them."

"Oh well," said Doris, "too bad."

"But if it's alright with your aunt, Gracie, we could take a walk round the Rec and meet her up by the gate in half an hour or so. Is that alright, Miss Mundy?"

"Yes, Windy. I don't see why not."

The four youngsters walked away. Florence sat down on the nearest bench, content to watch and listen. So convivial. Yet ... the raucous noise from that bunch of bully boys kept intruding. *Their assault's gone unchallenged ... I can't leave it there ...* She stood up. Shoving her hands into the pockets of her jacket, she strode off in the direction of the young men. She almost felt Andrew's spirit spurring her on.

The Wilkes boys eyed her disagreeably as she approached them, but she stood her ground. She had no idea what she was going to say. But she had to stand up for Fritzy.

"You got a problem?" one of the group asked.

"I'd like to speak to Billy Wilkes. I think he's here."

"I'm 'ere." A tall youth with unkempt dark hair sticking out of a scruffy cap sat on the back of a park bench, his boots on the seat. He was chewing on a matchstick. "What d'you want?"

"I've heard you may have been responsible for attacking a defenceless man on a bicycle a couple of weeks ago."

"Oh! You've heard that, have you?" Billy Wilkes said. "So what?"

"You should be ashamed of yourself. He's an innocent man."

"Oh yeah? Says who? You? But he's a German. A Hun. How do you know he's innocent? Jus' 'cos you ain't seen him kill no British boys don't mean he ain't. He's one of them lot. Our enemies."

"No," Florence shook her head. "You're wrong. He hates this war as much as anyone does!"

"Oh yeah?" Billy Wilkes said again. "Well, you'll have to prove it to convince me. As far as I'm concerned, he's filth. Vermin." He leant forward. Going to extravagant lengths to produce saliva, he summoned a ball of it into his mouth and spat. Florence looked at the glob of spittle as it ran down her lapel, speechless with revulsion.

"Be thankful I didn't spit in your kisser, Hun-lover. An' you better watch out no bricks come flyin' in your direction. Come on boys. No sense in wastin' more time on her."

They whooped and guffawed as they left. Florence took out a handkerchief and rubbed furiously at the damp trickle on her jacket. She felt sick.

On the way back to Factory Terrace, she was glad Grace, Doris and the two boys were there to talk about the clear night sky, the moon and stars, keeping the mood cheerful.

Later, when Grace had gone to bed, Florence sat with her sister in the quiet of the evening.

"Thanks for being their chaperone, Flo, I appreciate it."

Florence nodded and smiled a twisted little grin. "The Rec's got a lot of memories for me. It was strange going there after all these months ... How's Alf?"

"He's well on the road to recovery now. And having a good time. The nurses and patients all spoil him – he'll be a nightmare when he gets home."

"Mmm." Florence picked at her fingernails.

"Alright, Flo. Spit it out. What's happened?"

Florence winced at her sister's choice of words, but went ahead and told Nell the unpalatable story.

Nell shook her head. "Well what do you expect if you let yourself get mixed up with people like that? You're still like that Don What's-His-Name. Fanciful dreamer. So naïve."

"Quixote ... Is it naïve to stick up for people who aren't in a position to defend themselves? Is it naïve to speak out against wrongdoing?"

"Well, no, not as such, but you'll never make any headway with the likes of that riff-raff. You'll always come off worse."

Florence supposed Nell was right, but she still felt she had the moral high ground. "Does that mean I should do nothing?"

Nell didn't answer straight away. " ... You know, they might not be the only ones who would spit on you for consorting with a German –"

"I'm not 'consorting' with him, I just work with him!"

"Alright, alright, I know," Nell made a calming gesture with her hands. "Lots of people might agree with the Wilkeses where Germans are concerned. I'm not keen on them myself, if I'm honest, given the war they brought about has deprived me of a husband and my children of their father for all this time. And I still don't know if he'll come back in one piece – or when, or in what shape."

Florence had Alf's bed to herself that night. She lay awake till the small hours.

Chapter 52

Mostly, Wilf kept his one unbandaged eye closed so no one could tell whether he was asleep or not. That was fine by him. He was aware of a boy on the ward. The chit-chat with staff and other patients. Getting better, he was, curse him. No! He took that back. He wished the lad no ill will, but he did wish he'd just put a sock in the prattle.

Alf's round with the tea trolley became a highlight of the daily routine in Halstead hospital, and searching for variety and entertainment as his recovery progressed, the boy began to embellish it with little mimes. He had dusted off his Charlie Chaplin impression, improvising the famous moustache with a small square of brown paper stuck to his top lip with jam, and the bowler hat with an enamel chamber pot.

A little wave of laughter drifted across the ward to where Wilf Davis sat. He raised his head and turned it in the direction of the sound, and, without thinking, he opened his eye … Was he imagining it? He blinked, raised a hand to rub the eye and opened it again. No. As faint as it was possible to be, Wilf made out a shadow. A smudge. A hint of light and dark. And as the shadow moved, it synchronised with the sound of that boy with the tea trolley.

"Hey, boy. I'll have a cup of tea."

Alf moved towards him and the shadow got bigger. "Here you are, Mr Davis."

Wilf felt breathless. "Ta …" he said. But he knew. What he was seeing – *seeing* – was the nebulous image of another human being.

Chapter 53

So stupid, Florence kept thinking. She felt humiliated by the incident at the Rec. The self-doubt she thought she'd conquered came creeping back. She kept her head down, working hard, only passing the time of day with Frank, Annie and Holger when she had to. She derived solace in her communion with the unquestioning animals, whose closeness soothed her.

Things on the farm were going smoothly and there were no foreseeable problems, as long as the weather co-operated. It should have been a time of contentment and anticipation as the crops throve and the farm looked forward to boisterous haymaking, a promising harvest and the profitable marketing of its produce, but for Florence, the joy had gone out of it.

"I'll go up, then." She said to Annie and Frank after supper. "I want to write to Andrew."

Andrew. He'll understand. The only person she knew who would.

" *... and he spat at me, Andrew. It was so disgusting. I wanted those boys to see they'd acted unjustly, but they just called me a 'Hun lover' and threatened me with a flying brick. I felt so useless and humiliated. My sister called me naïve. Maybe I am, but I don't see why they should just get away with it. What they did to Fritzy was vicious – and cowardly.*

I miss you, Andrew. Keep safe.

***

Andrew's letters stopped coming. Florence felt it was the last straw. Did he disapprove of the last letter's revelations? *Surely not,* she thought. *Is he just too busy? Maybe. A casualty? Dear God, no.*

After another day in the potato field, Florence came in. Annie was waiting for her in the farmhouse kitchen. Florence took her boots off at the door and set them on the doorstep. "Have you got some old newspaper I can use to catch the mud off these boots when I scrape them? Please, Annie." Annie handed her a fistful of sheets.

"Here. Stick them on this. Then come in and sit awhile. You can toast some teacakes while I'm cookin'. Fritzy gone back, has he?"

"Yes. His time's up and he'll be on his way back into Halstead. I think he's almost as worn out as I am today. Those spuds kill your back."

"I can fill you a bath, if you'd like, dear. Frank's walkin' the crops with Jack, so he'll be a while yet."

"No, don't worry, Annie." She sighed. I'm happy just to sit. "Have you got any of that elderflower cordial you made? I'd love a glass – I'm really thirsty. Shall we sit outside? The evening's so lovely."

Florence sat on the farmhouse step, watching the sun dip toward the horizon, setting wispy clouds aflame. Annie soon joined her, passing her a glass of the sweet cordial. She eased herself onto the step.

"How are you, Annie?" Florence wanted to get in first. "How's Wilf doing? I haven't asked you about him for days … I've been in a world of my own … Sorry." She looked down at her hands, nails still mud-encrusted. She interlaced her fingers about her knees. "I promised to be a wise counsellor and try to help you cope with your worries with my sound advice. And I haven't been. Sorry," she said again.

"Don't you worry about us, Florence, dear. It was kind of you to offer your help. But you know, I take all my concerns to the good Lord. And if I'm honest, I don't need no other help, because I know He listens and looks out for us. It's worryin' times for a lot of folk, but we all got to make the best of it." She smiled a gentle smile at Florence and shrugged. "And as for Wilf, nothin' much new to report. But thanks for askin'." Annie smoothed her apron and looked out on the sunset, its radiance reflecting a glow in her face. "But Frank and me, we can see that somethin's not right with you. Don't get me wrong." She placed a hand on Florence's shoulder. "Your work's top-notch as ever – in fact we've been fearful that you've been overdoin' it. Even the German boy mentioned it to Frank the other day." She rearranged herself on the step and turned toward Florence. "Is it young Captain Forbes? Only I couldn't help noticin' his letters have dried up. But you were down in the dumps before that."

"Andrew not writing is the last straw, Annie."

"You know, keepin' worries to yourself ain't good for you … Do you want to tell me about it?"

Florence took a breath and the floodgates opened. "I've been bottling something up since well before I came to Halstead … Something happened to me back in London that I haven't told another living soul about. Not even Andrew. And certainly not my sister. What happened really shook me and I completely lost my self-respect. It was hateful. I felt violated … I still feel ashamed about it … It's haunted me ever since."

"Go on."

Florence took a mouthful of the cordial. "There was this man. Harry Bartholomew was his name … I can hardly bear to say it. He was interesting, intelligent, I thought. We went out together. I liked him – felt attracted to him. But he tried to force himself on me … in an alleyway … nearly succeeded …" Her voice dropped to a whisper. "I must have behaved like a … slut. That's what he called me …"

She looked at Annie. Was she shocked? The older woman's expression gave nothing away. But she reached out a hand and again laid it on Florence's shoulder.

"I felt loathsome. After that I came to doubt everything I was doing in life. It just seemed like a complete waste of time. Self-indulgent. Pointless. And, if I'm honest, I think it was. Tilting at windmills … That's why I jumped at the chance to come here with Nell and the children. And then the Women's Land Army gave me a reason to hold my head up again. Coming here has meant the world to me, Annie. You and Frank gave me back my self-esteem."

"It wasn't anythin' we did, Florence. You did it yourself with the way you've pitched in. We'd never have guessed you had so much unhappiness in your heart."

"I thought I'd conquered it – until last Saturday night on the dancing green, that is."

"Why? What happened?"

"Well … I confronted those louts who lobbed the brick at Fritzy. Grace and Doris pointed them out. The girls steered clear and I let them go off with their friends. It gave me the opportunity to give those thugs the length of my tongue – I just couldn't help myself! They spat at me, threatened me and laughed, Annie. Called me a Hun-lover … Naïve, Nell said. Why couldn't I just keep quiet and do the sensible thing? Now I feel all that shame and humiliation weighing down on me again."

"But now you've got Captain Forbes – he thinks the world of you."

"I know he does – he tells me in every … letter … But you know … you *do* know, because we've talked about it. In many ways I feel as though Andrew and I are a port in a storm for each other. Him for me because he's a fine person and he's offering an antidote to the shame of my past and a safe life. And me for him because I'm part of his vision for a sunlit future."

Annie nodded.

"But it's not real, Annie!" She broke off and studied her dirt-packed finger nails. Moments passed before Florence sniffed loudly and wiped her nose on the back of her hand. Annie sat patiently and stroked her hair. Florence straightened her back and cleared her throat. Her fingers played with the ring suspended round her neck. "I wrote to Andrew and told him about what happened with the Wilkeses. I thought he would think I'd done the right thing. But even he's gone silent on me. Without all this," she gestured towards the Colne Valley, darkening now after the sunset. "Without you and a proper job to do, I feel as though I'd go under. And it's all of my own making."

"You're bein' too hard on yourself, Florence. Standin' up to be counted, sayin' what you believe's right – that's *good*. And not enough people are prepared to stick their necks out – specially where the likes of the Wilkeses are concerned. It takes real courage to do what you did."

"Courage or foolhardiness?"

Annie rocked back and forth on the step. "I said courage, an' I mean courage." She paused. "In a way, your sister's right. You'll never get through to bullies like the Wilkes boys. But that doesn't mean you got to hold your tongue and let them get away with it. That's the coward's way out. And I know you're no coward." Annie paused to take stock. "I bet there'll be a letter on its way afore long … But you know, Florence, you're goin' to have to tell him sooner or later just how you feel. You've got to come clean, else it ain't fair."

Fair. The same word Harry had used. Only this time she knew it was legitimate. There would be no resolution, no restoration of self-respect without honesty. "I know. But I can't do it while he's over there. It must be face to face. When he gets back."

"You've been very candid with me, Florence. It can't have been easy for you to reveal them secrets you've been keepin' all this time. Specially as you've been so ashamed of the memories. But now you've got to convince yourself that it wasn't you're fault. Now. I'm no clairvoyant, but I'm inclined to think that now you've got it off your chest, you'll start to put it behind you. And if it's any consolation, what you've told me ain't shocked me at all. I think all the more of you for your frankness."

Chapter 54

"Have you seen any improvements in Lance Corporal Davis' condition?" Dr Gibbons asked the hospital Matron. The soldier's unwillingness – or inability? – to engage with anyone or anything perplexed him.

"None at all, Doctor. He's just as uncommunicative as ever. And there's no evidence of his sight returning."

"Hm. It must be the shell shock. Interesting. They're making progress with treating the condition up in Edinburgh, apparently. I read about it in *the Lancet*. A doctor called Rivers reckons it's all about repressing painful memories that's the main cause. If only we could get Davis to open up."

"I don't know how on earth you'd do that, Doctor."

"No. Neither do I. Our job's just to treat him for his lost sight. And it's all we've got the time and skills for. Pity."

Wilf had not trusted the evidence – of his own eyes – enough to tell anyone. What if it just as suddenly disappeared again? What if this was it? Vague shadows. Light from dark. What use was that ever going to be to him? Light at the end of the tunnel? He thought not.

When the day of Alf Ashford's discharge arrived, Wilf was not sorry to see him go. The ward would be a much quieter place without him.

The staff felt differently, though. "You've been a ray of sunshine round here, Master Ashford," Matron said.

"I'll miss you all," Alf said to the nurses, "but I can't wait to get back home." He sat on his bed, his belongings clustered around him. "I expect my mum'll be here soon."

Nell came in with Grace still in her school uniform, smiling at the prospect of Alf coming home. Grace ran across the ward to Alf's bedside, a piece of paper flapping in her hand.

"Look, Alf. It's a painting I've done – of poppies I saw growing in one of the cornfields at Valley Farm. I couldn't wait to show you. I'm quite proud of it. What do you think?"

"It's not bad, Gracie, but I'd say they're are a bit ... bright. Are you sure you've got it right?" he asked, holding the painting at arm's length, and screwing up his eyes. "The red's a bit strong for the rest of the picture, if you ask me."

"But they're *like* that, Alf. You haven't seen them – you were in here when they started flowering. You wait. They're *brilliant!*"

"Are you ready to go, Alf? Only I don't want to be too long. There's the twins' tea to think of, and I've left a hotpot on the range. Grace, why did you have to bring that thing with you? Couldn't it have waited till we got back? You'll have bags of time for all this then."

"Sorry, Mum. I …"

Grace felt a hand on her shoulder. It was Wilf Davis.

"Oh! It's Mr Davis, isn't it?"

"Yes …" he paused, hesitant. "Show me your picture … Please?"

"Of course. But you can't see … Can you?"

She put the piece of paper on Wilf's bed cover, laying it smooth and straight. He inclined his head towards it and laid an index finger on the painting where the poppies were clustered in vivid scarlet. His finger moved across the paper, resting on each splash of colour.

"Flanders. Like the blood of soldiers." He began to shake and tears welled up. The agonising memories. The harrowing sights. Real again.

Nell turned to face the young soldier. "Does anyone know that you can see? The staff here? Your parents?"

"No." Wilf wiped his nose on his hand and sniffed. "And it's my business. So I'll thank you to keep quiet, missus."

"If that's what you want. But you'll have to ask yourself what's the point of keeping it to yourself."

The point. The point. Wilf still didn't know.

Nell gathered Alf's belongings together. "Good afternoon to you, Corporal Davis."

"Goodbye, Mr Davis. Good luck." Grace picked up her painting. She turned and caught up with her family as they reached the exit.

Chapter 55

Florence felt a sense of relief since her conversation with Annie. She felt she was no longer living a lie. At last. She started smiling again. Everyone noticed.

It was a wet Wednesday in late June. Florence had seen to loading the morning milk churn onto Swank Everitt's cart and was just latching the gate when she spotted a figure limping up the lane. As he got closer, she could see he was leaning on a stick. The left sleeve of his greatcoat was pinned up and hung limply from his shoulder. The man wore a military cap. Her heart lurched. She opened the gate again and ran into the lane.

"It's Miss Mundy, ain't it?" the soldier said as he drew level with her.

"Yes."

"Thank Gawd. I thought I'd never get 'ere."

Florence looked hard at the man. He had a sergeant's three stripes on his sleeve.

"Of course!" she said. "I remember you from the Christmas party. It's Sergeant ..."

"Crawford, miss. Them was 'appier days."

"Sergeant Crawford. You must be soaked. Come on inside and dry off. It's awful weather for June." She led the way into the farm kitchen. Annie was busy in the dairy and Frank was out with Holger and Jack mending a gap in a hedge with a willow hurdle. "Can I get you a hot drink, Sergeant?" Florence took his wet coat from him and hung it near the range.

"If it's not too much trouble. And call me Arthur. Please."

Arthur Crawford sat down on the settle. His right leg stuck straight out, his heel resting on the hearth rug, no bend at the knee.

"Can I get you a stool to rest your leg on, Arthur? It looks uncomfortable."

"No ... no. Not to worry. It don't hurt no more."

Florence boiled the kettle and brewed a pot of tea, setting it by the range to keep warm. "You've been in the wars, it seems ... Oh! I'm sorry. Stupid thing to say ..."

"Miss Mundy. I didn't come here for your sympathy, welcome though it is. I've got some news for you which I promised I'd deliver in person."

"Oh?" Florence searched his face and saw only grief written on it. "It's Captain Forbes, isn't it?"

The sergeant still held his cap in his hand. He looked down at it and nodded. "Yes, miss." Crawford swallowed hard. He was unable to say more for a good minute. "I'm afraid he's dead." His voice was barely audible.

Florence poured the tea, her hand unsteady. Crawford put his cap down beside him on the settle and took the enamel mug from her.

"Can you tell me how it happened? When it happened? Take your time."

"Well." He cleared his throat. "We got sent to this place called the Chemin des Dames Ridge." He pronounced the place name in his London accent. "It was French-held territory since April last year. Funny thing, we'd gone there to recuperate after we'd been in Flanders. Horrible business. We was exhausted. Then, without warnin' the Germans attacked. We was under the command of a Frenchie. Stupid bloke, name of Duchene. He insisted the Tommies take up the front line trenches and Hamilton Gordon couldn't do nothin' about it. The Boche come at us like a hurricane. We hardly knew what hit us." Crawford drank from his mug of tea. "Loads of Tommies bought it that day – and Frenchies, too. The Boche seemed unstoppable. Anyway, they kept goin' and Captain Forbes was still commandin' what was left of our company. On the third day, 30th May, he went up to the Obs. Post. It was all quiet at the time. We don't know how it happened. Maybe the sun caught the lens of his field glasses – though he was always dead careful about things like that. Long and short of it is, a sniper got him. Clean shot. He didn't know a thing about it … Bloody waste, just like all of it, if you'll pardon my language, miss. The daftest thing is that the whole thing petered out a few days later. The Boche got so far ahead of their supply line that they couldn't go no further. Just like on the Somme back in March. The ruddy war's goin' nowhere. Except it's still claimin' brave lives like the Captain's."

He paused and Florence struggled to take it in. It was the Grand Old Duke of York thing all over again. She knew Andrew would have been thinking that.

Arthur Crawford put down his mug and reached into the pocket of his uniform jacket. He brought out an envelope and a flat tin. He handed them to Florence. "He asked me to give you these, if anything happened to him. He knew you'd never hear from official sources, not bein' next of kin or nothin'.."

The Snout Tin. She opened it and there lay the tortoiseshell comb she'd given him. As a good luck talisman. Her hand went to the ring, Andrew's grandmother's ring, still suspended around her neck. She fingered it for a moment, knowing in her heart of hearts that things would not have been any different if she had refused to take it from him.

"See, I lost the arm at Lys and was still recoverin' when we come to Chemin des Dames, so I was behind the lines, doin' a desk job. He thought I'd be more likely to survive. He wrote the letter when he found out our lads was goin' up front."

She turned the Snout Tin over and over in her hands, tears welling in her eyes.

"A man couldn't have had a better gaffer than Captain Forbes. He looked after his men like they was his own brothers."

Florence sat, her mind drifting back to her last view of Andrew lighting a cigarette under the lamp light.

"Well." Crawford struggled to his feet, his cane supporting his stiff leg. "Shrapnel wound. Bugg … sorry … messed up me knee joint. Won't get no better than this. It's what's held me up from getting to see you … I'm sorry I couldn't get here sooner. At least it's all over for me now. I think I've done me bit. Anyway, I'd best be on me way. You'll want time to read what he wrote you."

"No," Florence said, though he was right about the letter. "I can't let you walk all the way back to Halstead. You've more than done your duty by him – and me. And I'm so grateful. Please. Stay and have a bowl of soup. Then I'll take you back in the dog cart. Where are you headed?"

"I'm off back to the Smoke. Battersea. That's home to me. Family's expectin' me. I'll give you my address if you like – just in case there's anything I can do … You never know. Perhaps you'd like to write it down."

"Yes. I would. And then I'll take you to the station." She cut a thick slice of bread to go with the soup. While he ate it, she went out to harness the pony.

Chapter 56

By the time Florence got back to Valley Farm, the day was half gone and she was behind with her chores. She turned Cherry out in the paddock with the other horses and stowed the harness in the tack room. At least the animals were all living out now – fewer stable duties – but there was still plenty to do. She hadn't even swept out the cow byre since milking this morning.

There was still a good half hour before afternoon milking, so she went up to the hay loft, grateful for the absence of anyone else in the yard. The loft was almost empty, awaiting this year's hay crop. There was, though, a small pile remaining from last year at the far end. The scent of summer lingered. She made her way to it, making a mental note to sweep the loft before haymaking. She sat down, pulled the envelope from her pocket and ran her finger over her name, written in dark blue ink in Andrew's clear hand. Drawing the letter from within, she unfolded it.

My darling Florence, she read,

By the time this reaches you, you will know my fate. I've known we're in a really risky situation for some days now, and I'm aware that anything may happen. My trusty sergeant, Arthur Crawford, has promised to get this letter to you if he makes it out of here and I don't, and I know he'll do everything in his power to do so.

So, my sweet girl. The future we dreamed of is not to be. But I go to meet my maker a happy man for having known and loved you. I've told you enough times what it means to me to have you in my heart. There have been grim times these last few months, but always, dearest Florence, thoughts of you have kept me going and pulled me back from the despair of black moments.

When I think of you, I think of the clear summer air of the English countryside, fragrant with newly cut grass and noisy only with the buzzing of bees.

We have the song of larks here, you know. Right in the midst of this lunatic hellhole, the fluid notes of these little feathered specks of life are thrilling enough to keep my hopes up.

One of the boys lent me a volume of poetry by a fellow soldier by the name of Edward Thomas. He was killed last year before his poems were published, poor man. He did write about the war but he wrote much more about the country and the ways of country life. I have you in my mind whenever I read them. They've been a tremendous comfort, and I know you'd love them, if you can get hold of a copy. Read the one called 'Haymaking' and think of me, thinking of you as I read it.

Florence paused to wipe the tears from her eyes.

Now, my dear girl. I must speak of the future. Your future. Two things I would ask of you: to be true to yourself and to be happy. If you can do both these things, your life will be a fulfilling one and you will spread your infectious goodness to others.

Yesterday I received your letter about your contretemps on the dancing green. I was never more proud of you than when you told me about what you'd done – how brave you'd been in the face of a loutish mob. It confirmed to me that your spirit is as irrepressibly bold as I believed it to be. It's one of the reasons I love you as much as I do.

I hope you don't mind, but I shared that news with our Padre. Nice chap called Pobjoy. Quite difficult keeping the faith with what he's seen on active duty, I should think. He gave me a reference from scripture which confirms that you did the right thing – not only in my eyes, but in the prized estimation of none other than St Paul. It comes from 1 Thessalonians chapter 5.

I won't quote all of it; you can find it for yourself in verses 13 to 22, but here's a taste of some of the advice he gave those worthy people: 'Be at peace among yourselves; warn them that are unruly (just as you did, Florence, my love!); support the weak; be patient to all men.'

Now for the really important bits: 'See that none render evil for evil unto any man; but ever follow that which is good both among yourselves and to all men.' No arguing with that.

And now I must close. Heaven knows, I hope you never read this letter. But if you do, I want you to know that thoughts of you will be my dying comfort. Live your life, my dearest, but never forget your devoted

Andrew
Aisne, France
May, 1918

When Florence did not appear for supper, Frank set out from the farmhouse with Jack to look for her. Annie had known something was amiss, having watched from the dairy window as Florence ushered the injured serviceman into the kitchen and later as she drove him away in the dog cart. She'd seen her return, but sensed her need to be alone. *She'll find me if she needs me,* she thought.

Frank and Holger had fitted afternoon milking into the day's work. The farmer had sent the German off with a note apologising for his late return, explaining the reasons, and begging for him not to be put on a charge. But neither Frank nor Annie had any idea of Florence's current whereabouts, and she hadn't responded to their calls bellowed from the back door. Annie had checked the attic room. No sign.

The rain had stopped and the early evening was mild with the scent of damp soil and a mist rising from the fields. Frank was considering where Florence might have gone. But Jack crossed the yard at a run, his tail wagging. He stopped at the foot of the hayloft steps, looked at Frank and barked. "You reckon she's up there, do you, boy?" Jack looked up the wooden stairway, woofed and wagged again. "Alright. Let's have a look."

Frank took the steps two at a time and paused on the threshold of the loft. He could see her, coiled like a cat on the one remaining pile of hay. He moved towards her. Hearing not a sound, he thought she must be asleep, but as he approached her, he could see her ribcage convulsing with silent sobbing. He knelt beside her and noticed she was hugging a piece of paper to her chest. He laid his arm across her shoulders and let her crying work itself out.

It was long minutes before she lifted her face. She raised herself up and stretched out her arms towards Frank, who embraced her and stroked her damp hair. "Poor old tuppence. Life can be so cruel."

He could hear Annie in the yard calling his name, but he was sure his dog would make it clear to her where he'd gone, so he remained quiet, giving Florence all the time she needed. By and by, Frank's gentle cradling calmed Florence, and her sobs subsided, leaving her limp. He helped her to her feet and she carefully put the letter back in its envelope and then into her pocket. Supporting her every step, they made their way back to the loft door. "Let's get you back inside. But take care on them steps – we don't want no mishaps, now, do we?" He went down the stairway before her to catch her if she slipped. At the foot of the ladder, Jack laid a silky ear against her leg and whimpered. She felt the dog's warmth. Frank and Jack walked Florence back to the farmhouse. At the door, Annie was waiting, her arms outstretched.

"In you come. Sit yourself down. My word, this is a rum do and no mistake."

Florence began to regain a sense of where she was. "The milking ..."

"Don't you worry about that, Florence, my dear. Fritzy and me, we done it an hour ago. It's all took care of."

Annie handed Florence a nip of whisky and another to Frank. "I think we can all do with a tot of this. Normally I don't touch the stuff, but even I'm willin' to make an exception today."

The clock on the mantle ticked away the minutes.

"D'you know what?" Florence said, breaking the long silence, "it's such a silly thing, but all I can think of is that I haven't got a picture of him. You see, I always thought I'd see him again ... His family didn't know about me, as far as I know, and I don't know where they live. I ought to write to them ..."

"What about the sergeant that brought you the news. Could he help you?" Annie said.

"Yes ... He wrote down his address. In Battersea. I'll write to him ..."

"D'you want a bite of supper, Florence, dear?"

"No. Thank you, Annie ... I couldn't touch a thing."

"Can I get your bed ready? Would you like to turn in? You look worn out."

"Quite honestly I don't want to be by myself. If you don't mind, I'd prefer to sit here with you and Frank and Jack and just think. And remember."

Jack sat himself down at Florence's feet and laid his head on her knee. She put out a hand to stroke him.

Chapter 57

The fine weather returned and Florence took solace from the sounds and scents of the countryside. Andrew had been right, realising as she herself did how important the natural world was to her. Annie and Frank let her speak as the mood took her.

"I don't understand how anyone could be a sniper. How could you cultivate a skill intended only to kill? Just end a life you know nothing about …?" She reread his letter what seemed like a thousand times. "He thought I did the right thing about the Wilkes boys, Annie."

"See, I knew he'd be on your side. Didn't I say so?"

"Yes, you did. But I'm pleased to have heard it from him. To know for sure how he felt."

"Take your time before you get back to work, Florence. Don't knock yourself out," said Frank. "We want you in good shape for haymakin' afore long."

Haymaking. That poetry book Andrew mentioned, she thought. "I'm going to get back to work as soon as you'll let me, Frank. Work's like a dose of medicine to me."

"Let's say Monday, then. There's no denyin' we can do with the help, but what's happened will have taken it out of you, and you'd be mad to push yourself too hard too soon."

"That's sound advice, Frank, I know, but I need to be active."

Working in the kitchen garden in the pleasant summer sunshine fulfilled that need. Frank didn't try to stop her.

"You could pull some beetroots for me, Florence," said Annie, "I can get on with bottlin' them while they're nice an' young. Nothin' Frank likes better than a beetroot sandwich with plenty of pepper on … Come to think of it, it was one of Wilf's favourites, too."

The soil was easy to dig after recent showers. She pulled the ruby roots from the earth and laid them lengthwise in a trug, their leaves falling over the end of it in a glossy cascade. Holger crossed the yard and made his way to the vegetable garden, his boots soundless on the grass. It was the first time he'd seen her since he'd heard the news.

Florence looked up at him silhouetted against the blue sky, his shirt sleeves rolled to his elbows. "Fritzy …" She stood and leaned on her mud-caked fork.

"I have heard … what happened to your … friend."

She examined the freshly pulled beet in her hand.

"I want to say sorry. Not just for myself … but also for my country. I am ashamed."

She looked up at him. She could see sincerity in his eyes. "Thank you … I think there are many men on both sides who should feel ashamed. Not only your countrymen. I don't blame you."

He bowed and tried to click his heels together but the mud on his boots got in the way. "Ach!" He shrugged. Florence gave him a little smile. Holger stood where he was, shifting his weight from one foot to the other, trying to find the words to say something else to her.

"Go on, Fritzy. I'll help you out if you get stuck."

"Stuck?"

"If you don't know the words. In English, I mean."

"It is thank you I want to say to you, Florence. Frank, he tell me what you said. To ze boys who hurt me. It was gutt. Brave. Is all."

"It's alright, Fritzy."

***

"Now I come to think of it, we'll be goin' into Halstead on Sunday," Frank said to Florence. "After church it'll be another frustratin' trip to the hospital. But Annie, she's determined not to give up – or chide Wilf for the rudeness he hurls at her. I can't stand it, myself. I have to go outside and light my pipe to calm myself down. But what I meant to say is, you'd be welcome to come with us, if you'd like to. Only I was thinkin', you ain't told your sister yet, have you? D'you think perhaps it's time you did? Get it over with, like?"

"Yes, Frank. Thank you. Count me in. If I may, I'll come to church with you. I think I'd like to."

But there was one nagging issue she needed to address first. She sought a moment with Annie. "It must have crossed your mind, just as it has loomed large in mine, that I'll never have to deliver that painful message to Andrew. That I wasn't in love with him, I mean."

"Yes, of course it has, my dear. You must be feelin' very mixed up about that."

"Well, you know, actually I'm not. In fact I'm very clear in my own mind, and I wanted to tell you."

"Go on."

"I've asked myself again and again if I'm glad to be let off the hook, so to speak. And I'd be lying if I said I'm not relieved that I haven't got to do it. But. I'm absolutely certain I'd rather face him and tell him a million times if I could bring him back. His loss is a tragedy for me, for everyone that knew him or might have got to know him in the future. Unmitigated."

Annie squeezed her arm.

***

"Aunt Flo!" Grace said. "Did you enjoy the service?"

Florence nodded. She had found herself giving thanks (*to whom?* she wondered) for having known Andrew. She saw the difference he had made to her. The way he had loved her unconditionally.

"Yes, Gracie, I did. Especially the singing."

"Are you coming home to see us?"

"Yes, I am." They set off down the High Street. Doris stayed with them as far as her family's shop. "Aunt Flo, I know something really exciting, but I'm not allowed to tell you," Grace said, once they were on their own. "It's about Wilf Davis, but he swore us to secrecy and I haven't told a soul. Not even Doris."

"Well, that's good. You must keep your promises or no one will trust you. It's important. Anyway, I'm sure Mr and Mrs Davis will find out what there is to know. And really, it is *their* business. Not ours."

"I've got some news, too," Florence said after a short while. "But I'm not going to tell you till we get back to your house, so everyone can hear it together."

The roses were blooming in the border beside the path to the front door in Factory Terrace. Their perfume filled the air. Alf opened the door, and Grace barged in, cuffing him round his ear.

"Let us in! Let us in! Aunt Flo's here."

"Alright, alright! Keep your hair on – no need to push and shove." Alf jostled her as she crossed the threshold.

"Grace! Alf!" Nell's voice was strident. "Pack that in! I don't want you fighting. Remember, Alf's been very ill – you might do him an injury!"

"Hello there, young man," Florence said to Alf. "Long time no see! Are you better?"

"Yes, thank –" He was cut off in mid-sentence as his sister elbowed him to one side.

"Grace!" Nell, strode down the hall. "I shan't tell you again! Behave yourself! Go and put the kettle on, and be quick about it! Come in, Flo." Nell ushered her sister into the living kitchen. "Sorry about that. They've been impossible since Alf came out of hospital. So full of it! Shall I send them off to the Rec. so we can have some peace and quiet?"

"No, Nellie, don't do that. They might as well hear what I've come to tell you. Grace already knows I've got something to say."

"You have some news?" Seeing Florence's pinched expression, she was pretty sure it wasn't good.

They sat down in the garden at the back of the house while the twins threw tufts of grass at each other. Ellen brought the tea and some buttered fruit loaf, then sat on the low garden wall with Alf and Grace.

"Killed instantly, apparently," Florence told them. "He won't have known a thing about it. I suppose that's a blessing of sorts."

The children stared at their aunt.

"I remember him so well from the Christmas party," said Ellen. "I can't believe he's dead."

"Aunt Flo, I'm so sorry. You must be feeling very sad," Grace said.

"Flo. How dreadful." Nell held her sister's hand for a moment. "And what a waste of that poor man's life. You have my very deepest sympathy." She was quiet for a moment, then cleared her throat. "Will you stay and have something to eat with us?"

"Not this time, Nellie. I've promised to go back with Frank and Annie. They'll be ready to set off soon. I'd best be making tracks for the hospital."

"Well, let's hope they'll be getting some better news soon," Nell said, knowing full well they would. Grace and Alf exchanged glances. Florence noticed, but said nothing.

The moment she saw Annie and Frank outside the hospital, Florence could tell something had happened.

"Well, I'm jiggered!" Frank was saying, shaking his head and making much of the pony.

"I can't believe it, neither!" Annie was almost in tears.

Seeing Florence approach, Annie trotted towards her. "He can see, Florence! Wilf's getting his sight back! Just in the one eye, of course, but still. It's like a miracle."

"Oh! That's wonderful! I couldn't be more pleased for you all."

They climbed into the dog cart and Frank sent Cherry forward with a click of his tongue.

"They say he's known about it for days, but he hasn't let on. He said he thought he might lose it again, so he kept quiet. Then one of the nurses saw him light his own cigarette out on the terrace. Normally someone else does it for him – one of the other patients. He was a bit furtive-like, but she was sure of what she saw. So she told the Matron, and the Matron told Dr Gibbons, who came to see him. He shone a light in Wilf's eye, got him to follow his finger and suchlike. And he confirmed it."

"That's such good news, Annie. How is he in himself?"

"We-ell," Frank took up the story. "He's still pretty despondent. You'd think he'd be jumpin' for joy, but I don't think he quite knows what to make of it yet. I suppose the anger he's been feelin' all these months'll take a bit of shiftin'. We still don't know much about what happened to him in the war and why he's such a changed man – and he don't want to talk to us about it."

"What's going to happen now?" Florence asked. "Is he going to come home soon?"

"I hope so," Annie said, "I can't wait!"

Chapter 58

Dear Gibbons, wrote Justin Hoad,

Fascinated to learn that Lance Corporal Davis's sight is returning in his left eye. This fully vindicates the course of treatment we have been following. A very satisfactory outcome.

At this stage, we have no way of predicting the extent to which his sight will recover, but if you are happy with the healing to his facial wounds, I see no reason why he should not now be discharged.

I would, however, advise you to impress on Mr and Mrs Davis that too much exertion, disturbance, activity – call it what you will – should be avoided. The important thing is to keep him on an even keel and take things slowly.

Annie prepared for her son's homecoming as though royalty were expected. She cleaned Wilf's room, aired the blankets on his bed, hung the rug out on the washing line and beat it to within an inch of its life and washed and ironed the curtains. She had, though, removed the mirror from his washstand.

"Maybe next year, he'll be able to help with harvest," Frank said. "We're so short handed this time, I don't know how we're goin' to get done."

"Don't you go rushin' things. You heard what the doctor said. We got to take it slow."

Wilf, however, shrugged his shoulders. "So what?" he said to his mother. "I've had no say in what's happening to me. People talk about me, make decisions about me without ever askin' what I think."

Everyone was celebrating the 'miracle' of his returning sight, but he even felt ambivalent about that. Now he would be able to see his ravaged face.

"It'll keep on remindin' me," he said to Gibbons. "And I don't even know if I want to go home. My mother'll be fussing over me all day and my old man'll be goin' on about the farm. At least in hospital no one disturbs me."

"I'm afraid we can't keep you in here indefinitely, Mr Davis. You'll have to face the future sooner or later," the doctor said.

At Valley Farm there were so many issues to confront. Its familiarity. The backdrop to the life he'd loved as a child and later in his youth. All his hopes and expectations had been bound up with the place. His parents – so well-meaning, so utterly unable to understand what was driving his fury, his hurt and his fear.

And there was the German – a *German*, for God's sake. Well, he'd just refuse to have anything to do with the bastard. He didn't have to see him, talk to him, if he chose not to. And he would choose not to.

Dr Gibbons offered to drive him out to the farm in his car. Wilf took his leave of the nursing staff. "Thanks ... for lookin' after me."

"Good luck," they all said.

He glanced across at the view over the Colne Valley that he thought he'd never see again. It was still out of focus, but he could recognise it as the landscape he'd known all his life. And yet it gave him no pleasure.

He remained silent as the doctor's car pulled away, and the town was receding behind them before Gibbons spoke. "You'll have a lot of catching up to do."

"Hmm," Wilf grunted, saying nothing for several moments. "I don't quite see it that way ... I'm not the same man as left here to go off to the ... war." It took him every ounce of determination to say that word. It haunted his existence. The dreams, the flashbacks, they were part of what Wilf Davis had become.

"I understand."

Wilf could not see how he could possibly understand.

"I've read that talking about your experiences can help," Gibbons said.

"I can't do that. Never will." Wilf was emphatic. That silenced the doctor.

The car made slow progress along the track. Approaching the farm gate, Wilf could make out figures waiting there. His parents.

Oh, hell ... The next chapter in the pointless charade.

Frank and Annie stood at the gate, his arm laying lightly on her shoulder, her hands clasped together over her pinafore.

"Now, Annie," Frank said as they watched the motor approaching, "Don't go smotherin' the lad. Give him a bit of a breather. He won't like bein' chivvied."

"I know you're right, Frank, but I can' help wantin' to nurture him back. It's the only way I know."

"All I'm sayin' is give him some elbow-room. He knows you love him right enough."

Gibbons drew the car to a halt and let the engine idle while he helped Wilf from the passenger seat. He touched his hat. "I'll be coming out to monitor Lance Corporal Davis' progress in a few days. In the meantime, keep him quiet and calm. Good day to you all."

A cloud of dust billowed as the car retreated.

"See," Wilf said, "he's doin' it again. Talkin' about me as if I'm not here."

"Ma." He pecked her on the cheek. "Pa."

Frank held out his hand to his son. Wilf took it briefly.

"Come on," Annie said, "Let's get you inside. I expect you'd like a nice cuppa tea. And your room's all ready for you."

"For God's sake don't FUSS! I'm a grown man, not a snot-nosed kid. And I don't want to be treated like an invalid! Alright?"

Frank led the way across the yard and into the farmhouse kitchen.

"You tell us what you'd like to do, then, son," Annie said.

"I'll just go up to my room. An' I'll have my tea up there, if it's all the same to you."

His room. Just as he'd left it the day he went away. He stood on the rug by the bed and ran his hand over the bedspread his mother had made when he was just a small boy. The same chair under the window, the same washstand. But no mirror. *It must be bad,* he thought. The window in his room looked out onto the yard, the shadows lengthening now. He crossed the room to look out. He could just make out two figures outside the barn. One with copper-coloured hair seemed to be fiddling with a set of harness, while the other, taller and fair, was working on the horse-drawn rake, an oil can and a rag in his hands. The woman and the German. He turned away.

Chapter 59

Haymaking would soon start. Florence guessed there'd be little time to spare once it was under way.

She still thought a lot about Andrew – there were loose ends to tie up while she still had some free time. Now she had the Snout Tin and his letter – things she could truly call hers – she felt she no longer had the right to keep his grandmother's ring. So she wrote to Arthur Crawford to see if he could get hold of the Forbes family's address. He wrote back, having found it out from the regiment. Dorchester. The mention of the place had sparked off memories of the Rec.

They were Brigadier and Mrs Alexander Nicholson-Forbes. *Double-barrelled. I never knew that.* And his father a brigadier. She imagined the rigid discipline of Andrew's upbringing. *Brave of him to break free of all that* ... She sat by her attic window and began to write, explaining how she had met their son. As for the ring, she wrote: *"Andrew gave me this as a memento of our meeting, but now I do not feel I should keep it and so I am returning it herewith. It comes with my very deepest condolences for your loss. Captain Forbes was a fine man, and as I understand it, a fine soldier as well.*

How will they react to my asking for a photograph? she thought. *Oh well, the worst they can do is say no, or just ignore the request.* So she went ahead and asked. *That's enough.* She wrapped the ring in a piece of tissue paper, folded the notepaper and tucked them both into the envelope. She sat looking at it, her neat script spelling out the Dorset address: The Old Manor House. *Hardly my world. Nell was right there.*

She just had time before milking to cycle off to town to post it, and to fulfil her other mission, which was a visit to the book shop in the High Street. The woman who ran it had got hold of a copy of Edward Thomas' *Poems*. It was waiting for her to collect.

Later, back in her room, she unwrapped the book, untying the string and folding back the brown paper like a ritual. Turning to the contents page, she found it listed there: *Haymaking*. It painted a word-picture that was as old as time itself:

'*After night's thunder far away had rolled*
The fiery day had a kernel sweet of cold,
And in the perfect blue the clouds uncurled,
Like the first gods before they made the world
And misery, swimming the stormless sea

In beauty and in divine gaiety.
The smooth white empty road was lightly strewn
With leaves – the holly's Autumn falls in June –
And fir cones standing stiff up in the heat.
The mill-foot water tumbled white and lit
With tossing crystals, happier than any crowd
Of children pouring out of school aloud.
And in the little thickets where a sleeper
For ever might lie lost, the nettle-creeper
And garden warbler sang unceasingly;
While over them shrill shrieked in his fierce glee
The swift with wings and tail as sharp and narrow
As if the bow had flown off with the arrow.
Only the scent of woodbine and hay new-mown
Travelled the road. In the field sloping down,
Park-like, to where its willows showed the brook,
Haymakers rested. The tosser lay forsook
Out in the sun; and the long waggon stood
Without its team, it seemed it never would
Move from the shadow of that single yew.
The team, as still, until their task was due,
Beside the labourers enjoyed the shade
That three squat oaks mid-field together made
Upon a circle of grass and weed uncut,
And on the hollow, once a chalk-pit, but
Now brimmed with nut and elder-flower so clean.
The men leaned on their rakes, about to begin,
But still. And all were silent. All was old,
Older than Clare and Cobbett, Morland and Crome,
Than, at the field's far edge, the farmer's home,
A white house crouched at the foot of a great tree.
Under the heavens that know not what years be
The men, the beasts, the trees, the implements
Uttered even what they will in times far hence –
All of us gone out of the reach of change –
Immortal in a picture of an old grange.

She felt herself to be part of that timelessness – borne along by it.

"I can hardly wait for haymaking," Florence said to Frank at the supper table.

"Ha! You sound like a kid! Not long now. It's lookin' just right and the barometer's set fair. I was goin' to say we'd start cuttin' on Thursday. D'you think your niece would like to come out and help at the weekend? She can bring her pal and anyone else who'd like a couple of days' serious work out in the open air. They'll get a fine supper for their pains."

"I don't know till I've asked, Frank, but I wouldn't mind betting the answer'll be 'Yes'."

"Thing is, I got a reaper – that's a tool for cuttin' the grass – what the horses haul, and the rake what Fritzy's been workin' on. But everythin' else has to be done by hand. You've got to turn the hay over and over so it gets good and dry afore you stack it. And we're pitiful short of manpower. I tried hirin' a gang, but the hands just ain't there. At least I got the say so from the officer in charge at the old workhouse to let Fritzy work longer hours for the duration. He'll make a good stacker. He's tall enough, and strong."

"What job would you like me to do, Frank?"

"Well, I reckon to start with, you could get the young 'uns goin' on the teddin' – that's the turnin' – and keep an eye on 'em. Then, when we're ready to bring it all in, you could work on top of the waggon loadin' it all up and drive it to where we'll be stackin' it in the rickyard and the loft. Once I've done the cuttin', I can work with Fritzy. Stackin's quite an art. How does that sound?"

"Smashing!"

Thursday morning was clear and calm. She and Frank hitched up Clover and Campion and drove them out at first light to the furthest distant hayfield, towing the reaper.

"Farthest away first," Frank said, "and we can work our way back towards home as we go. I want you to follow on behind the reaper and rake it all up tidy. Pull out the big weeds like docks and thistles and we'll pile them up for a great big bonfire at the end. And fluff up the grass so the air can get to it. I hope you're feelin' chipper, young Florence, it's goin' to be a long day."

Florence made a fist and punched Frank's upper arm. They set to work and she was surprised how quickly they covered the ground, the tall grasses with their purple-ochre seedheads toppling like dominoes.

Holger arrived, his breeches girthed with a brass-buckled belt, a kerchief about his neck and his shirtsleeves rolled to the elbow. He was lithe and fit and worked ably with his pitchfork.

By mid-morning Frank was pleased with their progress. They stopped for elevenses in the shade of a tree. Florence unhitched the horses and offered them water from a half-barrel. ' ... *Beside the labourers enjoyed the shade/That three squat oaks mid-field together made ...* ' She drank the elderflower cordial Annie had packed in the picnic basket for her. It's coolness soothed her parched throat.

"Tell you what," Frank said, a jug of beer in hand, "you can have a go on the reaper, if you like, Florence. Ain't nothin' to it you haven't already done. Just keep it straight and the horses goin' at a regular speed. Then I can work with Fritzy separatin' out the weeds, and perhaps we'll catch a rabbit or two for a nice pie to celebrate at the end of haymakin'."

"You want rabbit?" Holger said. "I can catch. I see many already."

"You do that, boy!"

Come the weekend, the mowing was all but done. Grace and Doris had talked Windy and Lennie into cycling out to the farm to join in the hay turning.

"You bet!" Windy had said. "Nothin' I'd like better."

"We were up ever so early this morning, Mr Davis," Grace said, "we could hardly see where we were going, it was still so dark."

"Well, that's good. I'm pleased to see you here at this hour." Frank tried to look stern. He took a puff on his pipe in the interests of gravitas. "But you all got to remember there's a job of work to do here, and I don't put up with no laggards."

"We'll work hard alright," said Lennie. "Don't you worry about that."

They were like small dervishes, swinging their laden pitch forks. Every now and then they indulged in bouts of wrestling or a game of chase. At intervals, Holger dived off into undergrowth, chasing rabbits disturbed by all the activity. The haymakers advanced across the fields in a broad phalanx, leaving no blade of grass unturned.

Productivity had dipped a little by Sunday afternoon, but Frank was satisfied with the state of play, knowing that the hay was now dry enough to bring in. As the sun began to dip towards the western horizon, he shepherded everyone back to the big oak tree which stood in the corner of the home field. He and Holger had made a clearing under its spreading branches, where Annie sat buttering slabs of bread. There were candles in tin lanterns ready to light as it grew darker, and she had spread some old blankets on the ground for everyone to sit on. In the centre sat a rabbit pie giving off a rich aroma.

"Mouthwaterin'!" Frank said. "Come and get it, all you workers! Well done, Old Girl!"

"Not so much of the 'Old', Frank Davis." Annie gave out enamel plates to each worker. "Or you'll go without! Now then, you lot, line up here and I'll serve you each a piece of pie. There's some mashed spuds too. You can soak up your gravy with them. Perfect combination, if you ask me, so don't hold back."

Grace took her place on a gnarled tree root, taking care not to spill a crumb or drop of gravy from her plate. "Mmm! Mrs Davis, this is *so* delicious! Even my mother couldn't make a better pie than this."

"Well, that's praise indeed. But if truth be told, it's Fritzy we have to thank. It was him what caught the rabbits."

Holger inclined his head and the children gave him a round of applause.

Florence tuned up her mandolin.

"I've been trying to play something that sounds like birdsong but I don't know if I've come anywhere close … Would you like to hear it?"

"Course we would. Go on, Florence," said Annie. And so she played it …

Holger stood and put his hands together, and everyone else joined in the applause.

"That was lovely, Aunt Flo," Grace said.

Haymaking. Andrew's letter. He'd imagined this precise scene.

"Larks on the battlefields," she said.

"I have heard them," Holger said. "They are beautiful."

Light was fading and Florence looked at her watch. "Oh, heavens! I've got to get these children back home, or my sister'll be furious. They've got school tomorrow. Come on, you lot – get your bicycles, we've got to leave right now!"

The four youngsters got to their feet. Forming a queue, they thanked their hosts.

"It's been smashing," Doris said. "I'll never forget it."

"You've done a marvellous job, you young 'uns," Frank told them.

Grace walked with Annie back towards their bicycles, "Um ... I thought young Mr Davis would be with us for the picnic. He'd have enjoyed it, don't you think?"

"Well, you'd think so, wouldn't you? But I couldn't persuade him to come out. He don't seem to be able to enjoy anythin' at all at the moment."

"That's such a pity."

"Come on, now!" said Florence. "Take your leave and let's get going! Your mothers will kill me if you're not home soon!"

"I must go also. I come with you?" Holger asked.

"Oh, yes, Fritzy. Please do. We're all going in the same direction. You can help me keep this lot in order."

They rode off down the lane, in the sunset's afterglow. Frank and Annie watched them as they retreated in the gloaming, the children's voices shrill in the quiet evening.

"Reminds me of when Wilf was a nipper, how he used to love haymakin' and harvest time," Annie said. "Perhaps it's those memories that're too painful for him to be reminded of now."

"If he won't tell us, we can only guess, Annie."

"We got to play a patient game, Frank. Ain't no other way."

The cyclists stopped at the gates of the old workhouse to take their leave of Holger.

"Goodnight, Mister 'Olger," Doris said. Holger shook each of the children by the hand.

"Gute nacht," he said with his slight bow to each of them. The girls giggled and the boys tried to copy the bow. "Und danke – thank you for music, Florence, was wunderbar ... erm ... wonderful?" He pronounced the 'w' as a 'v'. Turning to Florence, he took her hand and bowed over it. The girls giggled again and Florence flushed.

"Goodnight, Fritzy. And thank you for the rabbits."

Chapter 60

"Right," Frank said. "Hay's dry enough to store. But now we got to rake it up together, pitch it onto the waggon and then stack it."

Frank, Florence and Holger were a good team and enjoyed seeing the hay harvest home and dry. First they filled the loft above the barn which Florence, as good as her word, had swept clear of the vestiges of last year's crop. It had been a cathartic act for her. Putting the past behind her. Then they set about building a stack on the rickyard, a skilled task that Frank supervised.

"You got to stack it secure-like else it'll be liable to collapse when the bad weather comes. I'm goin' to get Ted Fieldin's man, Henry, to come over and thatch the rick soon as he's got time. He's a good thatcher is Henry and always in demand this time of year."

Holger stacked the hay well, and Frank regarded his work, cap in hand, and nodded.

"You've done a good job there, young Fritzy. Now we're in shape to feed our livestock through the winter, no matter what the weather throws at us. May even have a bit left over to sell, if anyone's short come the spring." He turned to Florence. "And you, missy. You've done the work of a fully paid-up navvy! Come on inside and have some supper. You've earned it."

***

Wilf stayed in his room. Most of the time he lay on his bed, shutting out the world around him. He didn't want even to comment on, let alone participate in, one of the big events in the farming year happening within earshot of his bedroom.

Here at Valley Farm he had learned to believe in just rewards from hard work. He'd felt that same sense of satisfaction from a job well done that he knew his father, the woman and the German were feeling now. And farming was all about feeding people. Being close to animals. Husbandry. It was life as it should be lived.

But soldiering in the barbarity of trench warfare he had seen another world. Indescribable brutality. Land being laid waste. Oh, yes, he'd known camaraderie out there. The bonds he'd forged with pals in the trenches were deep. But so many of them were dead or, like him, ruined.

In the silence, he was aware of his own breathing, regular as the passing of the hours, as night and day, sunrise and moonrise. Lying in the hospital, it had all seemed so futile. He'd wanted no more of it.

Yet here at home, he'd made no attempt to bring his life to an end, even though he could, if he chose, now find the means. He realised for the first time in many months, that the desire to end his anguish by ending his life had lost its edge. He listened to the sound of his inhalation and exhalation and saw the rising and falling of his chest. *Strange,* he thought. The anger was still as acute and visions of horror still beset his nights. His life still blighted and meaningless, so why not end it?

"My mortal soul's damned to hellfire anyway," he said out loud, really believing it. But, if he took his own life, he'd die a criminal, his remains committed to unconsecrated ground. He imagined the agony it would mete out to his mother. *I've got no right to do that to her,* he thought.

A light tap on the door brought his thoughts back to the present. "Can I come in, son?" His mother's voice called from the landing.

"Yeah. Come in, Ma."

"I've brought you some supper." She set the tray down on the chest of drawers. "There's some cold pie and some bubble and squeak. I know you like it. And your Pa's poured you a pint of ale."

"Ta." He opened his mouth as if to say more, but closed it again with a slight snort.

"Is anythin' the matter, Wilf?"

He shook his head. "Nothin', Ma."

Chapter 61

'This summer's the closest thing to heaven I can imagine', Grace wrote in her diary, now into its third notebook.

And now there was another event to look forward to – the church fete to be held, as always, in the Vicarage garden on the third Saturday in July. The lawns were newly mown, and tables, covered in gingham cloths were set out around the garden. The organisers and a band of helpers had been busy since early morning, setting up stalls and hanging bunting from tree to tree. The custodians of the hoopla, skittles, white elephant stall, shove-ha'penny, cake and produce stalls were all in place. The tea tent was poised for action, and, above all in the estimation of the contenders, the cake competition had been judged.

Grace and Doris looked around the site. The children's choir was to sing 'Nymphs and Shepherds'.

"I'm not worried about that," said Doris. "We've rehearsed it – it's all in a day's work … But that duet … I'm so nervous. How're you feelin' Gracie?"

"Same as you. It's a nice song, 'Twelve Sang the Clock', but I'm worried people won't hear us in the open air."

"And it'll be noisy with everyone talking."

"And absolutely *everyone* will be here."

At 2pm on the dot Mr Curling the vicar declared the fete open and townspeople each paid their 2d and 1d for each of their children to enter.

Nell arrived early hoping to avoid the worst of the crush later in the afternoon. Iris and Renee were in the pushchair. Molly Cooper was with them, having closed her shop for the afternoon.

"There won't be much custom," she said to Nell. "Everyone's here."

"You're right there, Molly. On an afternoon like this, the whole town'll turn out."

Nell dropped off some jars of chutney she was donating at the produce stall while Molly looked at the white elephant merchandise.

"There's a nice cut glass bowl I'd like for puttin' fruit in." She pointed to it. "It'd look a treat on the sideboard."

"Yes, it is lovely, but isn't that a chip in the rim?"

"You're right, Nell. I hadn't spotted that. In which case, it's much too dear."

"Hello, Nell," came a voice from behind the women.

"Ivy! Good to see you." Nell turned to face her smiling cousin. "How's the little one?"

"He's doin' fine. Greedy little chap – growing like billy-o."

"What have you called him?"

"Sidney Albert, after his father and granddad." Ivy picked the baby out of his pram and bounced him on her arm. "I'm lovin' motherhood."

"I can see it's suiting you," Nell said.

As the afternoon wore on, the lure of the tea tent was increasingly inviting. Nell bought some cheese straws to keep the twins happy and the two women made for the shade and a sit down.

"Good afternoon, Mrs Ashford, Mrs Cooper. I trust you're enjoying the fete."

A man with a white moustache was raising his hat to them. Looking up from their seated positions, the two women had to shield their eyes from the sun to make out who it was.

"Oh! Mr Mathews! How nice to see you!" Nell said, attempting to rise to her feet.

"No, no, don't get up, I beg you," Morton Mathews said. "But seeing you there, I wanted to take the opportunity of making a suggestion to you both."

The women looked up at him.

"I'm pleased to say that all three of your children, Mrs Ashford, and also Doris," he nodded in Molly's direction, "are doing very well indeed at school. Ellen's aptitude in arithmetic is well above average, and, of course, Alfred's drawing skills are remarkable. And I'm impressed how he has responded to the challenge I set him to pay heed to his other subjects. Grace shows an admirable facility with the English language – her recitation of one of John Clare's poems in class the other day was enunciated beautifully and with great feeling. And as for Doris, she is not only an excellent all-rounder, but a personality of charm as well as determination."

Nell and Molly, naturally gratified by such praise for their young, wondered what it was all leading up to.

"Ladies, please don't attempt to give me an answer now, but I'd like you both to consider putting your children forward to sit the scholarship examination for the grammar school. In my professional opinion, they all stand a very good chance of passing. And now I must leave you to enjoy the afternoon. Good day, ladies."

"Thank you, Mr Mathews. Very much," Nell said. "Good afternoon to you."

Raising his hat once more he withdrew and re-joined a pleasant-faced woman they took to be Mrs Mathews.

"Well! What d'you make of that, Nell? I'm sure I couldn't possibly give him an answer at the moment. It'll all depend on whether Fred comes back from the war and what kind of shape he's in if he does. If he doesn't come back, or if he's in no fit state to work, God forbid, I'll need Doris to take on a share of runnin' the shop. It's a hard question."

"I'm afraid there's no argument as far as mine are concerned." Nell shook her head. "We only arranged to be away for a year, and it's almost up. I know the war's not over yet, but my place is back in Stratford. The air raids are a thing of the past, and I want to get the house ready for when George gets home. Please God he does get home."

"I had no idea you planned to go back so soon, Nell."

"Please, Molly. Don't say a word to Doris about it – it'll only sadden the children. They know we'll be going back, but I do want them to enjoy the time they have left here."

Molly reached out and squeezed Nell's hand. "You can depend on it. But Doris is goin' to miss your Grace like anything. And I'm goin' to miss you, too."

"Ladies and gentleman!" The vicar's voice, augmented by a megaphone, intervened. "May I have your attention, please? It is my great pleasure to introduce St Andrew's Church Children's Choir under the baton of Mr Oliver Davage, who are going to sing for us this afternoon."

Nell and Molly looked up to see their daughters amid an ensemble of boys and girls standing on a makeshift stage constructed of planks laid across a matrix of fruit crates, near the open window of the vicarage drawing room.

Applause crackled across the garden and, on Mr Davage's signal, the singers bowed.

"Thank you, thank you," Mr Davage said. Turning to the choir he raised his baton. A tinkle of piano music issued from the open window. It was just loud enough to give the children their cue and enable them to pitch their opening note. Once they began singing, they were carried along by the familiar tune.

"Nymphs and shepherds, come away, come away ... "

A cheer went up as the song came to its end and the singers bowed again.

"It's us now. Help!" whispered Doris.

The two of them stepped forward as the remainder of the choir sat down cross-legged behind them. They watched the choirmaster's baton. The sound of their voices drifted out over the crowd, floating on the breeze. *"Twelve sang the clock, and all's well ... "*

"Phew!" Grace said when the song was finished. "I'm glad that's over!"

"Well sung, you two," Nell said as they jumped down from the platform. Molly handed them each a penny. "Go and get yourselves a glass of lemonade. I reckon you've earned it!"

"Thanks, Mum. Come on, Gracie!"

"Molly, you shouldn't," Nell said.

"Oh! Don't be daft, Nell. Tuppence ain't goin' to break the bank. Besides, those lasses *have* earned it. Think of the pleasure they've given everyone. And they practised really hard."

"Let's go and have a look at the competition cakes."

"Yours looks good, Nell," Molly said, scrutinising the dozen or so entries.

"Not bad, but I don't hold out much hope of winning. Jane Mizen said she wasn't going to waste her time entering this year because Mrs Potter always walks away with first prize. It's because her sister's one of the judges, according to Jane."

At four o'clock, Mr Curling picked up his megaphone. "Ladies and gentlemen. I have pleasure in announcing the winner of this year's cake-baking competition. The rules are the same as always. Everyone has used the recipe as set out in the programme and all entries must have been baked in a regular, domestic kitchen. No professional entries allowed. Now. This year, we've had a bit of a problem on that score. After due consideration, the judges decided that the best entry in this year's class is the one baked by Mrs Ashford of Factory Terrace."

"Oo!" The crowd began to clap.

"But!" Mr Curling raised his hand. "In view of Mrs Ashford's work for Mr Broyd and the fact that her goods are sold in his shop, the judges deemed that she is ineligible to enter this competition and have therefore disqualified her entry, excellent though it is."

"Ahh!"

"I therefore have pleasure in awarding first prize in the 1918 St Andrew's Church Fete Cake Baking Competition to ... Mrs Potter of Parsonage Street. Congratulations – again, Mrs Potter!"

"Oh ..."

A smiling Mrs Potter approached the vicar to a crackle of applause and received her prize, a postal order in the sum of one shilling.

Nell and Molly looked at one another, raised their eyebrows and shrugged.

Chapter 62

Wilf found himself in a dilemma. If he was not going to take his own life, what was he going to do with it? He could see clearly enough now to know that his body had become flaccid, pigeon-chested. Once his outdoor existence had given him a muscular frame. He had never been vain about it, but now his diminished state caused him shame. In the hospital, when he couldn't see, the nurses had shaved him and kept his hair trimmed. Since returning home, his mother had tried to encourage him to tidy himself up. When, soon after his home-coming, she'd brought a bowl of water, a towel and a razor, he'd waved her away with angry words.

Lying on his bed, he put a hand up to his chin, now dark with weeks of growth. He wondered if many would recognise him the way he looked now. He even wondered if he'd recognise his own reflection if he caught sight of it.

"I'll have to do *somethin'*," he said out loud. He stood, went over to the window and opened it, letting in the breeze. The scent of the new hay was upon it and he could hear the fowl, pecking in the yard and clucking. He turned towards his washstand and filled the bowl from the ewer. He shivered as the cold water shocked his skin, washing the tears from his face.

Many minutes later, he opened the door and crossed the threshold, passing out of his self-imposed exile into the foreign land of the rest of his life.

***

The envelope was waiting for Florence when she came in from afternoon milking. It was lying among others left, as usual, on the bench inside the kitchen door. It was cream vellum with her name and the farm address written in blue-black ink. She looked at the postmark. Dorchester. It contained two pieces of card. One, deckle-edged, matched the envelope. She withdrew it. Printed in embossed script, it read:

Brigadier and Mrs Alexander Nicholson-Forbes wish to thank
Miss Florence Mundy
For the kind message of condolence
On the death in action of their son
Captain Andrew Geoffrey Nicholson-Forbes MC
30th May, 1918

Her name was written on a printed dotted line in the same hand that had written the envelope. That was it. No sign of curiosity about this woman with whom their son had become close. She thought it strange, for she had spent time with him more recently than they had. One might think that a bereaved parent – especially a mother – might want to know something about so recent an association. But then again, perhaps not.

"Hmm." She shrugged, picked up the envelope and pulled out the other piece of card. A photograph. It was the size of a postcard and showed Andrew in his dress uniform, smiling, his hand resting on the hilt of a ceremonial sword. It had been taken at the passing out ceremony at staff college. Not the pose she would have chosen, but it was a likeness she could keep.

She sat down on the settle and held it in good light. He looked so young. Well, he was young when he finished at Sandhurst. And not yet worn down by the war. An MC. Something else she hadn't known about him. Arthur Crawford had called him 'the best gaffer'. He'd never let his men down, in spite of his misgivings. Probably she was the only soul he'd admitted them to.

The door opened and a figure appeared in the doorway. Florence was caught off balance for a moment. This dark young man had a beard, chin-length hair and an uncertain look. And features marred by injury. He had a flowerpot filled with eggs in one hand and a bunch of carrots under his arm.

"Oh, Wilf! It's you. You've been outside." Florence felt rather foolish. "Are you feeling better?"

"Don't ask."

"I'm sorry. I didn't mean to intrude, but we haven't seen much of you since you've been back. Why don't you sit down? I was just about to put the kettle on."

"No." Wilf said again, though less aggressively. "Just went outside for a think. And I collected the eggs. Carrots were ready for pullin', too. I'm goin' back upstairs now."

"Have you seen your folks?"

"No, I ain't. And don't you go sendin' them upstairs, neither. I can't be doin' with that yet."

"Fair enough, Wilf."

Well, there's a turn-up for the books, she thought. And he'd said *'yet'*. She filled the kettle and toasted some teacakes. She knew Frank would be in soon – she'd seen him and Jack on their way back from checking the sheep and taking a look at the ripening corn.

Frank came back in, leaving the dog in the yard. "It's all lookin' good out there. This rate, harvest'll be on us afore we know it."

"That's good news, Frank. I'll see if the children can come and help again, shall I?"

"Ah! That would be good. They'll have broken up from school by then – with any luck they'll have even more time free."

"Frank. Frank!" Annie was breathless as she came running in. "You'll never guess who's been out in the yard. He's been pickin' up eggs and rootlin' round the kitchen garden." She bounced up and down. Every part of her bounced.

Frank pushed his cap to the back of his head. "You'll have to tell me, Annie. I can see you're dyin' to."

"It was Wilf. He's been outside. Of his own accord!"

"Well, I'll be!" Frank stroked the stubble on his chin.

"I was just checkin' on the latest batch of cheese, so I was out the back in the cold pantry. I caught sight of somethin' movin' out the corner of my eye. And when I looked up I could see him pickin' up the eggs in the chicken run. I could hardly believe it – thought I were seein' things ..."

"Did you come out and talk to him?"

"No. I didn't. God knows I wanted to, but I thought better of it. Didn't want to crowd him. Better if he makes the first move. But Frank! He's got up and gone out under his own steam. That's got to mean somethin's happenin' to him. Somethin' good ... hasn't it?"

"Let's hope so, Annie, my girl. If there's goin' to be a future for the Davises at Valley Farm, somethin' good's got to happen. An' I'm near wore out with waiting."

"Frank, we've got a long way to go yet. He's still so thin and ragged lookin'. He hasn't even seen what he looks like now. He's bound to be shocked. We've still got to box clever."

"I think Annie's right." Frank and Annie had forgotten Florence was there. Now they both turned towards her. "Wilf came through here while I was making the tea. It took me by surprise, too. My thoughts were miles away. I only managed some stupid comment and he just about jumped down my throat."

"I'm sorry, Florence."

"It's alright, Annie. You don't have to apologise for Wilf. I understand. And I think you're right to let him find his own way back to a life he can share with you, if that's what he is doing, and I really hope it is. He said he didn't want you to go upstairs after him, by the way."

"Pity," Annie said, "but I'm not surprised."

Wilf's forays out of doors became frequent and wide-ranging, though he was careful to avoid contact with his parents. And the woman. And the German. His limited vision did not impede his progress through copses and along field headlands, always keeping the hedges between himself and where he knew they were working. And he could make out more detail than he'd expected. He was recognising birds not just from their song, but also from the look of them and the way they flew. He'd even spotted a pair of wrens flitting in and out of the hawthorn hedge. Raising a brood. It made him smile. Smile.

He tried not to do much thinking; heaven knew, he'd been doing nothing but for months and it didn't seem to have got him very far. And the strange thing about his backing away from suicide was that it had not arisen out of any thinking he'd done. It seemed to have come out of nowhere. So why not just let events take their course?

Right now, he aimed to build himself back up into some semblance of a robust young man. He'd need to do more than walk, but at least it was a start. And he quite liked the sensation of just letting his mind run on in no particular direction. Observing. Meditating, almost.

But even out in the open air, he'd suddenly find himself in tears and shaking. He'd make for a tree to lean against, sit down on the dry leaf litter, draw his knees up and bury his head in his folded arms, letting the sobs come till the worst was over and he felt steadier. After bouts like that, he was tense, tormented, unable to speak.

***

"Have you got a photograph frame you're not using?" Florence asked.

Annie didn't ask to see the photo, but Florence showed it to her anyway.

"Aw, don't he look young?"

"Just what I thought." Florence looked again at the picture. "Well, it was taken a few years ago – and, in some ways, a whole lifetime ago. But I'm glad I've got it. And I want to put it on the washstand in my room."

Annie rummaged in the dresser cupboard, and brought out a dusty frame from the back. "Will this do? It's no great shakes, but it'll look alright if we clean the glass and dust off the cobwebs."

"Well, it's the right size and it'll do the job. I'll give it a bit of a polish." Florence took it to the sink, burnished the brass surround and cleaned the fly spots off the glass. "Perfect." She left the kitchen by the stairs door.

In the privacy of her room, she slipped the picture into the slot behind the glass and set it on the marble top of the washstand. She had made what amounted to a little shrine there, arranging the Snout Tin, still with her tortoiseshell comb inside, with the picture frame next to it on top of the two envelopes – one containing Andrew's last letter, the other the card from his parents. *That's all I have of him now*, she thought, *apart from my memories … Oh! And I have Thessalonians and Edward Thomas.* She reached for the poetry book, opened it and read aloud the verse on the page. "*In Memoriam (Easter, 1915):*

The flowers left thick at nightfall in the wood
This Eastertide call into mind the men,
Now far from home, who, with their sweethearts, should
Have gathered them and will do never again."

She closed the book, remembering.

Chapter 63

"Ma." Wilf stood in the doorway at the foot of the stairs. His mother was at the stone sink trimming and cleaning half a dozen cauliflowers she had brought in from the kitchen garden.

"What is it, Wilf?" She turned to face him.

"I need a shave. And I want to get rid of some of this." He flipped his hair with the fingers of one hand.

"Alright," said Annie, pleased. *Don't show your feelin's*, she thought, *keep it normal ... don't rush, don't fuss ...* "But I've got to finish these first. I've got a whole load of veg to get ready afore Swank comes for the churn. He's goin' to take it all to Mrs Cooper to sell in her shop. She's promised me a good price. So if you'll give me half an hour, I'll see to your hair and beard with the greatest of pleasure." *Fingers crossed he doesn't change his mind ...*

"Alright. Just don't make a meal of it."

"No, Wilf. I won't."

Wilf waited. Annie wiped her hands, and stooped to pick up the crate full of her produce. It was brimful, heavy.

"Wait Ma. I'll do that for you." The offer took him by surprise. His mother stepped aside to allow him access to the crate.

"Take it out to the churn rest, would you, Wilf? And ... thanks." She turned her back and began searching the cutlery drawer for the scissors she used for trimming Frank's hair. By the time Wilf came back in, she had all she needed for the job.

"Sit here, Wilf." She had shifted a ladder-backed chair to a spot where the light was good. Draping a tea towel about his shoulders, she began to soap her son's face with Frank's shaving brush. She took the cut-throat razor and felt him flinch slightly and his body tense as her free hand smoothed the contours of his face as she worked.

No small talk, Annie thought. The kitchen was quiet. The dark hair came away from his skin and fell in ragged skeins onto the cloth beneath his chin. She was moved by the still-youthful complexion of his left cheek. She took care around the ravaged right side of his face, scored with purplish scars. His sunken right eye socket brought her close to tears. Her lovely boy.

She handed him a towel she'd warmed in front of the range. He wiped his face. Picking up the scissors and a comb, she began cutting away the hair. It was like stripping back a disguise that had been hiding her son's identity. *Don't be daft, Annie*, she said to herself. *It'll take more than a haircut to put him right.*

She was trimming the fluff on the back of his neck. The back door opened and Frank, Florence and Holger came in.

"I was just wonderin' if Fritzy could have his dinner ..." Frank said, catching sight of his son. "Oh boy! You've got rid of the Rasputin look! Thank God! I was thinkin' you were turnin' into some kind of mad monk!"

Wilf got to his feet, shaking. He picked up the basin still with water in it, and flung it at his father. Water spun out in an arc and the bowl hit Frank in the chest. He gasped at the impact. The bowl crashed to the floor.

Wilf, his face crumpled with misery, pushed past his father and went out, slamming the door like a slap in the face.

"I'm goin' after him," said Frank. "He can't get away with behavin' like that!"

"No!" Annie raised a hand. "Don't you dare, Frank Davis. How many times have we said we've got to give him time? That boy's grievin'. He's wounded on the inside worse than he is on the outside. And them wounds take a lot more healin' than the ones you can see. How could you be so *oafish* as to make stupid jokes – about his looks, for heaven's sake? How *could* you, Frank?" She was in tears now. She sat down on the settle and covered her face with her apron.

Florence bent to comfort Annie, rubbing her shoulders through the coarse stuff of her dress. She held out a handkerchief for Annie. "That was crass, Frank." Florence said.

"I've just been gettin' a bit fed up with him bein' so moody." Frank studied his stockinged feet. "He's a man and he's got to start behavin' like one instead of all this wallowin' in self-pity."

"Frank, I know you're a good man, and an honest one. But you got to accept that sometimes – and this is one of them times and no mistake – 'snap out of it' just ain't the right approach. None of us has any idea about what he's had to go through." Annie sighed and wiped away the tears on her face. "And now look. He's gone. We don't know where, and I daren't think what he'll be doin'. Or how we're goin' to get him back."

Florence stood, her hand still resting on Annie's shoulder. "I'll go and look for him." She crossed the room to the door.

Outside as she put her boots back on, Holger slipped out through the still-open door. He closed it quietly behind him. "Frank and Annie, they must alone be, now. Is bad time."

"You're right. Very bad ... Um ... Fritzy, why don't you come with me and we'll look for Wilf together? Please? I could do with the moral support, and two heads and pairs of eyes are better than one."

Holger looked at her.

"You come with me. To find Wilf. Please?"

"Oh. Ya! I can do this."

"Where might he have gone? We can only follow our noses and hope for the best," Florence said.

Holger looked at her again.

"Sorry, Fritzy. Just thinking aloud."

"Jack can help, I think."

The dog stood facing the farmyard gate, his ears pricked and his tail wagging. He turned to face them and barked.

"Of course!" Florence said. "He knows much more than we do."

Florence unlatched the gate and the dog shot through it into the lane, turning right past the rickyard. He headed on. Now his nose was on the ground, his tail in the air as he pursued the familiar scent. Florence and Holger followed him as he trotted along.

"He to where lambs born is going."

"You're right, Fritzy. The shepherd's hut do you think?"

Holger nodded. They rounded a bend in the track and saw that Jack was lying down, tongue lolling, at the foot of the steps leading up to the door of the shepherd's hut.

"Good boy, Jack," Florence crouched to pat the dog's head. He woofed quietly and, in the silence that followed, Holger thought he heard a hoarse voice coming from inside the hut. He held a finger to his lips and cupped an ear with his other hand.

Florence stood and listened. A stifled sob. She nodded to Holger and he gestured that he should stay put while she followed the sound. She climbed the steps and stood with her hand on the latch, listening. Wilf was repeating something over and over again like a mantra, but his voice was so muffled, it was some moments before she grasped what he was saying.

"Thou shalt not kill … thou shalt not kill … God have mercy …"

Opening the door of the hut, she saw him, sitting on the floor, his back against the wall, his arms encircling his folded legs. His head was resting on his knees. With his face turned away, he did not see Florence's approach but he heard the door's hinges squeak. He fell silent, but did not turn his head to look at her.

Florence stood, searching for words that would not alienate him further. Kneeling beside him, she put a hand on his arm. "Wilf," she said, before he could react to her touch, "Wilf …"

Wilf raised his head. "Leave me alone! Just *leave me!*" He shrugged her hand away from his arm.

"Listen to me, Wilf. Just listen. For a minute. Please." She was quiet but firm.

"Just *go! Now!*"

"I understand why you must hate me, and Holger too. And you've got every right to resent us being here. But think of your parents. They love you so much, Wilf. And none of what's happened to you is their fault."

"Ma 'n' Pa." Wilf sniffed. "They don't know nothin'." He turned his head away again, but he didn't tell her to go.

Arguing in defence of Annie and Frank was her initial reaction, but she stopped herself in time. *This is not about them – or even about Fritzy and me,* she thought. *Something else, something from the war …* Those words she'd heard him repeating to himself: thou shalt not kill, God have mercy. *He's in a living hell.*

"Wilf." Florence took a deep breath. "Something happened to you at the Front that's causing all the fury and bitterness and *fear*, didn't it? I can see it's tearing you apart." She paused. The sounds of an English summer pervaded the silence that followed. Wilf sat motionless, his face still turned away. Florence moved away from him a little and sat on the floorboards. "You have to tell someone. To get rid of the guilt. Make a confession, if you want to think of it that way."

Wilf shook his head without raising it. "Never. I'm cursed to hell."

"Look, Wilf. I'm not much good on religion, but that doesn't sound like the God your Ma has faith in. Her God's all about – what is it? Forgiveness for all who truly repent? *All,* Wilf. No matter what. What I *do* know about is the power of coming clean. Of getting the things that weigh heavy off your chest. Your Ma helped me – *listened* to me and my pathetic, *puny* worries – a while ago. She made me realise there was a way out from the senselessness I was feeling. It was like a ton weight being lifted off my shoulders –"

His face, tear-stained and creased with pain, turned to her.

"Bet you never broke a commandment, eh?"

The agony passing across his features moved Florence to pity. She moved towards his slumped figure and made to kneel beside him again. He did not stop her.

"You know what, Wilf? I think we all break commandments. We can't help it."

"Not *killin'* though." Wilf's body convulsed with sobs. "I can't never be forgiven. Can't never tell no one … I wanted to finish it. Do meself in. I don't deserve to live."

He was quiet for a moment, but Florence felt there was more to come and waited.

"But now I can't even do that. Can't pluck up the courage. Can't lay the burden of it on my Ma. It ain't fair. That's why I tried to start puttin' myself back together. Pa's right. I did look like that Rasputin bloke. Bloody disgrace." He stopped for a moment and looked at Florence squarely. "But it won't do no good. I'm a bloody disgrace on the inside. An' that filth's goin' to be there for the rest of my life."

"Come on, Wilf. I really believe there's a way out of the dreadful blind alley you're in. The way it is, you're letting all the anger and bitterness and guilt become who you are."

He looked at her and frowned. "This *is* who I am … Now."

"If you'll let me, I'll try to explain how it was for me."

He nodded slightly.

"Something happened to me that made me feel ashamed and guilty. My life seemed futile. I despised myself. Those feelings lived with me, eating away at me, even though I tried to pretend otherwise. Until your Ma, and someone else I cared for made me see that the *only* futile thing was feeling the way I did about myself … But – and it's a big 'but' – first of all I had to make a clean breast of it."

Wilf said nothing. Florence took his silence to be a good thing. *Well, at least he hasn't thrown it back at me,* she thought.

"Now. Do you think you're ready to go back home? You won't have to say anything. I'll talk to your Ma and Pa. They'll understand, Wilf. Believe me."

She went over to the little window and looked out. There was no sign of Holger or Jack. It made sense for them to go back and put Annie and Frank in the picture and she assumed that was what they had done.

"Come on now." She held her hand out to him to help him get to his feet. With his dishevelled hair and pale cheeks, she got a fleeting impression of how he must have looked as a boy.

"No," Wilf said, "I'm stayin' here. I can think in here. You can tell Ma and Pa … Just tell 'em not to worry."

She left him to the birdsong and the sound of his own breathing, and closed the door quietly behind her.

Chapter 64

"You need help, Florence? I have all jobs done. Und I time have. And two hands pairs better than one are, ya?" Holger was waiting for her at the field gate when she went to get the cows in for afternoon milking.

She laughed a small laugh. "Well said, Fritzy. Yes, indeed they are. And thank you."

They walked the cows back to the milking parlour together.

"How Vilf now?"

"Well." She sighed. "He's very unhappy. And really angry. And I think he's afraid. He can't carry on the way he is ... Something dreadful happened to him at the Front, but he can't bring himself to talk about it."

"You think I help?" Holger said.

"You?" Florence looked at him. "How could you possibly? You're German, after all. You're part of Wilf's problem, aren't you? He'd never talk to you. And your English ..." She trailed off.

"Perhaps you are right." He frowned before he spoke again, trying to get his words in the right order. "But I am only person who knows war. What is like. So I understand. You can with my English help? Please?"

"Me?" She raised her eyebrows. "I'm no teacher, Fritzy."

"Nein, but you good speak."

"Speak well," she corrected.

"You see? You can help me."

She thought about it for a few moments "Oh, alright, then. We'll give it a try. I suppose there's nothing to lose."

Holger's acquisition of English had been slow, partly because of the long, quiet periods on the farm, and partly because he always spoke German with the other prisoners at the old workhouse. He'd learned quite a lot of words, but the way the English organised their sentences was very different from German, and their pronunciation was really strange. And try as he might to avoid it, German words kept creeping in.

Florence thought about how to help him get better. "I think it's best if you just talk to me as best you can, Fritzy. About anything you like – things you know about. And I'll correct you and help you get it right. What do you think?"

"Is good idea." He nodded and did the little bow.

"That's a good idea."

He repeated it.

Once Holger began, there was no stopping him. He took every opportunity to launch into an English monologue, pausing only to search for a word or a prompt from Florence. She realised how little she knew about him and his life before the war. Now she learned that his family were winemakers living in the country near the city of Wiesbaden on the banks of the River Rhine.

"It is lovely city." He tried to describe it. "Buildings are very beautiful. And it has hot ... baden – ah, yes! Baths. For medicine. Many famous people go ... Wine (he pronounced it 'vine') is very good. Is called 'Rheingau' because of river. I vork to look after horses in ... How you call field of grapes growing?"

"A vineyard." Florence laughed. "At last! A word where you can say 'v'."

"Ah! Yah. It is how I know about animal care. I very much like."

Florence found herself enjoying these sessions and liked the way the time passed agreeably, even when they were digging potatoes or mangolds. He asked her questions about herself ...

"You like London's big city?"

She shook her head. "I prefer it here."

Chapter 65

"Do sit down, Mrs Ashford." Morton Mathews closed his office door and resumed his seat behind his desk. The school year at Halstead National School was coming to an end.

"I wonder if you've had time to consider the proposal I put to you about entering your children for the scholarship examination for the grammar school? Only I'm more than ever convinced of their likely success. And it seems such a good opportunity for them all. You'll have read their reports and know what a very good year they have had. I must, however, press you for an answer as time is running short to put their names forward."

Nell leaned forward in her chair.

"Mr Mathews, I am very pleased indeed with your confidence in my children's abilities. And, believe me, in any other circumstances I would have been more than happy to comply with your advice. But I cannot." She paused.

Mathews looked at her. "Do go on."

"When we came to Halstead last September, I had arranged with my landlord in Stratford only to close up my house for one year. I have a commitment in writing to return. Besides, I very much hope that the children's father will be back from the war before too long. And I need to prepare for his homecoming." She flushed slightly and gave the headmaster a small smile. "I'm truly sorry."

Morton Mathews looked at Nell over his half-glasses with a candid expression. "Well, Mrs Ashford, I have to say I'm sorry, too. However, I can't say I'm surprised. Of course you must return. And I doubt very much I shall be the only one to miss you and your family here in Halstead."

Rising to his feet, he held out his hand to her. "Goodbye, Mrs Ashford." She took his hand and shook it. "I wish you all the very best of luck. And I would urge you to put Ellen, Alfred and Grace forward for your local grammar school when you get back to London. And see that Alfred keeps on drawing, won't you?"

"I doubt I could stop him if I tried. And thank you on behalf of all three of them – especially for Alfred's drawing lessons."

Walking back to Factory Terrace, Nell's mind wandered back over the events of her family's sojourn in Halstead and she felt a moment's satisfaction that it had turned out so well for them all. She had not considered the family's relocation in that light – she had, after all, left Stratford in blind panic without much thought about the quality of the life she was taking them to.

Now she was facing up to prising them away from this place that had been more than a port in a storm. Halstead had enriched all their lives in an unforgettable way. Hers included, she realised on reflection. Anxiety about George and the dangers he was facing were, naturally enough, ever present and her initial loneliness could have been her undoing, she thought. But Molly, Ivy and Jane Mizen, too, had proved to be friends she would miss. And the products of her kitchen she made for Bill Broyd were so popular. It gave her a sense of accomplishment.

She knew she must face up to revealing her intentions of returning to London before much longer. She was ready to give notice to Jane and Broyd, but it would be harder telling the children. And so she resolved to hold off for as long as she could so they could enjoy the summer without the prospect of leaving looming large.

Grace was looking forward with great joy to the long summer holiday. Doris, Windy and Lennie had talked of nothing else but roaming the countryside, abundant with flowers now, climbing trees, picnicking on the Brawks, gathering wild strawberries there and riding bicycles in the country.

Grace's contribution to the mix was the prospect of helping with the harvest out at Valley Farm. She had no problems selling that idea to the others and was just waiting on the word from her Aunt Florence that they were ready to begin.

In Grace's world there was nothing to equal the pleasure of the freedom to roam, breathe fresh air and share the company of her friends.

Chapter 66

"Well." Frank looked out from the farmhouse kitchen window. "I've checked the corn, the barometer's goin' up and I reckon that, come the end of this week, we'll be ready for harvest. Florence do you think you can get them kiddies up here to help us out?"

She, Annie and Wilf were sitting at the dinner table at the end of the working day. Florence nodded, her mouth full of pasty. "Mmm," was all she managed.

The room fell quiet and Frank took his place at the head of the table.

"Ma," Wilf said. "Where did you hide the mirror from my room?"

Annie was finding Wilf every bit as inscrutable as he had been since his homecoming, and Frank had failed to get a word out of him. But Wilf had started to come down from his room at meal times. A good sign, Annie thought, though his moody silence had cast an uneasy quiet over what had always been a time of good humour. Frank had found it particularly difficult to deal with. But he thought better than to voice any criticism or attempts at jocularity.

Annie folded her napkin and set it by her empty plate. "It's in the linen cupboard, Wilf. I put it under a pile of towels so it wouldn't get broke." She rose to her feet. "You want me to get it out for you?"

"No." Wilf's voice was sharp, like a slap and Annie sat down again. "I'll do it myself. Don't need your mollycoddlin'." He got up and headed for the stairs.

"But Wilf. You haven't finished your pasty."

"Bugger the pasty! If I'm goin' to do my bit harvestin', I need to know what kind of a state my face is in. It's time." He left the room.

Frank, Annie and Florence looked at one another, dumbfounded. Again.

"Well, I'll be!" Frank said.

The day of what Frank called 'the Rasputin tantrum', Wilf had stayed out in the shepherd's hut till well after dark. Frank had been all for fetching him back. Annie had physically restrained him. Wilf had slipped back into the house after his parents had gone to bed and silently made his way up to his room. Florence had explained to Frank and Annie what had happened out in the hut, but Wilf made no reference to what had passed between them. Their son's mute comings and goings continued to vex them.

But now. Now he'd committed to joining in the harvest.

"Heaven knows we can do with the extra help," Frank said, "but I'll lay odds he'll throw a dampener on the proceedin's."

"Never mind that, Frank – he's goin' to get involved. How long have we waited for this? And it's what you wanted, ain't it?"

In the solitude of his room, Wilf stood the mirror up on his chest of drawers, his good eye closed. He wanted the first view of his face to be at a moment of his own choosing. He would not be ambushed. He took a step back. His hands were clenched, his palms clammy as he stood before the glass. And then he looked.

He focused instantly on the mutilated flesh and sunken eye socket. "Oh ... God," he said. Grief welled up in him. For the forfeit of the years of his early manhood, for his ruined face, for the loss of his innocence. He would bear his disfigurement like stigmata all his life. The tightness in his chest gripped him like a steel band. But he remained dry-eyed.

As he stood before his reflection, he could not see how he could again engage with this world – the world of Valley Farm, of his parents, of his rural heritage. How was he to cope with meeting the people he'd known before the war? Drunk ale with? Played football with? And what about girls? What hope was there? His face was now his cage, his prison, stronger than steel. He did not know where to begin searching for the key.

It was many minutes before he tore his gaze away from the ravaged vision. He went to the window and, opening it, breathed in the summer's perfume in the evening light. Swallows dived and skimmed the surface of the duckpond, their calls piercing the air.

He had to do something about his appearance. Ameliorate the impact so people would not be taken aback by the shock, the ugliness. He rummaged in his chest of drawers and found an old red kerchief he'd once worn around his neck. He tied it about his head, covering his damaged features.

He leaned on the sill, lit a cigarette and blew a stream of smoke out of the window. The scene, the atmosphere – even the beauty and peace of this darkening tableau were just as they had always been. And yet irrevocably different. An irreconcilable paradox.

***

"Can you ask your friends if they can spare some time to help with the harvest at Valley Farm?" Florence knew it was what her niece had been longing to hear.

"Oh, *yes!*" Grace was ecstatic. "I'll ask them right away."

"Make sure they ask their parents. Mrs Davis says you can all sleep out in the shepherd's hut for a couple of nights. I'll be staying out there with you, so you'll have to mind your p's and q's. Come on, let's go and ask your mother if it's alright with her."

"*Yes!*" said Grace again.

"I know you'd never forgive me if I said no." Nell was keen for her children to drain the last drops from the cup of delight they had drunk from this past year.

"Annie suggested you and Molly might like to join us for the harvest home supper when we're all done, Nellie," Florence said. "She thought maybe Swank could give you a ride out to the farm."

Nell considered the offer for a moment, thinking it would round the year off memorably. "Yes." She nodded. "I'd like that. Very much. And I'll ask Molly."

***

"Now then." Frank sat the children down on a log. "Look here." He held up a handful of cornstalks, and took them one by one from the bunch. "This 'un's wheat – all spiky with nice fat seeds on it. That's for your flour." He put it down and pulled another stem from his little sheaf. "These're oats for porridge. And horse feed. They hang down all droopy-like. Quite pretty, I always think. And lastly we've got barley, with its bushy beard. It'll make good ale, will this."

He passed the stems round, so the children could have a good look at them. "We grow different crops in different fields, and change 'em round year by year so as not to wear the soil out. We have to keep 'em separate because they've all got different uses. But the actual harvestin's all much of a muchness. You have to keep the stalks all up the same way – with the seeds at the top for when we come to threshing – that's knockin' all the seeds off the stalks."

"Do we have to toss it all about in the air like we did with the hay?" Grace was hoping they would.

"What do you think?" Frank fixed her with a hard stare. The other children laughed.

"Come on Gracie – use your noddle," Lennie said. "All the seeds'd fall off."

"Umm. Yes, I suppose so."

"So don't let me catch you doin' that." Frank was smiling now. "You'll have lots of fun anyway. I want you workin' as a team, gatherin' up bundles we can bind into what we call 'shocks'. Then we're goin' to lean the shocks up against each other till we're ready to take 'em in. You all got that?"

They nodded.

"Here." Annie appeared with some old dungarees of Wilf's. Put these on, you young 'uns. They're old, but they're clean. Corn's scratchy stuff on bare legs."

"I can't wait to get goin'." Doris jumped up, dragging Grace with her. "Come on!"

The harvest proceeded joyously. Holger was able to do extra hours again for the duration. Wilf remained wordless and stony-faced, but his furious energy boosted their productivity.

"You're cock-a-hoop about the yields this year, ain't you, Frank?" Annie said when all was gathered together safely.

Frank stood, looking out at the shocks stacked against one another, golden against the sky and put his thumbs up. The pipe clamped between his tobacco-stained teeth did not prevent him grinning from ear to ear. "You know what, Annie, my girl? We done the right thing, ploughin' up that fallow ground this year and sowin' the extra wheat. Paid off handsome."

Frank estimated this would be the penultimate day of reaping and binding, and they were well on schedule. Once the shocks were dry enough, they could be stacked.

"The gang's workin' hard and it's goin' like clockwork. Wilf's thrown hisself into it like his life's dependin' on it."

"In a funny sort of a way, p'haps that's just what he's thinkin," Annie said.

"Still not sayin' much, though," said Frank.

Wilf had spent the morning 'shocking' and tying the corn into neat sheaves. It was a solitary job, which suited him. He could remain aloof as the others followed the reaper, raking the fallen cornstalks into heaps.

Annie brought cheese and hunks of bread and a jar of chutney to share. "Dinner time! Come and get it!"

The children had been playing hide and seek, full of energy still, despite the morning's exertions. They came and sat in the sheltered yard and tucked in.

It took Wilf a while to respond to his mother's call, and when he appeared in the rickyard the animated banter quietened. He sat down on a stump, and took a long swig of ale from the flaggon. Annie passed him a plate of bread and cheese.

"Ta, Ma." He began to devour it with what looked to Annie something like gusto. She raised her eyebrows but said nothing.

Florence unhitched Clover and Campion, stood them in the shade before she came to eat. She allowed them a drink from the water barrel and then attached nosebags to their halters. They were in need of a break, having worked nonstop.

"Mr Davis," Grace looked at Wilf.

"Wha' do you want?" he said, turning so he could see her. "And you can call me Wilf like everyone else."

"Wilf ... I ... er ..." She faltered, feeling suddenly shy. "I know a poem. I recited it at school and it's perfect for today. I wondered ... I thought you might like to hear it."

Hot anger shot through him. *What do I want wi' poetry?* If his mother had suggested such a thing, he'd have bitten her head off. But he could not bring himself to take his contempt out on the child in that way.

"Poem?" he said vaguely. "What poem?"

"It's by a man called John Clare. He's dead now, but he called himself 'the peasant poet'. I've got a book with this one in it – you can borrow it if you want. It's called 'The Wheat Ripening'. It's a sonnet." She sounded proud.

"Go on, then." He sounded weary.

And so she stood and began:

"What time the wheat field tinges rusty brown
And barley bleaches in its mellow grey,
'Tis sweet some smooth-mown balk to wander down
Or cross the fields on footpath's narrow way
Just in the mealy light of waking day
As glittering dewdrops moise the maiden's gown
And sparkling bounces from her nimble feet

Journeying to milking from the neighbouring town
Making life light with song – and it is sweet
To mark the grazing herds and list the clown
Urge on his ploughing team with cheering calls
And merry shepherd's whistling toils begun
And hoarse-tongued birdboy whose unceasing calls
Join the lark's ditty to the rising sun."

A crackle of applause rippled around the yard as she smiled and sat down.

"Very nice, that was, Young 'un," Frank said. "Am I s'posed to be the clown doin' the ploughin'?"

Everyone laughed and Grace flushed scarlet.

"Good," Wilf said. "Thank you." She smiled back at him.

"I like your scarf, by the way," Grace added. No one else had dared mention it. "It makes you look like a pirate."

Chapter 67

"How about a sing-song? I've got my mandolin." Florence unbuckled its case.

When the working day was over and Annie had fed everyone, Florence and Holger went back to the shepherd's hut with the children and built a fire with wood foraged from copses and hedges. Wilf stay on with them. He wasn't sure why, but the firelight beckoned him. They dragged logs into a rough circle around the fire, sat down on them and sang all the songs they could think of. Volume rising, mood hilarious. Holger clapped and nodded in time.

"I do not know these songs. What is mean 'cockles and muscles alive, alive-o?'"

"Not mu*scles* like in your body that make you strong," Windy said, "these mu*ssels* are fish that live in shells. Molly Malone used to sell them. In Dublin. That's in Ireland."

"Ah. You like I sing German song?"

"Yes, please!"

"Is called 'Grossvater Tanz' – is 'Grandfather Dance' in English."

He cleared his throat and began to sing. The richness of his baritone voice surprised Florence. *All this time,* she thought, *and I had no idea.*

The guttural consonants sounded strange to the children, but for Wilf, they were redolent of all the horrors he was trying so hard to bury. His hands shook and he began to breathe hard and fast. He was back in the trenches and thought of all the songs he and his comrades had sung there ... just thinking of them reminded him of all the boys who'd bought it. He got to his feet, turned on his heel and ran, quickly vanishing into the dark.

"Not again," Florence said under her breath. She strained her eyes in the direction of his departing figure, but the glare of the fire rendered the dark impenetrable.

"Is he ill?" Doris asked.

"Well, in a way he is. Look you youngsters, it's time to get to bed. We've got another long day tomorrow and we'll have to be up with the dawn chorus."

"Florence," Holger said. "You must here with children stay. I go to find Vilf – Wilf, I mean."

Without waiting for a reply, the German walked off into the dark. He didn't have to go far. He found Wilf retching and vomiting behind a tree. Holger knelt by him, took out the handkerchief he had in his pocket and held it out to him.

"Stick it up your arse!"

Holger stayed there with the square of linen still in his hand.

"Shit," Wilf said.

He took the handkerchief and wiped his face. Holger remained, patient, while Wilf composed himself.

"I wasn't runnin' off this time. I just didn't want to chuck up in front of them little blighters. But it was you singin' in German. I was right back there …"

"I am sorry, Wilf. I did not think."

A silence intervened before Wilf blew his nose on Holger's handkerchief.

"Is alright I call you Wilf?"

"S'pose so. You're here, ain't you? We got to call each other somethin'." He extended his hand to return the handkerchief, then thought better of it. "I'd best get Ma to give it a wash … But … ta, anyway."

"You are better now?"

"Depends what you mean by 'better'. I don't believe there's goin' to be any 'better' in my life."

"I also was there. I know the hell. I have seen the death and the … I do not know the right vord – word … injury is all I know."

"Injury! Huh! You mean *carnage*. You mean *mutilation*. You mean *massacre*. You mean blokes havin' bits of theirselves blown to kingdom come."

Wilf was shaking now, and he fixed Holger with a venomous look. Holger was wishing Florence would appear and help him out with these difficult words. He shrugged, shook his head and held his hands out, palms up, to demonstrate his lack of understanding. But he felt he must break the impasse.

"Wilf, I agree with you that this war is terrible. For all. And I apologise. For my country. Many wrong things have been done." He watched as the young Englishman's face creased in agony and his fists clenched in a gesture of supplication.

"It's me who should be sayin' sorry." Wilf's voice sounded strangled and Holger could barely make out what he was saying. "I killed one of your boys. Bayonetted 'im. Face to face." He buried his face in his hands and wept uncontrollably. "Ain't no forgivin' me."

"Hey, Wilf. What happens in war is not like ordinary life –"

"It *is*, though. It *is* life. Why should the rules be different in war? Men are men when all's said and done. I committed a *sin*, ain't I? I won't get let off just because it were in a war."

Holger put out a hand to show fellow feeling with the young Englishman. Before he knew it, Wilf had fallen against him and Holger found he was cradling Wilf who was shaking like an injured animal.

"You can tell me? You want say what happened?"

"No! No, I can't do that. I just want it all to go away and leave me in peace. But it won't. The memory's with me night and day. How can I live out my life like this?"

"Is like Florence said. These memories, they take over who is Wilf Davis. You must not allow." The German leaned his back against a tree with Wilf's head against his chest, waiting. Minutes passed, Wilf's sobs the only sound.

"It were at Passchendaele," Wilf said at last, his voice indistinct. "Last back-end. Not where I copped this lot." He gestured towards his marred features.

"Afore that. You wouldn't believe the mud there. It weren't possible for a man to walk. The water was chest-high in the shell holes. Horses was drownin' in them – men as well. We was tryin' to take the ridge. But we was goin' awful slow because of all the mud. Hell on earth, it was. And your lot's pill boxes. They was bristlin' with machine guns. We had to take cover in the shell holes all the time. And it went on and on till we was nearly mad with the misery of it."

Wilf fell silent, then sat up and wiped his face on his sleeve. He sat staring into the night for many minutes.

"You want say more?"

"I can still see his face now." Wilf breathed out long and slow.

He reached into his trouser pocket and pulled out a packet of cigarettes, extracted one and put it in his mouth. "Fag?" He held the packet out to Holger, who took one. Wilf struck a match and lit them. In the flare of the match, Holger could see Wilf's agonised expression. They sat and smoked in silence as the waxing moon rose, radiating its brightness through the overhanging tree branches.

"Whose face you see?"

Wilf sighed again. "Don't know his name o' course. Nor never will. Young bloke, he were. Like me. Could've been me … but German …"

He shrugged and trailed off for several moments, then took a deep breath. "I jumped in this shell hole, dodgin' the gun fire, see. And he were in there. Don't know why he were there. I've asked myself over and over what he were doin', and I can't think. Must have got separated from his mates. But he were scared alright. Shit scared. Same as me. We looked each other in the face. It seemed like an age. His eyes were grey, like your'n. They was piercin'. And looked straight into my soul. And there we was. Up to our bellies in water 'n' muck, starin' at each other … Then I saw him make a move. He were goin' for his pistol, I swear. I had to do somethin' – it were him or me. I was sure of that. I had my bayonet fixed. We all did. Matter of course. And I just …"

He stopped. He was choking on his own words and he struggled for breath. "I just … sank it into his belly. It went in right up to the hilt. It was a feelin' I'll never … never forget." He shivered. "Horrible. Bloody horrible … And the blighter's eyes were still fixed on me … Then blood started to dribble out of his mouth. It ran down his chin and spattered scarlet on his uniform. He started to keel over backwards – he was *still* lookin' at me as his face disappeared under the water … There was bubbles as the last of the air come out of his lungs."

Englishman and German sat together, backs against the tree. Wilf offered Holger another cigarette and they sat and smoked in the harvest moonlight.

"I don't know how long I stayed in that God-forsaken shell hole. I couldn't move. Just stood there, lookin' at his blood on my bayonet. I didn't dare move in case I touched his body. I'd have gone to pieces if I had. Then one of our boys come and got me and led me back to the trench."

He looked up through the filigree mesh of leaves and branches and fixed his gaze on the face of the moon. "*I'm sorry!*" he yelled skyward. "*I'm so sorry.*

Forgive me. If you're there, forgive me, please!" Burying his face in his two hands, he wept again.

Chapter 68

"I overheard it all," Florence told Annie. "After the children had settled down, I went to look for Wilf and Fritzy. I hadn't gone far when I heard their voices. They were in the copse near the sheep fold. I could hear Wilf talking and decided not to interrupt in case I put him off. He's had a terrible burden to bear all this time."

The two women stood together in the yard in the pale early morning light, the farm buildings casting long shadows over the cobbles.

"Did he say anything to you when he came back in?" Florence asked.

"No. He just took hisself up to his room without a word. But that ain't nothin' unusual. Frank was worn out anyway and needed to get to bed, so we turned in pretty soon."

"I'm in a bit of a quandary," Florence said. "Half of me wants to tell you what happened to him, but the other half thinks it would be better if he told you himself. He might even resent it if I reveal what's been haunting him all this time. In fact, he doesn't even know I know. It was Fritzy he told. He, Fritzy, I mean, got it just right. I even think his lack of English was a good thing – he couldn't say too much and just let Wilf talk. But believe me, Annie, what he had to say, what he's kept to himself all these months, explains it all. His silences, his fury, his despair."

They walked slowly back to the farmhouse and let themselves into the kitchen. Annie had left a big saucepan of porridge to cook slowly on the range over night. She lifted it down in gloved hands and set it on the hearth to give it a final stir.

"Here." She ladled a good half of it into a warmed crock. "You can take this lot over for the young 'uns. They'll need a good breakfast. Frank's already had his – he's out there gettin' ready for the day. Still a lot to do. As for Wilf, we'll see. He mayn't even show up this mornin'. But I think you're right, Florence, we must let him talk in his own good time. I've got a feelin' he will, now he's opened the biddin', so to speak."

Florence loaded a tray with bowls and spoons, a jar of honey and a jug of milk. "I'll drop this off at the shepherd's hut and get on with the milking." She headed for the door.

Annie busied herself with preparations for the harvest-home supper and began by peeling a mountain of potatoes. She hummed quietly to herself as she worked and was unaware of her son's presence in the room for some moments.

Wilf, dressed for work, his boots in his hand, crossed the room and sat down on the settle. He watched his mother's back view for a while as she worked at the sink. "Any tea, Ma?"

"Ooh, Wilf! You gave me a turn. I didn't hear you come down. Yes ... er ... I'll pour you a cup. And there's porridge on the hob."

"Ta. I'll help myself."

Annie handed him an enamel mug of tea and watched as he spooned sugar into it and stirred. He said nothing before he took a gulp of the hot liquid, so Annie turned back to the sinkful of potatoes. She resumed her humming, self-consciously this time, to break the silence of the kitchen. She could hear Wilf serving himself a portion of porridge from the pot and then the scrape of his spoon on the dish.

She had almost given up hope of him saying anything at all when Wilf said "I got somethin' I need to tell you ... Or maybe you already know."

"No, Wilf, I don't know ... But I'm listenin'." She turned to face her son, fetched a chair and sat down. She placed her hands flat, fingers spread, on her apron as Wilf began to recount his dreadful story. He spoke in a low voice which wavered now and then. His mother held him in her gaze, aching to embrace her boy, but waiting for his cue before she moved.

"It's been a livin' hell, Ma. Still is. I was goin' to do myself in to get rid of the pain of it. But I couldn't do that. When I thought about it, suicide bein' illegal and all ... and me not bein' buried in holy ground ... I couldn't do that to you and Pa ... It's why I've been so foul to you since I come back. It were like you were standin' in my way. I just wanted to get free of it ... and I still don't know how I'm goin' to live with it. I've been tryin' to get back to normal life. But ... his face ... that look ... it won't go away. It's not the damage to my sight and my face – I can learn to live with that. But I'm afeared I might be damned for what I've done. You brought me up Christian-like. An' I've committed this great big sin."

Annie let her son's words hang in the quiet room a while before she responded. When she did, she spoke with gentleness. Yet she was firm. She wanted Wilf to believe her, for her words to be of some comfort – and use – to him.

"This war," she said at length, "it's *not your fault*. Nor of any of the innocent young men what's been *forced* to do things they would never have dreamed of doin' in their worst nightmares. These powerful men, they've *used* other men's lives like pieces on a chess board, not carin' one *jot* about the pain and sufferin' they're causin'. And you. But twenty-year-old. You've had to do somethin' I can't even imagine. And all your life to live out in its shadow."

She stopped and put out a hand to touch Wilf's arm. This time he did not withdraw it.

"And the God I believe in, who's helped me in times of trouble all my life, He's a God of forgiveness. He knows you better'n you know yourself, Wilf. And He knows you're sorry, and that it ain't your fault. It'll be others – them that caused this terrible war – what'll get their comeuppance. Not the likes of you.

And never forget, Wilf, me and your Pa we're here for you. To help, if we can, whenever you need us."

They sat in the quiet and warmth of the familiar kitchen, not speaking further.

There was a noise at the door, and they both knew that Frank was outside, ready to get the last day of the harvest underway.

Chapter 69

"Morning, Fritzy," Florence said. He leaned his bicycle against the barn. "Did you get into hot water when you got back last night?"

"No."The German frowned. "It was too late for bath."

She laughed. "I didn't mean that, you idiot. I meant did you get into trouble. For being so late, was what I meant."

"Ah! No. Was alright because of harvest. Everyone is late back. No one minds ... 'Get into hot water' means 'get into trouble'? I did not know this. And I am not idiot, please."

"No, I'm just pulling your leg – joking. I know you're not an idiot. In fact I wanted to say what a marvellous job you did last night – with Wilf, I mean."

"I do not know. I hope so. His life will never be like before. And he is so young. He has to suffer this pain all his life. The war has done many terrible things to many men."

Jack ran behind the cattle, urging them through the field gate. Once they were safely back inside, Florence latched the gate and they walked down the track towards the rickyard.

"I can't wait for the whole dreadful mess to end," Florence said. "I don't think it can go on much longer, do you?"

"No. I think not. I think Americans will finish it."

They walked on in silence for a few yards till Holger spoke again. "What you will do when war ends?" He looked at her.

"I wish I knew, Fritzy. I'm signed up to carry on here till November in any case. I suppose it depends on whether it's all over by then. If it is I ... I'll just have to go back to London ... Nell's going back with the children very soon – we only came here for a year, you see ... What a year it's been!"

"Florence." Holger stopped and turned to face her. A lock of corn-coloured hair had fallen over his forehead. Florence looked at him and saw that his grey eyes were bright. He looked into her face with an intensity that took her breath away.

"Yes, Fritzy. What is it?" A small frown creased the flesh between her eyes as she looked back at him. His hand, trembling slightly, smoothed it away.

"I don't want you to leave here."

She held his gaze. And in that moment, she knew this was right. *Of course. Why haven't I realised before? What a fool I've been* ... "No ... I don't want to leave here either. Or ... you.

He took her two hands and the Englishwoman and the German stood facing one another, trancelike.

It was the dog who broke the spell. He ran forward and back, woofing impatiently each time he returned to them.

"Jack knows there's work still to do," Florence said at last. "We'll both have to leave if we don't pull our weight."

She ran her finger along Holger's forearm, tanned from the summer work and covered in golden hair, realising she'd wanted to do so for ages. It felt glorious and she shivered in the electricity of it. She held his arm as they walked on up the track. It felt the most natural thing in the world.

"Well, I'm blowed," Frank said to himself as he watched the two of them coming towards him. "Who'd have thought it?"

But work was work and they set to as if nothing unusual had happened to them, save for the slight smile they both wore all day long. By the end of the day, they were every bit as exhausted as on any ordinary day.

Wilf's contribution to the day's effort was as tireless as before. But there was something in his expression and his body language that suggested a release of tension. He was less the human embodiment of a steam hammer than he had been on previous days; he even took the time to engage with the children doing disappearing tricks with the young conkers he released from their prickly shells.

The harvest was in and Frank was elated. "Florence, Fritzy, all you young 'uns. An' Wilf, my boy. Well done, all of you. It's the best harvest for years! Them horses've earned a few days off. They've worked hardest of all, I reckon." And he slapped their chestnut necks for sheer gratitude.

"You know what, though, Pa," Wilf said, "If this farm is goin' anywhere in the twentieth century, we're goin' to have to get us a tractor. It's the future!"

***

Nell and Molly Cooper sat beside Swank Everitt at the front of his cart with Alf and Ellen in the back as the old horse made its way up the lane. The twins had stayed behind at Factory Terrace with Jane Mizen. When they reached the gate of Valley Farm, Swank drew the horse to a halt and helped the two women down from the cart. Nell paid him sixpence for the ride and slipped him a package of bread pudding wrapped in waxed paper.

"Ta, missus," Swank said with a chesty chuckle.

Molly produced a brown paper bag full of slightly rubbery carrots. "These're for the horse."

"Much obliged, missus," Swank said, and handed Alf and Ellen down from the back.

He swung the milk churn off the stand and into the cart, climbed aboard and turned in the farm gateway before setting off back towards Halstead.

"I expect this'll be the only time I ever come out here," said Nell.

"Yeah. Not long now an' you'll be on your way," Molly said. "Worse luck."

Annie came to the gate and ushered them in. "Welcome!" she said.

The yard was bedecked with bunting. Two long trestle tables with benches alongside, were covered in red gingham.

"You've made it look so cheerful and pretty, Mrs Davis," Nell said.

"Ah! Ain't no time like harvest. And we've got all you folks to thank, as well as tons of corn safely stacked to celebrate. Come and have a seat. I'll be bringin' out the food soon as Frank's back. The children've been cleanin' up. They'll be ready in a while."

Florence and Holger had rubbed down Clover and Campion, fed and watered them and led them out to the paddock. They leaned on the gate, their arms touching, as they watched the great beasts rolling on their backs.

"Is bliss for them," Holger said.

"Is bliss for us, too." Florence leaned her head against his shoulder.

He kissed her hair and breathed in the perfume of her. "You smell of country," he said.

"What, like cow dung, you mean? How dare you!" She slapped his arm.

"Like new hay and flowers. Is lovely. You are lovely. And brave. And funny. And wise. I watch you all this time and I think I am in love with you."

"Fritzy … You are my Gabriel Oak."

"Your what?"

"He's a character in a book I love … He's gentle and strong … Like you. I'll tell you about him … sometime. But right now, I've got a very important question to ask you. Now we're … together, shall I go on calling you 'Fritzy', or would you prefer 'Holger' from now on?"

"Oh dear. Is very difficult. Let me think." He frowned and rubbed his chin, whiskery now with pale stubble. "I think 'Fritzy'. Is how you always call me. And it will make me always remember now."

"Fritzy it is, then … and Fritzy, I do love you. And I quite like your straight nose and the cleft in your chin." And she knew then that she did love him.

"Cleft? What is cleft?"

"It's this." She touched his face with a forefinger and she felt again the frisson that gave her goose flesh.

The horses stood up, making grunting noises as they shook clouds of dry earth from their coats.

"I wonder how much longer horses like them will work the land," Florence said.

"Not very long, I think. Wilf is correct. Tractors are tomorrow."

"That's sad. Frank won't like it at all."

They joined hands and walked back to the farm.

"Hey! Nellie!" Florence ran to embrace her sister, releasing Holger's hand, but not before Nell had noticed. Nell fixed her sister with a curious look, the unspoken question hanging between them.

At that moment, Frank came in from the rickyard, dragging the branch of an oak tree.

"It's what we call 'The Orkey Bough'," he said. "That's 'H-HORKEY' with a 'H-HAITCH' on the front, like 'H-HOLGER'. It's the tradition round these parts to bring in a 'H-Horkey Bough' on the last waggon of the harvest. And that's what we've done this afternoon. So now it's time to celebrate. And we sure do have somethin' to celebrate. If all the farms in England have done as well as we have, we'll have kept this country from starvation, I reckon."

Everyone had sat down along the benches on either side of the trestles, and Annie was bringing steaming dishes of sausages and mash from the farmhouse kitchen.

"Sausages're Bill Broyd's," Annie said. "Ain't none better'n his."

Florence got to her feet, passing enamel plates round so that everyone could help themselves to the food. She filled the children's cups with milk and offered elderflower cordial to Nell and Molly, filling glasses also for herself and Annie.

"Now, I'm not one for speechifyin'," Frank began, lifting his tankard of ale, "but I just want to say to all of yous what've helped us, a great big 'thank you' from us Davises here at Valley Farm. Specially to our almost-kind-of daughter, Florence, who come to us like the answer to a prayer, and who's turned from a townie into a proper country lass. An' to our very own prisoner of war what's put in hours and hours of hard labour here without a single word of complaint that I've heard – mostly, I suppose, because his English ain't up to much. But he's a good lad. Even if he is a German! And then there's them young 'uns." He aimed a look at the children. "You've been a joy to have around. And your help's been like manna from heaven. Of course I want to thank my helpmate, my anchor in life's stormy seas. And this time I don't mean the dog, though he's a treasure in his own right, I mean – nat'rally – my old lady, my Annie."

He clamped an arm round his wife's shoulder as she dabbed her eyes on her apron.

"Silly old fool!" she said. Everyone clapped.

"But there's one person I've left till last. I don't mind admittin', there've been times when I've doubted that I'd ever see my son back here on the farm where he was raised. And even since he's been back here we've been worried sick about him. And I know he's got a hard road to travel. But still. He's here now. We hope he's taken the first step along that road. And we're all goin' to help him along his way, the best way we know how, by lovin' and lookin' out for him."

Frank cleared his throat and held out his hand to Wilf. "Son, welcome home. We hope and pray to God that you'll find peace bein' part of the future of this farm."

Wilf reached over, took his father's hand and shook it. "Well. Only if you'll consider gettin' a tractor."

A cheer and a gale of laughter went up around the table, then everyone pitched into the food.

"What're your plans now, Mrs Ashford? Is it true that you'll be leavin' Halstead afore long?"

"Yes, Mrs Davis, it is true, I'm sorry to say. But it can't be helped, I'm afraid. There's a lot I'm going to miss about living here. The children have had the time of their lives. And I really wish I could take my work for Mr Broyd back with me. I've enjoyed it so much and it's given me some independence … I won't have the chance of finding a job like that in Stratford. But we really have to go back. Our year's up and that's that."

"What about you children," Annie asked. "Are you lookin' forward to livin' in London again?"

"No, I'm not!" said Grace. "At all! Course, I'm looking forward to seeing Dad again, and I *do* hope it won't be long! But when I'm grown up, I'm coming back here to live in the country and be with my friends!"

"Ye-es!" said Doris and Windy and Lennie together. "You've *got* to come back," Doris added, wagging a finger.

"I'm going to miss my drawing lessons with Mr Mathews," Alf said. "They've been the best thing about being here. But I'm still going to be an architect, and I'll write and tell him when I am one. It was all his idea, you see."

Ellen shrugged. "I'm quite happy to go home with mum. She needs me, and so do the twins." Nell smiled at her eldest daughter. "Well," she said. "That leaves you, Flo." She looked hard at her sister, sitting close to the German. "Have you thought about the future?"

"Yes," Florence said, "I have. I'm staying on here till November in any case – I'm committed to the WLA till then and I hope Annie and Frank – and Wilf – will want me to keep on working at Valley Farm."

She drew breath and looked around the table. Annie and Frank were nodding, and even Wilf did not look hostile. "And then … well … it depends on Fritzy. I'm going where he goes. We'll be going together. He won't be a prisoner of war forever." She gripped his arm and looked into his face. "So, I'm afraid, Nellie, Gracie, Ellen and Alf, I'm not coming back to Stratford. I'm – *we're* – moving on together when the time comes."

Nell stared at her sister in disbelief, her head slowly shaking. "Well. Now I've heard everything! Unpredictable was always your middle name, Florence. But I suppose I must congratulate you." A smile crept across her face and she came round the table to embrace her sister. "You do look happy, I must say. Now. You must introduce me to … to … Fritzy.

"Nellie, meet my … my … *love,* Fritzy, alias Holger …" She trailed off. She did not even know his last name, she realised. She looked at him questioningly.

"Karsten," he said.

"Fritzy, this is my sister, Nell. You've already got to know my very dear niece, Grace, and these two are my older niece, Ellen, and my artistic nephew, Alf. They're the reason why I came here, so I can't thank them enough for that."

"Oh, Aunt Flo. I am going to miss you." Grace had a note of genuine sorrow in her voice. "But I do want you to be happy, so I won't be too cross with you!"

"Bravo!" said Annie. "Well said, young Gracie. Come on, Frank, let's fill everyone's glasses and drink another toast. To these young folks. All of 'em."

Postscript

"Aunt Flo."

"Yes, Gracie."

After a pause to organise her thoughts, Grace continued. "This has been the best year of my life. Golden and sparkling, like an expensive necklace, or something."

They sat on the steps of the shepherd's hut with meadowsweet fizzing all around. The girl had been going over everything she could recall about her Halstead life. She and her mother and siblings were all packed up and ready to leave for Stratford in a couple of days. Florence was going to the station to see them off, but Grace knew she would not be able to say what was in her heart in that public and probably tearful setting, and so she had pedalled out to Valley Farm for one final, intimate moment with her aunt.

"All my friends are like the precious jewels, and the things we've done together are the golden chain that joins them all together. And it's mine forever. No one can steal it. But isn't it funny? I've had the time of my life while the world is so messed up. You've lost your friend Captain Forbes, Wilf has lost his eye and is still so upset, and I don't know if my Dad can ever be like he used to be when he comes home. I might have to work really hard to cheer him up ... I feel a bit ... guilty."

"Don't," Florence said, wrapping her arm around her niece's shoulders and holding her close. "You've given as much pleasure as you've received, Gracie. And that's no cause for guilt. If you go through life doing just that, you'll have nothing to feel guilty about. Life might not always give you as much joy as you've had here, but just remember always to be true to yourself and you won't go far wrong. Captain Forbes told me that, and I think it's good advice."

The End